CATS AND DOGS

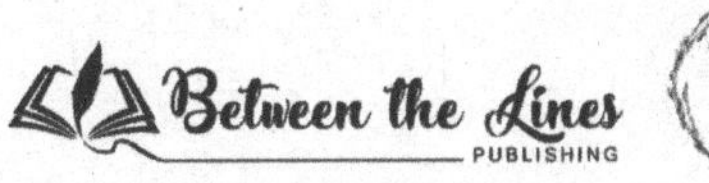

Liminal Books is an imprint of Between the Lines Publishing. The Liminal Books name and logo are trademarks of Between the Lines Publishing.

Cover design by Suzanne Johnson

Between the Lines Publishing
1769 Lexington Ave N, Ste 286
Roseville MN 55113
btwnthelines.com

First Published: February 2023

ISBN: (Paperback) 978-1-958901-13-7

ISBN: (Ebook) 978-1-958901-14-4

CATS AND DOGS

John Ouellet

If you love animals,
Read no further.
If you love horror,
Read on.
If you love both,
You decide.

CATS

One

If you were fire, this is how you'd want to burn, a true democracy of flame, all with an abundance and none with more than the other. They tried to fight it, tried to find an entry point, but all were consumed, as if fire knew they'd be coming and was tormenting them. All they could do was watch.

It was marvelously contained. It burned quick and tidy. Just the old house. It would be remembered as one of the most bizarre and terrifying fires in Kalispell's history. Five people dead. A child survived. A child and a half dozen cats that must have jumped from the fire. The child, a burnt-orange haired boy, seven-years old, his name now forgotten unless one cared enough to query the Internet, was found watching from the front walkway when the first neighbors arrived.

"He was quiet and unresponsive," one recalled. "Like in a trance." The interviewer suggested he was in shock, obvious to anyone listening to the report back then. When the fire department arrived, they had to work around him. He stood there on the front walk as if waiting to be asked inside. They tried to move him, but he kept going back, lifting the cats, and carrying them across the street. The chief asked the neighbors to take care of him. No one offered. They didn't know the boy, barely knew the family, even after five years on the block. "Cats seem to be the only friends the poor kid's got around here," the chief noted to reporters.

They kept to themselves, neighbors said. They were rarely out. They never spoke. We didn't even know how many people lived there. School? Guess so, if they had school-age kids. No, don't know where, never saw them at the school bus, I suspected their parents drove them. But I don't know, never saw them do that either.

An elderly woman took him. She'd lived across the street, same house for fifty-three years. She knew the family, enough about them anyway. Enough to talk to the media but she didn't. The things she saw weren't the type of things she wanted to share. Didn't matter that they were dead. It wasn't how she was raised, wasn't how she lived. She knew lots of things about all the neighbors, but she never gossiped and refused to repeat gossip.

Years back, her kids gone, she and her husband sat at the small kitchen table most of the day. Back then, she rarely took note of the outside. She drank tea and he tomato juice, they small talked while he read the paper, she her romance novels. He carved miniature soldiers; she crocheted. Then he died. After that she had plenty of time to watch the world outside go by.

The neighborhood was young, then old, then back to young again. She watched life in the streets, the holidays, the parties, the gatherings. That was a year before the odd family moved in. They did nothing, and that fascinated her.

She didn't have much luck with the boy either when she took him by the shoulders to lead him away. He came with her dutifully. There was no struggle, no reluctance. As soon as she released him, though, he headed back to the fire. Something was drawing him back. "His family," the chief said. "He's in shock; something inside is telling him he can't leave them alone. I've seen it before."

She didn't think so. She had been watching them long enough. Something else. She was too old to be chasing him down, but somebody had too, and no one else offered. Or dared, was a better word. She could see it on their faces. She watched them cross the street when passing the house, or grab hold of their child's hand when there was an absolute need to pass before it, and hurry their way past when on their own. And always with an eye on the house,, as if from a dark corner evil would come. It wasn't a fear of this peculiar boy. He was, after all, just a child, and all of them knew of children and childish things. And it wasn't fear of his family, as unsettling as they were. It was the unknown, and this family had become the boogey-men beneath their queen-sized beds.

At her third attempt she brought him inside her home to the barking of her Yorkie. For the first time he stood his ground upon being released. "You like puppies?" she said, picking up the dog. "Actually, she's small but not a puppy; she's almost eight years old. I got her for my birthday." She brought the Yorkie closer so he could pat him. But he didn't. He cocked his head, studying the dog. The Yorkie growled as it pulled away.

"JoJo stop that," she said. JoJo's hostility was not unusual, it being part of the breed, but like the neighbors she had an instant uneasiness around the boy. "Looks like you two need each other," she said, knowing the boy hadn't a clue to the reference, even if he was listening.

She tried putting JoJo into his arms; she wouldn't go. Just as well, the boy didn't seem interested in holding her. "I've got a few things to do," she said. "So, I need you to watch JoJo for me. Can you do that for me?"

He responded with the same quizzical look he used to study JoJo. But he followed her onto to front porch and stood in place while she fastened JoJo to her leash and the leash to the wrought iron post. She went inside and watched. The boy didn't leave. He gazed down at JoJo who was rubbing herself at his legs. It was the same empty gaze upon his face watching the fire.

She went to her chores in the kitchen. She was pleased to have reached him with JoJo, even as a momentary distraction. A new fascination to take him away from the horrors before him. Perhaps, she thought, he would never recover. She allowed herself to imagine his future without a family, perhaps without a mind. It would take time. She'd be gone before he either overcame or succumbed. At least in this moment, she had reached out and he had grabbed hold. If he can remember only that, maybe it will be enough to help him hold on longer.

Jojo was yipping madly on the porch. She finished washing her teacup and dried her hands. Within that time JoJo had stopped. *Let it go,* she told herself. The boy may be teasing or scaring the dog, but the interaction was good for him. It's what dogs did for little boys. But it wasn't that long ago her own were that age. Alone and quiet was a bad combination. She stepped into the front room. Through the window she saw his head. He was sitting contentedly but his stare was again across the street at his house. Time for human contact.

He was sitting with a cat nested on his lap, the source of JoJo's wild yips. "Ah, you have a new friend, I see. Make certain not to let Jojo off her leash again; she likes to wander. So where did she run off to?" She didn't expect an answer.

She stepped off the porch, calling out as she walked around the house. Her scream drew the attention of all those on the street. Even the boy took the time to divert his gaze to the dog. Of course, there was nothing she could do. The dog was consumed in dying flames; her charred carcass beyond help and recognition. She looked up at the boy, her mouth agape, her eyes hiding neither the horror nor the contempt. The boy had seen enough. He sighed and turned his attention back to the raging fire across the street.

Two

Libby, Montana – 27 years later

There wasn't much to love about Libby, Montana, but then, there wasn't much to hate either, and that was good enough for Alston. It was small; it was slow, it was country. There was plenty of hunting, fishing, and hiking. There were people, of course, but enough space between them so that he could avoid and ignore at his leisure.

When Alston Waters retired from the FBI, he had no plan. He could have hung on until mandatory retirement at fifty-seven but "hanging on" to anything was not a philosophy of life he embraced. Hanging on to his prior career as a Marine Officer, hanging on as a Supervisory Special Agent, or hanging onto his wife, entailed having to look back with regret. *Yeah life,* he would be saying, *I hung on.*

So, he dumped all three in rather quick succession. His military career was the first to go. He was an infantry soldier. When his promotion to major put him behind a desk with no respite in sight, he resigned his commission, to his wife's annoyance. She enjoyed the ten years of travel, especially the last billet at Kaneohe, Hawaii. When she asked, "what next?" he shrugged. She wasn't sympathetic.

She had reason. They had three children, two boys and a girl, all under the age of eight. The thought of heading back to live with parents in Akron, hers, or Grand Rapids, his, was not a happy one. The FBI was hiring. He applied and was selected.

That was over twenty years ago now. They were assigned to the Minneapolis Division, bad enough for her. After three years, he volunteered for the resident agency in Pierre, South Dakota. That made it worse. She and the kids lasted two years. The divorce was finalized three years later. "Self-destructive," she called him in the papers. He had no clue what that meant. Was that even grounds for divorce in Ohio? *Infidelity.* Surely that was grounds. *Extreme cruelty,* another good one. Or *Habitual Drunkenness.* But it didn't matter, he wasn't the one who filed.

She got remarried. It didn't take long. Truth was, he suspected it was in motion halfway through the Pierre assignment. He missed the kids and kept up on their birthdays and holidays. Two were married now. He didn't attend. Sad but he wasn't invited. Not being around to defend himself really hurt the relationships. If it was him with guardianship, he wouldn't have fostered such an atmosphere of hate, that much he knew. But what did he know; he was self-destructive.

He would have stayed in the Bureau if he could have rewritten the rules. He became Supervisor of the Pierre office. It wasn't a bad gig. Being a small office, he still got out to investigate, so the supervisor part just meant reviewing reports and going down to Minneapolis once a quarter. Then the seven-year rule came up. After his seventh year it was up or out, either up to FBIHQ in Washington or step down to be a Special Agent again. Washington wasn't going to happen. As for the step down, no big deal, and the pay stayed the same.

Only the step down entailed moving from Pierre; can't work where you once supervised was the logic. They needed him back in Minneapolis. They didn't need *him;* they needed bodies. And they needed them on the Counterterrorism squad. He had never worked CT, never been trained, never wanted to be. He was a criminal guy: bank robberies, kidnappings, gangs, drugs, Crimes on Indian Reservations. He lasted in CT three years, until he was fifty-two. With his twenty years in, he retired. Again, without a plan.

While on the FBI SWAT team, he took several temporary assignments around the country, several to Butte, Montana where he got to know a few of the county sheriffs. He was retired for less than a year when he received a call from Tom Vanderpool, perpetual Sheriff of Lincoln County. He was a gruff, old Vietnam Vet in his late sixties. As a retired Marine Gunny Sergeant, they hit it off when they first met about ten years back. He called Alston "decent" for an officer and Fed. Praise didn't get much higher from men like Vanderpool.

There was a job with the department. It was a three-year contract for a training officer, renewable, depending on funds. Sheriff Vanderpool had a man like Alston in mind when he introduced the concept to the Commissioners. When he met up with a mutual friend at a seminar in Butte and heard Alston had retired, well the timing couldn't be better. Would he be interested?

Alston's federal pension set him up pretty well, especially in South Dakota, especially for his simple needs. And his fly-fishing skills were getting serious attention amongst anglers. But he couldn't do that forever. He was only fifty-three, for crissakes. Some of his contemporaries were still in the Corps. Starting a life of leisure too early would make him real old, real quick.

Vanderpool suggested he drive to Libby to check it out, a fifteen-hour drive at most, fourteen or less if he badged his way through. But Alston didn't need to. He took the job before hanging up.

He closed up his small cabin on Bad River and was packed in less than two hours. No sense selling it; he wanted to come back. And renting meant worrying it would get trashed. He asked a neighbor to keep an eye out and dust it every month or so.

Training officer. He thought about it on the drive. Did that entail Equal Opportunity Training? Workplace violence? Community Policing best practices? He doubted it. Those words coming from Vanderpool's mouth would have sounded laughable. Still, he should have asked. Maybe Vanderpool was attempting to pawn such duties onto a contractor so as to free the real training up for a real cop.

He took his time, a leisurely lunch and dinner, a stop off at Custer National Forest. Letting his mind wander as it was prone to do on long road trips, he realized that for an out-of-the way state, Montana, like Ohio, had quite a few familiar cities: Billings, Helena, Butte, Missoula, Bozeman. And a few famous landmarks: The Little Bighorn, Glacier National Park, Great Falls Portage,

Upper Missouri Breaks, Bear's Paw Battleground. Well, except for the Little Bighorn, perhaps not so famous, except to the avid outdoorsman/history buff. Libby was not a city on many people's radar.

He made it in at one in the morning, seventeen hours. His GPS showed the Kootenai River just east of the downtown. His fly-fishing skills would not suffer. He checked into the first motel he saw, the Sandman Motel Down Under. Blurry-eyed and half hallucinating, who could pass up on a name like that?

He awoke at seven. Vanderpool told him to call him whenever and schedule a time to meet. He grabbed a bear claw and coffee at the breakfast bar and walked east to the river. Bumping into the Amtrak tracks, he meandered over to California Avenue and onto the riverbank. It was wide at this point, and not terribly scenic. It had a fairly fast flow and was no doubt pretty deep, not the best for fly fishing. Still, river like this had dozens of streams both north and south. Definitely needed to do some research.

He went past the Sheriff's Department on his return trip. It was close to eight-thirty. He asked a non-uniformed bleach-blonde woman at the front desk for Vanderpool. She informed him the Sheriff was out on a run. Alston assumed it was for breakfast. Vanderpool came in ten minutes later, sweating vigorously in his long-sleeved Green Bay Packer jersey. It had been nearly four years. He'd lost weight, a lot. He looked good, better than Alston. Fly fishing didn't keep one in Marine shape.

The sheriff sopped sweat from his neck with a face towel while offering his free hand to Alston. "Bright and early, huh? That's a good thing."

"I only did it to get a coffee and pastry," Alston said. "I'm not jogging."

"Not by choice for me. Got to, according to the docs. High blood pressure. Either I run or cut out the coffee, beer, and chocolate."

"Could do all four," the blonde said without looking up from her desk.

"Meet Bev? My mother died and left her in charge. Talk in the office. Want another cup?"

"I could use it."

He nodded to the corner. "Gotta get our own. Bev don't do coffee."

"Damn straight, hun."

The office, like the building, like the city, like the state, was austere. It fit Gunny nicely. "When you get in?"

"Late last night."

"So haven't seen much yet."

"I took a walk to the river. Good fishing?"

"So I've heard. Don't do any myself. So ... why'd you quit the Bureau."

"Didn't quit, Sheriff, I retired."

"Call me Tom or Gunny, Alston. So, why'd you retire?"

This was the interview *after* accepting the job. He wondered if giving the wrong answers would get him bounced before day one. The hell with it; the answers were the correct ones for him. "They pulled me down to the big city to work terrorism."

"And you don't think that's important work."

"Very important. Got a rash of Somalis going back to the homeland to learn how to do bad things. Just not for me, that's all."

"You're sounding defensive, Alston. Don't be. I'm the one who makes this decision and I made it. Just wanna know where your head's at."

Alston decided to hold his tongue and let the boss be boss. "First things first, don't know what your financial status is but I know Feds get a decent pension. You're divorced, right, and got kids?"

"She's remarried and the kids are adults, age-wise."

"Didn't remarry?"

Alston shook his head.

"I did. Twice. Got it right this time, I think."

Alston got it. They'd be working close together, and Gunny wanted to get inside his head a little. But he wouldn't, nobody did. Not his wife, not his fellow Marines, not his SWAT brothers, not his FBI co-workers, not the myriad of task force officers he worked with over the years or the tribal police officers.

"So anyway, salary. Best I could get you was twenty-nine grand. And that's bare naked. No medical, no dental, no matching four-oh-one. Days off and sick leave, that's left up to me, but trust me, I'll be liberal. I know how much you Feds enjoy your down time."

It was a joke, mood lightening. Alston gave in with a tight-lipped smile.

"Probably should have given you that input when we spoke, but I was hoping to get you more. Which I did, by the way. Originally they budgeted just twenty-five."

Alston was fine with it. He did his homework on Wikipedia. Median income for a family in Libby was about twenty-seven thousand. This pay and his pension put him three times above that, and he had no one in tow. Must make him the richest man in town. "Money's fine, Gunny. But I'll take you up on the liberal leave; I like to fly fish."

Gunny filled him in on the town, the county, and the department. The county was big but small; 20,000 folks crammed into 3,700 square miles. The department had twenty-seven sworn deputies. That raised Alston's eyebrows. "Don't take their law enforcement very seriously, do they."

"'Bout as serious as the rest of the country takes the military; not a damn 'til the shit hits the fan. But that's why I got the contracting bug. Too many additional duties for my deps, too many damn distractions. If it were up to me, I'd contract out the entire admin bullshit; dispatch, detention, community outreach, parking enforcement, process serving. Bam." He slapped his meaty palm on the metal desk. "Patrols and investigations, that would be it."

"So, I take it I'm gonna be handling all the gum-on-the-bottom-of-your-boot jobs?"

"Some. Kinda, yeah."

"EEO, community policing, type stuff."

"Not gonna lie to you, Alston."

"Not gonna lie to you either, Gunny; I'd rather be in Minneapolis working terrorism."

"Well, that boat's sailed, hasn't it?"

"You think that makes me out of options?"

"Look, Alston, I didn't call you just to be my PC officer. You have skills and experience. But you have no god damn – "

"Sheriff." It was Bev from just outside the door.

"Yeah, sorry. I meant to say, you have no gosh darn personality to speak of, and that's comin' from a Marine Gunny, mind you. But I've been to your tactics classes and seen you lead drug raids. I've listened to your op-orders. We need that here. So yes, to justify having you, I need to use you for the other stuff but trust me on this, your knowledge will be used and abused to the fullest of my power."

"When do I start?"

"Tomorrow. Eight. Unless you're up for an early morning jog with me."

"In my contract?"

"Nope."

"I'll pass."

Gunny flipped him a binder. "Read the policy manual. You have any recommendations, keep 'em to yourself for now. Wait till you learn where the bathrooms are before making yourself at home."

Alston stopped at Bev's desk before leaving. "I've been advised I have no personality. I guess I gotta develop one so I don't have to hear it for three years. I'm Alston Waters, new department training officer."

"Makes you feel any better, Mister Waters, I don't have much of one myself. Course I don't have to, I married the boss."

Three

Boning up on EEO and the like was mind numbing. Alston was always in compliance with the laws and rules as a Marine and Special Agent, but silly laws and rules had nothing to do with it. Those were just constructs mandated to ensure common decency, and since when did common decency need such oversight? Most of the stories the manuals gave as practical exercises consisted of behavior he associated with little boys pulling girls' pigtails and schoolyard bullying. The lessons, designed to drag on for two hours, he could sum up in two words. "Grow up." Still, EEO was a job creator for lots of people.

As for personality, he gave it his best shot. He enjoyed instructors who could tell a good opening joke. Of course, he enjoyed the drill sergeant approach, as well. He learned early on he was neither. He couldn't tell a joke; he couldn't curse. His lessons were peanut butter and saltine cracker dry.

Out in the field he was at his best. The county issued forty caliber Beretta PX4 Storms. Not a bad sidearm, but Alston preferred his forty-five. It also had two shotguns and two M-4 semi-auto rifles. One deputy was proficient with both, sixteen had never shot an M-4, and twelve had discharged a shotgun just enough to be dangerous to any good guys standing nearby.

The department's shooting drills consisted of static exercises at ranges of five to fifteen yards, and the entire day, from warm-up to qualification, took less time than the affirmative action classes. Alston introduced the use of barricades and drills for shooting from inside a vehicle. He constructed standalone doorways and window frames to simulate room and house entries.

He purchased three pepper popper targets, with his own dime, to develop speed and accuracy. He developed a close-range exercise designed to enhance their point-and-shoot skills. The range days went from ninety minutes to four hours. Not everyone was pleased.

"I get the training," Vanderpool said. "And so do the young deputies. But you got older ones out there. Standing that long isn't good for them."

"I hope to hell that's *their* bitch and not yours."

"Course it's coming from them."

"Some of those deps are sucking wind walking up to the firing line. Speaking of that, do you even conduct physical fitness tests?"

"Why? To put on record they're out of shape? They know that. It is what it is, so the saying goes."

"Agreed," Alston said. "And what it is, is those people have no business being in law enforcement."

"You've been giving the EEO lectures, just try getting rid of them."

"Just saying, Gunny, time to get serious."

"You just need to slow it down."

Alston nodded, more in understanding than agreement. "You got over thirty-seven hundred miles out there, and a lot of open spaces. Long guns are what you need. And good small unit tactics. Remember Leonard Peltier?"

"Out here, who doesn't?"

"Those two agents had a fighting chance if they had something better than thirty-eight revolvers."

"Getting bushwhacked didn't help," Vanderpool said.

"No. But I know Agents Coler and Williams would have changed the outcome if they had M-4's."

"That's a budget issue."

"But why aren't the M-4's and shotguns issued? They sit in the arms room; they need to be in someone's trunk."

"Yeah? Whose? You said so yourself, only Deputy Lester is proficient. You want him to be a one-man SWAT team?"

That was the opening Alston was working towards. Not a SWAT *team*, not for a twenty-seven person department, but a department that could function as one if the occasion arose. Alston, a team leader on the Minneapolis SWAT for twelve of his twenty years, was all in when it came to team tactics over individual training. He applied for the FBI's elite Hostage Rescue Team but was cut at the end. They gave no reason, they never do, but it was his personality again that did him in. He simply didn't mix well enough with the team.

When he returned to the office he was inundated with supportive texts and e-mails about how bullshit it was to cut him, that he was the most tactically proficient agent in Minneapolis, and the best marksman. It had to be politics again. But to Alston, peer relations were an acceptable reason to thin out the herd, and that had always been his Achilles heel. If it wasn't, why didn't any of the pity come via phone call or personal visit?

Knowing your partners capabilities, knowing they know what you know and are able to execute, that's the hallmark of any team in any field. So maybe Lincoln County didn't have the resources for a dedicated SWAT team; they could still be taught the weapons and tactics. All it took was time and training. In a crisis, that would serve them all well.

"I think your deputies need team building; they need some dedicated field training," Alston said.

"Sounds like you wanna take them out on an FTX."

"A field training exercise is exactly what they need. I'm not questioning your leadership or skills here, Gunny. But do you have a plan for your primary targets in this county? I mean, from a crisis management point of view, your hard targets, soft targets?"

"We have no nuclear power plants here, if that what you mean."

"No, but you have a big ass dam on that river. Closer to home, you have schools, hospitals, shopping centers, movie theaters. You need floor plans on file for those places, as well as wiring and plumbing diagrams. Whenever they change, you need updated copies. Your deps need to be knowing the entrances and egresses. I know you have festivals. You need tactical operation plans, not just plans for traffic control and parking enforcement. And by the way, you know none of them have any clue as to how to conduct house-to-house searches and clearing?"

Sheriff Vanderpool sighed and gave that look reserved for city officials who walked in with a parking citation. "Remember that hint I gave you about reading the policy manual and —."

"Really Gunny? That's the best you got? What I'm talking about here is exactly what you hired me for. You don't want it ... let me go. I got no dog in this fight."

"I guess I look at Lincoln County as a sleepy, old place that doesn't need stuff like crisis management and terrorist screenings. Maybe I could be more forward looking without going all Rambo on the place. But you gotta understand, you've been hired and I've been elected. Not your thing, I know, but I got politics to play by. I also have budgets and perceptions."

"You really think the people around here are going to fight you on this?"

"Hell, yes. I think it'll scare the shit out of 'em. What do I know that they don't? What am I hiding?"

"You don't need to tell them,"

"I make sure nothing goes on here in secrecy; it's how I keep my integrity and my parking spot."

"You don't tell them about my range drills. You don't tell them about my defensive tactics classes."

"Those aren't costing money."

"And neither will this."

Vanderpool sat up in his chair and cleared his throat. "Neither will what, Alston?"

Four

Montana is the fourth largest state in the nation, forty-eighth in population. The Missouri River originates in its southwest corner. Its flow drains most of eastern Montana to create a vast portion of the Great Plains. The western portion of the state is dominated by the Bitterroot Mountain Range which is part of the Rockies and the Continental Divide. The state animal is the Grizzly Bear. In the 1800's there were approximately 100,000 grizzlies in the west, now there are about 1,800; 800 in Montana. The state bird is the Western Meadowlark. There are plenty of Western Meadowlarks.

There are fifty-six counties covering more than 147,000 square miles. Lincoln County is the northwestern most county in the state, bordering British Colombia. Heavily wooded and mountainous, it also has the lowest point in the state at the Kootenai River.

Alston had been studying these facts and tidbits since his hiring. Being proficient at any endeavor means being a good students of all its aspects. He also reviewed and scouted for training areas months before approaching Sheriff Vanderpool. It gave him a lot of choices. There were mountains and flat lands, forests and plains, rivers, lakes, and national parks. The first consideration, bigger than terrain, was amenities. It had to have none. Restaurants, bars, movie theaters, malls, beaches, all distractions. As a team leader, back in the day, he could work around those, though not without a pushback. But with the advent of iPhone and such, distractions were omnipresent.

He'd have less of a problem here, but the reality was, these weren't the cowboys of the nineteenth century. People had come to love creature comforts and instant communication. He could get authority to conduct the training, authority to choose the time and place, authority to choose the deputies to train. But getting the deps to buy into it wasn't going to be easy. He'd set his Spartan plans in motion, then, being true to his quest to be more pliable, compromise and adjust as necessary. To a point.

Prior to Alston, Lincoln County training prep meant reserving the high school gym or putting construction barrels in the parking lot. Alston Waters didn't plan that way. He didn't waste his time or yours. "Go big or go home" could easily have been his personal motto. It had the Sheriff skirting their meeting for days. But at the end of April, eight months into the job, Alston cornered him.

"Time to make me earn the big bucks you folks are paying me," Alston said. "Just hear me out, is all I ask. If I don't have the answers you want, or at least good arguments, then shoot it down."

He started with the method: total immersion for four nights, five days; defined objectives using task, conditions, and standards; less instruction, more hands-on; relevancy and repetition; individual drills synched to team drills culminating in a field training operation; and all enhanced with minimal distractions. "And out here, there is no limit to minimal distractions." He thought it was a pretty good play on words, especially from him, lightly delivered and well timed to break up the concern he saw in his boss's eyes.

"That sounds ambitious," Vanderpool said.

"Yes."

"Well, I agreed to hear you out so I will. You have the details, no doubt."

Alston continued with the excitement of a young infantry lieutenant.

"It's out in a little town called Whitlash. Know it?"

"Liberty County."

"Yeah, that's where I might need you to come in."

"Don't say. Time for questions yet?"

"Sure."

"Why way out there?"

"It's got what I need. Good size hills, woodlands, and pastures for small unit tactics; wide open spaces for moving and shooting drills, an abandoned building for room-clearing exercises, and absolutely no distractions."

"Don't need to travel five hundred miles for any of that."

"It's three hundred ten miles, give or take."

"Who's paying the per diem?'

"I'm getting to that."

"And what's this abandoned building?"

"Sweet Grass Hills State Hospital."

Vanderpool nodded.

"You know the place?"

"I know it. It burned down, most of it."

"Not the part I need."

"You called on it?"

"I did my own recon."

"Course you did." There was a small commotion in the back parking lot, two guys arguing. Vanderpool used it as an excuse to casually lean back to catch the action. Only it wasn't casual. He stared out the window for a long minute. When he was ready, he returned upright and shook his head. "Hadn't thought of that place in a while. Nasty business. Twenty-three people died: seven staff, sixteen patients. Me and three of the deps went out there to help with the investigation, such as it was. Wasn't pretty."

"It's grown over now," Alston said. "Most of the damage looked to be in the upper floors, bottom two looked fine."

"You went in?"

"Brought out a ladder and looked through the bars on the windows. Even has furniture and equipment in there."

"Yeah, they closed it up tight right after. Not much worth saving."

"And the walls are intact, and the doors. Tight hallways, small and large rooms for entries. Good training site.

"Could be good for something, I guess."

There wasn't much passion in Vanderpool's voice. He was hoping the conversation would stop there but he knew it wouldn't. Alston was too far along in the planning stages to be concerned with events from over a decade ago, events he had not experienced and therefore could have no empathy for. It was just a cop-thing. One cop's nightmare was another's anecdote. Any cop in the business for any length of time had a story or two that disturbed them. They didn't need to adopt someone else's. The Sweet Grass Hills State Hospital was Vanderpool's.

"I don't think you'll get authorization."

"Why not?"

"Where to start? For one, it's state property. Then you got urban legends to deal with."

"You can make a call."

"It's almost summer," the Sheriff said. "Sure you wouldn't rather catch up on your fly fishing?"

"Gunny, you against the training or where I'm doing it?"

"Both, I guess."

"Since I've known you, you've been all about being direct. This hemming and hawing isn't you."

"Okay, I'm sure you understand the state bureaucratic issue."

"Just a phone call, like I said."

"You interested at all in the urban legends?"

"Not really."

"You'd better get interested; that's gonna be your big bugaboo. See, whether you believe in them or not, you have folks around here, good folks, who take them serious."

"You one?"

"Call it respect. You may have noticed there are a lot of American Natives here. Eight of them in this department.

"I've worked with Tribal police."

"I know. That's why I'm surprised, no ... disappointed you disregard their ways."

"Not so."

"No? Last July you scheduled three days of training during the North American Indian Days celebration."

"No one told me when I was planning it."

"You didn't ask. Then you didn't change it."

"I had things already scheduled."

"You had Clare Peone doing supply runs back in May, remember?"

"No."

"She does. She's from the Salish Tribe. And that was the Bitterroot Festival she missed."

"Never heard of it, and no one told me."

"Clare wasn't about to bitch, not to you, that's not her way. As for what the festival is all about, learn it. Do you know that river you fish in is named after the Flatheads?"

"Okay."

"Did you know there is no Flathead Tribe? It's three distinct tribes, and the Kootenai are one of them. Their aboriginal name is Kutanaxa, means 'licks the blood,' one of their hunting customs."

"I get it. You wanna throw some cultural diversity training on my shoulders."

"Yeah. But as a student." Vanderpool had lost that nervous spasm in his voice. This was important stuff to him, things he believed in. It made him feel a bit like Sheriff Andy Taylor. Sheriff Taylor didn't keep Mayberry safe because he enforced the law; he kept it safe by knowing the people.

"One Devil Dog to another, Alston, I love this town and this county. The people have been very good to me. I was a twenty-six-year Jarhead. At least half of those spent as a functioning alcoholic. When I retired and returned home to Helena ... well, I was barely functioning at all. Lincoln County hired me on as a dispatcher. Two years later I was the oldest cadet in the academy. Seven years later I'm running for sheriff, and damn if they didn't choose me.

"I'm not Native American, just grew up amongst them. Didn't give 'em much thought 'til joining the Marines. Then I understood. See we can get a bit miffed at soldiers, sailors, and airmen who slam us; it's part of the gamesmanship. But I won't tolerate a Marine who shames the Corps because the Corps is all about character. So, I won't tolerate a Native American who shames the character of their tribe. And I don't much care for outsiders who do the same."

That was it. He was getting his walking papers. Alston wasn't about to wait around for the formal presentation. He stood abruptly. It seemed the right way to handle the situation at the moment, but he felt childish and foolish standing there.

"Where you off to in a hurry? Sit the hell down, I'm not done." Alston took his seat. It was an order but with enough levity in it to relax him.

"I learned their culture; I'm still learning," Vanderpool continued. "We got high schoolers in this country don't know whose side Italy was on in World War Two; don't know who we fought in Vietnam or Korea, or that we even *fought* in Korea. Out here, most natives know about the Marias Massacre and the Battle of Rosebud. If you believe they've been conditioned to dwell only on the persecution, you're wrong. They know the tradition of the Round, Butterfly, Friendship, and Two-Step dances, and they can do them. They know the symbol for the bear and deer, and a hundred ways to use corn. They know the myths and legends better than we know American History.

"You understand why, Alston? It's not for arrogance or for protest. It's for the same reason the Marine flagstaff carries fifty-four campaign streamers; so no one forgets. Strange things happen when you really get to know a people's culture. You get to know their pride and their honor. Like their Fidelity, Bravery, and Integrity, the FBI motto, right?

"These Sweet Grass Hills, they're sacred to Native Americans, the Blackfoot in particular. They were hunting grounds, battlegrounds, and spiritual grounds. Now I guess you can go onto a plot of land or into any building in the big city and train without giving it much thought. But do that at Gettysburg or Antietam or the beaches at Normandy, and well ... I guess you just wouldn't. You'll get a lot of traction if you learn about these people you're training."

"Okay, Gunny, I've been schooled," Alston said. "Maybe I've been working this thing in a vacuum. Anything else I need know about this place?"

Five

On July 23, 2012, the Sweet Grass Hills State Hospital went up in flames. The hospital had its own fire hydrant, high pressure hoses, and enough extinguishers, if the people were there to use them, which they weren't. Being nearly six miles outside Whitlash, it took two hours before the volunteer fire department arrived. They would have been there much sooner had someone called immediately. No one did. It was contained to the top floor, the fifth. It was contained because the doors were locked. From the outside.

The fire began, they believe, after 12:30 A.M. The timeline was based upon a phone call made by Doctor Timmerman to his wife in Chester. They were newlyweds, having arrived from Seattle four months earlier. It was their ritual, him calling her as soon as he could after arriving for his forty-eight-hour shift. He was the rookie and had inherited the eleven P.M. to eleven P.M. The ninety-minute drive through desolation, with sketchy cell phone service, made his bride nervous. That night he called, the records showed at 12:33. According to his widow he was fine, actually bored already, all the patients sedated and asleep.

A volunteer backcountry ranger at the Mount Brown Lookout Trail was the first to spot the flames. He noted the time, 1:05. He couldn't get anyone at the Ranger station on his two-way until 1:15. The hospital was about half a mile away. He watched the flames, expecting them to diminish soon. He knew they had a staff of two doctors and at least five trained orderlies at night. He helped give their semi-annual CPR and firefighting training. They'd keep it under control until the trucks arrived. But they didn't.

The flames swept through the windows. There was nothing gradual about it. They moved as if swept out by an immense phantom broom. He couldn't see the building, but he saw the tips of the flames above the roof. Thank God it was confined to the top floor, at least the staff could usher them all out to safety. This he radioed to the ranger station. Still, he reported, better hurry. Wouldn't want the floors collapsing.

The floors didn't collapse; they were solid cement. And the walls were three feet of brick. The perfect furnace. Dry grass was the accelerate. Dry grass and benzoin. The benzoin the investigators from the State Police lab could understand. It was a topical agent used for burns, sores, and abrasions, common injuries at a state hospital of this type. But taking the time to spread what seemed to be piles of grass? It couldn't have been a patient. Had to be one of the staff, but all seven had perished. That was the initial report. But maybe there was an unreported eighth staffer present, someone on for an extra shift, one with a grudge, or a problem.

"We were asked to come in that morning," Vanderpool told Alston, "before any of the bodies were touched or removed. A fire in a state hospital, some fatalities, that's what I was told. I'd known Sheriff Abernathy since I was in dispatch. He was a Crow, not easily riled, but he was that morning.

"Somehow I thought it best to bring my Native American deputies along for this one. I don't know, the Sweet Grass Hills being scared lands. I thought, maybe they'd be good at interviewing witnesses and patients. I didn't know then there'd be none.

"We got there mid-morning. Abernathy met us at the driveway entrance. The firefighters were checking the structure, making sure it was safe for us to go inside. The flames were gone but the smoke billowed. 'Mattresses,' Abernathy told me. The fifth floor was where the patients slept. I asked him if he'd been in there yet. He didn't answer which gave me the answer.

"The elevator wasn't safe, so we walked the stairs. You know, Alston, how you do it in SWAT, climbing stairs slow, studying the next corner up ahead, staring upward, always expecting something bad to be waiting? We all watched Abernathy, a man who knew what was up ahead, and still he crept, as if it would change into something worse.

"I wasn't ready for it, none of us were. I couldn't tell a body from a floor lamp. It was brick and cement for crissakes, how much could burn? No one had any doubt it was arson. No, it was mass murder."

Vanderpool sat back and stared at the ceiling. Alston, still with a dozen questions, gave him his space. Having to relive this again, he deserved that much. Still looking at the ceiling, he continued. "Two of the deps had to leave the scene. One eventually left the department. Another I put on admin leave but she made it back okay. That was Clare Peone. Good dep still, but it changed her. Changed all of us." He snickered. "Except old Sonny Morning. Nothing changes Sonny Morning.

"We stayed on for three days, doing what we could which was little. Little cop work, that is. We bagged the bodies and the parts, made calls to family members, consoled those who came in. We did search the grounds for evidence. Later I learned the lab was able to ID all but two of the bodies. The staff wasn't a problem. They had their own dental records. But the patients' records were destroyed. Strange because they were kept on the first floor. We know they were lost in the fire because we found partials."

"So, it had to be a patient, one who escaped," Alston said.

"You'd think. There were sixteen; they think fifteen, maybe fourteen were recovered. Of course, could have been all sixteen."

"I'm confused."

"The bodies were cut up. We hope it was done after the fire, but who knows. Someone at the lab had the task of matching up body parts. Imagine that as your living? Christ. Never saw a fire that was so consuming. Must have been a lot of the benzoin used, must have gone up in a fireball."

"So, there's still the theory of an eighth staffer."

"Lotta theories, like the Kennedy assassination on a remote, rural scale. Could have been an eighth staffer, a rogue transient, maybe murder-suicide. I don't know. Doesn't make sense to me. But Abernathy told me later the hospital used temps. I'll call them transients. The place was so remote, and the hospital and its work was," he searched for the better word but found none, "inconsequential. It's done now."

"Didn't they track down all the prior workers, the temps, contractors? You know, investigate?"

"Abernathy did. He did a solid job. I kept up on it in the papers and the bulletins. Called him sometimes."

"He found absolutely nothing?"

Vanderpool's exercise regimen made it difficult for him to sit for long stretches. This was better than years prior when his sedentary lifestyle made it hard for him to stand for long periods. He stood to arch his back and stretch. "He found something," he said staring down at Alston. "But we'll never know what it was."

"He die?"

"You're gonna think we got the most inept police and labs in the country, Alston, but the coroner's ruling, he was killed by a wild animal."

"Why would I think bad about that? Plenty of bears here, right? Grizzlies?"

"It wasn't a Grizz. I spoke with the dep who found him out there, out at the hospital. Guess Abernathy didn't believe it was a rogue staffer either. It was an insane crime, done by someone insane. Someone sick enough to gather the doctors, staffers, and patients onto the same floor, litter the place with grass, spread highly flammable chemicals on everything and everyone, lock the doors to the floor, then vanish. Certainly, a staffer with that kind of mind would have been written up at some point. A worker would have brought stories home. That's not anger, Alston. That's insanity."

"Did the dep who found him have an opinion?"

"I don't know what he thought about who the killer was. I know he thought Abernathy was losing it, going back out there all the time. Searching around the place long after it had been closed up. It was the first place he checked when Abernathy's wife called saying he hadn't been home that night. Abernathy, or someone, had busted the lock on the front door. He was found in a back room. Not a place a Grizz would likely be, right? He was unrecognizable. His face, the dep described it as being sliced off in a very messy way. And innards pulled out of his stomach. A Grizz, even if it did follow him in, would have mauled him, not sliced him."

"Man with a knife."

"No, no knife. And the natives don't believe it was a man. That's the other legend you're going to have to overcome."

"What legend's that?"

"Cats. Lots of cats."

Six

Alston drove on with his planning with Vanderpool's begrudging approval. What could he say? Alston acknowledged his failure to appreciate the people he was working with. He made the rookie error of learning facts and figures but neglecting the people connected to them.

And he felt for the victims of the horrific events at the State Hospital. But to abandon training for a rash of legends and cats was dereliction of duty.

Vanderpool once again tried suggesting another location. For what purpose? To find another legend, another superstition? Would he need to become an expert on Native American lore, not to mention an environmental engineer, so as not to tread on another Big Foot or spotted owl? "As far as I'm concerned," he said, "I'll be the one most affected by this; I'm allergic to cats."

Vanderpool made the calls. It took some strategic navigation and arguing but he eventually received concurrence from the Public Service Commission in Helena. They didn't even know they had jurisdiction. For his part, Alston was able to obtain cartons of Meals, Ready to Eat rations from a National Guard unit at Fort Harrison. He also obtained scrapped sleeping bags, lister bags for water supply, canteens, ponchos, mess kits, and other individual items. He needed to make this as financially painless as possible for the county if it was to become an ongoing event.

And he had been working on a personnel list. He wanted ten on the first go-round. That made Vanderpool snap. "More than a third of my force?" Now I know you're crazy. Three."

"What kinda of team am I going to develop with just three? Besides, at that rate it'll take ten years to get them all trained. By then the first group will forget everything I've taught them. Eight."

On it went until six were allowed to attend, and it was cut from five days - four nights to four days – three nights. Alston was not happy to be condensing the training, but compromise was his new mantra. "I can tell you a few who won't go," Vanderpool told him.

He figured Clare Peone was one. And maybe Sonny Morning, which was a loss because Sonny was a monster of a man with unassuming leadership skills. It was his size, to be sure, but he was agile, quick, and amazingly coordinated. He shot as well with the left hand as the right; that was with his sidearm, shotgun, and M-4. And the M-4 he had never he held before. Alston had never seen a shooter combat load an 870 shotgun so quickly. He was firing round two before any other shooter was finished inserting the shells. He caught on to tactics, understood the principles, was an attentive student, was unflappable, and humble about it all. Least he was quiet about it, which didn't always equate with humility.

That was unlike Boyd Lester who wasn't as large, agile, coordinated, composed, or humble. But he had police and military experience. He was solid on tactics, and good with weapons. His brash demeanor didn't make him Alston's type of man, but this wasn't about Alston. If he could tolerate Lester for a few days, the department would benefit.

He wanted a female. But one wouldn't work so she needed a partner. There were four on the force. With Peone out, he needed the one he wanted least. Karen Stabler was solid. Not the best shot, a bit overweight, and mouthy, the PC term being "assertive." She was coachable, however. It was obvious she took the job seriously and wanted to improve her skills. Of all the deputies, Stabler was the one who seemed to most welcome Alston's new training regimen. He could use that type of attitude in the field, if for no other reason than validation.

Stephanie Mountain Star, however, had to be the most sullen, negative, and gloomy person he had met in Libby. He heard the story from another deputy about him and her being called to a domestic disturbance. It took twenty minutes of the husband being interviewed by Mountain Star to realize just how good he had it at home. Hadn't had a problem from the couple since.

The last two were a toss-up. He liked Terry Koopman. Alston had no clue as to why the kid chose a career in law enforcement. Actually, he didn't think he had chosen it as a career. He had an archeology degree from the University of Wisconsin. Alston wasn't sure if Lincoln County was a rest stop for him or a destination.

Mark Pratt would be good. He was an Oklahoma cowboy and mixed as well with Terry Koopman as he did with Sonny Morning. He didn't seem to take much serious, except Oklahoma Sooner football. His indifference would be a challenge.

Vanderpool surprised him by telling him to pick his team. He sat with them one-on-one in the break room after their shifts. He gave them the training rundown and proposed dates. He told them he was willing to reschedule, if possible, if there was a conflict. Part of his new gentler, kinder self.

Mid-July suited them all. Boyd Lester was the most enthusiastic, Sonny Morning, the least. Lester volunteered to be the range officer, tactical officer, and logistician. Sonny just shrugged his huge shoulders.

Koopman and Pratt were in. Koopman was single and Pratt was recently divorced. Alston had to wait on Koopman who expected to be invited to an archeological dig in Greece where an ancient Mycenaean tomb was found. When the funding fizzled, he signed on.

Since Sonny Morning seemed to have gotten over the state hospital fire (only thing he said about it was he still wouldn't eat burned bacon. Alston couldn't tell if was meant as joke), Alston ventured an attempt on Clare Peone.

She listened patiently without a nod or flinch. It made him uneasy. Was she having flashbacks? Was she working up the nerve to tell him to pound sand? Was she incensed that he dared to ask? "Course you wouldn't be the only woman there," he said. "Stabler's going."

"Yes, she told me."

"I know what happened out there. I know you were there."

"Sheriff Vanderpool told me you two discussed it."

Weren't many surprises left, except her answer. Of all the deps attending, Clare was the one he most wanted there. Not just to avoid a week alone with Stephanie Mountain Star. Clare was a survivor. He knew this from Vanderpool, who, as an old-school Marine, didn't lionize easily. Clare Peone was his champion. There was nothing sexual or familiar to it. He was thirty years her senior, well adjusted, content, and happily married. She was painfully plain, nervous, and uncertain in many things. But she was a fighter, and a Marine loved that in any person.

"What else did he tell you?" Alston asked.

"That I didn't have to go."

"Course not."

Most people Alston knew would take that as a cue to start a dialogue. But he supposed people like Clare spent most of their lives working out feelings internally. They were comfortable with decisions made without input. She thought on it for a night. After the next day's shift, she signed on.

Alston was willing to pay mileage from his own pocket for the use of someone's minivan for hauling the gear. It was Boyd Lester who told him no self-respecting Montana law enforcement officer would own a minivan. A local dealership supplied a Ford Econovan. This, along with the scavenger work done by Alston, allowed the training to be nearly tax-payer free, a benefit he made known to the Sheriff. "Tell that to the deps left behind who need to work double shifts, at time and a half, by the way."

The women drove in the van, along with Sonny Morning and Mark Pratt. Alston took his Jeep Cherokee, driving with Lester and Terry Koopman. In hindsight, he should have put more effort into the overall dynamics of the driving arrangements. But such things to him were like color coordinating a living room, just another thing he had no talent or interest in. Thirty minutes on the road had him realizing that four days was only a short time on paper. In real time it gave him everything ninety-six hours had to offer, both gratifying and agonizing.

It started with Lester trying to get under Koopman's skin. From the shotgun seat he twisted his head around to Koopman in the back. "Boneman, what happened to your boondoggle with the Raiders of the Lost Ark?"

"Cancelled."

"Cancelled or postponed?"

"I guess postponed."

"Postponed 'cause they didn't want you tagging along?"

Alston watched Koopman roll his eyes and feign interest out the side window. He wasn't sure Lester was the casual schoolyard bully, but he was sure Koopman was used to being the victim. He was probably competent and reliable. Course that's what the training was to validate. But up till now his quiet, almost apathetic demeanor made him unremarkable in a deputy's uniform. And his unwillingness to give it back to Lester made him this easy target. The truth, though Alston disliked bullies, he couldn't say he disliked them anymore than he did men who wore the badge, uniform, and gun without commitment, as if dressed for a Halloween costume party.

"No sweat, Boneman, we'll let you tag along. Course the only bone you'll be digging out there is your own." That made Lester laugh hard enough to satisfy him for a few miles.

"Hey Bones," he started again. "How did the skeleton know it was raining? He could feel it in his bones." He turned to look at Koopman, still staring out the window.

"Okay. Why'd the skeleton stop playing football? His heart wasn't in it. Get that one? No, nothing? 'Kay, last one I got. What does a skeleton order at a restaurant? Spareribs, right. Spareribs. Hey, I dug those up just for you. You could at least throw me a bone here." Koopman shook his head but otherwise refused to acknowledge him. *This was going to be a long week,* Alston concluded.

"Maybe those are too sophisticated for you, Bonehead. Here's some you'll definitely get. Two condoms are walking down the street and see a gay bar. One condom turns to the other and says, 'Hey, you wanna get shitfaced?' Why's it so hard for women to find men that are sensitive, caring, and good-looking? Because those guys already have boyfriends. Why did God create gay men? So fat girls could dance."

"That' s enough Boyd," Alston said.

Koopman turned to Lester, casually asking, "What are you implying?"

Lester shrugged and made a dopey *what-me?* face. "That you're an archeologist and you dig bones. What?"

"You saying I'm gay?"

"Damn guys," Alston said, "what are you, twelve-years old? You got guns and badges, for crissakes, act like you're old enough to carry them."

Koopman, back to looking out the window, said, "You're not only sophomoric, Lester, you're a dickhead."

"Oooh, interesting choice of words, Bonester. Whatta you think Captain?"

Telling them he'd turn the truck around and take them home would sound as if he was making light of it, but bringing them both back to Libby was just what Alston wanted to do. However, that would be another slap to his training program. It was like a scene from *Remember the Titans,* instead of Black and White it was ... hell, he wasn't sure what it was, really.

"Turn on the radio and shut the hell up, both of you."

"Relax, Boner, just having some fun, breaking up the trip." Lester said. "So, what should we listen to?" Right away Alston knew there was a punchline coming, "George Strait or Boy George."

Seven

They arrived at the state hospital a little after two. A county official was there to greet them, more than a bit miffed they were thirty minutes late. Alston tried calling the guy's cell but had lost service at Glacier National Park just outside Columbia Falls.

"I was gonna cut the lock but figured I'd wait," the man said. "No sense wasting a good rusty one if you weren't gonna show."

"No key?" Alston asked.

The guy, Loren Moore, Assistant Sanitarian from the Environmental Health Department, waved the large bolt cutters in the air. "Oh, I got a key."

He gave them an informative, though harsh commentary as he worked the bolt cutters around the lock. "Don't guess you folks could have found another building to use. No, none of my business for sure, just doing what I'm paid to do. Oh wait, this isn't what I'm paid to do at all."

"But you were the only one with bolt cutters, right?" Alston said.

Moore, having tried several times to snap the lock without success, held the bolt cutters to the ground and used them as a crutch to rest. "Didn't have no bolt cutters," he wheezed. "Matter of fact, didn't know I'd need them till this morning when I came to check the place out. Sure as shit, back to the office, ninety minute drive, searching for a pair, found them another fifteen minutes further south ... "

But Alston had feigned listening almost as soon as the bitching commenced. His last and only visit out here was purely for logistical purposes. Now he looked more at its tactical features.

He started at the top, the fifth floor, some sixty feet up. He couldn't help seeing images of the fire a decade ago. He didn't notice it last time but now he did, charred bricks outside. He looked up and down from first to fifth, all with barred windows. Some still had the old wire mesh behind them. Most were shattered. Kids with rocks, he figured.

The roof was flat. He brought ropes for rappelling exercises. More for confidence building than tactical use. He looked for posts for anchoring purposes but there were none in immediate view.

The area around the building was wide open in all directions. The closest grove of trees was thirty yards east, and what looked to be a partially collapsed well further beyond. There were small ridges and a depression that lead out to it. It would all be good for practicing approaches to a hostage rescue or armed stand-off situation. "Keep the damn kids away for a bit, anyway," Moore said.

"What's that?"

"There've been half a dozen car wrecks over the past ten years. Two fatals. This road and drinking don't go well together. Kids come up at night to drink and smoke, you know, weed. They know cops are using it, maybe they'll stay away. Maybe."

Alston looked on the side of the building. No fire escape?"

"Took it down few years ago, keep the kids from getting up on the roof."

"Doesn't look as if anyone's been able to get through that lock," Alston said.

Moore looked to be insulted. "I'll get you in."

"No doubt. But what I meant was, doesn't seem to be any other attraction here that would be of interest to bunch of local kids."

Moore raised the bolt cutters with a grunt to show he meant business this time. He was about Alston's age but long ago gave up trying to compete with the aging process, if he ever did. He was thin in the shoulders and arms. His distended belly was punching through his yellow Polo shirt. Guys with thick necks, shoulders, arms, and legs, could get away with pot bellies but on skinny guys, that was just a cruel joke of nature. Alston watched sweat pour from his forehead as arms and neck veins swelled. Moore leaned his full weight into it for a good fifteen seconds before giving it up.

"Catman," he said breathlessly.

"What?"

Moore took time to recover, wiping his soaked forearm over his soaked brow. "What the kids come for, the Catman."

Vanderpool told him about the cats. Dozens, maybe hundreds now, feral cats that populated the area shortly after the fire. The Tribes believed them to be the spirits of the children of the old boarding school and patients of the asylum, finally released to run free and wild. No mention of a Catman so he had to ask. "For real or stupid kid stuff?"

Moore was about to give the lock another try when Sonny Morning wedged his huge body between the two men. He grabbed hold of the bolt cutters and waited for Moore to let go. Sonny popped the shackle with the effort it would take most men to snap a pencil. He handed them back to Moore then excused himself.

"Big boy," he said to Alston. "So ... real? Real legend? Yeah. Real Catman? Like a wolfman? I don't think so. Been reports for years. Farmers in town have had cattle and sheep killed. Chickens, pigs, too. Claim they saw something big like a man but creeping like a ... like a cat, I guess."

"Any investigations?"

"County's come out. And some, whatta you call 'em, soothsayers? No, spiritualists, you know, mediums." He laughed. "Even had one of them TV ghost hunter shows set up here a few years back. Five nights, froze their asses off, and a group of them drunk kids stole their van and their equipment. Found the van, no equipment.

"And no Catman?"

"No Catman. Plenty of cats, though. Haven't seen any yet today, but you'll see them soon enough. My thought, and that of most rationale folks, it's just a Mountain Lion. Maybe stood on its hind legs at fences. Looks like a man if it's at a distance or you're high.

"Well, already wasted a good morning out here. I got another padlock in the truck you can put on when you leave. No need calling me; just snap it on when you check out. I'll keep the keys with me, so I know where they are next time you come up. I take it you will be using it again?"

"That's the plan."

"Enjoy. Oh, and a few rules the department wanted me to tell you. Stay off the fourth and fifth floors. There was a fire up there years ago, and they probably aren't safe. Also, the elevator's probably not going to be working but don't go messing with it. Fires and old age play havoc with elevators."

By now the entire team had gathered around, wondering what the long discourse was about. "Fires and old age play havoc with my dick," Boyd Lester whispered to Alston when Moore went to get the padlock "That guy like seriously takes himself serious." .

"Doing his job. Everyone get their gear together and bring it inside. And as I said twenty times, no ammo inside the building. And dig out your hiking gear and Camelbaks. We're taking a little two-mile walk." He didn't tell them those miles would be up Mount Brown. It was to be the first test of their mettle.

Mount Brown was the highest peak on the East Butte section of the Sweet Grass Hills, raising 2600 feet over three miles. He walked to the top casually in well under two hours. The slope was gradual, the terrain grassy with just enough rocks to make it more like mountain climbing. In July, it would be more strenuous which was what he wanted.

Once they turned east onto Black Jack Road, the mountain loomed dead ahead. Alston glanced in his rearview mirror to see the driver of the trail vehicle, Clare Peone, and the passenger, Karen Stabler, leaning forward to stare up at the peak. "That our hike?" Boyd Lester asked.

"That's it."

"Hot shit. Up for it Boner?"

"I've walked bigger," Koopman said.

"Great. How 'bout we jog it; make it interesting?"

"Get there walking just as well," Alston said. "And then you have energy for the mission."

Lester shot back. "If you're in shape, you can do both."

"Not a race," Alston said. "Walking's fine."

There was no moaning or groaning at the trailhead. Not that Alston didn't see it on their faces, all except Lester who was sickeningly excited and Sonny who he could never read. "Top off your Camelbaks from the five-gallon containers in the back of my truck. Conserve people. Like with your ammo in a shootout, every drop, every round counts. We start up in five minutes."

"Anybody want they can have some of mine; I won't be drinking much of anything on this stroll," Lester said.

"Everyone will get their own from the containers," Alston called out, avoiding eye contact with Lester. "And everyone will drink at regular intervals along the route. And we stay together on the mountain. "

Lester laughed. "That ain't no mountain, Captain."

"Rattlers all over," Sonny said.

"Okay, didn't know that," Alston said. "So, I guess watch out. We go up together, come down together. We'll take it slow. Just halfway up, that's less than two miles."

Lester protested. "Damn, hardly worth the drive for that."

Alston wanted nothing more than to ignore him and his running commentary, something he feared he'd be hearing all week. But this was a teambuilding exercise, and treating Boyd Lester as anything but part of the team was counter productive. Maybe like in an after-school TV special someone or something would put him in his place. He wasn't counting on it, though. "You want, Lester, hold your breath if you think it will make it more challenging for you." If nothing else, the comment loosened the team up and gave Alston a modicum of satisfaction.

Alston led them single file so he could control the pace. Every fifteen minutes he had them stop to drink. He could hear the heavy breathing to his rear but no one bitched out loud or begged to stop. That was what he wanted; see it through to completion. It was a good start to the training. "That rock outcropping," he said, pointing to his right at about the sixty-minute mark.

When they reached it and kept going, a few bewildered comments came out which he ignored. Three minutes later he pointed to a small grove of shrubs. The groaning grew in intensity upon passing them. After walking another ten minutes the line stretched thin. Sonny was at the rear sitting on a rock. Pratt, and the two women were stumbling badly over the loose rock. Only Lester and Koopman were keeping pace.

Lester jogged alongside him. "I know this game, boss. Psyche 'em out to make them quit."

Alston had him alone so he felt he could lay into him without alienating him from the team. "That what you think this is about, Lester, making people quit?"

"Thin out the herd."

"Herds already thin."

"Let's jog it, leave Bone-boy to look for his rocks.

Alston kept walking, his face to the front. "Anyone can get themselves into shape to run a hill alone. It takes a leader to get a team up it together. This is a team we're building. One fails we all fail. A leader would be back there encouraging them along, not up here scheming to leave them behind."

At that he stopped and started back down the hill, gathering up deputies as he went. "Everyone have enough water?" he asked. There were a few mumbles and head bobbings. "We were all doing fine until I gave you a stopping point, or what you thought was a stopping point. Then, even though you had water and stamina left, you gave up. Your bodies were able, but your minds weren't willing. Look down the behind you, you can see that first rock ledge we passed. We walked maybe two hundred yards passed it. It took walking just two football fields to make you to give up. Now you'll say, 'but you knew where the end was, we didn't.' Fair enough here. But in the real world, or a real mission, no one will know how long it will be or how bad it'll get. That's where you minds need to be stronger; that's where it needs to take control."

They stumbled back to the vehicles, all except Lester, cursing each small rock they tripped over, the same rocks they casually cleared on the trip up. Alston was about to remind them of that but held it, enough lessons learned this day. The plan was to rehearse squad movement-to-contact drills, but it was nearing four o'clock and by the looks of them, he wouldn't be getting their best efforts.

He broke open the MRE's. Amazing to him that only Lester and Koopman had ever eaten them. He was able to get three cases of twenty-four, plus portable stoves, mess kits, and cans of Sterno. It would leave them a little short, but he was sure some would prefer to go hungry than suffer four days of chicken pesto and pasta, southwest beef and black beans, and beef brisket, the only three entrees the armory had in stock.

He prepared his own southwest beef in silence; aware the uninitiated were following his moves. They were inspecting their food with both childish wonder and suspicion. It was Koopman who took the effort to show them how to set up the stove and assemble the mess kit into a usable tray. "Cheese tortellini and chicken fajitas are my favorite," he said. "Most people's, I think. And if anyone caught the dehydrated fruit, it's not half bad. Try it both ways, dry and hydrated, see what you think. Me, I like it dry."

He was beginning to like Koopman. Much of it had to do with how much alike he and Koopman were. Both quiet, speaking only when there was a need, both patient and composed. This he knew of Koopman based upon how he handled Lester. If Lester's jokes made an impact, you'd never know it by reading Koopman.

He wasn't the physical specimen Lester was, and Alston wasn't sure about his tactical skills, but those could be taught. Few police operations took the type of superhuman efforts Bruce Willis showed in *Die Hard*. And his simple act of showing them how to eat MRE's beat the leadership skills of Lester who was the first into the MRE case, insuring he had his pick. He sat on a rock preparing his meal, alone and detached. Seemed he only had something to say when it could be hurtful. He became involved when he could show his stuff as a way of boosting himself. His leadership style, if it could be called one, was to posture. Something in this man Alston hadn't seen since he was ten-years old watching torment on the playground. It was something he'd have to watch and control closely.

Eight

Back at the hospital Alston briefed them on the next day's training: preparing operation orders and small unit field maneuvers. The hike up Mount Brown didn't last as long as he had planned. They still had two hours till nightfall. The op order lesson plan would be a good way to spend the last rays of daylight. Other than flashlights and a portable Coleman lantern, the hospital promised to be pitch black. They could rest; they'd need it.

He assigned the small back room to the two women. It was a former examination room and had its own bathroom, for what that was worth. The plumbing was disconnected but it was a changing room if they felt the need. And there was a metal examination table they could use to lay out their clothes and built-in cabinets for their feminine things. It wasn't chauvinistic in his mind, just considerate. If they didn't think so and put up a fuss, they could stay with the men. They didn't fuss.

The front room was once the lobby, he assumed. Maybe a sitting room or library for the boarding school. There was once paneling for walls, now painted over with several coats. Still, the grain could be seen and felt through it.

It was stifling. Lester announced he was sleeping outside. Alston denied his request. "You do realize that with this many bodies in one room it will be unbearably hot," Lester complained.

"You want, you can choose another first floor room, other than where the women will be. But we'll all be together, inside."

"Why not all together *outside*?"

"All sorts of creatures and varmints outside," Sonny said.

"So what?" Lester countered. "People camp out all over this place. We're training to hunt down serial killers and terrorists, and we're freaking out over a maybe rattler?"

Sonny shrugged. "Grizzes and Mountain Lions."

"Sonny, you wimping out, too?"

"Mosquitoes. Hate mosquitoes."

"Four snake bites up here in the last two years," Clare Peone said. "One died. And two dogs."

"And that's out of how many campers?"

"There are Mountain Lions up here?" Karen asked.

"Where you from, girl?" Lester said. "Course there are."

"Ohio. I'm from Ohio."

"Yeah, home of the Buckeye chicken," Lester said.

"The Buckeye' s a tree, that's where the nickname comes from."

"Lots of bobcats and coyotes up here, too," Clare said.

"But the mountain lions eat bobcats and coyotes," Lester said.

"All right, all right, take a vote," Alston told them. "Inside or outside. I'll be the tie breaker."

"Secret ballot," Koopman said.

"We're not kids," Lester said. "Outside, raise your hands." His went up first. "Nobody? Seriously? Sonny, seriously?"

Sonny shook his head. "Too many mosquitoes."

Alston was in too much of a hurry to let this go on. For someone who didn't want to play childish games Lester was set on finishing out his. He went around the circle, browbeating everyone but Sonny, politely asking him to reconsider. The only one who gave him a hint of backing was Mark Pratt who said he didn't really care either way. "So that's two," Lester said.

"This isn't *Twelve Angry Men,*" Alston said. "It's settled. We're inside. I'm going to check out the training area we'll be using tomorrow, make sure campers haven't set up on it."

There was no way to reserve areas. He asked. There was hiking, biking, mountaineering all over the Sweet Grass Hills, especially in the summer. It wasn't a popular destination, but it had its enthusiasts who wouldn't take kindly to be rerouted.

He came across only two sets of hikers heading west to Gold Butte. He hurried back, intent on spending what would now be less than fifty minutes on his operation order lesson. He had the window down, Keith Urban up as he made the turn back to the hospital. He heard a gunshot, or thought he did. Around here, loose gunfire was probably common, but it was precariously close to where he was heading. He heard several more before the hospital came into view.

Lester was taking aim with his forty-five at the top floors. Alston bent his head below the visor to get a look at the target. From the corner of his eye, he saw Terry Koopman sprinting from the hospital and going for Lester with a recklessness Alston didn't know the boy had in him. Throwing the car into park, he jumped from it while it still rocked. As reckless as Lester was, shooting into an occupied building, having him blindsided by Koopman while holding a loaded gun would be all kinds of hazardous.

Fortunately, Koopman was in control and pulled up short. But his bellow made Lester flinch enough to miss his target, and he let Koopman know it. "You crazy, running up on a man shooting a gun like that?"

"Me? Me crazy? People are inside there."

"I'm shooting up top," Lester said pointing. "At the cats."

"Knock it off."

"You upset I'm shooting the pussies? You like pussies, Boner? Or do you like boners, Boner?"

"You know, I'm sick of you."

"How sick?"

"We're all sick of you."

That's when Alston stepped in. The war was on between the two of them. It would be disastrous to allow them to choose up sides. He took the weapon from Lester. "I counted six shots," he said.

"That's right, and five dead cats. Woulda been six if Bonehead hadn't gone PETA on me."

"I told you no live rounds."

"Inside. I'm outside."

The stories weren't exaggerated. Cats were slowly coming onto windowsills and the roof of the hospital. He turned to a rustling behind him. More cats. In the trees and laying along the dirt drive. In all, maybe fifty. The entire team stood motionless. A hundred cat eyes turned on them, waiting anxiously for a reaction to what had just occurred. Or perhaps waiting to judge. "Where the hell they all come from?" Pratt said.

"They live here," Sonny said. "Probably asking themselves where'd we come from?"

"What a creep fest," Pratt said.

"Yeah," Sonny said, "probably saying that about us, too."

A large cat, black and gray with gruesome patches at its neck and hind end, jumped on Alston's Jeep. It circled casually before laying itself down in sinister contentment. It broke the stillness with a soft meow at Alston, then watched his every move from atop the hood.

Taking an MRE carton from the back of the van and emptying it, Alston threw it at Lester. "Bury them."

Lester laughed. "What the cats? You shittin'? This is a forty-five, nuthin' left of them."

"Find what is, you and Koopman. "Can't leave them out here to stink and attract wild animals. There's a shovel in my Jeep. Take them out there," he pointed to a grove of trees near the abandoned well. "Rest of you inside for what's left of daylight."

He scooted the cat off the roof of the Cherokee for no other reason than, as Pratt said, it was damn creepy.

Nine

There was no sense beginning the class with a third of the team gone and thirty minutes left of daylight. He let them settle in. Clare Peone wrote in her journal, Karen Stabler read, Sonny Morning smoked while sitting at the doorway entrance, and Mark Pratt played harmonica. Lester came through the dark fields whistling *Whistle While You Work.* He stepped around Sonny, a broad smile on his face and the shovel over his shoulder. "Hee Haw, didn't know you played the harp. Sounds good. Merle Haggard, right?"

"Hank Williams," Pratt said. "*The* Hank Williams."

"Knew it had to be one of them hillbillies. Couple of guys in the One-O-First used to play that stuff all the time. Keep playin', keep playin.'"

A few minutes later and Alston had to ask. "Where's Koopman?"

Lester looked around and shrugged.

"He didn't come back with you?"

"No. I told him we'd take turns shoveling and we'd dump the carcasses together. He got derisive."

"Anyone see him come back?" Alston asked. Sonny and Pratt were silent. He went to the back room to Clare and Karen. They hadn't seen him since he went off with Lester.

He hadn't expected instant bonding between the two. He was sure they'd always be at each other's throats, and he didn't much care on a personal level. They had incompatible personalities. Lester was sarcastic but upbeat;

Koopman was cordial yet gloomy. They'd never work as a team but burying cat parts was Alston's way of telling them they'd better try.

He told Sonny to take a look around. As soon as Sonny left the stoop a chorus of cat wails went up. Like spring peepers in a swamp, the sound engulfed them. "Angry sonsabitches," Pratt said.

"Wonder why," Karen said.

"Honey, you can't handle shooting a cat you're in the wrong line of work," Lester said, spreading out his sleeping bag.

"Listen," Pratt said, "here that? They're upstairs, too. I mean, inside."

"This place is sick with them," Lester said. "Telling you, Captain, there's your target practice. Do the area a favor, too, cut down the population."

"Didn't see 'im," Sonny said stepping in.

"Shit, those cats gonna go on like that all night?" Pratt said.

"Play that harp of yours, Pratt. Drown them out."

"Gettin' noisy," Sonny said. "Gonna shut this door, no one cares." And as soon as he did, the cats ceased.

"Look at that, will ya. When Sonny Morning talks, folks and cats listen," Lester said. "Well, you old fogies can settle down, I'm going exploring."

"Where?" Alston asked.

"Here. Up, down."

"Wait till morning; we'll all go."

"I got a flashlight and I'm a big boy. You want us hiking hills and burying cats, that's one thing. But this ain't the army, and you're not my commanding officer. Hell, you ain't even a sworn police officer." Then he smiled. "No offense meant in any of that, but you're here to train us, not babysit us."

This was a serious challenge to his authority, but the kid was right, he had no authority, not officially. And Vanderpool was still wallowing in doubt when they left, establishing no pecking order. He was pushing it by ordering the burial but at that least had a health and hygiene basis. Letting this matter go could affect the training but fighting it would escalate the tension being built. Best to treat him like the insufferable kid in the classroom who can take up ninety-nine percent of a teacher's time. Treat him as if he wasn't there and he takes up none.

"Anyone game?" Lester said as he headed to the back stairwell.

None were willing to spend anymore time with him than needed. At least that's what Alston surmised. "Hey," he yelled out. "Stay off the fourth and fifth floors, and out of the elevator. It's not safe. That came from the county if you need authority to keep you in check."

Lester saluted as he passed through the fire door.

There was a thirty-foot hallway that led to two doors. The one straight ahead, Lester guessed, led to more rooms, more offices. This being a former asylum, perhaps he'd find a bed with straps, maybe a machine for electroshock therapy. The one to the right was either a door to the outside or the basement.

He lingered in the hall for a moment in the event someone decided to join him. Despite the warm night, the hall was cold, owing to the cement floor, brick walls, and lack of windows. Through the doors ahead was another empty room with no furniture and scarred linoleum floors. There was dust in the corners and grime on the walls, yet it didn't give the appearance of having been vacant for long. For one thing, the floors weren't dusty. And no cobwebs. Did dust and cobwebs proliferate in interior rooms without windows? He wasn't sure. Must be kids had found a way in, maybe used the room to drink, smoke weed, and get laid. Made no sense they'd take their empties out with them though; he never did. Why not leave a ratty mattress or sleeping bag behind; he always did. He gave an involuntary shiver as he passed through.

Onward and another choice. Three doors. "Easy to get lot in this place," he muttered. He checked each and was surprised to find desks, chairs, tables, and file cabinets. And all very nice and well preserved. "Could use this stuff in my place, better than what I got now." He opened a couple of drawers that contained file folders. Fingering through, he came across miscellaneous papers to include receipts, addresses, phone numbers, employee work schedules, and a manual for an IBM typewriter. "Nothing to see here folks, move along."

The Maglite beam flickered a few times before becoming noticeably weaker. Though he knew the cause he slapped it several times against a wooden desk. Something very quick and determined crashed through his legs, scaring him back into the darkened space as he dropped the light. Whatever it was was gone, at least for the moment, allowing him to catch his wits. "Who's there?" It was a hoarse whisper that lacked authority, which was fine. He didn't really want an answer.

He approached the Maglite which had fallen. His own shadow on the wall was a menacing sight as it slowly advanced, feet shuffling, shoulders hunched, arm outstretched. He snatched at the Maglite and plunged the beam into the corners behind him. It stopped on a gray cat watching him from atop a five-drawer cabinet, its back arched as it buried itself into the corner.

"You sonavabitch."

It hissed, sensing Lester's rage. Lester raised the Maglite and ran towards it. It gave an ineffective paw slap before leaping to the floor and pass Lester. "Should have plugged you like I did your mama, fuckin' thing," he screamed after it.

His light was nearly extinguished and admittedly he was unnerved being there. He went back through the hallway, intent on returning to the front room. The cat skidded out with him. It disappeared behind the door in the hallway, the one he thought went to the outside or to the basement. He noted it on his way in but didn't note it being open. It was now, only slightly ajar, barely enough room for the mangy cat to squeeze through. The hall was colder now, and it gave him a deeper chill he had to stop to shake off. He pulled at the door, hoping to see the fading light on a grassy hillside. But there was only blackness. That, and more cold.

"Shit, a basement," he muttered. "I hate basements." And he had a right. As a police officer in Des Moines, Iowa he got shot entering one. It was nearly six years ago. The bullet, a substandard thirty-eight round shot from an ancient Smith and Wesson revolver, lodged under his left armpit, skirting his ballistic vest, taking the damnedest route the doctors had ever seen. He must have had his arms raised at a perfect, or imperfect, angle, they said. And if the weapon was a forty-five, they'd be pulling it out of a corpse.

For sure the room clearing training exercise would have them entering this place at some point. If Waters knew about his past, he'd probably send him down first, just to humble him and bring him down a notch. "Sonavabitch isn't going to back me down," he said brashly. "Different place, different time. That basement wasn't empty; this one is. No one here but me and a cat."

He knew there'd be a time of reckoning when he would be forced to confront this fear. Not fear, he refused to see it as a fear. It was an anxiety only, like a dentist visit or his first parachute jump. The shooting review board from the state police suggested counseling but he knew the cure. It was sitting in the dentist chair and making that jump. Now, it was descending the stairs knowing this was a different time in a different place.

The timing was fortunate in that he was alone. He wasn't leading an entry team. He could approach this obstacle on his own terms. It wasn't an ego-thing. The reality was, having the confidence of fellow officers was paramount. It was why he despised Koopman. Koopman was just passing through; Koopman had no passion for the job; Koopman had no discipline to do what had to be done. Just as his own bluster didn't mean he was arrogant, Koopman's silence didn't make him humble. What Lester saw in Koopman was a condescension, and he was damned if he'd let a man like that see him wary of walking into a dark basement.

He was in a small alcove, no larger than a coat closet. The wooden stairs down were on his left. He moved ahead slowly. It was, he assured himself, because the Maglite was dying and basement stairs in old buildings were notoriously narrow and decrepit. He grabbed the rail as the steps shook beneath him. Talking to himself for comfort, he narrated the trip down. "Like this rail's gonna hold me if the stairs give out. Kitty, better be off the stairs or I'm gonna kick the living shit outta you. Holy cat crap, how many of you are living down here?"

Halfway down the stench of cat feces engulfed him. He was down as far as he cared to be. He shined the beam in all directions, to include his rear. The basement was extensive, probably the area of the entire building. There were numerous load-bearing brick pillars that looked as new and sturdy as if placed there last week. The cement floor had settling cracks but was otherwise in good shape. Dusty furnishings were scattered about. "Time for a garage sale, folks. Make a few bucks to pay some bills. Hey Kitty, where'd you disappear to?" He shook the railing, making enough noise to scatter anything in the dark. It upset a piece of metal that crashed to the floor and echoed long and loud.

He turned to leave when he spotted a large door built into the wall about ten feet behind the stairs. A vault. He descended the rest of the way. The stench was overpowering. He would have been satisfied enough with what he saw and smelled to tell Waters to forget about staging operations down here. But a vault? They left perfectly good, functional furniture behind. What else?

Whoever said cats were clean when it came to their own shit must have been selling them. The floor was covered with it. Wasn't much he could do about avoiding it. He didn't expect cats to sweep it up, but he thought finding an out-of-the-way corner was in their DNA.

The vault ended up being the elevator door. It was closed but he noticed it was stopped a foot and a half above the floor. He bent down and shined the beam underneath just as a cat hissed and jumped out from under it. It sent him spilling backwards. "That's it, I'm not going out by way of a heart attack." He picked himself up and made a straight line to the stairs, determined not be sidetrack by another intrigue. At the top he rested and composed himself. He had made it down and back. And his story of the cat smell was his proof. For those on the department who had their doubts, he had proven them wrong. Now, he just had to wait for the sweat to dissipate and believe it himself.

Ten

He didn't make eye contact with anyone when he came back into the front room. He was still shaking inside. It was from a lot of things, but he settled on the cats. Had they not been there around every corner and crevice, he could have stayed in his own mind, work his ancient fears out one step at a time. He feigned more interest in his dying flashlight, slapping the lens as he unscrewed the bottom. "Damn thing died on me back there. Batteries are almost new."

"I have a pack in my bag," Alston said.

"No, I got some in the truck. May want to rethink any training in that basement. Cats and cat shit everywhere. Stinks like hell. They're even jumping out of the elevator shaft."

"Unbearable?" Alston asked.

"I thought so."

"I'll check it out tomorrow," Alston said, a bit exasperated with another change.

Alston had a Coleman lamp in the center of the room, though only he seemed to be using it, scribbling notes on a pad. Pratt and Sonny were dead asleep.

"Hell, it's only nine-thirty," Lester said. He looked over the back room where a low light was shining through the cracked door. "Girls are up."

"Stabler's reading. Anything else down there I need to know about?"

"Furniture, cats. The elevator's stuck in the basement."

He saw Alston's questioning look.

"Don't sweat it; I didn't push any buttons. It's stuck between floors. Boner not in yet?"

"Maybe he decided to sleep out in the truck, get away from certain people."

"Getting a bit concerned about the lad, are you?" Lester said. "Maybe found himself an old Injun burial ground to dig up."

"Just check the trucks while you're out there. If he's not there we'll go hunting for him," Alston said with more than a hint of irritation.

"We're like little kids, huh Captain? I know, I know, if you boys would just get along. But you gotta ask yourself, you really want a guy like him as your wing man?"

"Enough, Lester, okay. You're right, I'm not the sheriff out here but it's my show, and I can tell you I do have some influence back in Libby."

Lester stepped over Sonny's sleeping heap on the way to the door. He pulled on it casually but it didn't budge. He tried twice more, little more oomph each time while looking for a deadbolt or latch he may have missed. "You got this thing locked somehow?"

"Shouldn't be."

"Then it's stuck like a mother."

Alston couldn't move it either, so he went for the big gun. "Sonny," he said. "Sonny, you awake?" When he didn't respond he told Lester to nudge him.

"Shittin' me. For all I know he wakes up like a hungry bear."

Alston knelt over Sonny and shook him. No hungry bear, he awoke gradually and with some effort. "Need your help," Alston said.

"What?"

"Door's stuck."

Sonny climbed to his feet. With an effort half that used by the other two, he managed to rattle the door. "Wait," Lester said. "Hear that?"

Alston put his ear nearer to the door. "No."

Lester told Sonny to pull on the door again. Sonny gave it a quick tug. "Not like that. Like before, jiggle it a few times. Hear it?"

"I hear something." Alston said.

"A banging, right, against the door."

"Okay."

"The padlock," Lester said. Alston looked at him in alarm. "That sonavabitch, Boner, put the padlock on the door. Fucker locked us in."

There was a barred window six feet to the right of the door. Alston shined his own flashlight through it but couldn't get a decent enough angle to see. He was joined by Lester who screamed through it. "Koopman open this fuckin' door. Koopman. Koopman, right now or I swear I'll kick your ass."

"Didn't the little county guy say he had the key?" Sonny said.

Lester looked over at Alston then continued cursing at Koopman though the bars. All this commotion awakened Pratt and got the two women out who didn't yet know the details but were sure of the problem.

"He wouldn't have latched it," Alston said.

"Why not, the little fucker?"

"There's sure to be another way out," Alston said. He saw the look of relief on everyone's face except Lester's whose concern was focused on despising Koopman. They had no way of knowing what Alston knew. That through his own reconnaissance, this place had no other way out, not an obvious one. By virtue of the building's purpose, the solid steel door was designed to keep one from breaking out. All the windows he saw were barred, with thick bolts anchored directly into the brick-and-mortar walls. Maybe hours of sledgehammer work could do the trick. He doubted a sledgehammer was conveniently left behind.

"We'll try to get these bars off."

"How?" Lester demanded.

Alston looked around. "I don't know. Maybe there's a hammer or pry bar around."

"Right. Maybe a few sticks of dynamite left behind, too, huh? I told you, didn't I? I wasn't the problem, it's Koopman. Deranged bastard."

"Enough," Alston said. Lester's antics were seriously disturbing others. "Go upstairs," he told Lester, "See if you can find another way out. Take someone with you. Sonny, you stay here with me."

"I'll go," Karen said.

Alston handed them each a handheld radio. "Alpha four," he told them, then conducted a radio check.

Lester recharged his Maglite with fresh batteries from Alston's stash. He couldn't control his fingers as he fumbled while he loaded. He couldn't get out of the room fast enough. Karen Stabler did her best to keep up. This wasn't the place she wanted to be, following the person she least wanted to be with. But she needed to make her bones with the department and herself. Leaving the state probation office may have been the mistake her mother said it would be. "You're a listener," she told her daughter. "You know how to empathize with people. And that's a good thing, it's a gift."

But Karen didn't think she was such a good listener. In listening too much, she got as many lies and excuses as she did atonements. In listening too little, she found herself making unfair assessments. On both extremes her empathy waned. A common theme from her probationers was the treatment they received when first arrested. It was there, with that arresting officer, that the offender most often developed their impression of justice, and no matter what occurred after, good or bad, that initial impression lingered.

But for the physical fitness portions, the academy wasn't much of a challenge. And she surprised herself on the range. She enjoyed the gentle balance between mind and body it took to place a bullet into a bull's eye at twenty-five yards. Still, the sterile environment of the academy was a long way from the streets.

Her first arrest wasn't pretty. It was a domestic dispute; an encounter they taught you could turn without notice. The young wife was beaten severely by her much older drunk husband. Her four children, two in diapers, were huddled in the corner. They weren't as scared as she would expect, leaving her to understand this was a typical Saturday night at home. Most times, if things seemed to have settled down, deputies were advised to just issue a stern warning. But the husband was in a bad way, going on about his wife being a whore. Leaving him behind wasn't a responsible choice.

When she cuffed him, it wasn't the wife who turned on her but the little ones, diapered babies included. Her back-ups said it was quite a sight. Two kids wrapped around each leg, biting, and clawing at her. One pulling daddy away while another slapped at her with a fishing pole. All while she tried reasoning with them in her soft, librarian voice. It took Stephanie Mountain Star lining the kids up against the wall, threatening to have them shot, to quell the house. "Sometimes," Stephanie told her, "You gotta use your outside voice when your badge won't do."

This was good, being in an environment where, according to Alston, she would be learning new things along with every other dep. Everyone was at ground zero, and everyone would be put in leadership positions. Here she could develop those skills in a controlled environment. If she couldn't walk-the-walk, then she'd quit. This she shared with no one. This test was hers to pass or fail.

"Maybe we should each take half a floor," she called ahead to Lester.

He turned and looked at her as if he hadn't a clue she was following him. "What?"

"We both have radios and flashlights. If we take one floor at a time we can move together, you know, make sure we check every spot."

"We're not looking for a fugitive; we're trying to find our way out. You do what you want; I'm going to the roof."

"But we're supposed to stay off the top two floors."

He shook his head in disbelief. Of course, stupid thing to say. Safety rules meant nothing at the moment. Thinking outside the box, not her strong suit.

He headed up the dark stairwell, his flashlight beam skipping across the floors, walls, and ceilings. Karen breathed hard in keeping pace. The airtight stairwell allowed them no respite, no place to rest and recover. It was cold cinder block and cement. Their feet dragged as the chalky echo bounced around them. Their throats had turned dry; their lungs ached. Lester couldn't escape fast enough. Karen was coaxing her burning quads to keep moving. Neither one thought of a third being in the stairwell with them. One who was quite at home there, who could sprint the steps without a dry throat, aching lungs, or burning quads. One who was waiting at each corner for one of them to make another wrong move.

Eleven

"You have a compact?"

Clare cocked her head. "A what?"

"A make-up thing, you know, with a mirror?"

"Yeah, sure." Clare ran to the back room and returned with her compact. She handed it to Alston. He extended his arm through the bars, the mirror at his fingertips. "Come up here, shine that flashlight back at the door."

Clare moved to the right of Alston and pushed the flashlight through the bars. She was blind as to where it was shining, relying on his directions. "Tilt your hand a little, towards the building. Okay up just bit. No, too far. Down. That's it. Hold it. Damn, yeah, it's the padlock. And it's latched."

He pulled his arm in. Clare didn't like the look of distress on his face. Sonny's jaws tightened. "If we find a bar, I might be able to get my arm out there, torque the lock off." Pratt suggested.

"Never get enough leverage."

Sonny pulled at the bars. "Buildings like this, built to last."

"Gotta hope they find an opening up top," Alston said.

"Yeah, then all of us can jump five stories," Pratt said.

"That'd be six, countin' the roof," Sonny added.

"Makes no sense Koopman playing games like this," Pratt said.

Clare was back in the corner, squatting in the dark, her hands wrapped tightly over her head, as if a terrible blast had shook the room. "Not him," she said.

"What?" Pratt asked.

"Not him," she repeated without looking up. She began swaying gently.

"What's not him?' Course it's him, who else is out there?"

Clare began shaking her head to the slow rocking of her body. Pratt looked to Sonny. "She okay?"

"What?" Sonny said. "Like I speak chick body language?"

"I don't know. Thought maybe this was an Indian medicine thing?"

"She obviously thinks she knows something."

Pratt turned to Alston. "What? What does she know?"

Alston flashed his light just above her head so as not to blind her. The color was gone from her face. Her eyes, what he could see of them, were dark and hollow. He may have gone with Pratt on this one, that this was a trance she had put herself into. But he knew where her mind was. And from the look on Sonny's usually unreadable puss, it was obvious he knew, as well. With Lester' s unwitting help, Alston could keep up the facade that soft-spoken Terry Koopman had a cruel, sadistic streak in him after all. But the truth - Alston was with Clare, sure that Koopman had nothing to do with this.

Crazy thing about a flashlight, it cut the world to a sliver. And by virtue of its power over darkness, it was in control. The hand may think it to be master, but it flicked left, right, up, and down in accordance with maddening nothingness beyond. The hand was connected to a mindless being that knew only what the light revealed. This coffin world with its narrow boundaries and low ceiling was a fitful place for Karen.

Old buildings were settled, she thought. The creaking floors and walls were done. But these weren't. Always, just outside the beam of light, life-threatening disturbances arose. And the flashlight pushed and pulled her hand frantically to keep them at bay. Yes, just walls and floors settling. It comforted her until she remembered the walls were brick, the floors concrete, and did bricks groan, did cement creak?

She was on the third floor, making her way around the outer rooms where the windows would be. There were dozens of rooms. Small closet rooms, large bay rooms. Rooms that led into hallways; rooms that led into rooms. Rooms she knew were lined with outside walls but no windows. The windows she did see were barred; heavy bars so tightly constructed that a fat rat would find it a challenge to escape. What threat thirty feet off the ground could so unnerve the architects to make captivity so complete? And where would an escapee go? She shined the light through the bars. Nothingness as far as the beam could throw.

She learned quickly to trust one sound, that of her own feet. Anything else would be a threat. She slid purposefully along the grimy concrete to accustom herself to it. She had no weapon, but she could let go a banshee screech that would rock these walls. She was alone; she had to be. It was, after all, the reason she was up here searching for a way out.

She couldn't escape the thought she was being followed and watched. That would be just like Boyd Lester. She knew the joke about never trusting a man with two first names. Boyd Lester cinched it. Not that she was a looker, though she knew from her training that looks had little to do with the crime. And the man was plain creepy. The way he spoke to people, the way he stared at them. Even his innocuous greeting felt intimidating, or at least challenging. It was as if he hadn't a socially conscious nerve in his body. But he was a cop, for crissakes. Brash, loud, obnoxious, insulting, but still, a cop. That should have comforted her.

This was part of the crazy inner monologue as she made her way. She had no clue as to whether she had checked all four outer walls, but nothing looked promising. Did Lester say he was checking the fourth floor? No, he made it quite clear he was going to the top floor. To the roof, actually, and he ran off as if being chased by a cleaver-wielding psychopath. Now that was an image she could have spared herself.

"Do what you want," he told her. Well, going back the first floor was what she wanted. The fourth floor was bound to be like the third floor, only higher. And the fact was he was probably right, getting onto the roof would be their best chance. Getting down was the issue.

She outran the flashlight beam on her way back the stairwell. A bad decision, she realized, as she was now disoriented. This was not like getting around an active hospital. There were no well-lit exit signs. The entire floor now took on the ominous expectations of the horrors lying beneath a child's bed.

"Settle down," she said to herself. "Breath slow. Like shooting. You need to control your breathing, steady your hand." At that she looked at the wall where the beam was gyrating uncontrollably. "Damn it," she said, grabbing the flashlight in a death grip with both hands, as if it was the neck of a prairie rattler.

Her breathing slowed as she composed herself. Then she heard it, deep breathing not her own. And, as Alston had told them while setting up, that was the problem with empty rooms inside a cement and brick structure, sounds echoed and moved, like referred pain. Concentrating too much and too long on the wrong spot could be detrimental.

She fought the urge to run. She focused her senses but the breathing she knew not be her own was now gone. "Lester, that you?" She heard a shuffling. She shined the flashlight from her ten to two o'clock. Nothing. A thick, suffocating musk odor hit her. It was heavy, like the scent her father would spread around the backyard to attract deer and elk. She paused for only a moment to determine its source. Realizing such an odor made little sense in a closed building, she backed off quickly. She made a right face and searched down to her six o'clock. Another right face to complete the circle. "Lester?" She'd have given anything for it to be him playing the asshole again.

She stepped back slowly until she struck a wall, then moved along it, with the hope it brought her back to the stairwell. The breathing began again, and that odor, now in her path. The flashlight showed her nothing, but she knew it was there. Something. "Damn you Lester, if you're fucking with me ... " Her words and tone were out of character, but they fit the moment. That, and they helped settle her, giving her comfort in placing a face on the threat.

She was at a corner. She knew enough about close combat tactics and horror movies to know that nothing good happened where walls ended. As she moved back from it to get a safer view, she was tripped by a skittering cat that screeched as it dashed between her feet. She spilled to the floor, losing the flashlight as she cracked her elbow upon landing. The pain couldn't compete with the panic that finally seized her. She scrambled on hands and knees to the flashlight which had bounced ten feet from her. The cat was crouching against the wall, coal black but for jaundiced eyes and flashing fangs. It greeted her with a sinister hiss while its six-foot shadow loomed menacingly above her. Unconvinced it was the only creature on the floor with her, she snatched the flashlight and came drunkenly to her feet.

She ran forward in the direction of her momentum. She stopped just short of an open elevator shaft. She turned sharply and headed back up the hallway. She let melodrama overwhelm her. But screw it. Something was out there, something that was trying to touch her, that would harm her if it did. This wasn't going to be how she ended; tossed down an elevator shaft or chopped up on a cold concrete floor. Then, as if breaking through the water's surface, she found the stairs. Her mind had her sprinting down, panic stricken, all the while chastising herself: *You're a cop, you can't be running from the dark like a child. You're the one people look for in a crisis, you're the one with the answers, you're the solution to the boogeyman.* Those thoughts, though, did nothing to slow her mad run to safety.

Twelve

She still wasn't composed when she entered the front room. And it didn't take astute observations to see the others knew something was not right. "What happened?" Alston demanded.

"Nothing."

"Don't tell me 'nothing.' I can tell —."

"I don't know, I mean, I saw something up there?"

"What?" It was Pratt, still spooked by Clare's chilling statement.

It was time for Karen to slump against the wall across from Clare, bookends in terror. She looked into Clare's eyes. This verification that she was right to be very afraid did not give her comfort.

"Where's Lester," Alston asked.

She looked around the room. "Still up there, I guess."

"Why didn't he come down with you?"

"We split up."

"I sent you two up there to work together."

"I know. But he wanted to go right to the top floor. I figured it made sense to recon the lower floors first."

"What was it you saw?"

Now that she had composed herself in the safety of the team, the truth of what she saw versus what she imagined made her sound more like a spooked teenager and less like a trained deputy. Her answer embarrassed her. "A cat."

"Shit," Pratt said. "A cat? There are cats all over this place. Get it together. Damn. A cat." He began laughing, a nervous laughter not met by others.

Alston was reminded of the Assistant Sanitarian's comment about the Catman legend that had evolved out here. And after Vanderpool's take on the legend, that the cats were souls of the children and inmates who died here, Alston wasn't taking the stories, crazy as they sounded, lightly. Not now that it was spooking half his team. "All right, " he said, more to change the topic, "While Lester's still looking let's give technology a chance. The sun's down, maybe that'll give better cell tower connection."

"Not in this building," Pratt said.

"Worth a shot."

Sonny was already working his. "I got nuthin'."

"Told ya," Pratt said. "Maybe out the window." He stretched his arms through the bars, resting his forearm on the cement sill. Within moments his cell phone spilled from his hands as a heavy weight crashed down. Before he could succumb to the shock and pain, he stood frozen before Terry Koopman's slashed and bloated face settling into a slow spin at the end of a rope. His eyes bulged from their sockets, staring down at dark purple cheeks that had been pared open in crisscross fashion. His mouth had been torn; the lips peeled back. Both ears had been severed. He wore no shirt. His torso had been savaged as if sliced through with razor blades.

No one in the room had noticed. The sounds coming from him were guttural squawks and croaks, urgent sounds coming from a man whose voice box had been removed. After an interminable wait, Karen Stabler glanced up at him.

"What's wrong?" She jumped up as she called across the room. "Something's wrong with Pratt."

He was stumbling as she approached, hands on his knees, the classic vomit position, which he did as soon as she grabbed his shoulders. The concern that surrounded him was broken by the frantic screams of Karen who had taken up the unfortunate position in front of the bars. "Sweet Naapi, what in hell happened to him?" Sonny said as he moved her back from the window.

Alston closed on them and immediately withdrew a four-inch hunting knife. He reached through the bars and severed the rope. Lester ran into the room, winded from the long flight of stairs. He announced that all the windows were barred, the exit doors were either frozen tight or locked from the outside, but there was a roof hatch he couldn't budge. "Someone puke?"

"What were you doing up there?" A rhetorical question from Alston, meant more to gauge Lester's reactions than to get an honest answer.

"I just fuckin' told you. Pratt just puke? Not good. Not good in a closed-up room. He's gotta clean it up; I can't take cat shit and that stink too." Which was an honest enough response, from a normal man, or a sociopath.

"You did this, you sonavabitch," Karen cursed.

"Did what? Make him puke?"

"And that was you following me upstairs."

"I was on —"

"Don't lie to me. It was you." She turned to Alston. "That's who I saw. He was up there, trying ... maybe what happed to Koopman, maybe he was trying to get me."

"Koopman come back?" Lester asked.

"Were you following Stabler ?" Alston asked.

"I never saw her after we left the stairwell."

"Fuckin' liar."

"You," Alston said pointing at her. "That's enough. Truth is you don't know what you saw."

"No. But it had to —."

"And Lester, you were never on a floor with her?"

"Never."

"So how did Koopman get tossed off the roof?" Sonny asked.

"Tossed off the roof?" Lester said. "No way. I told you, there's no way out up there, 'cept maybe that hatch. He went over that roof, he jumped is what he did."

Sonny shook his head.

"What?"

"Not the way he come down."

Lester stared into each horrified and accusing face. He ran to the window and shined his flashlight to the ground outside. "Good God." He turned to them. "And you think I could have done that? I can tell you this, we're not alone in here."

Thirteen

It seemed incongruent to be worrying about the dynamics of the group inside after what just transpired outside. But those dynamics were the very issues Alston had to address swiftly and firmly. All the plans he had for artificial stress were now OBE, overcome by events.

Clare was convinced of the evil residing here. Pratt was just a mess, his mind a weak link between realty and imagination. Stabler was anything but stable at the moment. She was a sudden loud bang away from hysteria. Like the others, she was needing to know that the killer was in plain sight, and that no one was waiting around the next corner. Alston was sure Lester wasn't involved in any way in the brutal killing of Koopman, other than bullying him into walking the woods alone. But he had made himself an easy target for the accusations. Sonny Morning was the one rock. But his type of asocial regard wasn't reassuring or endearing.

"You said there was a roof hatch?" he said to Lester.

"Yeah. Yeah, but it was stuck. Seemed stuck. I couldn't get to it, just jabbed at it with a pole."

"What are we going do with Koopman?" Pratt asked.

"Not much we can do," Alston said.

"We can't ... let him lie there," Stabler said.

"We won't. But first we have to get ourselves out of here."

"What about what Lester said?" Pratt said, staring at him. "That we're not alone in here."

Everyone was staring at Lester, expecting an answer, or at least an explanation. "Just makes sense, right?" he said.

"We'll stay together 'til we figure this thing out." Alston said. He looked at Clare who had offered nothing since earlier in the evening. She didn't get up to see Koopman, didn't react to Stabler's scare upstairs, didn't voice an opinion on Lester, and worse, showed no reaction to anything going on around her. Alston quietly asked her to her feet. She stood slowly without a word. "You okay with that? Coming upstairs?"

"I think so."

Lester would lead. Alston would follow. He had Clare third in line and asked Sonny to take up the rear. Lester and Sonny only would have flashlights, to conserve them in the event the ordeal stretched out. "Got ropes you want me to carry up?" Sonny asked as they lined up ready to ascend the stairwell.

"Left 'em in the truck," Alston said. “We know there’s one already up top.” He looked at each of them for a reaction. There was none. That was good, they were beginning to think realistically.

The convoy moved up slowly. "Hey, Sonny," Lester called over his shoulder.

"Yeah?"

"Keep your beam up the stairwell; I'll take care of the front."

Sonny did as directed. His Ace Hardware flashlight barely reached the next landing. Alston listened to and felt the heavy breathing from Clare who was practically in his back pocket. He glanced over his shoulder. If they all could have fit on the same landing, they’d have been asses to elbows.

Lester proceeded with caution, as if for sure there was a threat around each turn. "Pick it up," Alston told him. "There's nothing in here."

"So sure?" Lester said.

They reached the fifth floor. The pace had been laborious but all of them were out of breath as if it had been a sprint to the top. Alston let them recover and orient themselves before moving out. "Where's this roof hatch?" he asked Lester.

Lester brought them around the other side of the floor. It was a large room. Probably sleeping quarters. Alston noticed the walls with no charred bricks.

The fire must have been on the other side. Lester grabbed a wooden pole that was actually three, two-by-two wood strips nailed together, about twelve feet in length. With the first thrust at the hatch, it jumped slightly enough to show a string of stars and closed with a heavy thud.

"What the fuck?" Lester said. "I banged at that thing half a dozen times and nothing."

"Musta loosened it," Sonny said.

Lester's face showed his defiance. "Think I'm shittin'? Think I don't want outta here as bad as you?" Without waiting on a response, he continued, "I had nothing to do with what happened to Koopman. I'm a wiseass, I admit that, but that ... that was twisted. I ain't twisted."

"Find something to make a platform," Alston instructed.

There were rectangular examination tables, desks, chairs, and tall bookcases scattered throughout the top floor. Through the efforts of Sonny, they were able to construct a clumsy tower that nearly reached the ceiling. "Pratt, you think you can scale this thing?" Alston said.

Pratt shook the chair that was on the desk that was on the examination table. "Think so, if you can hold it steady."

With Sonny holding down the base, the others took hold of other furniture as Pratt made his way up. He was shaky enough to have Lester wisecrack to Sonny, "Don't know what he's afraid of, not near as far as the fall Koopman took."

"Just can't help yourself, can you boy."

Pratt tapped gingerly at the hatch once at the top. "Won't budge," he called down.

"You got to give it some effort," Alston said.

"I can't get any leverage." He was on the chair, the last piece of furniture in the pile. Lester hopped up to steady it. Pratt gave the hatch a vigorous push with both hands, and it flew open.

"Can you hoist yourself out?" Alston asked.

"Yeah."

As soon as he was up and through, Lester scrambled after him. He pulled himself through effortlessly.

"Anything up there?" Alston yelled.

"Fresh air." It was Lester.

"Everything all right?" he added.

"Give us a sec," Lester said. "Just checking it out now."

"Hold it steady," Alston told the remaining team. "I'll go up. You three don't move from this spot. Sonny, your flashlight still good?"

"Ah-huh."

"Conserve it. We won't be long and hopefully we'll have someone on the ground to get us out of here soon."

"Don't let it be Lester," Karen said.

Alston wasn't as sure on his feet and hands as he was in his SWAT days. Crazy how falling never entered his mind back then. He gave several looks to Sonny, signaling him to grab hold of as many pieces of furniture as he could. When he made it to the roof Lester and Pratt were nowhere to be seen, and yes, that made him nervous.

He saw the quick flash of a light at the front of the roof, two figures laying prone under the dim starlight staring over the edge. He jogged over. "What's going on?"

"He's gone."

"Who's gone?"

"Koopman. He's not down there."

Lester illuminated the immediate area and then some while Alston leaned over, following the powerful beam. "Try pinning this one on me," Lester said.

"Wolves drag him off?" Alston asked.

"Possible," Pratt said.

Alston pulled on the rope that once held Koopman. "What's on this thing?"

"Oil, feels like. And kerosene by the smell," Pratt said.

"Who wants to go down?"

"Better be you Pratt," Lester said, "I'm sure the boss still wants me on a short leash."

"Doesn't matter to me who goes down, you or Pratt."

"I'll go," Pratt said. "Then what?"

Alston dug into his front pocket for his truck keys. He then tore a small sheet from a memo binder and handed both over. "Call Loren Moore at this number; he's the assistant director of something or other, the little guy who met us out here."

"What if I can't catch a cell tower?"

"Drive south towards town. Shouldn't have to go more than a few miles. And better call the Sheriff, fill him in."

"How 'bout trying to bust us outta here first," Lester suggested sternly. "We all rappel down the rope."

"Not sure we're all capable of that. Short of breaking that lock —"

"Worth a shot."

"Maybe."

"What about Koopman," Pratt said, "his body, I mean."

"Not a priority at the moment," Alston said.

Pratt grabbed hold but couldn't get a solid grip on the oil-soaked rope. He took off his s shirt and wrapped it around his hands. "Should hold for sixty feet or so," he said.

"Just take your time," Alston said. "Don't outwalk your grip.

Pratt took a deep breath then started down.

Fourteen

Lester directed the flashlight to guide Pratt down the rope. "Don't let yourself hang," he told Pratt. "Brake and squat."

"What?"

Lester guided him on how to drape the rope over the tip of his left boot while clamping the rope tight with his right boot, creating an "S" loop designed to support his body.

"Hey, it works."

It was slow going. Alston stood to stretch his legs. From behind he heard a small commotion. Believing it to be the others coming up to investigate, he continued to stretch. It was the mounting chorus of low hissing that made him turn abruptly.

It was half a dozen cats not ten feet from him, crouched low as if ready to pounce, yet seemingly content to study him. From the shadows came more. At first one at a time, then several at once. They oozed in from the dark edges of the roof like an overflowing vat of soup. They floated in in hypnotic waves, now a hundred sets of yellow-green eyes staring up at him.

"Shit," he muttered, loud enough for Lester to hear as he rolled over onto his back. "More damn cats."

"Not just more, like every one in Montana," Lester said. "Musta come out of the roof hatch. Why didn't they yell out to us?"

"No," Alston said. "They came from the sides."

"They climbed the building? They can do that?"

"I don't know." Though they didn't look likely to attack, Alston knew enough about cats to know how instantaneously they could. And the notion of so many doing so made him very nervous.

"What are they doing up here?" More of Lester's nervous rhetorical chatter.

In an instant there was a sudden flash of light from down below and Pratt's maniacal scream. Lester flipped back to his stomach; Alston fell onto his. The flashlight wasn't necessary as the rope was ablaze below Pratt who scrambled madly up it. "Wrap your leg!" Lester screamed. "Wrap and pull! Climb, damn it, climb!"

But as Pratt's panicked face stared up at them, they all knew how this was going to end, and so Alston shouted the only advice he thought could work. "Let go. Let go, Pratt. Drop!"

Lester turned to him. "What the fuck you tellin' him'?" He shouted back down the wall. "Just climb you bastard."

"He can't out climb the fire. He has to drop."

Lester looked back down. The fire was engulfing Pratt's boots. "Drop!" he screamed. "Drop you stupid bastard!"

He was only halfway down, another thirty feet, at least. But he dropped and fell hard, his legs folding uselessly under him. He was alive; they heard his scream, but he wasn't going to be much use for a rescue mission.

"Can you move?" Lester wanted to know, but Pratt was in no condition to answer. They could see he was on his side, his torso twisting but his legs motionless.

"Had to have busted up his legs," Lester said.

Alston remembered the clowder of cats on the roof top with them. But when he turned, they were gone. Every one of them was gone.

After a few minutes Pratt regained a semblance of composure. He stared up into the beam of light Lester was offering. "I can't feel my legs," he yelled.

"That's a good thing for him," Lester said to Alston, "Don't think he'd wanna be feeling anything down there."

"I gotta get down there," Alston said.

"Yeah, no, don't think that's a smart move. Not until we know what the hell caused a spontaneous fire under his ass."

"We don't have a choice. How much rope is left?"

Lester pulled on the rope. Its end was still bright with embers. "About half as much as we started with."

"Least I can prepare myself for the fall."

Before he could grab hold of the rope, a black wave churned in the shadows beneath them. It came from the grove of trees beyond the parked trucks. Silent but relentless it crested beneath them where Pratt lay. The flashlight beam followed it in as it reached Pratt, consuming him amidst his bloodcurdling screams.

"Cats," Lester said. "Hundreds."

Alston had scraped a handful of gravel and hurled it below. It was a pathetic gesture that did little to scatter enough of them. He grabbed handful after handful and rained them down without looking. Then he heard the gunshots from Lester. He let go four or five shots. Alston looked down. Several cats lay dead ten feet from Pratt's writhing body, obliterated by the forty-five caliber rounds. Others scattered, but many more casually moved just a safe distance away in wait.

"You brought in live rounds."

"Now is not the time to write me up for disobeying a stupid order," Lester said while combing the ground in short bursts, an Ayoob grip on the flashlight and handgun.

A commotion behind them had Alston turning quickly while Lester let go two more shots. "What's he shooting at?" Sonny asked, puffing mightily after his short jog.

"Cats."

Sonny leaned cautiously over the ledge. Clare Peone and Karen Stabler joined him. The cats were crowding in on Pratt again. The noise from the gun was no longer a novelty for them, or perhaps they understood the odds in their favor, so many of them against the occasional gun shot. Lester spotlighted Pratt. The three newcomers to the scene stood in shock to see him covered with blood. Peone suspected it to be splatters from the several dead cats laying nearby while Stabler accused Lester of hitting him with errant shots. "They're eating him," Sonny said.

In unison, like the marching of an army, the cats closed the circle. They were being drawn, or perhaps pushed, towards the thrashing body whose pleas for a rescue hadn't subsided. None of the onlookers offered advice or encouragement; there was none to give. Pratt had no weapons. He couldn't even battle back with his legs. Swinging his arms was a futile gesture, as useless as Lester's gunshots. "Somebody get down here," he called into the light. "They're coming. They're coming back. God, please get down here."

Alston took the rope. "I'll tell you when I'm ready to drop. Soon as I do," he told Lester. "Spray the area."

"Then what?" Stabler said.

"I'll try to get him back to the truck."

"Never happen," Sonny said. "Look." He lifted Lester's hand and directed the light onto the two trucks parked close by but not close enough. Like stadium bleachers dozens of cats, possibly more, sat on the hoods and roofs.

"It's the only chance he has," Alston argued.

"You don't put out a fire by dousing it with gasoline," Lester said.

But Alston was already gathering the rope in. Below there came a mad scream. They could actually hear the trampling of hundreds of paws. Pratt was nowhere to be seen, under mounds of spinning cats and flailing tails, undulating like lunging snakes. While the others watched in horror, Stabler grabbed Lester's weapon from his hand. She fired a shot into the mad melee. The cats scattered. Pratt lay immobile and now silent. Even from the distance they saw most of his face chewed and clawed away. Stabler aimed carefully and put two well placed shots into his chest.

Karen Stabler held the weapon limply out to her side. Lester slipped it from her fingers. "I had to," she told no one in particular. Her confession was flat. If this team was to be her judge and jury, she offered no hint of a defense. If she were expecting repercussions, she didn't seem to care. Sonny wrapped his meaty arms around her shoulders as he gently escorted her back. Lester and Clare readily followed.

Alston took Sonny's flashlight but didn't dare illuminate the scene below. The sounds were sufficient. There were none from Pratt. He could hear cats jostling for position. There was the occasional screech and hiss, but it was the lapping, that usually innocuous noise his ex-wife's cat made at its milk bowl, that horrified him most. He could see that tabby now, crouched low and compact while it ate, its sandpaper pink tongue darting feverishly into the bowl, yellow eyes glancing menacingly up at Alston, daring him to get too close.

Across the way by the two trucks, a figure stood beneath a tree branch. The light caught it for the briefest of moments but it freeze-framed in his mind's eye as it stared back at him. Not human, not animal. Something ... else. It was thin but there was no fragility to it. It stood at the ready, erect, and defiant. Its arms long and cocked at its side. But Alston's focus was on its wild mane of red hair and a thin beard that hung patchy and jagged. Then it smiled. No, not a smile, a scowl, held long enough for Alston to see something not quite right. He stared back hard to confirm what he was seeing. Its teeth, he was certain of it now, glared like fangs.

Fifteen

"Bring all your supplies and rations over to this corner," Alston said, pointing behind him.

"Why?" Lester asked.

"I want to inventory what we have."

"What *we* have? You plan on some kind of redistribution?"

"Rationing Lester. We'll need to ration."

"Rationing's fine, just don't go throwing all our supplies into one pile. We were both in the military; we know how that experiment works out."

Alston ignored the critique. "Sonny, get Koopman's and Pratt's stuff, too."

"Let's look at what we have here," Lester said. "We have a self-proclaimed leader who leaves an unlocked padlock on the door with all of us inside. He leaves the basic supplies outside: ropes, batteries, guns. He sends a man down an oil and kerosene-soaked rope with a half-digested plan to get help. He has no ammunition so when it's needed, it's up to me and a woman to jump into action. Now he wants to take charge of what we have left. Anyone else see an issue here?"

No one spoke up and that was enough confirmation for Lester to continue. "Here's a plan. Cats get in and cats get out. My thought is they use the basement. I know they've been down there; I smelled their shit."

"We'll do nothing before having an after actions report," Alston said.

"You shittin' me? You still got us in training mode? You think that ... animal, that thing out there is gonna give us time to mind-fuck this? How 'bout we get operational?"

"Didn't we just try that?" Sonny said.

"Okay, correction. How 'bout we *stay* operational."

Stabler, her body still trembling, her voice feeble, asked, "What thing out there? What'd you see?"

Lester saw nothing, and Alston wasn't about to give up his apparition. "Somehow the rope Pratt was on caught fire while he was going down," Alston said.

"Didn't just catch fire," Lester said. "Someone lit it on fire."

"We don't know how," Alston said.

"Use your head, man, it wasn't spontaneous combustion. And I think we can all eliminate me and Koopman now. And don't be trying to protect us as if we were kids on a field trip. Now, is the basement the plan or not?"

"Give me your extra rounds," Alston demanded.

"Like the man said, 'from my cold, dead hands.'"

Another battle brewing. One that based upon recent events Alston would have a hard time winning support for. He issued a compromise. "Then keep it holstered."

"Until I need it."

Sonny tossed two A-bags behind Alston, letting the team know where he stood. "You want," he said to Lester, "you go down there, tell us what you find."

Six sets of gear were put into the circle. That was all of them minus Lester who dragged his gear to the far corner of the room, his literal and figurative statement of defiance and isolation. There wasn't much to distribute other than assorted snacks led by Pratt's beef jerky and Sonny's Little Debbie's cakes. Clare had two large sandwich bags of sliced carrots, celery, and cucumbers. "Hope we're not here long enough to make me a vegetarian," Sonny droned in mocking dry humor.

"Hope we're alive long enough," Stabler said in fear or her own dry humor.

Alston had had to make unpopular decisions before, though none this closely connected to life or death.

"Just so you know, I appreciate you having my back on this. You know, with the gear and stuff," Alston said to Sonny.

"Yeah, no big whoop. Truth is, I'm not sure you know what the hell you're doing, but I really don't like that guy."

Alston turned out his lower lip and nodded at the less-than-reassuring endorsement. "Guess he thinks he has a better plan."

Sonny looked at him expectantly. "Better than yours?"

"Guess he thinks so."

"So, what is yours?"

Alston shrugged. "Dunno."

"Yeah. Well … better get one. You got a nut with a gun and a lady 'bout to slit her wrists."

"Clare?"

"Oh, yeah."

Sonny pulled a camouflage Gerber hunting knife from its sheath and worked on balancing it in his palm. He twisted its point into his thick, brown callused hand, pulling it out and repositioning it just before it broke the skin. "So … what the hell did happen up there?"

"You saw."

"Ah-huh. Saw what happened. Don't know how."

Sonny wasn't one to talk much. Pregnant pauses and silence didn't bother him. He seemed to welcome them, like a jogger waiting for traffic to clear at a street corner. He spoke when he had something to say or a question to ask. So Alston wasn't concerned about opening up to him on what he had seen or thought he saw.

"I can tell you what I saw," he told Sonny, "but I'm going to have to wrap my head around it before I can explain what it was all about."

"Soundin' like an Injun, now."

"Did you see any cats on the roof?" Alston asked.

"No."

"None came out off the fifth floor? Up through the roof hatch?"

"Uh-uh."

"Well, that's the first crazy thing. They were up there on the roof just before Pratt fell. Jumped, I mean."

"Why would he jump?"

"I told him to; the rope was on fire."

"Guess that's the second crazy thing that happened."

Alston took the knife from Sonny. He slapped the side of the blade against his own palm. "It was like the cats were a diversion," he said, staring into his open hand. From the corner of his eye, he could see Sonny staring at him. "They came out of nowhere. When we turned to look at them, that's when the rope went up in flames. Then just that quickly they were gone."

"Then they got all over Pratt."

Alston nodded. "Think that's crazy?"

"Whole thing's crazy. Where you wanna start?"

Alston laughed into his cupped hand at first. And softly. He then dropped his hand and rolled his head back, letting go with a loud burst of laughter. The others, sitting pensively along the wall on the other side of the room, looked on as if he had lost his mind.

Sonny's comment was worth perhaps a smile but certainly not this high-energy reaction. But it was just what Alston needed to release his bottled-up tension. From Clare, it came out as her detachment. Stabler used hostile agitation. And it had Lester's provocations ratcheted up several notches. Sonny just stayed Sonny.

"Sonny Morning," Alston said. "Your folks had some sense of humor."

"Sunukkuhkau," he said.

"What's that mean?"

"He who crushes."

Alston shrugged. "Okay, didn't mean any offense."

"That's my name, Sunukkuhkau Morning Gun."

Alston deciphered. "Got it. Sonny Morning. He who crushes the morning gun."

"It's Algonquian."

"I thought you were Blackfoot?"

"The language is Algonquian. Really, it's a family of languages. In the plains it's called Arapaho. Confusing shit. I don't know how they figure it. Some language guy with a federal grant and nothing better to do."

"Still, parents had the good sense to shorten it."

"My grandmother did that. My old man named me. He was bigger than me and a wild man. He came across Sunukkuhkau somewhere and thought it fit him, so he gave it to me. Only he didn't stick around so he had no say in what I was called. Feminine side won out. Wanna know about 'Morning Gun?'"

"Good story?"

"I think so. Know about the Marias Massacre?"

Alston shook his head.

"Eighteen-seventy. Soldiers were out looking for some hostile Blackfoot. 'Stead they came to a Piegans village. This Piegan tribe was part of the Blackfoot Nation, but they were a peaceful one that had a treaty with the government. It was January twenty-third, early in the morning. Cold as a bitch, heavy snows. The braves were out hunting. Yeah, the soldiers knew it. At least one soldier recognized the band as a peaceful tribe. Yeah, he told the command. In the end, they ambushed and killed 173, mostly woman and children, and a few elderly. My great-great-great-grandfather was one. Not before picking up a rifle and killing twelve soldiers, least that was the family legend passed down. So ... Morning Gun."

"And someone along the line dropped the 'Gun.'"

"I did that. Nothing particularly Sonny-like about a gun."

"Nothing particularly Sonny-like about you," Alston said.

Sonny cocked his head. "That was uncalled for."

"Sorry, guess it was. Why become a cop if guns aren't your thing."

"Never said that. Just don't want them connected to my name. And cops do lots of good things that don't involve guns, right?" He leaned his blockhead back against the wall and closed his eyes. "What I wouldn't give to just sit out there."

"What wouldn't we all?"

"My uncle worked at this place for like three years."

"Really?"

"Custodian. He had some wild stories."

"Such as?"

"The patients, the staff, its history. Creepy most of it, so I can see how Peone could go off about ghosts. The staff though was the worse, the part that scared me most. To hear my uncle tell it, this place wasn't much better than a Vietnamese POW Camp. Supposed to be that the sane fix the insane. Sounded to me like insanity won out. Don't believe anyone ever came out cured, but there were those who worked here that came out infected."

"Your uncle being one?"

Sonny shrugged. "He wasn't too stable to begin with, but this place ... yeah, it did things to him. He told us he left because he could, and he was afraid there'd come a time he wouldn't be able to.

"Anyway, I used to come up years after he left to camp, just out there on Mount Brown. Not all the way up, of course. I'd go up Gunsight Pass Trail, oh, 'bout two miles then find a spot. Younger then, and lighter. It was nice. Hopin' to do something similar this trip. Guess not."

"No, guess not."

"So, what'd you see up there on the roof?" Sonny asked.

"I told you."

"Something else. I saw it on your face. And I know the legends."

"I'm not sure, nothing probably."

"Suit yourself, boss, you're the one who has to handle these folks. But you do know it wasn't Lester creeping Stabler out upstairs, right?"

He wasn't ready to let on to them about what he saw, but there was no sense outright denying it now and insulting the man. "Yeah. I know."

"And you do know we were being watched climbing the stairs."

"Probably were."

"And that I know it, and you know it, and Clare knows it. Course, Koopman and Pratt know it now, too, but they don't matter much."

"Your point?"

"Only two who don't know. Just something to keep in mind when making that plan of yours. And deciding when to put it into effect."

"Can I make a small fire?" Clare asked. She held up a box of Swiss Miss. "I can't find any Sterno. I always have a cup at bedtime. I have enough for everyone."

The Sterno was another thing Alston left in the Jeep. He looked around. The ceilings were high. Small fire with old, broken up furniture wouldn't smoke too badly. "Go 'head. Find some furniture pieces, stuff that's not treated or at least looks natural."

There was none in the room. Clare looked nervously through the door that led to the back room where the women were to sleep. "Sonny," Alston whispered. "Mind giving her a hand?"

When Sonny stood, Alston handed him the knife. Sonny tucked it under his belt. He tested it, sliding it in and out several times before taking the Maglite and escorting Clare into the back.

Sixteen

"Keep 'em occupied." It worked with little kids and Marines, no reason to think it wouldn't work here. Alston put Lester in charge of security; Karen and Clare maintained supply and logistics, such as they were; and Sonny had escort duties. That was the extent of his plan. He was hoping the light of day would reveal the door they had overlooked, the unbarred window, the hole in the wall that let the cats in and out.

They sat in a tight circle and drank Swiss Miss, even though the room was steaming hot with no air coming through. The mood turned mercifully light for a few moments when Sonny announced he had never had hot chocolate with marshmallows. "Never?" Clare said.

"No. Only thing we put in it was rum."

"Seriously?"

"Haven't had it much but when I did, yeah, rum. Haven't had any since I was a boy."

"That's like child abuse," Karen said.

"Nuthin' like child abuse, not where I come from."

"Look in his A-bag," Lester said, "Bet you'll find rum in there."

"No, I came up clean."

"Shame," Stabler said. "I could use some right about now."

Alston set them up in shifts for sleeping. Lester, as security officer, assured him they were safe inside. "All the action's happened out there. Less you think we'll get mauled by cats."

"Happened to Pratt," Sonny said.

"Little different," Lester argued. "He kinda fell into their laps."

But that was Alston's concern. He knew little about cats, especially feral ones. But of all the nursery rhymes he'd heard, and the nature shows he'd seen, he never heard tell of them as predators of anything bigger than field mice and small birds. Nor had he heard of them having a structured chain of command, one that could make them move and attack on orders. Wasn't that the meaning of, "trying to round up a herd of cats?" Someone was out there controlling them.

"Even so, make up a schedule," Alston told Lester. "Two at a time for two hours each. Fifty percent security for each team. It's twelve-thirty, daylight's about six. First two shifts bring us to four-thirty. I'll take it from there."

"Anyone hears anything wake me up. I got the gun and live rounds, and I'll be keeping them." Lester looked to Alston for a challenge. He got none.

Alston got his bedding ready while Lester barked out his orders, teaming himself up with Clare Peoné and Sonny with Karen Stabler. "We're staying put, right?" Stabler clarified. "No making rounds."

"I want the two back rooms covered," Lester said.

"Not by me," she told him emphatically.

"You don't need to go into them, just flash a light once in a while. Don't know what you're afraid of; whatever's out there is out there, not inside."

Alston listened while staying uninvolved as the two barked back and forth, who was going first, for how long, where to sit, where to check, who kept the gun. It was really of no consequence as Alston had no intentions of falling asleep himself. It was just an exercise in staying active, their minds on something else for moments at a time. Even fighting sleep and each other would prove worthy adversaries.

At quarter to three he was awakened from the sleep he had fought against. It was a scream from across the room. Clare was standing just this side of the open doorway, the flashlight hung low, spotlighting the floor just in front of her. Her body convulsed as if being electrically shocked. He climbed to his feet. Sonny was at her side, taking the flashlight from her. "There," he heard her say. She pointed beyond the doorway.

"What's that mean?" Sonny said.

Alston pushed past them into the room. *You all must* was written in crooked, broken red lines on the far wall. "Hand me the light," he said to Sonny, reaching his arm behind him without taking his eyes off the wall, fearing this creature coming back to finish his warning.

As he suspected it was blood. And still wet. Clare had disturbed the writer in mid sentence. He spun the flashlight to his right where he knew the other exit doorway to be. Then, aware it could be sitting in the shadows, he scanned the room with quick bursts of light. "What do you see?" Lester yelled in.

"Nothing in here now."

Lester was at his side, reaching his hand to the wall. "That blood?"

"Yeah."

"He's in here with us," Clare said.

"Who?" Karen asked.

"The wendigo."

"It's not a wendigo," Sonny said.

"Well what the hell is a wendigo ?" Karen demanded.

"A man-eating spirit," Sonny said. "Punishment for the nastiest sins. It's just a legend."

"It's real," Clare said.

"It's crap."

"We've both seen it," she said.

"Whoa, whoa, you've seen this thing?" Karen said. "Here?"

"She's talking years ago," Sonny said. "And we didn't see a thing."

"We saw plenty, Sonny. You know it, and you know what people have been seeing since, and what happened to the sheriff out here."

Lester and Karen listened intently, throwing glances back at Alston.

"Tell me what's going on," Karen said. "What's this all about?"

Rather than let them hear Clare's ghost version or Sonny's thinned-out one, Alston gave them what he had learned from Sheriff Vanderpool.

When he finished his sanitized version, Clare let them know, "He's not telling all of it. Tell him Sonny. Tell him how the patients were all locked inside the room to be burned alive, the way the sheriff had his face ripped off, just like Koopman."

"Not denying any of that but it wasn't a wendigo," Sonny said. "It was something very human. Evil, yeah, but still human."

"And he's not telling the history of this place as an Indian boarding school" Clare said. "The draconian methods of assimilation they used. How children were stripped of their native clothes, had their hair shaved, were trained like rats with bells and whistles to be less Blackfoot. They were beaten, locked in closets, and starved as punishment. They were beaten for the smallest things, if they didn't learn fast enough or well enough, if they didn't embrace Christianity and throw off traditional ways. 'Kill the Indian, save the man,' remember."

"That I do," Sonny said.

"So why this Mandingo-thing," Karen said. "Kids being beaten doesn't sound like their sin. Why would they be haunting this place, or whatever?"

"It's not them," Sonny said, knowing Clare was not about to let up. Legends, like any other type of history, were understood best by telling, not by burying. To him, the legend was silly but no sillier than some the history lessons he learned in school. And smart people like Clare had a degree of faith in them. "Blue Elk is the wendigo that Clare is talking about. He worked with the administrators of the school. He was Blackfoot but bought into the assimilation. Maybe a little too much for everyone's good. They made him responsible for school discipline. Maybe he was trying to impress them; maybe he was a natural sadistic sonavabitch. Either way, he was as ruthless as any death camp Nazi."

"How do you know all this," Lester asked. "Were you here as a kid?"

"Way before my time. Blue Elk was killed in 1923. Murdered was the story. Fell from the roof, just like … well."

"They know it was murder?" Karen asked.

"No, legend again 'cause no one was ever caught. It's believed it was a father of one of the students here."

"It was murder," Clare said. "I know because the murderer was a family friend. His twelve-year old daughter was raped here. She was called Ainih kiwa. 'To sing.' She jumped from the roof, so her father made Blue Elk follow her. Everyone knew but the school wanted it kept quiet to keep the atrocities from being found out. Ainih kiwa's father vowed to expose it all but he became a hopeless drunk before he could. When he finally did speak out, no one would listen. So Blue Elk lives on as a wendigo who guards this place against intruders. To do this he is given an army."

"Of mangy cats?" Lester said.

Sonny shrugged. "So, it's said."

"And knowing this, you came back here? And brought us?" an irate Karen Stabler said, her eyes darting between Sonny and Alston.

"It's just a legend," Sonny said.

"But it's happening damn it, you're seeing it happen. Clare, you must have believed it. You've been freaked out since the door bolted shut."

"I wasn't sure."

"And now?"

Clare was about to answer when she was cut off by Sonny. "It's not supernatural, okay. If it is, then we're a bunch of cocky teenagers in a slasher film who have no way out."

"Sonny's right," Alston said. "Deal with what we know, what we can find in the real world, and work from there."

Seventeen

"It's in the basement," Lester said.

"Could be anywhere," Karen answered.

"No, the basement. It's the only way in, and," he added, "the only way out."

"Stop calling him an 'it,'" Sonny said. "It's not an 'it', it's a 'he.'"

"Could be a 'she,'" Karen said.

"Yeah, a she who can drag a full-grown man up five flights of stairs and toss him off a roof."

"And a hellavu powerful he," Sonny said. And at that they stared helplessly at each other, the specter of the wendigo looming large.

It was dawn now. The endless night finally closing. No one slept the past two hours. It was like a slow, tedious elevator trip. Heads bowed, eyes diverting. No one spoke but they wondered along with their worries. What would the dawn bring? Hope of a way out or confirmation that they were indeed trapped?

The first finger of sunlight came through the front window by the door. It crawled along Clare's leg. They all watched it slowly move across her to Sonny's boot, onward across the floor to Karen's chest and face until it rose above them and was gone.

"My ass is sore, I'm tired, I'm hungry, I'm pissed," Lester said, looking to Alston. "We have any semblance of a plan here?"

"Anyone have any luck with their cell phone?" Alston asked.

"I've been trying all night," Karen said. "Mine's dead."

"Same here," Clare said.

"Ditto," said Sonny.

The only ones with any juice left were his own and Lester's. Both tried with no luck. "Shut 'em down, then, save what we got left."

They stood and turned gravely in unison at the sound of a cat's long drawn screech from the bottom of the stairs. Two more appeared and sat contentedly behind the first who was much larger. It had thick tufts of gray fur under its ears, like heavy sideburns. It stood to parade along the step on powerful hindquarters and thick paws. "It's a damn bobcat," Lester said.

"No, a mix maybe," Sonny said.

"Look at it? It's twice the size. And the way it walks."

"If it was a bobcat, those other cats would be bone and gristle by now. Besides, look at its tail and ears; they're white. A bobcat has black tips."

Lester had his pistol out and at his side. He raised it slowly, but Alston was on him before he got it past his hip. "What the hell you think you're gonna do, shoot the whole damn herd of them?"

"All that I can."

"That's why this is happening," Clare said, "Why we're being killed."

All eyes were on her. She stood trancelike, watching the big cat patrol the step. The cat, likewise, locked its gaze on her. "It's you." She was looking through Lester. "It's you they want."

"You're a fuckin' nut," he said.

"Let's settle down," Alston said. "We're letting our imaginations get the best of us. It's daylight. Whatever it is, whoever it is, we have the advantage in numbers. And we can see now." He glanced down at Lester's right hand, holding his semi-automatic in the low ready position. "And we do have a weapon."

"Boss, might wanna see this." Sonny had wandered away while Clare made her sinister accusations. He was now in the doorway to the back room. When Alston made his way over, he pointed to a thick brown folder laying in the corner by the room's other entryway. "Wasn't there before," Sonny said. "I think he left his calling card."

Alston bent over. The folder was open, a photograph stapled on the left side, the cover to a dossier on the right. He picked it up. "Stand down," he called to the rest of the team.

Lester made his disagreement loudly known. "We got no time to stand down."

"For this we do. There may be something here we can use."

"Like he's gonna leave us a map outta here."

Alston ignored him, He ignored them all. He didn't feel their anxious eyes on him as he walked, head down, flipping pages, back to his corner in the room. Nor did he feel the penetrating stares of the three cats. He paused before sitting when he turned to the photograph of a small red-haired boy whose vacant eyes showed no trace of humanity.

Walter Bradford Hill, born July 24, 197- in Lordsburg, New Mexico. Parents, Mahlon and Ruth Hill; two older sisters, Lucille, 10, and Karin, 11. One younger brother, Winston, 4. The report continued in chaotic, blue-inked script:

HISTORY: Orphaned at eight after a fire at home in Kalispell, Montana in 198-. WH lone survivor. No known relatives located. Five foster homes until committed to SRH Hospital at age 11.

VIOLENCE OF RECORD: Fire investigation in Kalispell revealed WH possible source. Kept by neighbor day of fire, set neighbor's dog on fire. Committed for psych eval 60 days. Brought to foster home ten weeks later. Family (protect identity) reported bizarre, then horrifying behavior almost immediately. Issues of unprovoked violence began after three months. At first, WH uncommunicative, standing on walkway in front of house for hours until brought inside. Began walking circles around the house, always on the same route, wearing a beaten path. Would begin at precisely 6:45am. Family, to see if he would come in on his own, let him go one day. Had to bring him in at 7pm. Violent tantrums began shortly after, mainly if not allowed outside. Had fixation on cats that led him to behave as such. Walks around house became more consistent with prowling. Began communicating with cat-like noises. Hissing and clawing as acts of aggression. Attacked family's 12-year-old daughter, termination of foster care. More of same at other homes. Violence became more of the norm, oftentimes unprovoked. WH found/befriended/nurtured feral cats in neighborhood. Often stayed out overnight in wooded areas in cold/rain environs to be with them.

DIAGNOSIS/TREATMENTS:

Initial diagnosis of psychotic break caused by family social disorder and feelings of abandonment, alienation resulting in escalating uncontrolled anger issues. (SEE family history under separate report 92-8675-FH). Current diagnosis of Dissociative Identity Disorder as offshoot of Borderline Pers Dis. Mood controlling meds: Olanzapine, Aripiprazole and VPA.

There were then dozens of pages concerning Walter Hill's weeks, months, years at the hospital. Alston read only a few but each showed episodes of violence that resulted in restraints, solitary confinements, and electroshock treatments. There were innumerable attacks on other patients and staff. Alston noted with interest that never was there a mention of a weapon involved. There were several entries that highly recommended performing a leucotomy, which reading further, he inferred was a lobotomy. Most though, recommended lifetime institutional confinement with limited contact with outsiders or other patients. It seemed that only one or two doctors were allowed access to him.

"Jesus," he muttered. "Reads like a script for *Silence of the Lambs."*

"Good stuff?" Sonny was looming above him.

"For Hollywood, not for us."

Eighteen

Shattered nerves frayed still further with the harsh metallic grind of Lester's semi automatic slide being pulled and released. He charged at the cats; the gun outstretched. He swept his arm at them as if brushing away a mass of cobwebs. The largest one stood its ground while the other two scattered. Its large paw clipped the end of the pistol as it made a low hiss. "Demon or man," Lester yelled up the stairs, "someone down here has firepower to deal with you. So come on down and take it, Beelzebub."

"Don't talk like that," Clare admonished.

He shook his head and gave her a twisted smile.

Alston stood. "We'll try the basement."

"Finally, a command decision worth a damn," Lester said.

Alston watched Clare's shoulders sink. She didn't want to venture down there. "Lester and I will take a look, you three sit tight," he announced.

"Why?" Karen said. "The more eyes we got down there –"

"You might see something up here in the daylight we missed."

Sonny, Karen, and Clare stood in the center of the room. It was warming up fast as the sunlight filtered through the windows and cooked the cinderblock walls. This would have been a hellacious place to train in the heat of the day, on gritty concrete in such cramped quarters. An open door or two could supply some relief if this desert had a breeze to spare. And they could come and go, stop for a breather, wander the grounds. All three of them now were feeling the isolation, the despair, the hopelessness of the patients and the children who stood here before them.

"What does it mean?" Karen asked softly, as if sinister ears were close by and listening. "'You all must' We all must what?"

"I don't know," Clare said. "But it scares me."

"He's communicating with us," Sonny said. "maybe that's a good thing."

"Nice. He writes in blood after slicing up two of us," Karen said.

"Yeah, that is a problem."

"Whatever he's saying, it's meant for all of us," Clare said, her eyes darting around the walls as if they were steadily closing in on her.

“Least we can all agree it isn’t supernatural,” Sonny said.

“Why? ‘Cause of that?” Clare nodded at the folder left behind on the floor by Alston. “That doesn’t prove anything.”

“Like the wendigo left it there to throw us off?”

“Why not?”

“What kind of demon needs to plant red herrings.”

“A demon will do all sorts of things when we’re not paying attention. Besides, just because it’s in human form doesn’t mean evil isn’t in control.”

Karen was flipping through the file. “Cute kid, in a Twilight Zone kinda way. Damn, he's been here for almost twenty-eight years."

"That's crazy," Sonny said. "Place gone up in flames years ago, fire department and police all over it, and this kid, or guy, manages to stay hidden?"

"So, what's your theory?" Clare said.

"I don't know; some homeless guy, or guys. Comes and goes. Just a nut."

"He stays hidden," Clare said. "He knows his way around here."

"Least now you're using the right pronoun."

"Listen to this," Karen broke in. "Says here WH, that's the kid's name, Walter Hill, was caught in the basement with over two dozen cats."

"What's that mean, 'caught with?'" Sonny asked,

She shrugged. "Doesn't say. Says all the cats were euthanized."

"Let me see that." Sonny took the folder and read further.

"That's it then," Clare said. Karen waited for her explanation. "Don't you see; he's protecting his family."

"That's insane" Karen said.

"Crazy *was* the theme of this place," Sonny said.

"Look at this," Sonny brought a photograph over to hem. "This him as an adult, you think?"

The image was of a thin, pointed man, crouched in a corner. He appeared naked but for a red scarf around his neck. His back flared at the shoulders; his oblique muscles twisted into a taut fold. The thick quad muscles of his left leg contorted beneath him as he sat in a full squat.

He was half turned, staring at the photographer with contempt, as if having just been scolded, or perhaps interrupted in some deeply personal moment. His flaming orange hair was wild, mangy, and in tangles down his shoulders. He gripped something in his hands. "What's he got?" Karen asked.

"A sponge," Sonny answered.

"No. Look," Clare said, pointing to the concrete floor in front of the squalid man-boy. "Those are crumbs; he's eating bread."

"Sweet Jesus, he's living and eating like a beast and the best they can do is take his picture for a scrapbook?" Karen said.

"So, what is it he's wants from us?" Karen wanted to know.

"He doesn't want a damn thing," Sonny said. "We're on his hit list, and he wants us to know he's serious. You two be okay up here alone for a while?"

"Where you going?" Karen asked.

"I need to tell those two in the basement something that may get us out of here."

"What?"

"Cats and this Walter Hill, or whoever he is, have to be coming and going from somewhere. I may know about a room that leads outside. You'll be okay." He said it with no air of confidence. To provide some assurance he added, "We're only a flight of stairs away."

"Why don't we just all go down," Karen said.

"I'm not going down there," Clare said.

Karen stayed behind with her, arming herself with Sonny's knife. "I hate that clown Boyd Lester like no one I can remember," she said, "but damn if he isn't right about needing a gun in here." Clare wasn't listening. She had sunk into the corner where she had spent most of the night. She drew her knees up and wrapped arms around them. Fine, Karen thought, make yourself small. But small means vulnerable. And building a nest may give comfort but it's no defense.

Holding down the fort while the menfolk go out hunting the savages, or some-such analogy, wasn't what she signed up for. They were sworn deputies. If they made it out, when they made it out, it would be clinging to the shirttails of the men, of Lester Boyd, no less. These were not the kind of anecdotes she was prepared to hear for the remainder of her career. She knew that if she didn't participate to any greater degree than babysitting, she would need to quit the department. She could see the recommendations that would follow her. "We need to do something besides cower up here; can't sit on our asses." She said it aloud, though it was mainly an urging to herself.

"No, I don't think we should."

"You don't, huh? Like this room is off limits to ... whatever that thing is? You got some kind of weird Ouija, voodoo, totem figurine that keeps us in an out-of-bounds bubble?"

"I ... I just don't know."

"I know. The thing I know is, if Walter or whoever comes in here, I'm on my own. I can't count on you. How 'bout at least helping me find a couple of metal pipes to beat this guy's skull in."

She shook her head. "We should wait here."

Clare was beaten down by what she knew and what she thought she knew. There was no convincing her they had control of their fate. They were trained to handle hostile situations. They had some skills in hand-to-hand combat, and if it was possible, they knew a bit about how to talk crazies down.

Karen pulled the knife with dramatic flair from its sheath. "That's the last thing we should do. Just you remember what we're paid to do."

Nineteen

The big man stepped on a piece of rotted timber which had Alston and Lester spinning around in terror. Lester lit his face with the flashlight beam. "Scared the fuck outta me," he said, "you're lucky I didn't shoot you through the head."

"Don't think that flashlight's loaded." Sonny said.

"The gun was right behind it, brother, make no mistake."

"Where are the other two?" Alston asked.

"Upstairs. Remembered something that might help."

Alston's look showed his concern. "I left them my knife," Sonny said.

Lester's smirk told them what he thought about that.

"What is it?" Alston asked.

"Reading that file, the kid was caught with a busload of cats down here."

"Ya think?" Lester said. "Can't you smell the damn things."

"Not the point. He wasn't just down here because he could hide them, I don't think. I think he had a place to control them and hide himself."

Sonny took the flashlight from Lester. He shined it slowly around the room. "This the elevator?" he asked, halting the beam in a spot behind Alston and Lester.

Lester turned. "Yeah."

"My uncle told me about a room down here. It was part of the original building. A tiny, four-wall, no-window, low-ceiling room that was sealed off when the elevator was put in. So, it wasn't in use when this was an asylum."

"When it was still the Indian School, then" Alston said. "And for what? Storage?

Sonny shook his head. "It was their version of solitary confinement."

The light was still on the shaft. From what Lester could see the elevator hadn't moved since he last saw it, still poised about a foot off the floor. He approached and knelt over it. "Gimme that light." Lester held his hand out behind him. Sonny obliged and Lester fumbled with it in his anxiety to explore the undersides of the shaft.

"See anything?" Alston asked.

"Nothin'. Just a hole."

The flashlight dropped from his hand and rolled beneath the elevator when he heard the shrill scream of a woman from upstairs. It landed with its beam pointing back into his eyes. He cursed it openly and spun away to see the mad scrambling of four boots on the gritty cement as Sonny and Alston raced up the staircase.

Karen had moved cautiously through the maze of rooms on the first floor. She twirled the knife in her sweaty palms, out of nervousness and to get the feel of its weight. Several times she spun left, right, and to her rear at some unexplained sound to find it was nothing, or at most, nothing there.

Leaving Clare behind wasn't an issue to her. To her mind they should have left her three hundred miles behind, back in Libby where life was slow, and crime was prevalent but easy. She wanted to dress the quiet, demure, feckless girl down. *Just why had she come? What was it she wanted to accomplish? To prove?* She knew from her own short interview with Alston Waters that such questions were not asked but should have been. Here was a woman who believed in ghosts which was great puff material for a campfire and smores, but not helpful to any tactical plans. Yeah, girl, stay behind in a room that's no safer than anywhere else in this rat hole, cat hole being more apt.

She followed short, narrow hallways that pushed her from tiny rooms and closets to open bays. Breadcrumbs is what she needed now. Breadcrumbs to drop behind her like in the fairy tale. Hansel and Gretel, was it? She chuckled to herself. Her luck cats would come behind her and eat them, just like in the story.

Some rooms had windows but like all the others she had seen, they were barred. She gave them all a good shake in the hope time had loosened them. The interior rooms without windows were disturbingly dark. They couldn't have been offices, she thought, who'd have put up with such a depressing space? Maybe examination or waiting rooms, but still. A longer corridor took her in deeper as if into a vast cave. It was cold and the floor was no longer scuffed vinyl but a cement slab. The hallway dumped her into a room where, to her left, was a small cage, a holding cell. It was an unexpected sight but considering the work done here, she could envision its usefulness.

The door was open. She swung it gently. Its hinges ached with rust. She rocked it rhythmically, the joints emitting a high-pitched squealing that brought a scruffy gray cat to the doorway of the room. It announced itself with a quiet wail. "They let you out alone, damn thing," Karen said. "No blood-thirsty friends with you? Shoo." She stepped towards it with a stomp. It responded by sitting and staring attentively up at her.

At the back of the cage was a small industrial desk, marred with scratches and carvings. A drawer was partially open. You could outfit a good-sized government office with the shit they left behind, she thought. She took a few steps inside the cell. Behind her she heard the cat hiss loudly. "Shoo." She turned to toe tap it but found herself staring into the bony chest of a sickly-white figure. He towered over her, long and lean, wild hair of flaming orange. His eyeballs bloody red, lids crusted over. Random tufts of hair covered his cheeks and chin, the skin mottled and deeply splotched, as if he had pulled the whiskers out by hand. His soiled T-shirt, torn and filthy, hung sheet-like over his bony shoulders. She could smell wet dirt. He cocked his head slightly at her, the way an intrigued cat would do. Yes, like a cat. Of course, this was him. Walter Hill.

He had her cornered. Though he looked every tissue the animal she saw in the photograph, he was human. He had a mind, a conscience. He could be reasoned with. "Walter," she managed to squeeze through her tightened throat. "Walter Hill."

His eyes, once penetrating as if wanting to understand, went suddenly cold. He leaned down, dangerously close. She felt his breath, smelled it, a sour, incapacitating stench, and at that moment, she knew that what was once human was no more. His lips parted, exposing bulbous, black gums surrounding gray teeth, fashioned into a row of stunted but lethal blades. His hands rose slightly, enough for her to see the long, dagger-like nails. "I know who I am," he snarled.

And at that he slashed at her face, tearing away a portion of her cheek and nose. Her scream was followed by another swift rake, this at her mouth and neck. She fell back over the desk, but he stayed with her, slashing at her chest, neck, and arms, paring away flesh as if gutting a fish. He crouched over her, his teeth flashing as he curled his lips. His breathing was heavy, not from the effort but from depraved exhilaration. Karen drew her legs in and kicked to keep him at bay. She was screaming. Was she screaming? She wanted to but why wasn't anyone coming? She had been here for five, ten minutes. Five, ten minutes of this brutal attack. No, it had been mere seconds. The rivers of blood came into view. Glancing down she saw her chest and arms coated. So much blood in such a short time. Her face stung as if salt had been poured into razor blade wounds.

Walter Hill stood with his head casually cocked. With an imperceptible strike of his hand, he grabbed her outstretched foot. He gripped her ankle. She pulled and pushed to no avail. He took hold with both hands and with a quick twist, snapped it. She heard the pop, the pain so great she must have passed out momentarily. When she came to, he was down over her, his hand raking at her chest and midsection, dissecting her as she lay there, hoping, praying to pass out one last time.

Twenty

She didn't hear screams. It was the whining of cats, or a crazy blast of wind through the bars or a vent. Maybe Karen was singing wild and off key to comfort herself. Clare rose and paced the floor. Any moment Karen will be back here, telling her she checked the area and there was no way out from here. Clare wouldn't tell her *I told you so*. They'd content themselves to sit and wait to see what they found in the basement.

But Karen didn't come back, and the grisly noise continued. Clare moved towards it but quickly retreated, like a circus animal being forced back by the snapping whip of a domineering trainer. There was no denying it to herself now, that somewhere back in the confines of this hell Karen needed her help.

The men would come up, surely, they heard it. Lester had a gun; that's what they needed, something to kill with. But they were down below; Karen was rooms away, behind concrete walls that trapped noise as ruthlessly as it had trapped them. What she was hearing were the echoes moments after Karen's screams. These were not cries for help, they were extracted from her in a most vile way. They were sounds not meant to come from the living but from the dying.

She found herself moving through the door now, towards the screams, leaving the surroundings she had come to trust. She surprised herself with the ferocity in which she hurried through the maze of passageways and rooms, stopping for mere moments to gain her bearings until she saw the next hallway down which a river of feral cats poured.

She bounded through them, into a room with a small holding cell. Cats were congregated in the back by an overturned desk. Behind it she heard the fading sounds of Karen's cries. The cell door was shut, locked. She shook it violently, more cats shot through the bars. Karen's body was undetectable, but she knew it was there, buried beneath the writhing cover of motley fur, like maggots on exposed garbage.

She called to her. The cats jumped, and she could see a shredded, bloodied pant leg kicking weakly and vainly. She ran hysterically to the basement stairs, shouting, her stomach churning, bile burning her throat, seeping into her nostrils. Alston raced up to her, his eyes trying to read hers. She heard him demanding an answer to a question she couldn't remembering him asking. Sonny stepped around him and held her firmly by the shoulders. He shook gently, then more forcibly while she tried to settle herself.

"Back there," she pointed down the hallway. "Karen."

"What is it?" Alston demanded.

Sonny, still holding her by the shoulders, calmly instructed her, "Clare, you'll have to show us. You have to."

She hurried them back to the hallway and pointed. "She got locked in somehow; I don't know, you'll have to ..."

They ran past her, Boyd Lester now at their heels. "Holy Christ," Alston muttered.

They could see Karen's legs plainly now, what was left. The cats had stripped them nearly to bone. As cats do, each had taken their share and scattered into corners to feast in private. They paid little heed to the humans who stood open-mouthed at the ghastly sight.

Sonny pulled frantically at the door. He stretched through the bars to scatter the scavengers but those he could reach merely moved away. Alston raced to the side of the cage where he could see Karen's sprawled body behind the desk. Her face was flayed apart like Koopman's. Her chest too, covered in blood. He couldn't look further. "Shoot," he said to Lester. "Shoot what?"

"The fuckin' cats, shoot the fuckin' cats."

"For what? She' s gone, and I don't have many rounds left."

"I ordered you to shoot." His voice trembled. He was sweating. He was losing it, he knew. Of course, shooting a cat or two would do no good. And he was sure a time would come when that gun would be better utilized. But someone needed to die, someone, or something besides them. It was a notion born out of frustration, fear, and anger, three emotions Alston rarely gave into.

"At what? There, that scraggily one?" And Lester shot one in the corner, chewing contentedly before being splattered against the back wall. The echo of it rang through the room, even vibrating the steel bars. "How 'bout there?" He pointed the gun at a larger black one. "Fatter, hey? Should be an easier target; big wide spray of blood and guts, that what we're going for here?" He fired even before the echo of the first subsided and now the waves of sound rolled over them.

The cats were scattering frantically now. Some carried their gruesome meal with them, others abandoned it, leaving the floor of the cell looking like a butcher's shop. Clare ran in, her hands over her ears. "Stop, stop, you idiots, don't you get it now? He's after us for shooting them."

"Talk to the man, his idea to waste ammo," Lester said. He looked to Alston. "Thought I was the bloodthirsty one? Seems you got a sadistic sliver up your ass, after all."

"It's all of us now," Clare said. "He wants the ones who killed his babies. Karen, Lester, now Alston it will be you for ordering it done." She raised her eyes to the ceiling. "What is it you want us all to do?" she called out. She turned back to the doorway. "We'll leave you alone. Just let us out and we'll leave you all alone. What is it you want from us?"

The four of them stood silent, as if expecting an answer or a sign. "Let's get out of this room," Sonny said. "Nothing we can do." All four had visions of what would go on here once they left and the cats returned. No one spoke of it, no one wanted to. They wandered back to the front room. Lester took the lead, holding his pistol at the ready-gun position. As he entered the front room, he held his hand up. "Stay back till I've cleared the back."

"Nothing here," Alston said.

"Yeah? Betting our lives on it?"

He moved slowly around the corners, peering into the shadows and recesses of the ladies' sleeping quarters. He lowered the weapon slowly. "You're right, Captain, nothing here. Now."

Alston came up behind him. "Whatta you mean, now?"

"He finished his threat."

On the wall, the message completed in blood read, *You all must die.*

Twenty-One

"It's only been twenty-four hours."

She startled him. "What? I'm just dozing."

"With eyes wide open?"

Sheriff Vanderpool, reclining wormlike in his chair, staring at nothing in particular out the back window into the department parking lot, scooched himself upright with a grunt and a groan. "Shouldn't have let them go."

"They're big boys and girls; they can handle themselves,"

"They should have called in by now."

"You know full well that area of the state swallows up cell phone signals. Besides, was that part of the plan, to call in?"

"Of course, it was." He spun around in his chair to face his wife. "Maybe not implicitly, but checking in, that's a given."

"You're not trusting that Waters guy, are you?"

"No, I trust him well enough. He knows his stuff, good head for training."

"But not for people?"

That was Beverly Vanderpool's first and lasting impression of Alston Waters. He had that air of a man who digested field manuals like M&M's in a single sitting. A man who saw square holes and would cut and sand the edges and curves off anyone who wouldn't fit into them. Even his smile took on a custom-designed look when he penciled it on. She wouldn't call him plastic; he was what he appeared to be, and if you thought otherwise, you weren't paying attention. It seemed now that her husband hadn't paid attention.

"It's not that he's not capable," he told her. "Just maybe it's too much too soon for these deps."

"Like Clare?"

"You know, she told me she still sleeps with the lights on. I wasn't supposed to tell anyone that. She won't even go into the storerooms or those outbuildings alone. She wanted to quit the department. I told her to hold on, that it would get better. Guess she took this training to prove to me she was ready."

"Could be she needed to prove it to herself."

"Could be. And Sonny. He acts tough and hard but he's no hero."

"And you think this training is out to make them heroes?"

He stood to stretch. "Training doesn't make a hero. Circumstances make a hero. And I don't see a circumstance in Lincoln County needing one. I think this training's gonna make me look like a frustrated dad living his glory years through his kids. Tell me I'm over thinking this."

"Good training is never wasted time, isn't that what you always said?"

"And it shouldn't, not in an ideal world. I just don't know if it's really needed or if I want it to be needed. And what scares me is a cowboy like Lester Boyd getting all this kinda good training. I can just see him creating a circumstance we don't need."

"Well, what is it? You worried about the training or who's getting it?"

"Both." He put his hands on his hips and laughed. "You did it again."

"Did what?"

"Made me figure out my problem without telling me a thing."

"Darling, I just asked the questions you wanted to ask yourself."

"And made me answer them."

"Sheriff, you know I could never make you do a darn thing."

"They're gone," Clare said softly.

"The cats?" Lester said. "How can you tell?"

"Not them. Karen, Pratt, Koopman."

"Shit. That's still news to you?"

"No. But it's still a shame because they didn't do anything wrong. The one he wants most is still here."

"Come get me," Lester shouted.

Clare shot him a mournful look. "Koopman wasn't even serious about being in law enforcement."

"Mistake number one," Lester said.

"Person can't have other interests?"

"In this job, you better have your head in it."

"Don't think he was anticipating running into a psycho up in the hills of Montana," Sonny said. "Walter Hill, that is."

"Pratt was thinking about moving back to Oklahoma," Clare said.

"Was he?" Alston said, surprised it didn't come up when the two of them spoke about the training.

"He was going to try smoke jumping."

Lester laughed. A disturbing cackle that unnerved the group. "Guess he went out with a taste of that then, huh?"

"Hate to say this," she continued, "but I didn't like Karen. Worst of it, I didn't know much about her other than I didn't much like her." She allowed herself to look across the room, through the walls, down to where the holding cell was, where Karen lay dead, still bleeding, in pieces, even now being eaten by cats who knew nothing of the ghastliness of it all. To them it was a natural event. Food, just food, to keep them alive another day. Tomorrow they'll search out more. Or perhaps be given more. She may well be the next meal. "I couldn't even write an obituary for any of them." She looked at Alston. "Could any of us?"

"That's a maudlin thought," Sonny said.

"Big word coming outta you," Lester said.

"Not a big word at all. Know what it means?"

"I would guess it means crazy."

"No, it doesn't."

"Yeah, well I'm just not the English wiz that you are, chief."

"You know any polysyllabic words that don't involve the nomenclature of a gun?"

"Yeah. Go fuck yourself."

"It doesn't take much to reduce you to that, does it?"

"Thing is, Koopman may have been the one to make a great archeological find, the origin of man," Clare said, ignoring the tension rising between the two men. "Maybe Pratt saves a family in a forest fire. And Karen ... I don't know. And it doesn't matter, anyway, about us writing obituaries. None of us are leaving here alive. I don't think any of us will be leaving here at all. He's serving food to his children. When they're finished with Karen and are hungry again, he'll come back for another one of us. And another.

"Well, that's not how I see my demise playing out," Lester said. "Sit here and wait to be sliced and diced if you want to but I got an elevator shaft to explore."

"He's waiting for you down there," Clare warned.

"For once I'm with Lester on this," Alston said, slowly getting to his feet. "We know who we're dealing with. He's one man whose only weapon is his knowledge of this building."

"Don't forget his family," Clare said.

"Okay, time to shut her up," Lester said.

"Let her talk," Sonny said. "It's good for everyone to have something to say about this."

"She's creeping me out. First it's mythical demons, now it's a man who controls a pack of killer cats."

"He doesn't control the cats," Alston said. "They come to feed, not to kill. We keep him away; we keep them away."

"Maybe. But you oughta read about him before you go," Clare said. "He left us his life's story, after all. Strange huh? We end up knowing more about him than we do about each other."

Twenty-two

Alston picked up the file on Walter Hill to review while Lester ranted. "We're wasting time."

"You on some kinda schedule?" Sonny said. "Let the man read."

Sonny's long, slow fuse had been lit. Not by the heinous events of a registered madman but by the abusive, often cruel, performances of one of their own. One of their own with a loaded gun.

Sonny knew that if it came down to it, Boyd Lester wouldn't hesitate to turn the gun on one or all of them. If they were to find a way out, a way out and a small window of time to do it, it would be the man with the gun going first. If there was just one round left, would he use it to save another or himself? Sonny was sure of the answer. Better that the gun be lost than in the hands of a man who would use it so recklessly.

He had it in him to wrestle it way himself but that would only widen the divide Lester was creating. It would divide them into two groups, weakening them in the long run. The best he could do was to unleash a little of his own bravado to let Lester know that he was not a friend and would not stand by idly if a need arose.

"We're low on water and food," Lester said. Maybe what, another day? It's almost noon. Feel it? The sun? It's baking us while we sit here." He moved to the small window and put his hands up to the bars. "Nothing. No breeze, just heat."

"We're out of water," Clare said.

Alston looked up. "No. We consolidated it all right there in those canteens."

She overturned two canteens in her outstretched hands.

"Nice," Lester said.

"What about food?" Alston asked.

Clare bent down and rifled through the canvas bags. She held up a handful of bars and bags.

"Sure, he leaves us the food," Lester said. "That ready-made crap is filled with salt. The more we eat, the more we need to drink. This creature's got better tactics than you, Waters."

Alston looked down at the folder.

"And still he reads. I'm checking the rest of the basement," Lester announced.

"Stay put," Alston said. "We're not splitting up again."

Alston knew their situation had just gotten gravely worse, and that Lester's assertions were correct. Walter Hill had a strategy. Crazy as it sounded, it was not something he read or was taught. And most probably not something he had devised on the spot. It was how he had survived and allowed his population of cats to survive all these years. It was classic warfare; divide and conquer and cut supply lines. It was done on the battlefield; it was done in nature, by creatures of cunning and audacity with a will to survive at all costs. "You said there were cats under the elevator shaft."

"Yeah. One."

"That's where he is."

"We looked there."

"From what I've learned reading the file, Walter Hill didn't just live with the cats; he lived like them."

"No man could squeeze through that space," Lester said. "You saw how narrow it was."

"A cat can." Alston said. "And maybe a man who thinks like a cat."

"Thinking like a skinny fifteen-pound cat don't make him one."

"I seen a three-hundred-pound man doing ballet," Sonny said.

"Where's that fit in? Lester said.

"Just saying, thinking it done is getting it done."

"Clare, Sonny, grabbed what's left of our gear," Alston commanded. " How many workable flashlights left?" Three and a half, they counted. That included Clare's, Lester's, and his own, and the half belonged to Sonny. He gave Lester's to Sonny and left Lester with the gun. "Order of march will be me, Lester, Clare, and Sonny in the rear. Lester, have your gun at the ready and follow my flashlight."

It seemed silly, having an order of march for a trip into a basement, but it seemed to be just the piece of preparedness they needed to comfort them. Even Lester fell in without so much as a snicker or sneer.

The movement was slow and deliberate. Alston wasn't concerned with a Walter Hill direct attack. No, it would be a multitude of cats sent at them as a distraction or perhaps like a probing attack to draw indiscriminate fire or make them break ranks. It would probably work, frazzled as they were.

It was alarming that he was viewing this man, institutionalized since childhood, as a tactical mastermind, a practitioner of Sun Tzu. But in his own right, Walter Hill had amassed an army, kept it fed and thriving, and had taught it how to follow orders without question. And it was formidable. All this he had to keep to himself. He stopped midway down the stairs and called back quietly to them. "Whatever happens, stay together, and Lester, unless it's him, save your ammunition."

Twenty-Three

Lester exaggerated many things but not the overwhelming odor of cat. It may have been droppings on the floor, but it hung in the air like fog on the Scottish Moors. Efforts to walk over the piles were subjugated by the need to keep their heads up and on a swivel.

He could see cats sitting along the basement walls as if they were spectators watching them enter a great arena. None of them moved. Alston had a terrifying notion they were being commanded not to. "Take a look underneath again," he told Lester. "See if there's something there."

"Didn't see anything last time."

"Humor me."

Lester got to his knees and handed his gun back to Alston. "There's two left, with one in the chamber," he said. "Just make 'em count if it comes at me." He lay out on the floor. "Nuthin'. Don't even see any cat shit in there." His voice straining as his chest ground into the cement floor. He shined the flashlight around the small cavern.

"Cat won't shit where it sleeps," Sonny said.

"Can you get in?" Alston asked.

“I can’t squeeze through, I tried.”

Alston turned around.

“I know you ain’t looking at me,” Sonny said.

“Clare?” Alston's directed the flashlight low and to her right to avoid destroying her night vision. It left the other three in shadows. The cats, sitting silently, moving only slightly to lick a paw or make room for another, added hauntingly to the surreal backdrop.

She didn't suffer claustrophobia, but then, she'd never been in a place such as this where escape wasn't a given. Even here in the dark basement, she knew there was space beyond. But through there, the place where they suspected evil to be ... it made no sense to the part of her that sought self-preservation.

But there was that other part of self, less narcissistic, more idealistic, more attune to an outer being than an inner being. What was she read on the wall of the analyst she was seeing, *the strong cannot help the weak unless the weak are willing to be helped, and even then, the weak must become strong by their own efforts, to develop the strength which they admire in another. Only they can alter their condition.*

She had nothing to offer Koopman or Pratt. Their deaths were out of her hands. But Karen, she had let Karen down. Her recklessness was her own doing, but Clare knew she could have protested harder; she could have gone with her. If she couldn't stop what happened, she could have sought help quicker. But she didn't protest at all, she didn't go, and she was hesitant to answer the cries for help.

She admired Karen Stabler for her assertiveness in dealing with the likes of Boyd Lester, for her outspoken nature, for her impetuous style, and in her heart, Clare knew she also reviled her for all of it. Stabler was eight years her junior, and with only four years on the job, but she was the bar females in the department sought to reach.

Clare had heard the talk, that she was easily spooked and unfit, carried along by her Sugar-daddy Sheriff. And it was true, that much she could admit to herself. She could blame her edginess on her experience at this place all those years ago, but Sonny had been through it, and the Sheriff. They were fine, or so they seemed. Really, she was more like Koopman, sworn into a duty she didn't measure up to, only he had the integrity to admit it.

"Clare," Alston whispered as he slid up beside her. "You don't have to."

She shined her flashlight at the ground around Lester, and at the thin slit of space she was to crawl through. Lester rose to his knees and bid her to take his spot. "Do I get the gun?" she asked Alston.

"When you get inside; if you think you need it."

She knelt and leaned heavy on the elevator floor, testing its steadiness soon to be just inches above her. Satisfied, she crept under it on her belly as far as she dared without committing herself. She fit rather easily, making her wonder mockingly why Lester was so sure he couldn't. She switched the flashlight to her outstretched right hand and scanned the area. There it was, a jagged hole in the side wall, and again, she wondered how Lester could have missed it.

She slid through and low crawled towards the back. The hole was to the left about fifteen feet. After two seconds, when the suffocating stench hit her, she was forced to stop and bury her head into the cement floor. Sonny was wrong; cats did indeed shit where they lived. There was no way a person could exist down here; the toxic air alone would be fatal. It had to be a passageway, she reasoned. It was the only thought that made her move on.

"Toss the gun in here," she called behind her.

"See something," Alston asked.

"Nothing to shoot at but there is a hole in here. Could be a passageway."

She heard commotion behind her. She twisted her head to listen. It was Lester going at it with Alston. She was sure of the topic, the gun, he didn't want to give up. When she tried to straighten her elbows, she clipped her head on the bottom of the elevator. Dragging her body around one-hundred-eighty degrees, she crawled back, poking her head through the opening. "I'm not going further without the gun," she advised, "so make a decision."

"I didn't see a hole back there," Lester said.

"It's there."

"I don't think so."

"See it to believe it." She was on the high ground on this one. It felt good to back the blowhard down.

"I can't get through there."

"I think you can. It's a little tight underneath but the hole's no more than fifteen feet away."

"Then what?"

This type of back and forth could work in a conference room or a patrol car but it was maddening as hell here. Her shoulders were cramping, and her neck ached under the strain of staring up, and none of them had the good sense to at least crouch. "I'll go back and see what's behind the hole, but I'm not going further without the gun." She spun around quickly, to let them know there was indeed enough room for anyone of them but Sonny.

"Go in with her, man," Sonny said to Lester. "unless you're scared."

"Course not."

"No big whoop if you are. Claustrophobia, shit, I got that. Never catch me down there."

Clare was nervous approaching the hole but determined to go back with good news. She paused to hold her breath to listen. Hearing nothing disturbing she moved on. It was several degrees cooler in here which she wanted to attribute to fresh air coming in from a soon-to-be discovered escape tunnel. But it could just be typical basement dampness.

It was more than a hole; it was a very rough doorway opening for cats or skinny humans, of which she was one. Caution foremost on her mind, she stopped two feet away and held the flashlight on the opening. As always happened in the movies at this point, a cat would jump out and hiss. She waited but nothing moved. She crept closer and reached her hand, then arm. through, bending the flashlight hastily at every possible angle.

It was a room. Narrow, low, and long, but not a tunnel, definitely a room. The walls were old red brick, some missing and broken. Water was dripping from somewhere inside. She could hear it; she could smell it. She could drop through the opening but not knowing how far the floor extended, or if she could get out again, she called for back-up. "I got something, but I need some help." With no response after ten or so seconds, "You guys still there? Somebody, anybody?"

She heard the grunting of an aggravated man behind her. Then the thud of a head against the bottom of the elevator. Then it was Lester's muffled cursing as he dragged himself through the crawlspace.

Twenty-four

It didn't take much inner coaxing to put him on the road east, and Beverly didn't do a thing to dissuade him from going. Nothing much happened in Lincoln County that needed his immediate attention. He'd just drink coffee all day and mope. A trip away for a day would do him good.

He tried for the first hour of the drive to raise one of the team on his cell phone but nothing. He loved the tranquility and remoteness much of Montana offered but damned its dark-ages inconveniences.

So, he tried to relax on his drive along US 2. He knew what it was that was pulling him out there, it was that damn school-slash-asylum-slash-burned out hulk of cement and steel, though he wouldn't admit such a thing to a soul; they'd pull his badge.

He was fortunate that Beverly thought the training was his source of angst, as well as pitiful Clare Peone and bombastic Boyd Lester. And those were ancillary concerns. But what happened out there over a decade ago had never left him. He told the others to let it go as he had; he told them it was a freak-thing, done and gone. When asked, he feigned forgetting the details when answering those inquiries from reporters and crime writers that kept coming. But he hadn't let it go and the details were there, always right there. He had nowhere else to put them.

Sheriff' Abernathy's grizzly death had everything to do with the fire. The cause of death ruling still infuriated him. Shit, no animal could have done that to him, no animal would have a need to. Horrific fire, locked doors, destroyed records, mutilated bodies, someone was very sick and very pissed off. Not a cheerful combination. And having that person locked in with a bunch of feel-good doctors who believed they could alter hearts and minds was this disaster waiting to happen. Armed guards are what they should have had, and plenty of them. But that would have entailed putting a detachment out there, state or county, and they weren't about to spend money on a problem that was hundreds of miles from upstanding folks. Like crime in the inner cities, leave it there and leave it alone so good people could say it never happened.

One would think that whatever evil had passed through there was long gone. Whatever occurred now was built on legend and superstition. But he paid attention to the stories coming over the years. The ones from kids, drunk and high, he could dismiss. The ones from farmers and police reports about lost cattle and pets at an alarming rate had more credence. Credence, not coincidence. And he had told all this to Alston Waters, and still Waters went, and still he let him. Admitting he was spooked was not good police work, but knowing he had deps out there ... yeah, he was spooked.

"You said it would be easy for me to get through here," Lester said as dragged himself beside her.

"Never said, 'easy.' Just that you could do it."

"That the tunnel out?"

"I don't think so."

"Whatta mean, don't think so? You said you checked it; you said it led to outside."

"What is it with you telling me what I said? I said I *thought* it was a passageway but now I think it's a room."

She saw only bits and pieces of his face when she lit him up with the flashlight. But she heard him hyperventilating. "You okay?"

"Fine. So ... a room. Okay, why we laying out here? Whatta you waiting for?

"It's tactical SOP to clear a space before entering. That's why I —"

"Damn, screw that shit. We gotta ... gotta get outta here."

"I don't know if it's going to get us out, I told you."

"Not the building, here. Just get us outta here, damn it."

He was flipping out. Claustrophobia. It was why he chose not to see the room, or to not disclose it. Better to stay locked inside than to face his fears. The arrogant sonavabitch. Slamming everyone then losing it when it counted. Clare knew better than to challenge or even patronize him on it. But he was on the verge of a full-scale fit, and she had to get him out of it fast by going forward, not back. Diving through that hole where a maniac could be waiting was suicidal. Come up with a plan that is quick but sound, gets him moving forward, keeps him in the moment. "Lester, I can get a look at most of the room from just outside the break in the wall but there are blind spots, okay."

"Yeah. Blind spots."

"So, you'll need to ease through the hole, just your head; you should be able to view nearly all the space."

"Okay. Okay, let's go."

"Wait. Give me the gun to keep you covered."

"No. I keep the gun."

"But this will be like you clearing and me covering, Lester. I'll have the flashlight; I can see the long angles."

"No, I keep it."

"Your hands won't even be through; you have no fields of fire. From where I'll be I can –"

"Let's go."

And he pulled himself forward as if a thirsting man towards a waterhole. Clare was able to thrust the flashlight into position just as his head breached the opening, not that it would have mattered had Walter Hill been waiting there with a meat cleaver.

"Clear," Lester said as he frantically began to scramble through the hole.

"No. We haven't scanned the whole area." Clare grabbed him at the collar.

"I did."

"How could you without light? Just stand-down another fifteen seconds, will you?" Dumb, scared shit would rather get disemboweled like the others rather than stay another second under the elevator. Of course, being trapped in a tiny room just beyond would offer little relief. Again, she kept this to herself.

She flipped over and switched hands with the flashlight, making sure Lester was following the beam and not just giving the "all clear" for the sake of his comfort.

"Hold it, hold the light there," he told her.

"There?"

"There's another break; I think it's a tunnel. Move the light left and right. Slowly. No, keep it up where it was, just left and right. Yeah, another break in the back wall."

Her shoulder was numbing for leaning on it and holding the flashlight in place. "Okay, I gotta take my arm in." She rolled onto her stomach and massaged her arm back to life. "That has to connect to the pipe back to the well."

"What well?"

"To the west, I saw it when we were on the roof. You and Koopman must have passed right by it when you went to bury the cats."

"No, we didn't pass a well."

Let it go, she convinced herself. *Not the time or place, and you need him focused.* "You drop first," she said, but he was already dropping, arms first.

She turned herself around, dropping her feet, feeling for the ground with no help from her wing man who was off exploring the wall. The floor was hard cement, so it was, in fact, a room of some sort. But it was only about four-by-eight; she'd seen larger jail cells. She thought it wise to keep Alston and Sonny apprised. "Hey?"

"Yeah?"

"We're in. It's a room, and a tunnel. I'm thinking it leads out to a well."

"The broken down one west of here?" Alston asked.

"Yeah."

"That's a good quarter mile out; think it's passable?"

"We're gonna give it a shot," she said. "Stand by."

"I'm betting they're in that room," Sonny said to Alston. "The one they kept the kids in."

"Well, right now their hell may be our salvation."

Twenty-five

"Whatcha thinking about?"

"Nothing."

"It's something, and it worries ya."

Alston scratched his chin. "There are two scenarios here. Either Walter Hill is behind us, watching, or he's in there, between them and the well."

"And watching."

"And watching."

"Yell in there, tell 'em to be careful?"

"They don't know that much by now, Sonny, they shouldn't be in there."

The cat odor wasn't as strong inside the room but there was no mistaking they had been there. With the dampness and dripping water, Lester couldn't help but think of wet cat shit smeared along the floor and walls. How it would get on the walls he hadn't a clue but in his mind, it was there.

It was good to be on his feet. It was still tight, no more than a walk-in closet, and dark, but at least he could stand and stretch. The notion of going back out using another suffocating low crawl wasn't one he wanted to dwell on. Going forward didn't offer much more comfort.

The pipe went left and right. Inspecting the opening he saw that the brick wall had been chiseled through to the hardened clay pipe. In high school he had a summer job back in Wabasha, Minnesota with an excavating company that was replacing sewer pipes. Tree roots had grown into the old clay pipes, those that hadn't disintegrated. He learned clay pipes went out of use in the 1920's. He tapped his flashlight against it. Flakes of clay rained down.

It was tall enough to squat in, and wide enough to touch side-to-side with bent elbows. He stared down it. No daylight was coming from the other end. Clare called it a quarter mile length. Not far if you were a track sprinter, a little tougher for a swimmer, downright torture on hands and knees. And though there were no noticeable cracks, how safe could this ancient pipe be?

All sorts of reasons not to go but someone would have to. He was the most tactically proficient deputy, former military, and he was keeping the gun, so it was logical he be the one to lead. Besides, Clare had done the hardest part.

"Does it go out?" Clare asked.

"Can't tell. I can't see any light at the end."

"It does lead to a well, meaning the pipes are laid at the bottom so probably won't be seeing light."

"Says you, huh."

He had been staring down the long, narrow pipe, contemplating how insufferable it would be to crawl through. He was aware of his heavy breathing, his profuse sweating in spite of the chilling temperature. Clare was aware of it, too, which explained her questioning his resolve. "Sure you want to chance it? I can —"

"Stay here," he said. "I'll be back in a bit."

She took hold of his arm. "Lester, we all have our fears. You don't have to go."

"You'd like that wouldn't you?"

He gingerly climbed into the pipe, turning right. "Wait," Clare said. "These pipes go north and south; the well is west. So, these must be connectors for something." She stared ahead, as if through the wall. "South, the well is south of the elevator shaft."

"Sure?"

"It was dark, but I know it's south of the elevator. Then there should be a connector going west."

"So south; I go left here."

"Yeah. Left here."

He stepped back out and turned himself around. Tight, as he thought, and smothering. His plan was to duck walk through, to create some sense of space. But that wasn't going to work; his quads burned after ten seconds, and his knees were so tight to his chin the shuffle would take him hours. On all fours he went, flashlight left hand, weapon right hand, dragging both along clay and through puddles.

What if it didn't bring him out? What if Clare was wrong? What if she was fucking with him, and the well *was* north? That would be like her, and like the others. They hated him. Maybe he could see it; he did ride Koopman hard, even if jokingly. And he had no sympathy for Clare's wild demon fantasies or tolerance for Stabler's accusations when they scouted the upstairs.

Okay, chill, breath, relax. This is the start of the freaking out. You let your mind wander to the darkest sides, letting you believe the tunnel has no end, that it's actually getting smaller and smaller until at last it crushes you, and no one's there to save you.

Clare called back to Alston and Sonny, "Lester's going through now. Problem is, they're old clay pipes, may be collapsed. But if not, I'm hoping it'll take us out to the well."

"I'm not liking it," Alston said to Sonny. "Look." Alston turned around and shined his flashlight along the walls. "Cats are gone."

"Had to go upstairs, right?"

"I'm thinking that. But where and why."

"What's your guess?"

"That Walter Hill doesn't care about you and me trapped in the basement. He's more concerned about us getting out." Alston lay down before the elevator "Clare. Clare, you still there?"

"Yeah."

"And Lester?"

"No, he's heading down the pipe."

"Stop him. Don't go down the pipe 'til we have a plan."

"Copy." Clare leaned into the pipe to call to Lester. In mid-call she stopped and recoiled at the sound of a low hiss just behind her. Slowly she eased herself back, not daring to turn towards the sound, knowing it to be at least one of the cats. Not knowing how many or their intentions.

It was just the one, the one Lester called a bobcat. It looked bigger on this level, eye to eye, and damn if it didn't look like a bobcat now. It was crouched as if setting itself to attack. At less than five feet away, it could be on her head and tearing at her eyeballs in less time it took for her to blink them.

Slowly she backed out, being careful not to rise to her full height, not knowing if that would scare the cat or challenge it. Her grandmother talked soothingly to her two cats, but they responded like cats were supposed to. She didn't trust uttering a sound to this one. She had seen enough of what these cats could do to know they were not ordinary. Which made her wonder how many others were behind this one, or behind her at this moment, awaiting their signal from Walter Hill. She dared not look back to check.

Behind her was a cage, windowless and doorless. It reminded her what her brothers did for fun as boys. They would take one of Eema's cats and put it in a three-by-six pen with a prairie rattler. The cat always won. So here she was, without even the defenses of a rattler.

Her Maglite was back at the crawlspace under the elevator shaft. It was heavy and damn near unbreakable. It was the choice of most cops for that reason, a flashlight and nightstick in one. Backing out would expose her face and neck; turning would expose her back and neck. She wasn't fast or even quick, but adrenaline would count for something. If she could get halfway to the Maglite before the big cat jumped on her back, that would be workable. She could smash her back against a brick wall if that's what it came to. Course if it grabbed hold of her leg.

As soon as her head cleared the opening she ran to the crawlspace. Reflexively her shoulders drew up to cover as much of her neck as possible. She ran furiously but under control. She couldn't afford to lose her footing when the cat took hold. The seconds it took were agonizing minutes. She reached the Maglite before the cat could pounce. She turned violently, swinging the full weight of the weapon with both hands in the desperate hope the cat's head would bisect the arc.

But the animal stood back stalwartly, its magnificent profile centered on the tunnel entrance. This was no escaped housecat. Its size and demeanor told her, and all other creatures nearby, that it was indeed the alpha. It was certainly the kind of beast that could shred a face and chest apart. The thought of it being amongst the animals that killed Karen had Clare wanting to beat it senseless regardless of its immediate intentions.

It turned to look at her as if an afterthought. Then, slowly it crouched, the muscles of its haunches, shoulders, and neck firing under the thin, gray coat. It was focusing down the tunnel where Lester was crawling. Its intentions made plain; Clare had precious little time to react.

Twenty-six

There was a loose brick in the elevator shaft. With her arm, it wasn't the best weapon, but she didn't want to chance throwing the Maglite and losing it. All she needed was a distraction, something to piss the cat off and redirect it to herself. Her plan went no further than that. "Guys," she yelled over her shoulder, modulating her voice so as not to get the cat agitated, and not daring to take her eyes off it. "Got company in here."

"What?" It was Alston. Must have been down on his belly, his voice coming back to her with an echo.

"Ahhh, 'member that big cat? One Lester said was a bobcat? Yeah, he's in here with us."

There was a long pause where she knew Alston was contemplating things. "Is it ... aggressive?"

"Yeah. From the little I know of cats, it's aggressive. Listen. I don't have time to discuss it and we don't have time to make a plan. Lester's in a predicament and I have to watch his back, if you can picture the situation."

He could. Lester heading down the pipe, Clare close enough to the elevator shaft to hear him clearly, that put the big cat between them. "Hold on, I'm coming through."

"Gonna be too late."

The extra pounds and inches Alston added since retirement were not making it easy. Just three feet in, he wedged firmly between ground and elevator. He cursed as he undulated his body worm-like. Getting stuck forever was not his concern; getting through to Clare and Lester in time was. He stopped struggling to catch his breath.

"Stuck?" Sonny yelled down to him.

"No, just slow going."

"Maybe you should back out."

"Can't."

"Can't or won't?"

"Both. I could use you in here with me."

"That ain't gonna happen."

The floor on his chest, the base of the elevator on his back, Alston was reduced to slow, shallow breathing that made him understand just what an asthmatic went through. "I fucked up."

He thought he was confessing to himself, but Sonny heard. "How's that?" he said.

"I saw him. I saw the Catman."

"In there?"

"No. On the roof, when we were on the roof." He should be conserving his breath. He should be resting to save his energy and strength. He was a mere fifteen feet from the wall but with the weight on an elephant on his back. He continued talking as if in a confessional. "He was in the wood line. Watching us, watching me. Should have told you all then. Made us stay together."

"You should have done that," Sonny said.

Of course. Old Sonny Morning was not the man you confessed to if sympathy was what you wanted.

"Yeah, shoulda. I saw it in him, he's not letting us go." He pumped the floor with his fist. "Now a fuckin' crawlspace is keepin' us from freedom, like he knew this was where we'd end up."

At that he heard screaming on the other side of the wall. Lester, in clear panic. And all Alston could do was hold his breath to listen and wait.

Clare leaned into the pipe and waited. It was chest high to her. Hearing Lester's frantic screams, she pulled herself up and in. She must have pulled herself up nearly two feet. She didn't remember doing it. If she banged a knee or elbow, she didn't feel it. There was no time. She was racing down the pipe on all fours, moving like the big cat. It helped that she was small and thin, but her agility surprised her. Each time her right hand came up she shined the light down the tube. She could see the hindquarters of the cat thrashing about, and Lester's feet outstretched as he worked at kicking it away.

The pipe was wide enough, and she was slight enough to wield the Maglite with some force. But it would be just enough to piss the cat off. When she reached the melee, she grabbed its back legs and dragged it off Lester; then it turned on her. It wasted no time in latching onto her left shoulder. It's claws easily made their way through her light sweatshirt.

The pain was intense and unremitting. She held the cat at the neck, knowing it would soon work its way to her face. It was too powerful and too frenzied to hold back for long.

She pressed deep into its neck with her fingers, feeling for the artery. At last, the cat let loose. It was winded and disoriented but far from dead. It collapsed onto its side. Before it could right itself, Clare put her knee in its midsection. She grabbed both ends of the heavy Maglite and pressed against its neck, grinding hard as if rolling out bread dough. It kicked and clawed futilely at the air between them. She didn't relax a muscle until it stopped.

Clare had pressed and rolled the Maglite to the point she twisted the cap from the case, spilling the batteries. Lester had dragged himself away, somewhere down the pipe. She heard his heavy breathing. She called to him, "Lester."

She swept her hands along the floor of the pipe in the blackness, poking under the edges of the carcass. "Lester, shine your light over here. I lost my batteries."

A dim beam hit her. "Lower it just a bit." The beam landed on the dead cat's body. It stayed there for a few seconds.

"Is it dead?" Lester asked.

"Yeah."

"Sure?"

She lifted it. "Here they are." She shoved the cat to her side. It landed as a dead cat should. Lester followed it with his flashlight, leaving Clare in shadows.

Clare fumbled with the four batteries, having to flip them several times. Her arms and shoulders were like rubber, and they shook uncontrollably now that the adrenaline was receding. As she stuffed the batteries in, she conversed with Lester to keep him in the moment.

He was possibly still in shock. She was fortunate in that she was the aggressor in her battle. And though it took less than three minutes, she had time for mental preparation. Lester's situation was different, and she imagined he was feeling much like the cat did when she was squeezing its neck into the ground. "You cut bad?" she asked.

"I think so."

"Slide up here, let me check you."

Lester didn't move. "Just give me a minute."

"I know you need to collect yourself but it's not safe in here. These cats, they don't travel alone."

"Yeah. Okay. Just a minute."

"Waters wants us back. 'Sides, we know this is here; we can come back when we have a better plan. Let's go."

She turned her light on Lester. He had been ravaged good. She looked down at her chest. Lotta blood for such small claws. It took seeing it for the sting to really hit her. "Might wanna kill your light," she told him. Mine's got more juice."

"Mind?" he said. "You're blinding me."

She clicked it off. "Coming then?"

He was composed now, enough to feel the wounds from the cat and the insult of being rescued by the faint-hearted Clare. Won't that be a story for her to bring up whenever she felt the need to castigate him.

He heard it. Slow, shallow breathing coming from the darkness up ahead. It wasn't Clare. He could hear her maneuvering herself around, the Maglite tapping on the pipe. He was about to tell her to hold still and listen, he really was, but she turned on her light and directed it back down the pipe. There, not a foot away, and blocking their path, was a creature, a man who resembled one in only the rudimentary way. Clare's light illuminated him for mere moments before she screamed and dropped it.

Lester watched, frozen in place, as the shadows wrestled in the oblique glow of the light. The creature tossed her against the side. It growled, no hissed and spat, an enraged man-cat. Its hands swiped madly at her like a scythe cutting wheat. The attack was mindless and relentless.

"Shoot Lester, for God's sake shoot." Clare begged incessantly, again then again, yet the words weren't reaching him. The voice didn't seem connected to the moment. This butchering was beyond any reality he had seen or imagined.

Finally, she stopped begging. The monster was leaning in on her, and in the shadows, Lester couldn't distinguish the two. He dug the forty-five out from the holster. He prided himself on the speed of his draw, but here he was all thumbs and nerves. He sat up and held the gun in his right hand between his knees, admonishing himself to relax and steady his aim. He held the Maglite in his left and crossed it over his gun hand.

The creature turned defiantly into the dim light coming from Lester. There wasn't enough to be blinding, just a soft glow. It hissed, displaying teeth carved to razor points. Long red hair, thick and wild, soaked with sweat and blood, hung matted to its neck and forehead. Its hands, with long dark nails, gripped Clare' s neck. She was unconscious, or dead, and looked like a battered rag doll. Her face was unrecognizable, sliced open like Koopman's. It grabbed up Clare and quickly backed down the pipe with her ragged body as a shield.

"Sorry, Clare," Lester muttered, "I don't have a good shot and I can't waste the bullets."

Twenty-seven

Alston waited in the crawlspace until Lester climbed back in. Without Clare. "Where's Clare?" Alston asked.

Alston's presence in the dark startled him. "Shit," Lester said. "Where'd you come from?"

"She behind you?"

"Didn't make it."

Alston was about to go off on him, tell him he was just talking to her. But Lester crawled past him before he could. "Can't talk in here," he said breathlessly, meaning he couldn't get out fast enough.

"I told her not to go in there; I tried to help," he told Alston and Sonny when the two were safely out from the elevator shaft.

"That so," Sonny said, stealing a glance at Alston who listened attentively.

"I couldn't fit in the pipe. She said she'd try it. There was this ... creature, thing. It must be whatshisname, Hill, that crazy you were reading about. It was bad."

"You give her the gun?" Alston asked.

"Huh?"

"The gun. Did you give it to her?"

"Ah, no. No, I didn't. I told her ... it wasn't a good idea, but you know how she is."

"Yeah, I do," Sonny said, his voice booming with rage. "She was scared to death of this place. She wouldn't be taking chances."

"Whatta you mean, she was the first one to crawl under there," Lester protested, "I had to chase her down the pipe. Look." He lifted his shirt. "The wild bastard got me, too."

"She went in 'cause you were too chicken shit. But she wanted the gun, you wouldn't give her the gun. Besides, that's bullshit, she was talking to –"

"Not helping," Alston interjected. "Not helping, Sonny. Is she alive or not?"

"No. I mean, I don't know, not for sure. She was being dragged off. She didn't look good. She looked –"

"Did you shoot the thing?" Sonny said. "I didn't hear a gunshot. You had the gun, why didn't you use it?"

"I didn't have a clear shot. It was tight in there. It was dark. And he stayed behind her the whole time."

Alston couldn't allow Sonny's interrogation to continue, though he was in step with the reasoning. He wanted to snatch the gun from Lester, blow his head off, then toss his body in the elevator shaft for Walter Hill to take apart.

Maybe Lester couldn't have saved Clare, but he could show character. He could have integrity, not make Clare look like the crazed radical, when in fact, she was the one who ran in to save his ass, and most probably did. But there were just three of them now, and the unstable one had the gun. Alston didn't want to fight this battle on two fronts. Imperceptibly he glanced at Sonny and nodded. It didn't ease the big man's ire, but he sucked it up for the moment.

The Econovan and Jeep Cherokee were out front of the asylum. No sign of the team. Sheriff Vanderpool got out of his pick-up and stretched. It was warm but the trees made a nice canopy. If not for the memories the old asylum brought, he'd agree with Waters, great place to spend a few days training.

He looked the building over from his safe distance. He felt a spasm of panic while looking up at the fifth floor. It looked the same yet encouragingly different. Maybe time was being kind, allowing him to forget bit-by-bit.

"What the f–?" he muttered as he leaned his head forward and squinted to get a better look. Yeah, the door was padlocked. Why would Waters feel the need to lock the place up while out training? Must be hikers out and about. Couldn't have gone far on foot. He laughed, picturing big Sonny Morning mumbling under his breath while plodding through the hills. It had been a long drive. Knowing they were safe, and the training was in motion, he went back to his car for a well-needed rest.

"She had to come back, something she had to do," Sonny said. "Had nothing to do with you or what you said."

"She tell you that?"

"Didn't have to. It's why I came, can't escape fear by hiding."

"You afraid of this place?"

"Guarded. That's kind of a fear. I've come up here to hike the hills, but never came near here."

Lester was asleep in the corner. Alston and Sonny watched him as they spoke. "I could sure use a cup of good coffee," Alston said.

"Any type of coffee," Sonny said.

"Don't know how long we can last without water." He nodded to Lester. "He's gotta be dehydrated after all that."

Without caring if Lester was listening, Sonny said, "Why'd you shut me up down there?"

Alston waited to see if Lester stirred. He looked to be asleep, but Alston whispered low in the event he was putting it on, making Sonny lean into him. "This is not the place to pursue it. But if we get out, we have enough to bring him up to the sheriff for dereliction. If we don't get out, it doesn't really matter, does it?"

"Hear that?" Sonny said.

Alston did. "Squealing noise. Human?"

"No," Sonny said. "Like bad breaks. Coming from the stairwell."

"The elevator?"

"How? There's no electricity."

"Hand crank or pulley system? Way out here, electricity sketchy, manual option would make sense." Alston said.

"Okay. So, one guess who's doing the pulling."

"Lester. Lester." Alston was on his feet, nudging him with his boot. "Get your gun."

"What?" He heard the squealing right off and was on his feet. "What the hell's that?"

"Elevator, we think, being hand cranked."

"How's that work?" Sonny asked. "Can he operate from any floor?"

"I think so," Lester said, "long as there's access to the shaft where the pulley system is. No access from the basement with the elevator on the ground. He's gotta be on a floor upstairs."

"Or on this one with us," Alston said.

The elevator shaft was down the hall, past the stairwell. A small amount of daylight made its way in but much of the interior was in constant shadows no matter the time of day. It added to the depression and hopelessness that came with this place. Madness. It was not only confined here, it procreated here. "My flashlight's had it," Sonny said.

Alston watched his flutter. "Stabler had the last batteries."

"Mine's okay," Lester said.

"You mean Clare's, don't you?" Sonny said.

"Here, you take it, take the lead. I'll be in your hip pocket with the gun." The boy was a bit more humble this time out, a bit of conscience eating away that hard shell.

The elevator was stopped a bit less than midway between the basement and first floor. They did a quick scan of the hallway. It appeared they were alone. "Must be on a floor above," Lester said.

"If we know anything about him it's that he could be anywhere," Sonny said.

"Why'd he bring it up, the elevator?" Alston said, rhetorically.

They all three stared at the door as if awaiting the rising of the curtain to start a play. Sonny approached and attempted to pry the single door open. "Wait," Alston commanded.

"For what? Him to tell us what to do? Tired of waiting. He gives us a ride, we take it."

Alston saw evidence of the powerful man Sonny was. His shoulders and trapezius muscles swelled as he worked at the door. Though he couldn't slip his sausage fingers in enough to get a solid grip, his ferocious manhandling had it nearly bending.

"Let me get a grip," Lester said. "I'll pull and you push. Thing's old enough, it just might work."

Lester felt a give and directed Sonny to grab hold of the door. He moved to the side as Sonny tore the door back. It was halfway open when he stopped, his hands resting on his knees. "Oh, shit," he said. "No, not her."

Alston and Lester gathered behind him. Clare was slumped in the corner, sliced and blood covered. "Sweet Jesus," Alston muttered.

"Sonavabitch is mocking us now," Lester said.

Sonny stood and turned to him. "He ain't mocking; he's killing. Been killing since you shot his cats. Should be you in there."

He stepped down into the elevator. "Watch it, might not be safe," Alston said.

Sonny gave him a *you shitting me* look. "We're not leaving her for his cats."

He took her up gently, as if she was merely sleeping. He swept her mottled, tangled hair from her unrecognizable face. He cradled her in his arms, mindless of the blood dripping from her. Effortlessly he stepped out and brought her into the front room but wouldn't set her down.

Alston touched his shoulder. "Sonny."

"She was a good person," he said.

"We need —"

Sonny turned to Lester. "Tell me what happened."

"I told you. I ... I'm not sure."

"Sonny, we need to move fast," Alston said.

"No. I want to hear it from him. I want him to say she saved his life."

"She went into the pipe —"

"After you. She went in after you. You went in and she had to save your ass."

"You weren't there."

"We were talkin' to her just before she went in. Now you give her her due; she earned that much."

Lester shook his head. "I don't know what she told you, but she didn't save me."

Sonny, determined to protect Clare's body and spirit, would let go of neither. The anger building up in him reached its peak with the dead body of Clare Peone resting in his arms and Lester's repeated denials.

"Sonny, the elevator's up here. Means there's room for us to get under it and into that tunnel," Alston said. He didn't know if he was reaching him. Sonny stood in place, and if the big man didn't want to move, no one here was going to make him. "Set her down in the back room," Alston said. "We'll close the doors, get her when we come back."

Sonny took Clare into the back room that was to be her and Karen's sleeping quarters. He lay her down at the wall where Walter Hill had scribbled *You all must die*. "I need to be alone," he told them.

"Make it quick," Alston said. "We've only got a short window here."

Twenty-eight

"What are we waiting for now?" Lester wanted to know.

"Sonny."

"How long he gonna take?"

"He'll be out soon."

"We can't afford to—"

Alston grabbed Lester at the neck and pinned him to the wall, his thumbs wedged into his brachial plexus. He waited for a reason to bury them up to his knuckles. "You're damn lucky these aren't his hands wrapped around your throat," he said through clenched teeth. "You have no right to make demands. We'll wait until he comes out, thirty seconds or thirty minutes. And if we get out of here alive, better hope you don't meet one of us in a dark alley."

He released and stepped back while Lester held the sides of his neck and gasped for breath. Lester straightened up quickly and reached to his hip. "Go 'head, waste a round on me," Alston said. "And another on Sonny when he comes out for you. That leaves just you and one round. You like those odds?"

"We'll finish this later, Waters. I may get bounced from the department, but it'll be worth it."

Sonny came out of the back room. He waited for the two to finish their confrontation, then decided it wasn't worth it. "Let's get downstairs."

"Gonna close that door?" Alston said.

"No. He comes up, I want him to see inside."

Alston peered around him. On the wall, written above Walter Hill's warning, in blood Alston suspected came from Clare, Sonny painted a warning of his own. *Walter Hill will die.*

They hurried down to the basement. Not sure, and at this point not caring, if Walter Hill and his army were waiting. The elevator was about four feet off the ground, enough room for all of them to make it through. "Gonna be tight going through that hole in the wall," Sonny said.

"It'll work," Alston said, "We'll make it work."

Sonny knew this was not the time to worry about details such as bending and crawling. As Alston said, it was something he had to make work. There was no way that psycho was going to let them out without a fight. "You two through first; I'll stand watch."

Lester entered first, his pistol out at the ready. As they neared the access hole into the room, the elevator dropped nearly a foot. Alston, anticipating such a tactic, went to his knees. Lester was caught unaware, his head colliding with the elevator. He crumpled to the floor as it quickly descended. Alston crawled to him and yanked at his collar. He was groggy but not out.

Alston yelled but the screeching of the rusted cable drowned him out. Lester was frantic and disoriented. As Alston attempted to pull him towards the break in wall, Lester made a mad scramble towards the front. Alston pursued him too far and too long. He could see Sonny on his chest, reaching in for any hand he could find but he was too far away. The elevator was now pressing upon their backs. Lester's feet were kicking against Alston's head. They weren't going to make it; they weren't getting out of there.

Another foot, Lester was nearly there. He pulled with his hands, propelled with his feet. Sonny's hand was looming closer. At one point they swiped at each other, their hands crossing over one another's. Lester put his left arm out straight and held it there. Sonny would find it. He'd feel it, grab hold, and with one huge tug, slide him out from under. Or the elevator would stop. As soon as it felt him beneath, felt him as resistance, it would stop itself. It would have to. It's how they were made. But this one wasn't being operated by such rules. It wasn't programmed to be safe. It didn't care that it maimed. So, when Lester first felt the car on his back, he knew that without Sonny he had no chance.

Their fingertips touched but his could go no further. Sonny leaned in, frantically screaming at him to reach, reach further you sonavabitch, you're almost there. And Sonny's fingers raking over Lester's, trying to get a grip, but the car had Lester's shoulder pinned to the floor. And now, with life nearly squeezed from him, Lester pulled his right arm forward enough to switch the gun into his outstretched hand. His fingers worked it forward towards Sonny. "Get the bastard," he muttered.

Sonny could see nothing but darkness under the car now. It was as low as it could go, with Lester and Alston's bodies wedged beneath. And still it continued its descent. Lester's outstretched hand lay exposed to his wrist. It twitched, balled to a fist, then relaxed. Reflexes. Sonny knew there was little life left in it. Whatever was would soon be gone.

And the car was still falling, Walter Hill was still upstairs somewhere cranking it. Maybe he didn't know he had caught them underneath. Maybe he would continue to work it until it would fall no further. The thought infuriated Sonny. It was always said of Sonny Morning that to piss him off, really piss him off, would be a horrific experience for his antagonist. He didn't know if that was true, having never been really set off before. His mother and grandmother called him a lamb inside a grizzly. He liked it usually, the lamb protected beneath the grizzly facade. At this moment, however, he wanted the bear.

He raced up the steps, determined to search out every room, every hallway, on every floor, for Walter Hill. To hell with a stray cat or a clowder, it was a man he was after. Mental case or not, Walter Hill was a calculating murderer, a thrill killer with a sadistic streak off the behavioral science charts.

He slowed as he turned the corner on the first floor. Though his mind was still out of control in the chase, he had to regain tactical advantage. If not, it was two madmen chasing each other and the results were left to chance.

He removed the magazine from the forty-five. Two rounds left. He pulled the slide just enough to see inside the chamber where a third sat. He replaced the magazine, and though he attempted to do it quietly, the click of it seating echoed like a cannon shot down the hall.

He gripped the weapon tight. From the front room there came the shuffling of feet, too heavy to be anything but human. Little doubt who it was. He moved quickly, coming to the entrance, cautiously inspecting the room a sliver at a time. His heavy breathing and galloping heart rate were not in keeping with his temperament, but he gave himself a reprieve. He'd been in life-or-death situations before, but those were places he just found himself in; never before had he entered so knowingly.

The shuffling continued but Hill was nowhere to be seen. The back room, Sonny knew, with Clare's body. The thought of his cats being called for dinner had him wanting to rush in firing his last rounds. He was law enforcement; killing outside the scope of deadly force, to protect from death or grievous bodily harm, was not an option here. Clare was already dead. But an arrest was not on his mind. Like his namesake, revenge was his motivation.

Too much movement was happening in there. Was Hill moving the body? Was he preparing it? Although angered and anxious, Sonny kept his approach methodical, stopping just outside the back room. One step to the left and he was targeting the center of Walter Hill's back.

Hill was frantically scratching out the message left for him by Sonny. He was using Clare's blood. Perhaps he was signifying the war continued; perhaps it disturbed him and erasing the words erased the threat.

He was tall and thin. His four limbs worked quickly but the efforts seemed constrained, the actions not fluid as he stumbled each time he moved laterally. Watching him, Sonny's fear subsided. No matter how he tried to behave cat-like, he was subject to human frailties. And years of crawling through tunnels, living in cold basements, scavenging the woods and farms for food, not to mentioned being totally insane, took its toll on his body.

Hill must have felt him standing there. He turned slowly. What a gruesome final vision he must have been for Koopman, Stabler, and Clare. He wore ancient jeans, unfashionably ripped, and a black "Timberwolves" sweatshirt. His feet were bare, swollen, and black from dirt and neglect. The nails repulsively long, scraped to rough points. His face was ashen, covered with red, puffy welts. His eyes were swollen and thick with crusted mucus. But they were piercing and jaundiced which gave them a green hue. He swept his matted red hair from his face with pencil-thin fingers tipped with dagger-like nails. He cupped his right hand over his mouth as he stared back at the gun. Slowly he bent down and cradled Clare in his arms.

"Put her down," Sonny commanded.

Hill extended her out to Sonny.

"What, you offering me a gift? Sonavabitch. Cat bringing a mouse as a peace offering? You sick piece of shit. I said, put her down!"

Hill stood staring. Sonny moved forward, the forty-five directed at the floor at Hill's bare feet. "You know what I'm saying, you can write, you can read, you can understand, so don't play the fuckin' insanity ticket on me. Save it for the court. You'll need it if I don't waste you right here. Put her down!"

Hill bent slowly and placed her on the floor. He seemed ready for the next set of instructions. Sonny looked at the wall. "That unnerve you, did it? Don't like being called out or you just like playing in blood." He took a few steps forward. Now just less the five feet away. With a quick snap he pointed the gun at Hill's forehead. Hill didn't flinch or bat an eye.

"I should just shoot. One round to the head. Done. Who'd blame me?" he said. "Who'd even care?"

"Go," Walter Hill said, exposing his sharpened teeth.

"So, you talk, too. Sit down."

Hill complied into a squat.

Sonny's shoulders ached. He lowered the gun but kept his hands wrapped tightly around it. "Guess lots of folks out there like to study you, the freak that you are. Me, I don't want you walking outta here. You lit this place up back then, didn't you? Killed all them folks. Why? They mess with your cats, that it? Killed Sheriff Abernathy, too, I'd lay money. Your folks back when you were a kid, fried them too." Hill stared up at him. Not defiantly, not sadly. Empty.

"Look at you, dead inside. Not much without that army of cats. You want me to go, huh. Where? Through that drainpipe? You and those cats follow me? Not likely. 'Sides, you think I'd let you go after the shit you've done. I should just shoot you now. I just might."

Twenty-nine

Hill leapt on Sonny from his squatting position. Walter Hill had his army, he had his fangs and claws, his honed reflexes. Sonny had his size and strength. Let Hill fight like a feral cat; Sonny would fight like an angry Indian. Peering through his raised elbows, he waited for Hill to get close enough. But even in his ferocious attack, Hill seemed always aware of his proximity to the danger posed by his much larger foe. There was no finesse to his punches, but his long nails and whip-like slaps were lethal. Unless Sonny made his move soon, his arms would be of no use. He reached out to grab Hill's arms, missed, but managed to hurt him with a solid block with his hambone forearms. He took advantage of the momentary lull to bear hug him around his gaunt shoulders.

He squeezed as he lifted Hill and swung him around, slamming him against the door. He was vaguely aware of the congregation of cats hissing as they mounted the bookcase. Then they were on him as he pressed his full weight into Hill. He felt a dozen claws digging into his calves and thighs. They didn't tear; they held on tight, as if injecting a toxic venom. The intense pain did its job. He was unable to hold the gun as he loosened his grip long enough for the madly struggling Hill to break free.

He broke through the door and ran back into the labyrinth of the building. Sonny fought off the dozen cats left behind as a painful diversion. He shook, kicked, and threw them off as he ran for the gun. He cursed himself for allowing the tide to turn against him. He was back to the start of this nightmare with less resources.

With the cats gone, he shut the door for a temporarily respite and time to think. Not many options. Three bullets left. He'd better be true with the first two or the third he'd need for himself.

"Where's everybody?" Vanderpool asked, looking back behind Alston.

"Just Sonny. He's still in there." At that, Alston broke away.

"What about the others?"

Alston was at the barred window by the front door, calling to Sonny. If not waiting in the front room, he could be anywhere. And if anywhere, he could be in danger.

"You have a bolt cutter?" he asked the Sheriff.

"No."

"We have to get in there."

"How about where you got out?"

"Can't."

Vanderpool stepped back to stare up. "Gotta be someway —"

"No. No, there's no other way."

"Okay," Vanderpool said, grabbing Alston hard by the shoulders. "You need to regroup here. You know what's going on, I don't. Doesn't sound like you can handle this on your own so you'd better fill me in."

"They're all dead."

"What?"

"Except Sonny. So far."

"How did that —"

"Walter Hill. He's the Catman or whatever it is you wanna call him."

"Why would he be killing *anyone*?"

"He' fuckin ' crazy, Gunny. And Lester was shootin' the place up, killing his freakin' cats. Thing is, I got out through pipes, but the passage is blocked now and Sonny's alone without a weapon."

"Someone has a gun; I heard a shot inside."

Alston stopped to reflect. Lester was at the entrance with Sonny trying to pull him through. But the elevator was pinning him to the floor. He couldn't move. At that moment Alston slid through the hole just as his leg was smashed and nearly removed completely. "I don't see how; Lester had the gun, and he was crushed. I'm sure of it."

"Jesus."

"Unless somehow he got it out to Sonny. We gotta get in."

"Wait here." Vanderpool raced back to his truck while Alston clung to the bars and continued to call through the window. Vanderpool returned with shards of a soda can.

"What are those for?"

"Shims. I got two. This is a double-lock shackle."

"How long's it gonna take?"

"Not sure. Been a while since I've done this."

"Gunny, we have no time."

"Got another plan?"

Vanderpool manipulated the lock so that he could work the shim down the shackle. It was a painfully slow process, twisting it into the lock's body. "Can't you speed this up?" Alston complained.

"Dammit," Vanderpool cursed.

"What?"

"Broke. I'll need to cut up another can."

Vanderpool jogged back to his truck, Alston at his heels. As Vanderpool fished around the cabin for an aluminum can, Alston spotted a heavy rusted chain and hook in the pick-up bed. He dragged it up to the door and hooked it to the shank of the padlock. Backing up the Cherokee, he attached the chain to the trailer hitch. Vanderpool watched. "You're gonna tear the bumper out before you break that lock."

"Hell I will," and at that, Alston put the gas to the floor. It caught earth and jolted forward with just a slight burp that was the padlock snapping free.

It was like a bomb. Sonny thought that's what it was, that Hill had saved some of the explosives he used for the fire and was bringing the building down on him. Damn if he would go out that way. He rushed out the door of the back room just as Sheriff Vanderpool was charging through the buckled front door,

Alston Waters stumbling along. Sonny Morning nearly fainted at the sight of the men and the smell of fresh air. "I thought you were dead," he told Alston.

"Close. Just you?"

"Yeah."

"How'd you get the gun?"

"Lester came through. Let's get the bastard.'"

He looked down at Alston's leg. "You're a mess."

"You ain't any better.

"Let's get outta here," Vanderpool said.

Sonny was adamant. "No."

"You crazy?" Vanderpool said. "After all you've been through? Look at you. Looks like you fell into a stack of razor blades. You and Waters need to get down to a hospital."

Sonny shook his head. "Can't leave."

"I know Clare and the others are dead; we'll come back."

"Not gonna be that simple or tidy, Gunny," Alston said.

"Ain't just about the bodies," Sonny added.

"Look, I don't know all the details here but I'm giving an order. We're heading out."

Sonny looked at Alston for support. "I'm with Sonny on this," Alston said. "Walter Hill, insane or not, crossed the line in there."

Vanderpool looked at the two men who had just survived a devastating experience. Sonny Morning, a legend for his tranquil nature, was bent on vengeance. Waters, a calculating practitioner of tactics, was with him. Both had been badly mangled and had seen friends and associates no doubt killed in horrific ways. He hated the men behind the desks, whether in the Corps or in law enforcement, who, for the sake of exercising authority, barked orders countermanding the front-line troops who knew firsthand the dangers and consequences. He swore never to be that man, yet here he was. "Sit tight then," he said. "If we're going in, we're going in hot."

He gave Alston his 12-gauge shotgun he kept loaded with slugs in the event he crossed paths with a bull elk. He kept his own nine-millimeter. Sonny went back to the Cherokee for Maglite batteries and a box full of forty-five cartridges. "We need this much firepower for one man," Vanderpool said.

"No, but we will for his army," Sonny said moving back into the asylum.

Vanderpool looked inquisitively at Alston. "'Member those cat stories you told me about? They're true."

"Check the basement first," Sonny said. "See if he's moved the elevator." Alston told him and Vanderpool to go ahead, he couldn't make the climb down.

Sonny was his stalwart-self again. Reserved, grounded, controlled. He was focused on just one thing. Alston could see there'd be no negotiating. The Sheriff, the law of the county, was with them but he'd better adjust to what was about to go down. Fortunately, he hadn't asked many questions. Maybe he had too many, or maybe he just didn't want to know.

Sonny came back alone. "What?" Alston asked.

"Car's still on the floor."

"Where's the sheriff?"

"Still down there. Barfed when he saw Lester's arm sticking out."

Sonny moved slowly down the hall while Alston waited for Vanderpool who came back up, sweating hard and walking slow. "Holy shit. Lester's arm." He shook his head.

"Nothing's pretty in here, Gunny. Be careful, those cats, they come from all over and they swarm."

"How? Why?"

"Hill was a patient here. My guess is he caused that fire and set up house with feral cats."

"We need to take him in."

"Don't go there, Gunny. You don't want to witness what goes on; I suggest you wait outside."

"And leave you as Sonny's wing man, fucked up leg like that?"

They followed Sonny. There was to be no tactical discussion here. Sonny was on a seek and destroy mission. Best to stay back as his security and extra firepower. But Alston knew, and Vanderpool suspected, that Sonny was moving forward without a plan. He marched the hallway, kicking the doors of the rooms they passed hard enough to unhinge some. He bathed the room in light then moved on. There was no thought of security, no thought of a retreat plan. And that's what Hill was relying on.

They were heading down to the room where Karen Stabler was attacked. "Just to warn you Gunny, Karen's in there," Alston told him. He got it and didn't ask questions.

Turning, Alston noted the long "L" shaped corridor, the one that spooked them when Clare came running. As it was then, it was dark with shadows, and disturbingly quiet. Something stirred him, not deja vu. If he was setting up an ambush, this is where he'd do it.

Thirty

"Sonny," Alston whispered. "Not good."

Sonny kept moving. Alston quick-stepped to grab his arm. "Sonny, I'm serious. We're too exposed."

"Fuck it. We gotta find him."

"Or he finds us."

Vanderpool elbowed Alston. "Look," he whispered.

Alston turned. Crouched on the floor behind them, on the banister and stairwell, dozens of cats. More he was sure, just beyond. Even Sonny reconsidered. "Move slowly," Alston said. Vanderpool led them back out. A large tabby reached up and attached to his leg until he shook it off, ignoring the sting and stifling a scream. Another swiped at Alston's head from its perch on the railing, puncturing his ear. Vanderpool held his left hand up as he made the turn in the hallway. Alston and Sonny gathered at his side. Cats covered the length of floor before them. They were still but deliberate in their posture. "They aren't gonna let us go," Vanderpool murmured.

"No. They're not," Alston agreed.

There were many more to their front than to their rear, but a battle loomed either way. "That back room," Alston said to Sonny, "door open?"

"Ah-huh."

"Okay. Could be a hunk of cats in there, too, but we're gonna have to chance it. We're gonna turn back, slow, and easy. If they attack, beat it to the back room."

Alston made his half turn when a cat sprang from nowhere onto his shoulder, the first shot of the ambush. The three sprinted forward as cats hurled themselves. Knowing the gauntlet included cats on the railings, they did their best to keep their heads covered. Shredded arms and legs they could survive, protecting their eyes was vital.

They were on them like a swarm of Killer Bees. Five were still with them when they got to the back room. Sonny tore one from his hamstring. It clutched hold of his pant leg so tightly that Sonny had to snap its neck. Seeing this as a tried-and-true tactic, he did the same to the three on Vanderpool and the one at the nape of Alston's neck.

Vanderpool collapsed, bloodied, and badly wounded. A cat had torn through his jeans at his inner thigh. While the others merely dug in and were content to hold firm, this one seemed to understand the predicament it had Vanderpool in. Minutes more and Vanderpool would have been nullified. He looked up at Sonny. "What the fuck you get me into?"

The stench of Karen Stabler's decaying corpse hung heavy. The cats having finished with her had abandoned the room. Perhaps the odor was too much for even them.

"We can't stay in here for long," Vanderpool said. "That stench will kill me if I don't bleed to death first."

Few things are more painful than shallow slivers of the skin. Hard to think that a wound as imperceptible as a paper cut on a fingertip could stop a person who could otherwise walk a half mile on a shattered leg as Alston had done. Something to do with the thousands of nerve endings, Alston figured. That made an army of feral cats an effective enemy if torture, more than death, was the objective.

And he, Sonny, and now Sheriff Vanderpool had their share of cat scratches which were already causing reactions. After an hour, Vanderpool's leg was noticeably swollen. As was Alston's neck. Hard to tell with Sonny but the skin on his arms was deep purple even in places not torn open. The cats had not left the hallway. Each time they opened the door to check the cats would arise en masse. They didn't attack or edge forward; they were content to stay in place, knowing they had their prey corralled.

Vanderpool found it difficult to stand but forced himself to walk to keep the blood moving. On one occasion he dared to peer into the cell at Karen who resembled a torn bag of garbage dragged from a barrel on trash day. He nearly vomited a second time.

"I hope to quit this shit for good someday," he said to no one in particular, pulling a crushed pack of Marlboros from his front pants pocket. He looked up. "Sure you guys won't mind. Nothing else, might cover the stench, huh?" He removed the Bic lighter from the pack and lighted the cigarette.

Alston surveyed the room then jumped to his feet. He ran past Vanderpool, grabbing the lighter from his hand even before the cigarette was fully lit. He tipped a wooden chair over and began pulling and pushing one of its legs. "Help me with this," he said to Sonny.

Sonny pushed gingerly off the floor. He put a foot in the center of the upturned chair and kicked a leg twice. It snapped free from its corner bracket.

"Feel better," Vanderpool asked.

"Yeah. Yeah, I do," Alston said. He pulled his shirt off and demanded the others do the same. "Got any more of these?" He asked, holding the lighter up.

"No."

Understanding where this was going, the two gave their shirts to Alston who tied them haphazardly but securely to the chair leg. "Don't know how long this flame's gonna last so we have to get through those cats quick."

"What about Hill?" Sonny asked.

"Forget it, Sonny. For now, just forget it."

"And Clare?"

Vanderpool stood before him. Sonny dwarfed the sheriff in height and width, but in his depressed state, he appeared much smaller and frail. "Sonny, best we can do for her now is get ourselves out of here and get some help."

"How's that help her? I mean, yeah, she's dead but leave her here to end up like that?" He nodded to the cell and Karen Stabler.

"So that she didn't die for nothing, Sonny. So that somebody lived through this because of her."

Alston ignited the shirts, twisted the top off the lighter, and poured the fluid on the unlit section. As he waited for it to catch, he issued his plan. "We're going straight through. I'll head out first with the torch." At that the fluid caught fire. It was an impressive flame, hot and bright. "Don't stop. Keep your head down. One jumps you, keep moving." He grabbed the door handle. "Ready? Move."

The cats scattered immediately but stayed within striking distance. Sonny was in the rear, head down but peering over his shoulder, hell bent on following orders, until from the corner of his eye he saw Hill leaping down on him from the second floor perch. Sonny leaned far enough to his left so that Hill bounced off his right shoulder before colliding against the wall while remaining on his feet.

The other two had turned the corner, pushing waves of howling cats ahead of them. What remained behind were a dozen or so on the stairwell and railings. You'd think that with Hill flailing at Sonny they'd be caught up in the frenzy. But they sat back as if awaiting a final victor to step out of the melee.

Sonny didn't cover up this time. Sensing this was to be a one-on-one match, he flew at Hill, grabbing him at the shoulders and tossing him across the hall. Rather than counterattack, Hill raced up the stairs. His cats watched him with curiosity but no willingness to involve themselves. Hill stopped at the landing, eyeing his army, willing them to attack. Sonny stood below, his gun now out and scanning the scene before him, ready and willing to kill anything that made a move at him. None did.

He tucked the gun back into his belt and gave chase. Hill dashed up the stairs at incredible speed and lightness. He'd have outrun Sonny and disappeared back into to the asylum had he not turned abruptly to rake Sonny across the face. The slash blinded Sonny but he continued his own assault.

Temporarily stunned and hurting, he led with outstretched arms and barreled straight at the spot he suspected Hill to still be occupying. Thinking he had turned the tide, Hill hadn't moved. Sonny could feel his boney figure but had a hard time wrapping it up, the deadly hands sweeping in concert like pair of scythes.

There was a mad rhythm to Hill's swings, like a boxer on a bag. Sonny's arms were strips of raw bacon, but he stayed on target. Reach-slap-pull; reach-slap-pull; reach-slap pull. Sonny had it now. At the next "pull" he stepped in and wrapped his hand around Hill's wrists, torquing them until he saw the grimace in Hill's face. "Look at them," he sneered. "They're waiting for your blood and guts this time."

Pain was in Hill's eyes but also seething hate. He had a demonic stare which he used on Sonny as if it could control him as it did his army. "Shit don't work on real people," Sonny said. He pulled out the forty-five and worked it savagely into Hill's mouth."

From below he heard Vanderpool. "Not like this, Sonny."

"Only way."

"He's insane; you're not."

Hill was attuned to Sonny's sudden lack of focus and the nearly imperceptible loosening of his grip. He responded without hesitation by slapping the forty-five to the side, digging the nails of his right hand into Sonny's forearm. The nails of his left planted deep into Sonny's face, letting them nest there, daring Sonny to pull away and risk having sections torn out.

Alston's torch was nearly extinguished, but he still had a hefty table leg. He plunged ahead, up the stairs. Seeing reinforcements arriving, Hill spun from Sonny and headed up the steps in hopes of making it into the asylum to be lost once more. Sonny, near blind but crazed with rage, moved with him. In a bear-like move he corralled him with his arm. The rest was reflex. Never would he admit to himself or others his true intent, but the momentum of that powerful blow lifted Hill up and over the railing. Hill dropped headfirst down the two flights, his head exploding on the edge of a cement stair.

The cats scattered as the body fell. It was not Walter Hill, their alpha. It was now just a body whose head was no more than a mass of brain matter and thick jelly. They closed cautiously, sniffing the body. Several pawed at the brain puddle, then licked it from their paws. Vanderpool moved aside frantically as dozens of cats poured back into the hallway to inspect and partake. "Fitting end," Sonny called down from above.

They still couldn't get into the locked cell for Karen Stabler. Boyd Lester's body was too broken to be moved neatly. They looked for Terry Koopman and Mark Pratt but didn't spend much time, knowing there was little hope in finding enough of them to bring back to Libby. Clare Peone was a frightful sight, but Sonny lifted her gently and carried her to Alston's Jeep.

"Sorry, Sonny," Vanderpool said softly, his hand on Sonny's shoulder.

"She didn't run away, Sheriff."

Vanderpool nodded.

"It's why she came back here, to prove it to herself. And us, too."

"She did real good, Sonny. Folks will know that."

"I could use some water."

Vanderpool gave him the Igloo quart-size cooler. He drank greedily as did Alston. "Any more?" Sonny asked.

"Just a can of warm Diet Pepsi."

Sonny and Alston were sitting beneath a grove of Quaking Aspen, catching their first breeze in several days, more cherished for being the one they thought they'd never feel again. Vanderpool stepped around them to get the Pepsi from his pick-up but stepped back abruptly onto Alston's hand.

"Careful there, Gunny."

"They're watching us?" Gunny said.

Sonny and Alston turned to see hundreds of cats at the windows, on the roof, at the front door, and on the grounds of the asylum, more than they had ever seen at one time . "What are they thinking?" Vanderpool asked.

"I've been staring at those mangy things for two days now," Alston said, "and hell if I know."

"Sheriff," Sonny said.

"Yeah?"

"I'm ready to get outta here now."

Vanderpool hugged the sides of his pick-up as he made his way around to the driver's side. "Boys, you don't mind we're gonna wait on this SWAT thing. When I get back, I'm spending money to get the department a few mean-ass dogs."

DOGS

One

"And in the fifty-ninth minute of the twenty-third hour on the sixth day, God created Maine." Tabitha half-grinned at Trent, indicating she was only half teasing. He smiled back, enjoying her commentary as they sped forever north.

"I feel like Lisa Douglas from that old TV show, going off to Green Acres," she said.

"You've been using that joke since Connecticut. And it doesn't even fit; that was a farm."

"She was someplace desolate, Kansas, Maine, makes no difference."

Trent rolled down the window and stuck his head out.

"Put that up," she screamed above the wind. "You'll wake the kids."

He heard but feigned temporary deafness. He was joined by Mop, their Biewer Terrier, who jumped into his lap to hang her head out the window. Trent turned to Tabitha. "Put your window down and stick your head out."

"I will not."

Trent took a deep breath. "Smell that?"

"Ewww, I think Mop took a dump." One of the twins, Ricky, had been awakened by the wild rush of air.

"It's the ocean, low tide."

"What's that?" Ricky asked.

"Put the window up," Tabitha told him again.

He did, and it was as if the car had plunged into a vacuum, it was so suddenly quiet. "It's when the ocean is closest to the moon, so the moon pulls the tides away from the shore," he called over his shoulder.

"Nah," Ricky said. "It's Mop."

"This smells nothing like poop. This is seaweed and dead fish ."

"God, dad, we gonna be smelling that every day?"

"If we're lucky."

They were leaving Reston, Virginia. Tabitha, his wife, was hoping Maine was just something he had to get out of his system. Reston, he declared, was what he had to get out of his system.

The nine-year old twins, Ricky and Jeremy weren't old enough to be familiar with leaving family and friends behind. They had been traveling nearly thirteen hours, but to them Autumnwood Drive would always be just minutes away and around the corner. No one but Trent was for the move, but they were given little choice.

Trent Aress was the Washington front man for a California lobbying firm that represented several defense contractors. He won his bona fides as a grant writer for several small midwestern colleges. He had been a lobbyist for sixteen years, five of them pre-marriage. He enjoyed most of it, but the work, the location, with the cross-country travel and intense stress, was never his dream. That was here in Maine where he spent his boyhood summers on his grandfather's potato farm.

In his heart he was a relic from the nineteenth century even as he hobnobbed with the power brokers of D.C. Over drinks or coffee, the talk would most always turn to life-after D.C. Few had visions of staying in town for long. The capital was little more than a staging area for politicians, civil servants, and lobbyists. Most were heading out to join big firms as captains of industry. He used to hide his humble ambition until he became comfortable in his skin. Now, it drew stares, mostly blank, and questions that usually ended with raised eyebrows and a shake of the head.

It wasn't a whim, he told Tabitha early on. She wanted kids right away, two would be optimum. He obliged. His plan? They'd be raised in Maine when the time was right. They'd learn to work boats on the ocean, sail, deep-sea fish, maybe even be lobstermen. That time had nothing to do with OBD, One-Bad-Day on the job. It would be right when he felt it. He'd let her know.

Meanwhile, he kept abreast of the Maine business environment and real estate, more specifically the service industry and motels. He had the money, saved and invested since before his marriage, he told Tabitha on the day he quit his job.

"You'll like it," he told her. "No, you'll love it."

From the age of seven to fourteen, he spent his entire summers in Maine. He couldn't pack fast enough from home in St. Louis to get there, and he hated leaving in August. "The life grows on you," he said.

"So do liver spots."

"No, it does. This shit I'm working, it doesn't touch me. I have no ownership. It's a way to make money, that's all."

"Good money," she said.

"Is money good for the way you make it, or the way you use it?"

"Well, from my end that's a no-brainer."

She was from Vienna, Virginia, a town that boasted of great schools, a thriving downtown, a Metrorail station, and a chunk of the Washington and Old Dominion railroad which they tore up to make a biking and hiking path. "They had to make a place to walk and ride a bike," he would chide her. "They had to tear up railroad tracks so you could walk without getting run over. What's that tell you?"

But she loved it. Even Reston was too far away at ten miles. "That's because ten miles around here is a an hour drive," he'd say whenever she rose to applaud her hometown. "In Maine ... " And she could fill in the rest, so often had she heard it each time he cursed the D.C. traffic, people, buildings, noise. *In Maine, you can walk for ten miles and the only vehicle you'll see is a John Deere. In Maine the loudest noise at night are the waves crashing against a jetty. In Maine, you can watch a bird fly for ten miles and then some.*

The only things she ever found remotely interesting about Maine was that it was the only state with one syllable; and Eastport, the eastern most city in the country, was the first one to see the sun in the morning. "See," Trent said, "that's kismet." "No," she said, "that's fifth grade geography."

For so many years she heard it as bluster born of frustration. But as the time drew closer, it worried her. He began perusing the Internet for motels-for-sale. He was subscribing to magazines like *Yankee, Mainebiz, and Down East.* And he was reading them. Cover to cover. Dog-earing pages on industrial kitchens and cabin renovation. He even had a Bedandbreakfast.com icon on his desktop.

He would attempt to impress with such tidbits as, "you know ninety percent of the country's blueberries come from Maine?"

"Hundred percent of ours come from Safeway."

"And ninety percent of the country's toothpicks. They have a state cat. There are over thirty-one-hundred islands. York was the first official city in America. It has enough deep-water harbors to dock every naval fleet in the world. Most people don't know this stuff."

"Most people don't care," she'd say. "Anything in those magazines that might remotely interest me?"

"It's home to LL Bean."

"Not even close."

A month ago, he sprang it on her at breakfast. He tossed eight, 5-by-7 color photographs on her strawberry jelly covered English muffin. Whatta ya think?" he said.

She wiped the jelly off the glossies. "Looks like something from Somalia."

"It's a vacant motel," he said.

"No wonder."

Trent held one up. "Know what this one is?"

"Smudges on a windshield?"

"Our motel from space."

"*Our* motel."

"Six guest rooms and three cabins."

That was when he told her about his life savings; the one they could have used to replace their worn carpets, their ancient refrigerator, their scarred living room furniture, their outdated master bedroom set. He told her his timing couldn't be better. Interest rates were low. Unemployment was down. Property values were heading up as was expendable income.

Stryker John Island of Washington County, off-season population 43; seasonal population, about the same, eastern-most county in the U.S., encompassing Eastport, the only place in Maine Tabitha knew a thing about. It was twelve miles from the mainland, Nuthatch Cove, another metropolis of 500, swelling to near 2,500 in summer.

The motel he purchased wasn't nearly as bad at the photos suggested, the realtor assured him. Trent checked it out himself the weekend before he bought it. That was his emergency trip back to St. Louis, the story he gave Tabitha to avoid another argument. Good thing he went too. There was a near-binding offer that he trumped with an amount twenty-five grand over asking. Still fifty thousand below what he was willing to spend. He'd used that to rehab the old place.

Tabitha was incensed he would do such a thing without her knowledge, input, or concurrence. She was taught by her father to be skeptical of all things she couldn't inspect for herself. That included people, places, and things. "This island doesn't even have a Wikipedia page," she said.

"Yeah," he said, "Isn't it great?"

"Do we get our own house?" she asked.

"There's one."

"You have photos of it?"

"No."

"I see. Not a priority for you."

"Not really, but you'll love it. If you think it needs work, I'll do it, or we'll get it done. Mainiacs love helping people out. It's the bartering system. You got a skill, you can trade it for food, labor, equipment, just about anything. My grandfather did it all the time. He was a wizard with farm equipment."

"And just what is your lobbying expertise gonna get for us?" she asked.

"Lobbying might come in handy, never know."

They drove Maine's undulating topography that rose and fell as if it were the waves of the nearby ocean. The kids and Mop were antsy. Tabitha was uneasy. Trent was immersed in the rapture of the journey. This coastline, rich and abundant since the beginning of time, had been a bounty for generations. To centuries of early travelers who passed through, it offered little more than fish and forest. But there was more. Much more. As much as each heart and mind could hold. The distance he and Tabitha had traveled could not be measured in miles alone.

Two

Trent hadn't looked at a map since leaving Reston. There was no need. The route was as natural to him as cradle to grave. He pushed off and drove his family as did the stalwart pioneers before him. He was on the move, looking for space, fulfilling a restless spirit to live beyond what life had to offer, demanding instead what he could take from it. Instead of expanding with the mass of humanity, Trent was looking to be solitary. In a world big with complexities, he wanted only its vastness.

Their last stop before Stryker John Island was Eagle Grove to fill up and eat at Lewright's Deli. They then sped fifty-five miles north to Nuthatch Cove and the ferry. It took them an hour and a half, though there were few stoplights and fewer cars. Trent drove slowly, insisting on taking in the scenery which Ricky said hadn't changed a darn bit in the past three hours.

It was early April. Trent wanted a solid two months on the ground before tourist season began. January would have been his choice, but Tabitha wanted to be home for her mother's birthday and the birth of her first niece. And winter in Maine had less appeal to her than the state itself. Only Trent delighted in the transformation spring would bring.

The boys perked up when their father said they had just five short miles to go. They passed a service station that quadrupled as a feed store, bait shop, and grocery mart. There was just one road down to Nuthatch Cove and back out. From their vantage point the town looked old and run down. Tabitha's heart sank. She was holding on to the smallest of hopes.

Trent marveled at the slices of glacier rock still coated with scattered layers of crusted snow and fast ice. Seagulls cut the sky like the mighty aircraft out of Andrews Air Force Base. This entire world was thick with the smell of ocean. It was a kingdom. The buildings that lay upon it were ancillary to the land, pedestrian structures meant only to assist in any way deemed appropriate by the people who ruled here.

They sat quiet and long in the vehicle as it made its way on the ferry across the bay. "They knew we were coming," Tabitha said.

"These are all good, caring folks. You'll see; they're all about helping one another."

Really? All good folk? She wasn't feeling Trent's kinship. The ferry boat pilot greeted them with this head-bobbing discourse, "So you the folks that bought the motel. Busy winter, bringing all those workers and equipment out there. Haven't seen the place yet but will. Lotta work done looks like. Gotta be nicer than it was. Don't go asking Abe Carver if he likes it. He don't."

He didn't sound excited about them or the motel. He spoke only to Trent, his tone dull and disinterested. And when Trent spoke, with the lobbyist voice that never failed to charm and cajole, it fell flat on this man who appeared to have gone suddenly deaf. Even those extra fares he had been taking over to the island during the long winter sounded like a nuisance. And who was this Abe Carver? If Trent knew, he wasn't saying.

Out of excitement or fear, Mop bounced left to right, from lap to lap, panting and whining through the partially open windows. Tabitha put them back up to deaden the roar of the twin 450 horsepower engines. It didn't stop Mop from her frantic dance as she licked, pawed, and banged her snub nose on the glass. "She's gonna pee," Jeremy said.

"She's not going to pee," Tabitha hoped.

"Yes, she is, she always does."

"Well take her out on the deck."

"Cool," Ricky said, "I'll take her."

"Both of you go," Tabitha said.

This was sure to be a big world for Mop. Ricky gave her the name. As a puppy, the twins would slide her across the kitchen floor to each other. When

Tabitha scolded them to stop, Jeremy would tell her they were helping to clean the house. "She's not a mop," she told them, "she just looks like one."

"She is today," Ricky said.

Though she no longer allowed herself to be so abused (she'd scurry behind Tabitha's legs to escape) she never grew out of squeezing her full seven pounds into the tightest places. They'd find her under the sofa cushions, between the cushions and armrest like the TV remote, under furniture and beds, and behind the dryer. Finding her was never easy. She heard the calls and whistles but ignored them. No one fretted when she didn't respond; she eventually came out, but there was always the fear they'd sit on her or worse.

She was Tabitha's dog, bought for her by Trent when the twins were five. It was meant as a joke when Tabitha complained the boys were no longer infants. "Wouldn't it be nice to have a little one around again? One who never grew up?" He brought Mop home a week later.

Tabitha was a good sport about it. It would be great for the boys to learn responsibility and to not fear dogs like so many of her friends' kids. It was certainly an added benefit that Mop would never get heavier than a handbag.

Tabitha named her Alice, after her great aunt who died when Tabitha was six. But with Trent and the boys calling her Mop it was senseless to add another name. Though she fed and coddled her, and the boys wrestled with her, it was Trent's near neglect that Mop most gravitated to. It was if she was working hard to earn his attention.

The engines shot into reverse as the ferry approached the island dock. Tabitha rolled down the window and called to the boys. They jumped into the backseat and Ricky dumped the shaking dog between them. "You should have seen her, mom. We put her on the floor, and she vibrated all the way across it."

"The deck," Trent said. "The floor of a boat's called a deck."

"Yeah. She just kept vibrating and couldn't stop," Jeremy said, "It was so funny."

"Oh, she's still shaking." Tabitha reached around and pulled Mop onto her lap.

"Home," Trent murmured when they landed.

There was something very childlike in the way he spoke the word, like Dorothy in *The Wizard of Oz,* awoken from her frightful dream. Maybe he had been, too. At the breakfast table that morning he broke open his inner child. "I thought I went to the farm because my grandfather wanted me there," he told her. "I was ten before I realized that wasn't the case. Summer was the time my old man used to get away from us. He'd go off to God-knows-where. I don't know if it was to the end of the world or the end of the block. My mother sent me up to Maine so I wouldn't notice. My two sisters were too young to get it. By the time they did, none of us gave a crap about him or the family. But I kept up like I didn't know. I kept it up because I loved being in Maine as much as I hated being home.

"I know you have all your family here," he continued, "but Maine is all I have worth holding onto. This is my chance to take something and make it mine. And really, it's not that far away. And with the motel we can block off rooms whenever we want so they can come stay with us. They'll love it up there, you'll see."

She couldn't argue his point. It was the only event of his past he showed any passion for. He didn't even display photos of his parents, both now deceased, or his sisters whom she had met only twice, last time at their wedding.

Trent knew what it took to put window dressing onto the most desperate situations. It was, after all, how he had made his living. He had the place fixed up from what he told her, and the ferry captain confirmed. The island was cold, barren, and lonely during the winter months, he warned her, but at least the living would be comfortable. So, while he tended to the harsh realities it would take to make this business thrive, she could maintain the family with a modicum of security. But that was to be another miscalculation.

The main house was a circa 1850 cedar-shingle structure which had been empty for nearly six years. Someone had been back to clean out the cobwebs, mouse droppings, and anything else you'd expect to find, but it had seen its last serious renovations somewhere in the 1970's. It was linoleum, wrought iron, faux wood paneling, and sculpted carpets of assorted greens, harvest gold, and aqua blue. There were several hanging lamps left behind. As the wind rattled the looser parts of the structure, Tabitha stood by the ancient windows. The cold bit through her. Hence, the need for the heavy, dark drapes.

"It's big and sturdy," Trent announced. "The way they used to make 'em."

"It smells," Ricky said.

"Go upstairs and pick out your bedrooms."

"Not alone," Tabitha yelled behind them as they bee-lined for the stairs.

Ricky halted. Trent shot her a quizzical look.

"You don't know what kind of shape it is up there," she said.

"Fine, I'll go with them," Trent said.

It was getting dark. Outside a cold, wet blanket was being drawn over them. There was a small porch, more of a platform, off the kitchen door. She looked out at it dispassionately. The old movies her parents adored, she watched with no romantic affection. That banging screen door and the steady breeze that sensually teased the heroine's loose strands of hair had no effect on her. She saw it for what it was, what she was feeling now. Isolation. Emptiness. A feeling that whatever was pulling her husband in was pushing her away.

The boys bounded downstairs having caught their father's enthusiasm. "Can we sleep here tonight?" Jeremy asked.

"No. There's no furniture."

"Dad packed our sleeping bags," Ricky said.

"How thoughtful."

"That was the last ferry of the day," Trent said from the stairway. "We're stuck." He tried to smile his way out of it, but her harsh stare struck him down.

"We need to talk," she said.

Trent waved the boys upstairs as the last rays of sun vanished. "Take Mop with you so she can get comfortable."

"That makes me feel good," Tabitha said, "concerned with the dog's comfort but not mine."

"The movers will be here tomorrow; I paid Hack an extra hundred to make an early trip over."

"Who?"

"Hack, the ferry boat pilot."

"But this place, I thought you were fixing it up?"

"Not the main house, just the rooms and cabins. We need to be ready for tourist season."

She spread her arms. "But — "

"It's livable enough for now. We'll get it done; you'll see. It's just ... not the priority."

"Oh, okay, I'm not a priority."

"No, see? I *knew* you'd twist it that way."

"There's another way to interpret that?"

"Tabitha, we're running a business. All businesses when they start out need certain things, and they can't be done all at once. So, you prioritize."

"Don't patronize me, Trent."

"I'm not; I'm explaining. What good is it if this place is done to the nines but the guest areas are trashed, and trust me, Tabitha, they were trashed. I mean, not even livable. Mold, dead bugs, water damage, I mean, you don't even wanna know."

"And you bought it why?"

"The potential." He went to the window and pulled the drapes back. The sunlight was gone. There was a dim light a half mile north. A neighbor. The closest one to them. "Well, hard to see now but the ocean, the beauty, the solitude. So many people are looking for that."

"So many aren't."

He stared at her as he let the drapes fall. "Why you doing that?" He saw that puzzled look on her face. "And that. First you say something very argumentative, then you come on with a look like you don't know it."

"You're serving a lot of masters here, Trent, I don't think you can accommodate them all."

He walked outside, what he had planned to do since getting into the house, this early confrontation just making it more urgent. He started down the road to the neighbor. Three days a week, thirty minutes each day, he hit the treadmill at *Fitness First.* But after just half a mile on this gravel road his inner thighs ached. He smiled. This world would test his mettle on many levels.

He was breathing hard when he arrived at the house. He wasn't even sure anyone was home, but then, where would one go? The town center, if it could be called one, was nearly four miles away. He walked around the side which ignited the bark of a serious dog. Then two. The thick-coated German Shepherds jumped from the shadows behind the house. Trent heard the rattling of the heavy chains, but even so, the temper of the animals threatened to tear them loose. He had no time to regain composure or to settle his heart when the front door crashed open and an old man who normally wouldn't have the legs for such a thing, raced forward with a shotgun. "Who the fuck are you?" was his greeting.

Trent threw his hands up. The dogs strained mightily against their chains. "Neighbor ... from up there," he said in a panicky twitter.

The old man thrust the right side of his head towards him. "Who?"

"Trent Aress. I just moved in up the road."

The shepherds continued their offensive, digging at the ground to their front, leaning on their haunches for traction. The old man poked the muzzle of the shotgun into a dog's face to force them back. He lowered the shotgun, much slower than Trent would have liked. "Yeah?"

"I saw your light on. Thought I'd come down to pay a visit."

The man eyed him cautiously. "Put your damn hands down."

Now it was cold. The adrenaline had left him, and his muscles remained tense. He began to shake, and his teeth chattered uncontrollably.

"Whatsa matter," the old man asked, "got some kinda palsy?"

"It's cold."

The man looked around. "Suppose it is."

"That's quite a pair of dogs," Trent said, nodding to the corner of the house. "Kinda aggressive."

"Very aggressive."

"Yeah. You got anymore hanging around I should watch out for?"

"Huh? Yeah, could be." Even with the absence of light the old man squinted. He pursed his lips and tightened his jaw, making Trent very nervous.

"What are their names?"

"Names is dog."

"Okay. I'm Trent Aress. Guess I already told you that. And you are?"

He turned his back to Trent and walked away. With a slight wobble, he disappeared back into his house muttering, "Don't want no visitor; don't want no neighbor."

When Trent got back home Tabitha was sitting, her back against the wall. The boys were laying on the floor, their heads resting in her lap. They were tucked away into the furthest corner of the living room. By flashlight she was reading to them, *Love You Forever*. She stopped as the three looked up at him. "I think I just met Abe Carver," he said.

Three

Stryker John Island was named after its first full-time resident, whose true name was never known. It measured eleven miles at its longest, by five and a half miles at its widest. The Passamaquoddy Tribe was its first known inhabitants but were driven off over the centuries to a plot of land that measures just over two miles squared.

That left behind a man who called himself Stryker. No one knew if it was his first name, last name, or nickname. And since the island offered nothing the mainland didn't have, no one much cared. The curiosity of him existed only for being the one white man on the island allowed a plot of land by the Passamaquoddy. If he had a secret for it, he didn't let on to outsiders.

He lived alone on the island until his death in 1796 or 1797. His remains were found in his small shelter through the misfortune of a fishing boat crew forced onto the island by a winter gale. Among his few belongings was a letter from Germany, addressing him as John. The details of the letter were lost to time so only urban legend exists. And it was only natural that a ghost tale grew up around it.

The people of this harsh coastal region had enough to worry about in the present; history was just that, gone and soon forgotten. So, the exact whereabouts of Stryker John's cabin was never recorded. He was buried on the island, that which remained of him, and his gravesite, too, was long lost. But islanders swear they know where he lived then and where he haunts now.

All this was known by Trent. He heard it from the realtor. It wasn't a warning, nor was it an informal and unwritten disclosure statement. "Might be a great marketing tool," the realtor suggested. "Tourists love a good spook story." Trent didn't think so; such things were a niche market, and definitely not family fare, which is where he was heading with this venture. But when Tabitha continued to balk, he tried it out on her. She didn't believe but warned him, "You dare tell that to the boys, and I swear I'll swim to shore with them on my back."

The motel was near the northeast tip of the island. From sea to land, this was an archeological dream in horizontal; ancient green, blue, and foamy white waters pounding eon-old glacier rock that cradled and guarded young brown sand and younger brown earth. Trent stood in awe. Not of its power, but of his new union with it.

From the backyard Trent could see across the Bay of Fundy to Nova Scotia. But not this first morning, not this early, not until the sun's morning rays stretch themselves along the furthest ends of north and south. He watched as their brilliance lifted the clouds that moments earlier seemed so anchored there. They fled upwards until they ran out of sky, and oranges and reds lay in their stead.

In the mornings to come Trent would watch to see whose sky it would become. He saw in it an epic battle played out by the Norse gods. If the pressure was right, it could have easily gone the other way. Today it was for the sun, but the clouds could have hung on and smothered the sunlight like a fat, wet thumb snuffing the wick of a candle. Soon it would be so and being a man who enjoyed give and take, Trent was anxious to wake another day to be part of it.

What he thought was the rustling of the tall grasses behind him turned out to be Ricky racing to his side. "Kinda early for you to be up," Trent said.

"I couldn't sleep; the dogs woke me," Ricky said through a shiver and a stifled yawn.

"Who? Mop?"

"No, somewhere out here. They barked all night."

Trent hadn't heard a thing. As a matter of fact, he hadn't slept so well in a long time, even on the hard floor in the sleeping bag. He worried that thoughts of what he wanted to do and had to do would keep him awake for nights on end. But he cracked the window just a bit, in spite of his wife's protests, and fell dead asleep to the crashing waves and sweet ocean smells. "You like it here, champ?" he asked his son.

"It's okay, I guess."

"Okay? Just, okay? Look at this ocean?"

"There's no beach like in Virginia Beach."

"There are better things about the ocean than beaches."

"What?"

"Well, we can fish, deep-sea fish –"

"Can we go on a boat?"

"Sure we can. Sailing, too, if you want."

"Today?"

Trent had no desire to make promises he couldn't keep. Ricky was an intuitive boy. Lies didn't sit well with him, and they sat with him for a long while. "Well, not today. It's a bit cold and rough out there during the winter. Besides, we don't have a boat."

"We can rent one, or have an instructor take us out."

"We'll buy our own, how about that? And when we do, we'll teach ourselves; we don't need anyone out here teaching us anything, do we?"

Tabitha called out for breakfast from the kitchen door, cold sausage sandwiches and hash browns. Trent and Ricky ate ravenously, while Jeremy picked through the hash browns with great skepticism. Tabitha quipped about how they'd survive out here, dependent upon cross-island runs for fast food that wouldn't make decent fare at a Burger King. Trent told them all their fast-food days were behind them.

The moving company assured them they'd be there by nine. They arrived at close to one. "You folks know how far out this place is?" one of them asked.

"Yes," she said. "Didn't you?"

"Not exactly. I don't know, we might have to charge you more."

"The rate is by the mile, not by the isolation."

He scratched his head. "You don't even have cell phone service out here, you know that?"

She didn't, but she wasn't surprised. "You're late, and we'll be spending the entire night putting ourselves together."

"Nuthin' much else to do out here," his partner muttered.

As the two workers moved at a feverish pace to get the hell out, Tabitha found herself alone in the house with them. She put on her coat and went to the back porch. Trent was nowhere in sight. She called to Ricky and Jeremy. She thought she heard a high-pitched call in return but it was just the wind. Would the wind always be so omniscient? She knew so little about this place.

It had to be getting warmer. The movers wore lightweight sweaters and no gloves or hats. But like the native animals, they were accustomed to the climate and adapted easily to it. Tabitha shivered and dug her fisted hands into her coat pocket. She called out for the boys again before venturing away from the porch towards the water. The sight of the waves beating the rocks with such fury scared her more the closer she got. Two figures were but commas on the shoreline up ahead.

She was running now, to the edge of the property, just before the broken seawall littered with algae-coated shingles and cobbles. In her suede clod slippers, she dashed across the stones, losing one, not stopping to retrieve it.

Ricky and Jeremy were two hundred yards ahead, traversing jagged rocks that to Tabitha may as well have been the ridge of Mount Everest. Ricky was jumping from edge to edge. Water sprayed up against him. She was close enough to hear his defiant laughter. He taunted Jeremy to keep up. Mop needed no encouragement, but the wicked winds were having their way with her, and Tabitha cringed at the thought she could be swept out to sea, Ricky too preoccupied and Jeremy too overwhelmed to notice.

She managed to reach them, negotiating a few rocks herself, alarmed at their slickness and sharp edges. "Get down from there." She sounded more frantic than she wanted to, but no more than she was.

It startled both boys. "We're just playin'," Ricky said.

"It's not safe. Now down, all of you."

As usual, Jeremy was the first to comply. He walked gingerly over the slick ridges. "I told him not to go up there, mom, I did," he said, relieved to be on solid ground.

"That's 'cause you're chicken," Ricky teased, racing up behind. In contrast to his brother, Ricky made the return trip with reckless abandon.

There was a sophomoric pride in watching him. They were not identical twins. Jeremy was thick and squat. Ricky was two inches taller already and much thinner. Whereas Jeremy shuffled heavily and noncommittally, Ricky was lithe and moved as if there was a purpose to every step.

The differences were apparent from birth. Ricky was the first to crawl, to teethe, to say his first words, to walk, to be potty trained. Then, he walked further, ran faster, and talked more. Heaven help her, but it made her more attune to him, and she wondered now what came first: Ricky's development or her attentiveness.

It was her dirty little secret. Certainly nothing sexy. Nothing a tabloid would find juicy enough to print if she were a celebrity. But it unsettled her. How much does a nine-year old understand? How far back can he reach? How much can he pull out? How much does he dare?

There were times, like now, when Jeremy stared at her knowingly, and she had to look away. Tonight, it will be Jeremy asking her to read a bedtime story. It will be Jeremy asking her to leave the light on. Endearing for a mother to be sure, but in comparison to Ricky, it made her wonder what made them so different; Ricky so daring, so independent, so reckless, while Jeremy's spirit was firmly grounded.

"There are rats here, mom," Jeremy said.

"Rats?"

Ricky hopped back onto a rock. "Yeah, big ones. That's so cool. Let's find one," he said.

"Let's not."

"Betcha they came off a ship that crashed here like a hundred years ago. Like a pirate ship. We're gonna go sailing."

"You are, are you?"

"Yep. Soon as Dad buys a boat and no one needs to show us how."

"Never, ever come down here without one of us with you. These rocks are dangerous. One slip and you're out there," she pointed. "Back to the house to help unpack. And where is your father?"

"He went walking down there." Ricky pointed down the road to the nearest house, the one Trent said Abe Carver lived in. Ricky turned to dash off in that direction, but Tabitha was anticipating it. She grabbed the collar of his coat to hold him, but it took a swat across his bottom to get him back in line.

When Trent returned her disposition hadn't changed much since getting the kids into the house. "We're gonna love living here," he said.

She held him off at the door. "Jesus, Trent, do you know where the boys were?"

"Playing down at the water?"

"You left them there?"

"I went for a walk; they were fine, it's our backyard."

"Like being in our backyard makes the ocean less dangerous?"

"Not like they were *in* it."

"Trent, think of the ocean here like Reston Parkway, do we want the boys anywhere near it?"

"Oh c'mon, what fun can they have on an island if they can't get near water?"

"Don't make me out to be the bad guy," she said. "This is all new to them; it's new to all of us. There's a learning curve here. And what's this about us getting a boat?"

"Need one," he said as he hustled past her into the kitchen. "We live on an island."

"But a sailboat?"

"Where are the boys?"

"Upstairs unpacking. And we got rats here."

"No rats on an island. Just field mice."

"The boys saw them."

He put his hands on her shoulders. "Let's go out for dinner."

"We got work to do."

"Later."

"We have to at least set up the beds."

"Sleep in the bags like last night. They kids loved it."

"No, not again. Not when I don't have too."

The men finished moving in the last piece of furniture. One handed Trent a bill he didn't even bother to look at. You guys live near here?" Trent asked.

"Nope. Wells. We picked this load up in Augusta; the closest storage facility we got."

"That's a long ways back," Trent said.

"Over two hundred miles. I take it you folks are new to Maine," his partner said.

"Ah-huh."

He snickered. "You folks gonna find that a lot. Ain't nuthin' close enough way up here."

She looked at Trent who obviously found this further evidence of isolation a bonus.

Trent shook their hands. He still hadn't looked at the bill. When they were out the door but before they left the driveway, she chastised him. "Read it. Make sure they didn't overcharge us because we're out in the sticks and if they did –"

"It's fine."

"You don't know that."

"Don't sweat it. Besides, how would I know if I was overcharged? "

She looked at him in shock. He wasn't one to count every penny, but he did his nickels and dimes. And in this new venture, which she knew so little about, they would need to save because there were no guarantees. This cavalier attitude was deeply disturbing to her on so many levels.

Four

She'd give it a year. Just twelve months from the day. All four seasons; what more could he ask of her? She'd home school the boys as she had always wanted, but they wouldn't finish a school year here. Before spring next year, her and the kids would be gone. She'd suffer quietly through this spring mud, the stifling stench of rotting fish and seaweed in the summer, and barricade against the frigid winds and snows of winter only once. If she had too, she'd meet the neighbors, just the once, and spend the rest of the months avoiding them. Not that she was antisocial or adverse to meeting new people. Back in Virginia, she could be as social or as solitary as she wished. Here, Trent was demanding that she spend her life obliging others, and that just wasn't in her.

She wouldn't learn to sail. She wouldn't catch or bone a single fish. She wouldn't collect seashells. She would do what she must to get through the days until that final one when she could tell him, "Trent, I gave it a shot and now it's about me."

All this was unspoken, of course. She came to Maine with reservations she shared with her husband, but she kept this resolve to leave to herself. To discuss it with Trent would be a prelude to endless, heated arguments on the matter. Things that went right would be his evidence to stay; those that went wrong would be blamed on her willing or encouraging them.

She strolled through the house, him on her heels telling her how they could caulk the windows, replace the faux paneling and green carpet, tear up the linoleum kitchen and bathroom floors. This from a man who wouldn't jiggle the handle of the toilet to stop it from running.

The next day they drove across the island into the last rays of sun. It was a dazzling red that even the kids took notice of. It spread across the horizon like tomato paste on the windshield. She insisted they take Mop with them. She hadn't left their heels and trembled uncontrollably since they arrived.

The first spot of civilization was a sign for a dog kennel nearly three miles out. The small downtown was about a mile beyond. It was a town in the sense that it had an intersection and storefronts commensurate for the need. Hard to tell when its heyday was or if it had such a day. Its half dozen brick buildings, faded and chipped, were seemingly put up in a hurry by men as anxious to move on as their delivery drivers. They were fitted in squares and rectangles, not an arch, cornice, or column to them. Walls and roofs were flat without a gable, corbel, or dentil molding. Defenders would call this utilitarian, but even builders should have an opinion of themselves grand enough to leave behind for the ages.

"We'll eat breakfast here," Trent said, pointing to Averill's, a squat brown-brick structure that shared space with a barbershop.

Trent slowed. "Closed," he said.

Two blocks down and nearly out of the downtown limits, there was a family restaurant. It had no name, just the words "Family Restaurant" in red above the plate glass picture window. Perhaps it was so popular it didn't need one. "Good eats, here, I bet," Trent said pulling into the side parking lot.

He wanted it to be so, and so, it would be. Like forcing down his mother-in-law's pot roast that was always tough and heavily peppered. Strange the things a man can ignore when in a situation he finds pleasant; the corollary to how little it takes to irritate him in a bothersome place.

Tabitha saw the restaurant was nearly deserted. There was an old man paying at the register, and a woman and small child at a table in the front. The man was coming out as she was getting Ricky and Jeremy from of the backseat. She heard Trent greet him.

"Abe," he said.

She looked up as the old man stood by the driver's door. The man ignored Trent.

She stared at him from over the top of the Land Cruiser. He was a curious man, or maybe not so curious, only very typical for a Mainer, or Mariner or Mainiac, whatever it was they called themselves. He was perhaps a fisherman who retained the eternal tan, ruddy in mid-winter. His face was hard as he stared at Trent, laugh lines around his mouth they were not. Trent alongside him was a comical sight. Maybe not to the casual on-looker who may have mistaken Trent for a gentleman farmer. But Tabitha knew his smooth hands, his trick knee, and his back that gave out while carrying trash bags to the curb.

"Your new neighbor," Trent said to the man. "We met a couple of days ago. This is my wife and —"

But Abe was in his truck and closing the door before Trent could complete the introductions. Fine by Tabitha and the boys who found him creepy. Abe cracked his window and called out to Trent in a voice that sounded to be speared by a dozen fish hooks. "That your dog?" he said, nodding to Mop.

"Yeah," Trent said.

Abe nodded thoughtfully. "Ain't no kinda dog at all."

Trent turned to Tabitha and shrugged. "Abe, our neighbor."

"Sweetheart."

"No sweat. No different than a senior senator on the Armed Services committee. He'll loosen up."

Inside Trent made small talk with an elderly waitress. Sheila, which she pronounced as "Sheiler." He introduced them all around. Sheila thought the twins were cunnin.' Jeremy blushed while Ricky asked her what it meant. "Cute, darlin. Means you're cute. You folks from away?"

"Virginia," Trent said. "Just bought the motel down east end."

Tabitha smirked. *Down east end.* Like some kind of native. She didn't understand fully why these pretenses bothered her. His glib manner and stories of wheeling and dealing while a lobbyist titillated her. So did the name dropping of Senator so-and-so and Representative him-or-her; the late-night dinner deals with senators, congressman, and CEO's of national and international corporations. Some she attended when the CEO's or politicians wanted to put on the air of family-first. Even when she knew his talk was more puff than truth, she hung on every word. Not only was it stirring, it was his job, and a well-paying one.

"This place have a name?" he asked Sheila, meaning the restaurant.

"Fingal's," she purred, beguiled by Trent's attention. "For Fingal Donnelly. He's dead but it's still Fingal's to most of us."

"Well, this here's a fine place. Since we live down the road, we'll be regulars, I'm sure."

This here's a *fine place*? Was he patronizing or submitting? No, she couldn't, wouldn't see herself at Fingal's on Saturday nights chumming with the Sheilers and Abes.

"What'd that man mean, Mop's no kinda dog?" Ricky asked.

They all looked expectedly at Trent. "Beats me," he said.

There were certain aspects of this place Trent wasn't ready to tell his family. He doubted he'd ever tell them. Like the John Stryker ghost story, and what went on in Abe Carver's backyard.

Last night, when he left the boys at the beach, he took a walk along the rocks to Carver's farm. It was just under a mile by road, but closer to a mile and half along the ocean. He wanted mostly to make amends for the initial meeting on that first night. Perhaps he came on too strong, though he couldn't imagine what he said or did to alienate the man in such short order. But also, he wanted to explore the layout of his neighbor's property.

His plans did not begin and end with his small motel. He wouldn't have begun this journey with such small dreams. He had a five-year plan which he knew he could whittle down to three if the stars lined up. Part of the plan was to purchase adjacent property; Carver's was the most obvious and functional.

According to public records it was just over twenty-nine acres with a 905 square foot house of two bedrooms and one bath. Carver purchased it in 1969. It was listed as farmland which made no sense to Trent, the entire island being mostly rock and gravel, suitable for his purposes of a three-story condo complex, nine-hole par three golf course, health spa and pool. Next, he'd get licensed for his own ferry boat operation, one a few rungs above of the hillbilly operation running now.

He came up the backside of the property and was surprised by thick pastures of tall golden grass in the midst of turning to green. But there were no plowed fields being readied for planting. There appeared to be no plots for gardening past, present, or future. What he saw were fat, thickly woolen sheep.

He cut a perpendicular path from the rocky shoreline that had been built up with an unnatural placement of boulders, not unlike a stone wall found in a New England cow pasture. Only these boulders were man-sized and larger, as if meant to keep back whales.

The ground was spring soft beneath him with shallow pockets of mud where grass would soon flourish. The sheep moved across the field ahead of him. Twenty, he counted. A few lambs scurried madly behind in an effort to stay with the flock. He approached a small shed that wore the Maine coastal weather. Beyond it was a large barn equally weathered, then the house on towards the main road.

Although he was treading on the private property of a man he barely knew and didn't much care for thus far, he felt as if he belonged there. It was an island and it invited him from all sides. He envisioned it as a world of its own, his world. He could encircle it on foot in a day. He could walk it east to west in an afternoon, north to south before breakfast. He would walk the land and learn the lay of it on all its levels. He was a man who knew how men worked. He would soon know all the residents. He would know their families and their stories. He'd know their secrets. He would become the island's soul.

The shed had a nauseating odor. He figured it to be sheep droppings. He had never been on a sheep farm though his grandfather had neighbors who kept them. His grandfather once had a small herd of them brought onto a new piece of property he purchased. It was covered in weeds, vines, fallen trees, even poison ivy. The sheep had it cleaned out in less than a week.

At the flimsy door of the shed he heard the buzzing of flies. Opening it had the flies greeting him as additional fodder. The stench was peculiar to him and nearly debilitating. In the thin light he saw two small shapes hanging from the ceiling. Sheep. No lambs. Woolless and headless. They spun slowly, as if by an invisible hand showing off a butcher's handiwork. The flies were buzzing piles of entrails that had oozed from the long slice made from neck to scrotum.

The kill was recent, or so he reasoned, the innards still moist, the odor still strong. It was only the curiosity of the image that made him stay a moment longer in spite of the nausea rising inside him. Then he heard the dogs.

They sounded far off. Then he realized even the thin walls of the shack could mute noise. He backed out quickly and stared down at Abe Carver's house where the barking dogs were pacing frantically in the open pasture not a football field away. They spotted him as quickly as he did them and came racing his way.

As they closed in, he counted only two but the snarls and barks that echoed throughout the pasture and off the piles of rocks made it sound as if a pack was onto him. Heeding their warning, he hurried back to the shoreline, behind the safety of the rocks. He didn't remember scaling the piles. More like heaving himself over them. He cracked his knee and shoulder but didn't dare stop to inspect the wounds. The dogs mounted the stone peaks just as he gathered himself off the cobbles. Like hounds of hell, they sneered down at him yet didn't dare advance. Well trained or held back by some demonic force, Trent thought as he stumbled down the beach towards home.

That night Tabitha listened to the endless wind. Ferocious. Nothing soothing or comforting came from it. The world out here was so barren that sound and movement traveled unencumbered, and an old beach house was not about to stop it or even slow it down.

She snuggled in closer to Trent for warmth and reassurance. She was soon joined by Mop. "I'll miss your stories," she whispered.

"What stories?"

"About your work in Washington, the name-dropping."

"I won't."

He never called it that himself; name dropping. He had met them all. The powerful who stayed on, the weak who left. The honorable, the shamed. It was a life made for a movie, really. A hardworking, self-made man who created an idyllic life for his family. Least that would be Tabitha's tag line. And how was this updated ending: self-made man recreates himself on a remote Maine island where his wife is driven mad.

"Hear that?" she murmured.

"What?"

"Howling."

"The wind."

She thought so too at first. But throughout the days she would intuitively stop to collect herself after being struck with an apprehension that went beyond the cracked plaster walls and cold dead space, beyond the man-made world. This isolation was meant to be their destination, but it was a fitting ending only for an old racehorse, not a young family. "Are there wolves out here?" she asked.

"Not on an island."

"I've heard of wolves on islands."

"Dogs," he said. "Just dogs. I've seen some around."

This was comforting. Dogs, like Mop, sounds of civilization. She closed her eyes listening to the howl that was wind, dog, or wolf. She fell asleep, not knowing at the time that real sleep was far away in another place in another time.

Five

The first month was lonely for Tabitha, exhilarating for the twins, and cathartic for Trent. Furnishings for the motel rooms came in, then for the cabins, while the main house waited impatiently for the promised updates. Even the littlest annoyances such as the dripping kitchen faucet, the bedroom window whose upper sash seemed to pick the coldest nights to slip down, and the peeling linoleum floors of the kitchen and bathrooms bothered her terribly while Trent deemed them to be reasonable nuisances.

He came north without so much as an electric drill. A hammer and an *As Seen On TV* screwdriver set had made their way in the trunk of the car. She found it while wading through it for a roll of paper towels, so now she could at least hang things on the walls. One of the delivery boys, a young Greek or Italian kid, had his eyes on her all day. She took advantage by having him fix the sash and faucet.

There was a roar outside like one would hear changing a flat on the beltway. It started out a low moan she immediately picked up on, these past days being so deathly still. She waited until it grew menacingly loud before racing to the front door for a look. The twins joined her to see a long flatbed heading towards the house. "What's that?" Jeremy said.

"Truck. Carrying something."

At the base of the small hill that led up to the motel, the air brakes squealed. A sound that had Mop scurrying under the kitchen table, Jeremy pressing his palms to his ears, and Ricky racing down the road to meet them.

Tabitha saw it clearly with two flapping tarps holding down several huge crates. It stopped in front of the house but kept the engine running. The driver got out and headed for the door. *He's going to ask for directions,"* she insisted. *Please tell me you're going to ask for directions.*

He yelled to her before he reached the door. "Trent Aress live here?" She read his lips but feigned deafness.

He held up the bill of lading. "Aress," yelling again.

She nodded.

"Where you want us to put 'em?"

"Too big to stick up his ass, you think?"

"What's that?"

"I don't know what they are," she yelled. "Back there's fine with me." She pointed to the rear of the motel, meaning into the ocean. The driver gave a three-finger salute and headed back to his cab.

She shook her head, feeling idiotic and helpless.

She met Ricky and the driver around back. Mop was still terrified and vocalizing it from the safety of the underside of the kitchen table. "Any chance this is a mistake?" she asked.

The man ripped several bills of lading from a clipboard. "Nope. Bought and paid for." He handed them to her.

She looked at each bottom line before yelling. "Holy shit!" It startled Ricky and the driver.

"I'm just doing my thing, ma'am. You think you're ticked; you should talk to the ferry boat pilot who had to dump all his gear to get us on board." He looked to his assistant, and both laughed, enjoying the memory.

The flatbed tipped while hydraulic cables lowered several wood boxes into the backyard. It took all she had to keep Ricky from jumping onto the trailer and slipping beneath the cargo.

In the deathly quiet that remained behind after the tractor-trailer left, she and the boys stood in the shadow of the implements. "Dad bought them?" Jeremy said, holding his mother around her leg.

"Ah-huh."

"What are they?"

"Pieces of his lost mind."

Trent was ecstatic.

"You bought a lighthouse! Really, a freakin' lighthouse?"

"It's a replica of the West Quoddy Lighthouse."

"The what?"

"Tabitha, you need to get with it and do some reading. You need to know these things."

"Why?"

"Because it's our home. Our guests are going to expect us to know these things. Like the West Quoddy lighthouse is right here in Maine; it's the closet object in the United States to Europe. That's cool stuff."

She gave him a look that told him she didn't get it.

"Why can't you see it. It's our gimmick. We put it up in front of the motel."

"Are you insane?" she demanded. "I mean, not casually, but like, certifiable?"

"No."

"You see how much it costs?"

He laughed. "Yeah. I paid for it."

"Trent, twenty-three thousand dollars."

"That includes shipping."

"It should include fifty feet on the Chesapeake Bay. Where did you get —"

"I've told you, it's money I've been saving, and I started long before we got married so don't go thinking I've been squirrelly money away all these years, well ... not a lot anyway."

"Is it even legal? I mean, what if a ship crashes up here?"

"It's legal. No different than having a pink flamingo. And its signal isn't a beacon; it'll be the motel name in green neon."

"Green neon. Really? And don't tell me you've hired a dozen illegal Mexicans at three bucks an hour to put it together."

Ricky was listening from up on the box above them. "Not here," Trent said. He tugged at her arm.

"Get him down first."

Trent hauled Ricky down as he told him and Jeremy to head inside. "You don't like it here yet?" he said.

"*Yet* hasn't entered into it. I'll never like it here."

"You don't know this place."

"And you do? You say 'this place' as if it's legendary. Trent it's been thirty years for you. You were a kid; your grandfather was the farmer, not you. Now you think it's hereditary."

"Ricky loves it."

"He loves the game. In a lot of ways, he likes it the way you like it."

"Why not give him and Jeremy a chance?"

"I thought we were doing that in Reston."

He threw his arms skyward. He turned and walked towards the rocks on the shore as if he were heading out for good. He turned to her abruptly. "I can't do this alone, without you, without the boys."

"So why the mysteries?"

"What mysteries, Tabitha? What have I held out on you, besides this lighthouse? Which, as I said, is going to be the coolest thing on this island."

"This whole move. It's something you'd expect a crazy old uncle to do, I don't know. You didn't ask; you didn't discuss it with me, you —"

"Didn't discuss it? That's all I've done."

"But *at* me, Trent, not *with* me."

"Now what's that supposed to mean?"

"It's like getting married: A girl wants to be asked, not told."

"That's romance, we're beyond that stuff."

"You're never beyond that stuff."

"So, every day, for the rest of our lives, we have to be coy with each other. I have to whisper, 'I love you' before I, I mean we, make a damn decision?"

"That wouldn't be so bad, would it?"

He came back to her. She looked the way he dreamed she would out here. Windswept and crisp in the late afternoon air. She wouldn't admit to it, but it made her more radiant than ever. It was the island. In time she would come to know it, too. There'd come that summer morning she would greet as if it was the first day of her life. Everything new, everything with a promise. The world outside would be of their creation.

"Aress Acres," he said.

"As a name?"

"Or I was thinking of Aress Landing. What do you think? You choose."

She shrugged, not wanting to say what she thought of his gesture of letting her choose between names. But he read her face. "Please, Tabitha, don't destroy this dream."

Six

It wasn't a group of illegal Mexicans who came in to erect the twenty-eight-foot lighthouse. It was a crew of five from somewhere on the mainland who cost three times as much. Trent was there to supervise the fourteen-hour ordeal which had them calling in another crew to level the front yard with slag, for quite a bit extra since it was a last-minute request.

As predicted, it brought islanders out. Tabitha saw them come and go with none approaching the work site. Trent wandered out to greet them. She saw a lot of pointing and arm spreading by Trent, a lot of nodding and toe-ground scratching by the onlookers. Whatever small talk transpired, he didn't share it with her.

She could have prepared drinks and snacks for the event, had the boys set up a table to feed their neighbors. It would have been hospitable; it would have been what Trent wanted. But Tabitha wasn't in that mood. Regardless of her husband's other predictions, she wasn't feeling the onslaught of love from those of Stryker John Island.

Out of necessity, not partnership, she made trips into what she had come to call the center of the island, downtown being just too much of a stretch. Twice a week she was at *Tingo's Market*. It was the only grocery store available, another stretch. It was owned and operated by Marla and Todd Barber. They were friendly enough in that they special ordered Kashi Vanilla Graham Cluster cereal and green tea for her. "Most folks make monthly trips to the mainland for anything we don't carry," Marla told her. From Tabitha's viewpoint that included everything outside of milk, white bread, Oreo cookies, and an assortment of beers and liquor whose inventory seemed inordinately large considering the island population.

Small talk and concern had her asking, "Do you have a large summer population on the island?"

"Not *on* the island," Todd said. "Day trippers mostly, come for the novelty. Artist-types and photographers. Used to have a marine biology class from the community college stay a few days down at the place you folks live. Don't come around no more."

"So, most of your clients are islanders."

"Most," Marla agreed.

Yes, they answered her questions, but she sensed the relationship would never evolve into one where they asked many of her. She had her theory on why. *Tingo* was a unique and strange name, Native American, or maybe a people from a South Pacific Island, or an African tribal word. So, she asked. Todd shrugged. "It was the name when we bought the place twenty-two years ago."

So just like *Fingal's Restaurant,* nothing here changed even when the people around it did. An island custom; an unwritten rule, perhaps. Or laziness. No, security. There was a reassurance in knowing life could go on and still stay the same. She shared this with Trent who said she was over-thinking things. "I'd do the same thing," he said. "People know it as one place, they figure, why change it?"

"What people? There are what, twenty people on this island."

"More than that."

"So why don't you keep the old name of this motel?" she challenged.

"Don't know what it was. And just because they see it that way doesn't mean I do," he said. "Look, they're happy with their way; I'm all about making it my way."

"These people don't seem the type to let someone walk in and change things."

"Who's changing? I'm making something."

Trent's skill at multi-tasking was a benefit to him. No motion, no thought, no deliberation, lacked coordination. Chess was a suitable metaphor; play it several moves ahead. The island had no formal government, having been annexed by Nuthatch Cove with most services coming from the county. But that didn't stop them from meeting bi-monthly to discuss issues that needed to be raised to the township and county. There was one pub on the island, next to the only service station. *Trugards* had a long bar, usually full, and four tables, used mostly on nights like these when talking face-to-face was more advantageous than to a row of profiles.

Trent came twenty minutes early but found he was the second to the last person to arrive. The last being Hack Corlin, the ferry boat pilot, who took a seat at the end of a table. The captain doffed his greasy John Deere cap to him as he sat.

There were twelve people besides Trent and Corlin: ten men, two women. They opened by thanking the pilot for coming. Again, he doffed his cap. The issue was the ferry schedule; it was due to reduce to only two trips on Saturdays and Sundays, down from three, with the last one being at 3PM. "Don't need it," Hack Corlin said.

"I work on the mainland Sunday nights, Hack, you know that," one of the younger residents said.

"You got a boat."

"It's not always working, and I like to leave it for my wife."

"Won't make it happen for one man, not worth it."

"C'mon now, Hack, you know damn well most of us travel far away as Banga on weekends. Shuttin' down that early doesn't work. For us that doesn't work."

"I can start later, 'bout an hour, and extend it the same hour. But for three or four folks, and that's all it is on weekends, Les, so don't go telling me there's a mad rush. Just isn't worth the expense."

The give and take went back and forth for nearly an hour. Hack Corlin didn't budge. The islanders became surly, telling him the dock needed repair, and the ferry listed to the left and its vibrations were putting their trucks out of alignment. There were also complaints about exhaust build-up on board, an issue to which Trent silently concurred.

"You folks are making my point," he said. "Lots of maintenance to do. More unnecessary runs I make the worse it'll get."

Todd Barber stood. He was as gangly as an old-time basketball center with plenty of bony points from his cheeks to his knees. He didn't like the confrontation going on. He admitted as much when he told Corlin and the group they weren't children and shouldn't act like them. "None of us are up here to make lots of money," he said. "But none of us are up here to lose it either. Hack's got his points; we got ours. Best thing is to go to the Cove, see if they can't lend us a hand."

"For crissakes, Barber, we been there before," Rachel Kusenie said. "Ain't no help comin' from there. Wastin' our time is what it'll be. Lot like we're doin' here."

Rachel Kusenie lived with her partner, a quiet, petite woman ten-years her junior who rarely came outside the house and was known never to leave the sheep farm the two operated on the far side of the island from the motel. Rachel had auburn hair and skin so fair the freckles stood out in stark relief even under the early spring sun. She spoke through a toothpick which she shifted from corner to corner while she ranted at Barber.

Trent listened as the sides bickered on the issue. He couldn't have picked a better night to make his debut. Hack Corlin looked to be bored of the evening already. He pulled back his denim jacket sleeve to see his watch. Then he looked to the bar which was not serving until the meeting was adjourned.

Trent stood and cleared his throat. "You folks know Mackinac Island?"

No one spoke but they were listening. "It's a small island in Michigan, about half the size of ours, just eight miles around."

"I know of it," Marla Barber, an irate tone for the disruptive newcomer. "They got ferry problems?"

"I don't know but the point —"

"There ain't no point if it ain't about ferry problems."

"Well, I don't agree," Trent said. "My point is thinking outside the box."

"Who are you?" a squat, grizzled man asked.

"He bought the motel," Todd Barber said.

"Oh, right. And put up that god-awful lighthouse."

Trent smiled but the man didn't. "Trent Aress," Trent said.

"Yeah, well, Aress, that lighthouse it's ... I don't know the word."

"Fucked-up," Rachel Kusenie offered.

"No, that ain't it."

"Tacky," came the word from a tall, thin man leaning his chair against the wall. He tapped the toes of his boots lightly to rock himself. He smiled tight-lipped, a dip of Skoal bulging his lower lip .

"That mean ridiculous?'"

"Kinda."

"Then that's what it is, tacky."

Trent wanted to defend himself but realized the best defense was always a good offense. Defending the lighthouse would play into their childish hands. How many times he wanted to come back to a haughty Senator with a spiteful line when asked what the messenger boy had in his mail bag today. Or, "what marching orders have you been given, soldier?" Here he had a dysfunctional group who thought it worthwhile to rail against the reduction of a single ferry boat run when everyone on the island had their own boats. An entrepreneur would have come up with a plan to run his own operation on the off times. Backwoods islanders or political hacks, it made no difference. The number one, two, and three rules for both car salesman and lobbyists was smile before, during, and long after.

"Well, leave it to a mainlander to bring a piece of vulgarity up here to you folks," he said, then smiled. No comments. They didn't know for sure whether it was a put-down or a compliment which was just the reaction Trent was going for.

"This Mackinac Island," he continued, "it's strictly a tourist island. No commercial fishing, no industry, no manufacturing. They have just a couple of motor vehicles on the island for police and safety. Transportation is by horse-drawn carriage, bicycle, and foot. It's the vacation destination of hundreds of thousands of people worldwide."

"You want us to get rid of our trucks? "The grizzled one said.

"Worse than that," Todd Barber said, "he's suggesting we start living for tourists."

"You own a market; wouldn't that be great for you?" Trent asked.

"Yeah, and you own a motel," Marla Barber said.

"It can work here. Stryker John can become that kind of destination."

Trent then listened to the panel deride his plan for reasons he found hard to rationalize. The meeting ended with Rachel Kusenie saying, "Thought it was strange you coming over here to build up a motel with no tourists. 'Build it and they will come,' that it? Wasn't that from some movie? Well, if they come, good for you, and if they don't, you just wasted a lot of time and money. Either way, you'll get no help from us."

The official meeting broke up and the group left the tables for the bar; all but Trent who was sat licking his wounds. "Looks like the visiting team could use a drink," Hack Corlin offered.

"Didn't know I was."

"Shit, I came up here from New Jersey four years ago, and I'm still the new guy. Or was."

"You took a pretty good beating yourself."

"Think so? Beer?"

"Sounds good."

"Preferences?"

"No. Yeah. How 'bout that *Mean Old Tom* stout I've been hearing on the radio."

"Now that's how to begin making friends around here. You'd have set yourself back light years if you ordered a *Sam Adams*."

Seven

"These folks, they're not like other folks you know down in Washington," Hack Corlin was saying. "In many ways they're like rugged survivors. In some ways, they're like clueless kids."

From his tone of voice in the stories he shared, Trent understood that Hack Corlin liked it very much living across the bay from Stryker John Island. In Trenton, New Jersey, he owned several apartment buildings. Now, he didn't want the hassles of either extreme, the unreasonable demands of the rich or the unreasonable apathy of the poor.

He told Trent that in Jersey, whenever he could, he headed for the eastern shore to sail his thirty-six-foot Sabre sailboat. Trent wasn't a boat enthusiast but much of his job required him to be knowledgeable enough to listen and add a few tidbits. He knew the name *Sabre,* and knew they weren't cheap. "You gave up that life for this?" Trent said.

"I could certainly ask you the same thing. It wasn't so much the life as the lifestyle. My wife left me four years before I made the move up here. I loved her; I loved my three kids, I loved that boat, but none of it topped work, which I didn't love but had the mistaken belief I needed if I wanted the other three. But, I lost two anyway and sold the third to live some semblance of my dream."

That dream was to work full time on a boat. He was too old for the Merchant Marines and too soft to be a fisherman. He had to go someplace along the ocean where the cost of living wouldn't bankrupt him. A stroke of luck, the man he was selling the *Sabre* to had a brother-in-law looking for just the opposite, a job with advancement potential in a fast-paced city. Seems his wife left him for not being enough like Hack Corlin, and Corlin laughed at the irony. Corlin sold his apartments along with the yacht, righteously split half with his ex without legal pressure, and bought the rundown ferry boat operation from Nuthatch Cove to Stryker John Island. "Never looked back," he said. "Wonder if that brother-in-law does."

Trent guessed Corlin to be in his mid-fifties. He certainly had transformed into an islander in these four years. "It's because I let it happen," he told Trent. "I didn't come up here to be me. See this little exchange we had tonight, they would have bitched if I decided to add a new run instead of eliminating one. Clueless little kids? Just out for a good argument. But survivors, too, because they fight to stay as they are."

"Stubborn," Trent added, staring over the bar, determined to see only the cluelessness in them.

"Never gonna win doing it your way, the old Trent Aress way. See if I wanted to be the old me, I would have just raised rates. But." He took a relaxing sip, as if the conversation was over. "Soon enough they'll be accepting the new schedule. Then it will become the old schedule and any changes to that will bring us down here to argue and drink again. May sound crazy to you but it's no big deal to have things taken away from them; they're used to that. Just don't go adding anything."

"No offense, Hack, but you made a small change, what I'm suggesting is a whole new identity for the island."

"Sure. And it scares 'em."

"How?"

"You a bit scared moving up here?"

"Not at all."

Corlin tilted his head. "C'mon."

"Apprehensive."

"New will do that to ya. You think these people came out here because they wanted to reinvent themselves, because they welcomed change? I tell you it's just the opposite; they're tired of reinventing, nervous of change, scared of people trying to bring it."

"What is it with you people?" Trent said, louder and more agitated than he should have been considering the company he was in. He dropped it a few decibels. "I mean, change, change is good. It's what life's about. Without it, things don't get better, people don't get better. Look at you; look at me, talk about drastic moves. People are better when they change. And I'm not even talking about them. It's this island; it has so much to offer."

"It changes, they change. That's how they see it. And people here feel better for the lack of it. Capitalism isn't a dirty word up here; it's just not a goal."

"Crissakes, whenever non-believers talk about capitalism they point to the negatives; when they talk about socialism, they can't go further than the philosophy."

"These folks are far from being socialists; anarchists, maybe. Or maybe just people who don't give organized government any more thought than they do organized religion. Take your neighbor, for instance."

"Abe Carver."

"Notice he isn't at this thing tonight."

"Expecting him to be?"

"Not at all. I see him on the ferry twice a month bringing his slaughtered sheep and wool over. Never talks and doesn't seem to listen. You think he's gonna want tourists traveling to the island; you think he's interested in seeing change?"

"That why you mentioned that he wasn't happy with us buying the motel?"

"Partially."

"That's one person," Trent said, "And one I doubt people like."

Corlin laughed. "You're right. And how'd you like to be the one person on this island disliked more than Abe Carver? I overheard a phone conversation from your realtor on one of his few trips to the island. See, there were as many bites on that old motel as there were on the ferry. So, Carver made an offer but wanted a land contract deal. The sellers weren't thrilled with the idea but were ready to take it."

"Until I showed up. Couldn't see Carver operating a motel."

"No," Corlin said. "Not the motel, the land, for his sheep. Your coastline has some of the best sweet grasses on the island. That's that tall grass with purple stalks. It makes lambs raised near the ocean very tender and more expensive."

"You said my buying the place was partially his issue; what was the other?"

"The man's just plain crazy."

"Man's not crazy, just comes from a long line who were." It was a man at the table behind them, the tall thin guy who called Trent's lighthouse tacky. He was rocking his chair lightly again, a big smile barely filled up with crooked, brown-stained teeth. He held a large mug of stout beer in his lap. As during the meeting, he was alone, and Trent knew why: that smile did nothing to make him look friendly, attractive, or approachable.

"Whatta you know, Dutch?" Corlin said. "Thought you'd be back on the mainland by now."

"Well kinda can't, Cap'n, need the ferry tonight, if you don't mind."

"Ah-huh. How many mutts you got this time?"

"Three, and they won't all fit on my skiff."

"Ah-huh, can't fit 'cause they're too big or too wild?"

"C'mon Cap'n, one bad experience was all."

Even when Dutch was trying to make small talk and be nice, it came off as slippery. Trent could see it right off; Corlin knew it from experience.

"Dutch every time I see those dogs of yours it's bad, but I'll tell you what, you chain them down below and pay double for my trouble."

"Double?"

"That's the offer, and it's not a bad one considering I could deny you passage with them, and I can still sue you for what the last pack did to my arm."

"Barely broke the skin. You didn't even get no stitches."

"They broke skin enough, and I have the hospital bill for the rabies shot to prove it. And don't go crying poor mouth; I know you got the money."

Dutch's laugh slivered from between lightly clenched teeth. He eyed Trent as he took a long, slow sip. "Sorry 'bout that crack on your lighthouse," he said. "Just my personal opinion."

"One you could have kept to yourself," Trent said.

"Suppose so. But it was nicer than what others are saying. Like Abe."

"Hearing a lot of not nice things about Abe Carver. I met him; seems odd and standoffish but I've met those types in Virginia," Trent said. "How well you know him?"

"Enough I suppose," Dutch said.

"Good friends?"

"Just business."

"Have to do with dogs?"

"That's right. Matter of fact just sold him another one tonight, said he needed more security."

Trent shot Corlin a look as if asking for an explanation. Corlin shook his head and drained his glass. "Want another?" he asked Trent whose mug was still half full and warm.

"I'm okay."

Corlin left them alone.

"Own a pet store or something?" Trent asked Dutch.

"A kennel, here and on the mainland."

"Between here and my place? I've driven past it. The sign that is. Didn't see a kennel."

"Down that dirt road a bit. Keep a few dogs there for raisin' and trainin'. Sell them on the mainland."

"Market for that?"

"It's a livin'. Been doing it long enough; I have customers down east. A lot inland, even Boston and parts thereabouts."

"Kind ya got?"

Trent had fallen into the speech pattern of truncating his questions and statements, a habit that put Tabitha into fits while trying to teach the kids proper English. "Treat it like cursing with the guys," she said. "Bad enough you do it, just leave it at work," Only home was work, and Trent found curbing it not only difficult but unnecessary since this was where the boys would be raised. To talk King's English would be to talk down to these people, a sure way of getting their asses kicked.

"Shepherds, mostly, but I get boxers, bull terriers."

"Don't see much use for guard dogs 'round here."

"Like guns," Dutch said. "Folks feel comfortable having 'em."

"What makes my neighbor feel he needs to augment his pack?"

"If what you mean is why's he wanting another dog, can't say. See, we don't have that kind of relationship. But he bought a bull terrier."

"A pit bull."

Dutch twitched his mouth. "Some folks call 'em that. How 'bout you, you need a dog?"

"Have one."

Dutch grin widened, showing the black holes where molars once sat. "Yeah, I heard about that one of yours."

Trent catalogued people as friends or opportunities. Rarely since he had grown up did he ever use the words "hate," or even "dislike." It wasn't a wise thing to do in his former business where associations made all the difference. Still, he wished he had the luxury of having throwaway people, people he could love, like, dislike, hate, ignore, with all the sincerity of a real person. It was with Dutch he felt the urge to begin.

Trent read people better than most. If the money was better, he would have gone into the FBI or CIA. But you didn't need skills to read old Dutch. And the gall of it, Dutch knew it and played it like a game in which he had nothing to lose and everything to gain.

"You're a big dog kinda guy, I take it," Trent said.

"Don't gotta be big, just gotta get the job done."

"What job's that?"

Dutch shrugged. "Whatever the man wants," and flashed his thick, brown smile.

Corlin came back to the table. "What about it, Cap'n, I get that lift?" Dutch asked.

"I'm shoving off in thirty minutes."

"Give me sixty; I hitched a ride up here so don't have my truck."

"I'm gone in thirty."

"I'll drive you," Trent said.

Corlin shot him a severe look meant to intimidate which only made Trent flash a devious smile of his own.

Eight

Trent drove Dutch back down to his kennel. There was no assurances Corlin would give them even the thirty minutes he promised. Trent wasn't exactly mystified as to why Corlin had issues with Dutch and his dogs. Only an exceptionally dysfunctional individual would have any kind of relationship with someone like Abe Carver.

But Corlin's immediate angst seemed to be with Trent for offering to lend a hand. The guy was a fare, and he was paying double the rate. He didn't even put up a fuss. Certainly, the guy's company for the twenty-five-minute ferry ride wouldn't be insufferable. There was something more, something Trent wasn't grasping, but that was for another day for while Corlin was getting a bigger fare for his efforts, Trent was angling for something more enduring.

Trent knew he had no connections and no contacts, but now understood he had no common ground with these people. That is, no common ground when it came to his vision. Vision was a personal matter, much like the five senses. Everyone with fully developed senses knows what the color red looks like, what an orange tastes like, what a wood fire smells like, just as everyone knows the sound of a barking dog and the softness of a cotton ball. Yet how red, how tangy, how smoky, and just what is a bark and what is soft? There was no defining such matters to any satisfaction. The best Trent could do was to expand his vision of the island and the people. Dutch, could be that opportunity.

"Turn here," Dutch said. The road was narrow and potholed. Trent took it slow, expecting Dutch to give him further directions. But half mile down the black road Dutch said nothing while Trent saw nothing.

"Say when," Trent said.

"Bit further." Two minutes later, "here's good. Leave the headlights on."

Dutch jumped out and headed to a red pole barn dead ahead. Trent heard howling dogs inside the barn. He killed the engine to get a better listen. The howls were long and haunting, and echoed chillingly through the metal confines. Dutch was gone from sight, somewhere inside. Trent listened to the howls, now more mournful. He shivered in quick jolts as if bolts of ice were stabbing at him. He heard Dutch before seeing him as he wrestled with metal leashes and cursed his animals into some degree of obedience.

The dogs, three of them, two pit bulls and a German Shepherd, didn't know where they were going but they were violently anxious to get there. They pulled and reared like the dogs at Carver's place. Unlike Trent, who at the moment was regretting this decision, Dutch showed no fears of them and in fact, was more violent and aggressive than the trio.

"Open up the back, will ya?" Dutch commanded.

Trent sat while Dutch wrestled them in. One-by-one the dogs climbed over the seats to inspect Trent with sniffs and licks. Satisfied he was either a non-threat or a snack to be saved for later, they left him alone to investigate the rest of the vehicle. Dutch had worked up a sweat and was breathing like a sprinter when he sat back down. The dogs were still agitated, stumbling around the back, occasionally leaning their huge heads into the front compartment like Mop, but not at all like Mop. "You gonna tie them down or something?" Trent asked.

"Be fine for the short drive."

"But two pit bulls and a Shepherd, won't they kill each other?"

"They do we'll have less to unload, won't we?"

Trent, determined to make the ride as short as possible, sped down the trail to the main road at a speed designed to keep the snorting, drooling animals preoccupied. As it was, Corlin wasn't even at the ferry when they arrived ten minutes after his scheduled departure time. "Knew he'd stick around," Dutch said. "Wants that money."

The dogs were worrying Trent on many levels, the least was the soiling of the SUV while the worst was having his head torn off. Though it was cold this evening at the water, it was more comfortable than staying inside. He got out without announcement to stand by the dock. He heard Dutch behind him strike a match and moments later smelled his cigarette. "Nice night," he said. "Not skittish from that drive, are ya? Look kinda flush."

Like the proverbial wing puller, Dutch enjoyed watching Trent in distress. "Drive didn't do it," Trent said.

"C'mon, everyone loves dogs. You got one."

Trent was looking at the bobbing ferry but from the corner of his eye could see Dutch staring at him for a reaction. He was determined not to give one.

"Not everyone," he said. "And them that do don't like the kind you got."

Dutch took a long, slow drag, blowing back out casually. "What's that country song, somethin' 'bout some folks don't like boys like me, but some folks do?"

"That was about girls, not mad dogs."

"Whatever. Yeah, that's me all right, Mister Aress. Some folks do."

Trent was rethinking using this man as a marketing tool. There was little doubt the type of clientele he would flush out. Why did he ever suppose he could collaborate with a man who could carry on a relationship with Abe Carver. "Not a fan of the dogs or the man who does like you," Trent said.

"Who? Abe? He ain't bad, just a product. Know Malaga Island?" Dutch asked. Trent looked at Dutch for the first time since the dog ride. He was happy for the change of topic.

"No."

Dutch tossed his cigarette against the side of the ferry. It burst into an orange plug, like a miniature aerial bomb before crashing to the water.

"People don't talk much about the island or what happened to it. 'Bout a hundred years ago Maine threw everyone off it and put some of them away in a crazy house."

"Why's that?"

"Few reasons. Racism for one."

"Were they Indians?"

"Blacks. Or them with mixed blood. They called them 'feebleminded' because they didn't know things like what a telephone was. This was in like 1905 when not many people even had 'em. So, they told them to leave the island, or they would be burned off it. Most left, some didn't."

"I'm guessing from your intro something bad happened to them."

Dutch dramatically struck a match and lighted another cigarette. "The mainlanders even went back and dug up the island graveyard to take the dead ones off. Buried them bodies at the school for the feebleminded in New Gloucester. Guess they figured even dead half-breeds were crazy. Come to find out none of them, the live ones that is, were crazy at all. They found things from the school on Malaga. Papers written by the kids, books they were reading. Better handwriting, better spelling, better papers than kids on the mainland. Guess you can imagine what they did to that school?" He took a deep draw on the cigarette bringing the cherry embers to an intense glow.

"Funny thing was those folks mostly kept to themselves with lobstering, little fishing. No farming: the soil was for crap. They were poor, wretched things better left alone. What they couldn't get on their own was given to them by folks who sent over food, clothes, books, stuff like that."

"So, race wasn't really the issue," Trent said.

"Never really is, is it? More of an excuse."

"You said there were several reasons they were forced off the island," Trent reminded him.

"Casco Bay."

Trent knew the name but didn't make a connection.

"Malaga was a little place. Insignificant. Can't hardly find it on maps no more. But it was just off the coast of Portland. All them bigger island's beyond; Peaks, Great Diamond, Long Island; were ripe for development. Tourism, Aress, and Malaga and its people were an eyesore, freaks, an embarrassment. No matter now, but no one's lived on the island since."

It was a nasty piece of history that the country was full of. Ignorance run amuck. But Trent didn't understand the reason for such small talk, unless it was another one of Dutch's quaint traits, scaring the uninitiated with ghoulish stories. "He's really late, isn't he?" Trent said. "Wonder if he changed his mind about leaving tonight."

"Some of the ones taken from the island, the ones who weren't really crazy, most of 'em lived and died at that school in New Gloucester."

"Maybe he got himself drunk," Trent said, refusing to let Dutch freak him out with more of the story.

"Like you don't find the island on the map; you don't hear talk of the descendants. Like they don't exist. But they do, you know."

"That so."

"That neighbor of yours for one."

"You saying Carver's a descendant? You know that for a fact?"

"Now Mister Aress from Washington D.C., don't tell me after all I just told you you'd malign one of the descendants?"

"No, just that —"

"Makes you wonder if the folks *were* right back then, that crazy *did* live on the island, and that maybe it's hereditary. Or maybe it's something they learned and passed down. Either way, you wonder what it is you've gotten yourself into, don't you, Aress?"

"We're running late." It was Corlin walking up the road behind them. "Get those mutts loaded down below. Got my money? Up front."

Trent stood back as the dogs were handled and the two transacted business. Corlin came by saying, "Stayed away a bit to give you time to get to know old Dutch."

Dutch leaned over the back of the ferry rail, the dogs pulling in three directions on the heavy chain leashes. "Hey, Aress, maybe you're wondering, too, just how many of them descendants are out and about, hey?"

Nine

Memorial Day weekend was a week away and in spite of it being advertised in green neon on a lighthouse.

twenty-five feet high, *Aress Landing* had not one reservation. It wasn't for Trent's lack of effort. He knew his target audience was on the mainland so spent his days in the towns around Nuthatch Cove and even down to Portland. Leaflets and flyers as if looking for a lost cat weren't his style. He visited local newspapers and radio stations, even wheedling a few free minutes from a local morning show in Augusta. It was hard to know if he was leaving a significant wake behind, but he was confident in his methods.

While Trent was doing his damnedest to fill the rooms, Tabitha did the bare minimum to get them ready. She was tasked with keeping them clean and working on theme designs. She did a little of both, but mostly, she threw herself into the school year with the boys. After all, one way or the other, she and they would be back in Virginia by spring. Regardless of what became of *Aress Landings,* the boys would need to move forward. It was an added benefit that business being what it was, Trent would be heading south with them, leaving this miserable failure far behind.

She had the notion home-schooling would be as fruitless an endeavor as the motel. Ricky was too energetic whereas Jeremy was too reserved. She couldn't see settling Ricky down to study the ecology of the island any more than she could see Jeremy venturing into the rocky surf to experience marine life firsthand. But it wasn't working out that way. The outdoors was a mystifying yet hospitable classroom. And being an island made it more so. Even teaching was more inspirational. Nothing was done in the house. No matter the weather or the subject matter, they'd sit on the huge rocks along the water or walk the cobbles. They'd bring no books, papers, or pencils. There, more questions were asked than answers given, which had the boys fighting their way to the computer to research. Dependent, as always, on an Internet connection.

Math, science, history surrounded them. Poetry and art came to life with obvious allusions. So adapted had they become to their classroom that they railed against their father's plan to clear the kelp and stones to create a tourist-friendly sandy beach. "You can't do that," Jeremy told him. "Bugs eat the kelp and birds eat the bugs." Ricky added, "If nature wanted sand to be here instead of rocks, then the waves wouldn't be so big. Big waves take the sand away." If it wasn't for so many negatives of the place, she could see them graduating from this school.

This day she convinced Trent to stay home. He fought it, as she knew he would. He had been traveling the mainland four long days a week for the past month. His nights on the island were spent readying the place. It was becoming easy for him to lose sight of her and the boys, and this was bothering her. In Virginia, he had control because he knew the game and the players. When things went sideways, he had little trouble righting them; it was just a matter of pulling the strings he had been pulling for years. Here on the island, with people he privately referred as "ocean-front hillbillies" and "water trash," he hadn't learned what strings to pull, if any. These people hadn't warmed to him. Charm meant little, perhaps nothing. She felt it the day the lighthouse went up and told him so. "They don't know what they don't know," he said, parroting a now trite phrase. "Maybe, Trent, these are people who don't want to know," she told him.

He and the boys spent the morning replacing shutters on the cabins. Later in the day they took shells from the beach which Trent was crushing for a sunken path from the rooms to the water. "I see math in that," she said "which is great because that's their game for tonight."

"Math? That's not a game, that's homework."

"They don't think of it as homework, and I don't call it homework so don't you."

She ran out to *Tingo's Market* for things that could have waited until the next day, but she wanted the night to be his with the boys. The owners of *Tingo's*, the Barbers, who once seemed to embrace her as a new neighbor, had cooled towards her. The atmosphere at *Tingo's* grew to near belligerent. There were cross-eyed looks between mister and missus when she came in. And a lot of silence. Usually, the twins were an icebreaker, but the Barbers were not into charming and delightful. But it was the whispers that killed her, and paranoia wasn't behind it.

It was nearing eight and *Tingo's* was about to close. She chose to believe this was tonight's reason for their coolness. She turned away from Marla Barber and the counter just as Todd Barber called out a hearty welcome to Rachel Kusenie, whom Tabitha met face-to-face when the two collided. Tabitha dropped her bag of assorted vegetables and box of Prince spaghetti, then braced her hands on Rachel's shoulders. Rachel shook her loose and Tabitha was sure Rachel deliberately shoved her back against the counter.

"I'm terribly sorry," Tabitha muttered before breaking into tears.

"Shake it off girl," Rachel said. "Couldn't possibly have gotten hurt."

"I'm not hurt."

"So why the ballin'?"

"That's Aress's wife, the man from the meeting," Marla said, as if that was reason enough for tears.

"New girl in town, huh? Feelin' a little out of place, that it? I get it."

Rachel bent down to pick up the bag and groceries. Tabitha wiped a final tear, brushed back a wisp of hair, and bent over to help, but Rachel had the mess righted just as Tabitha reached for a Macintosh apple. "You new here, too?" Tabitha asked.

That brought a touch of laughter from the Barbers and a quirky smile from Rachel. "I was once."

"Everyone's new to a place once," Tabitha said. She shot a look at the Barbers. "Nice to know there are people who remember what it feels like."

Rachel handed her the bag. "Chickie, if you're talkin' 'bout me, you couldn't be more wrong. I never allow myself to feel like a stranger, and I never let anyone make me feel like one."

That cutting remark took Tabitha by surprise. She thought this queer little woman with the butch haircut and short, gnarled fingers was to be the first person who could show her empathy. Instead, she was just one more person to avoid. That list was growing gravely longer with each day. "Didn't mean to offend you," Tabitha said as she stepped around her.

Back in the Land Cruiser, she heard a hard rap on the driver's side window. It was Rachel. Tabitha's heart raced as her eyes locked onto Rachel's face. This attack was bringing it to a new level. But surely Rachel wouldn't start something here. Then again, why not, considering the only witnesses? And who would it be reported to? This was wild west stuff in the furthest reaches of the east.

Rachel made the universal hand crank motion for Tabitha to roll down the window. When Tabitha hesitated, Rachel barked that she wanted to talk. It was enough to break Tabitha's fight or flight dilemma. She threw the vehicle into reverse and traveled no more than five feet before creasing the rear quarter panel of a Dodge Durango, Rachel Kusenie's Durango.

Tabitha jumped out. "What did you do that for?" she screamed at Rachel. "Look what you made me do? This is your fault."

Rachel inspected the damage from her original spot. "Guess I should thank myself then," she said, pulling a toothpick from her mouth to use as a pointer. "I think you just straighten out that fender for me. Now, 'fore you get all whiny again, how 'bout grabbin' a beer like I was trying to ask in the first place."

Ten

Tabitha followed Rachel down the road to *Trugards*. Rachel insisted, but not in the sinister way she spoke in the grocery shop. "That crack I made about me not being new," she said, "didn't come out right. It was meant as a kindred spirit kinda thing."

Trugards was that type of place she thought it would be, the kind she avoided. It was a place made for drinking with little thought into making it appear otherwise. Unlike the sport's bars, there were no leather booths, no high-back stools, no brass railings or fixtures, no microbrews on tap, no big screen TV's, no electronic darts, certainly no wi-fi. There wasn't even a full menu. Burger, hot dog, cheese pizza, and fries was the menu, in block letters on a chalk message board above the bar. She didn't know why she expected anything more from the place but was surprised to get something much different from Rachel Kusenie.

They sat at the end of the bar. There were two others there: a woman in her late sixties and a young man in his thirties. They sat at the other end, though not together. Rachel acknowledged them both with a "wassup" for him, and a "hey darlin'" for her. Rachel introduced Tabitha to Mel Cready, the bar owner and the only person currently living on Stryker John Island who was born there. "Right in the back room," Mel said. "I figured I may as well stay for the duration, so I bought the place when I was two."

"For real?" Tabitha said.

"God, girl, no, not for real," Rachel said. "He uses that line for every new visitor."

"I take it not too often then."

"No, so I bust up the regulars with it whenever they need a laugh," Mel said. "It never gets old."

"Spare us," Rachel said, then introduced Tabitha. Mel nodded and extended his hand. "Didn't see you at the meeting. That fifty-foot lighthouse," he said, "that what you're gonna be calling the place now, *The Lighthouse*?"

"Aress Landing. That's our last name, Aress. And it's twenty-eight feet."

"Yeah, it's every bit of fifty."

Rachel ordered a glass of Chardonnay to Tabitha's surprise. "What? You expected a shot of Jack Daniels?"

"No. I mean, yeah, I did. I'll have the same then."

"Seems the lighthouse has a life of its own around here," Tabitha said when Mel left. "Complete with gossip and intrigue."

"That it does."

"I notice how no one asks me about me, or us as a family."

"That's just us; we like being left alone. Figure others do, too."

"I don't feel like we're being left alone at all" Tabitha said. "Matter of fact, just the opposite."

"The truth? New people come here very seldom. When they do, they do it quietly. I think that's a good policy for most places."

"This why I was asked here tonight?" Tabitha asked. "A little nudge from the island welcome lady?"

The wine arrived in surprisingly tasteful and delicate wine glasses.

"Me? Welcome lady?" Rachel found that a hilarious punchline. "Sister, I'm no welcome lady. Back home I was voted most likely to scare a wolf to death. And that's no lie, I really was." She removed the toothpick and raised her glass to toast. "You know, Mel brings this stuff over from the mainland just for me. Maybe he'll need to double up on the order, huh? How 'bout this one: to the Aress Motel, or whatever she be called, and the lady who makes her run, may she become the heart and soul of Stryker John Island."

A touch of melodrama, Tabitha thought. Or a touch of sarcasm with a dash of something disturbingly more. Out of hospitality, she tapped her glass to Rachel's. "So *why* am I here?" she asked again.

"Because you're new. And I *do* know what that's like."

Tabitha finished her wine quicker than she had done in her college sorority days. Rachel was just a sip behind. She called out to Mel for two more and Tabitha didn't argue. The wine added further blush to Rachel's ruddy cheeks. Tabitha was finding herself at ease with this come-to-life Peppermint Patty.

Rachel Kusenie had a style. She could bust into a place at closing time and still get service. She had specially ordered wine at a broken-down bar. She had her truck dinged and blew it off as if she had three more just like it at home. She could refer to new acquaintances as *girl, sis, chickie*, and get away with it. Such traits tested Tabitha's nerves. Even requesting *Tingo's Market* to specially order Kashi cereal and green tea was out of her comfort zone. Maybe it was her environment back home, her upbringing, her personal boundaries. "You from the mainland?" she asked Rachel.

"Yeah. The mainland three thousand miles away. Oregon. Small town outside of Bend," Rachel said. "Before that I came from Hoquiam, Redlands, Baraga, Ossawatomie, and Ottumwa. And when at the end of that list Ottumwa is the most recognizable place you've been, if you don't want to be shit on you need to arrive early and stay late, if you catch my drift. I came here with my partner six years ago."

"So, I need to make some noise, that what you're saying."

"Nah, noise is just noise. It's what you do, how you do it, bring something to the table. I got this feeling you have things to bring. Just like your old man."

"Back to the lighthouse again, huh?"

"I give him credit for the way he's come in here. I like that. Just that it ain't gonna work, Not here. Again, nuthin' personal. Had a guy come on the island 'bout the same time I did, tried to put aluminum siding on the hardware store. Didn't last six months."

Tabitha hunched forward, wrapping her palms around the newly filled wine glass. "What was that Mel said about a meeting?"

"Your old man didn't tell you? Wow, heard of guys lying to their old ladies 'bout screwin' other chicks but never knew one that did it to cover up a town council meeting. Guess he didn't want to tell you about how we practically ran him off the island."

Tabitha didn't know whether to be angry with Trent for not telling her, or with Rachel for telling it as she did. Surely Trent wouldn't have said anything to get on the bad side of these neighbors. He was much too astute for that. So, Tabitha picked sides and turned defensive. "If he went to your meeting, he did it to get to know you, not to be browbeaten."

"Well, he got to know us, all right." Rachel reached over and cupped Tabitha's hand with hers. "I know what you expected, that this island would be filled with witty, educated folks who read a lot of poetry, played classical violin, and painted sunrises on the beach. Just like in those North Carolina beach-romance books."

"So at least you read."

"Only the Almanac and owner's manuals. I got dragged to one of those movies just the once. Thing is, I came to this island like most of the others, to avoid the kinds of things your old man talked about."

"He's my husband," Tabitha slid her glass from Rachel's reach, "not my old man."

"Sure, just hillbilly-speak, don't mind me. Change of topic, how do you like it here so far?"

"I don't."

"Didn't think so. How do you spend your days?"

"I have my boys. I'm home schooling. And helping to set up the motel."

Rachel took a final sip from her glass, letting her lips linger on the rim. They were luscious, thick, and red now from the wine. "That's good. Won't find much else to keep you occupied here. You aren't into this motel-bit, are you?" she said.

"Just because I don't like island life doesn't mean I don't like ... what my husband does. I mean, it's my dream, too, the motel. It's our dream." Tabitha heard her sentences trailing off, fading. She couldn't be sure it was the wine.

She hadn't had a glass since New Year's Eve. Even then it was Champagne and just two or three sips. "Why would you even suggest such a thing?"

"My partner wasn't into the island routine. She wanted to buy that motel, turn it into a bed and breakfast. Me, running a B&B, can you even see it?"

"I can see that."

"Yeah, well, I thought about it. Even went to check the place out. That had to be three, four years ago. Place was a wreck then. Can't fathom the amount of work you folks are having to put into it. But I couldn't give up sheeping."

Tabitha slapped the bar, startling Rachel and the two at the end. "That what that is, that smell? Sheep? I can smell it all the way down to our place."

Rachel laughed. It was delightful. High-pitched, unaffected, and still very childlike. Not at all what Tabitha expected from a woman so worn. " Heck, I don't reek that bad. That's Abe, your neighbor, girl."

"Abe Carver?"

"Yeah. Meet him?"

"No. Just saw him once."

"Better you don't. He's mean and he's a deviant."

"Oh, my god, you mean my kids are —"

"No, not that kind of deviant. Don't think anyway." Rachel closed her eyes and pursed her lips. "No, don't see it, not with no human anyway. Hey, Mel, two more."

"Not for me," Tabitha called down to Mel.

Rachel shrugged. "Cheap date."

"I have to be getting home. But what's it about this guy I need to know?"

"Guess I don't really know, which is a good reason to stay clear."

"I don't get it."

"Around here everybody knows everybody and everybody's business. You'll see that for yourself if you don't hide in your house like Abe and my partner. I know Abe only 'cause we're both sheepers. He's been doing it longer than me, but I get most of the orders 'cause people just don't like the man. And don't much trust his sheep either. "

"He angry at you for that?"

"The only reason we haven't killed each other is 'cause he stays at his end of the rock, and I stay at mine. Even avoid the days he's using the ferry. Hey, that motel of yours, you need a hand cleaning, fixing, call. Here's my number." She handed her a yellow business card with black print, *Kusenie Sheep Farm.*"

"Thanks. But my husband's getting pretty handy around the place."

"Really? Wouldn't think so by the looks of 'im."

The boys were in bed with their dad resting on the sofa when she got to the house. Mop curled on his crotch. Trent was struggling to either sleep or stay awake. He readjusted himself as he cupped his hands over a contented Mop. "I'd say you took the long way home but that would still be no more than thirty minutes," he said.

"How long was I gone?"

"'Bout three hours. I called your cell."

She pulled it from her coat pocket. "Cell coverage here is like getting a decent cut of meat at *Tingo's*."

"Okay, so you bought the market out or went to the mainland."

"Why don't you just ask instead of making idiot guesses."

"Where were you?"

"Now you're being accusatory."

He grabbed Mop up in his hand and stood. "I can't win here."

"I met a person who met you and we had a drink."

"Never would have been one of my guesses. Who?"

"Rachel Kusenie."

He rolled his lower lip down as he thought before shaking his head. "Don't know that name. Where'd you meet her?"

"At the market; I ran into her truck."

He tossed a still contented Mop onto the couch. "Christ, Tabitha, there's like twenty vehicles on this whole —"

"Relax. It's fine, she's fine. It was a ding and, she didn't care." She collapsed on the couch and gathered Mop into her arms. She put her head back and appeared to fall into an instant sleep.

"How much did you have?"

She drowsily held up two fingers.

"You don't even drink."

"Don't fight it, may get you lucky tonight. The boys do their math game?"

He sat next to her. "Their homework? No, we watched *Yankee Workshop."*

She let out a sigh and shook her head.

"So where did you go, what did you drink, and who is this, Rachel Kudzo?"

"*Trugards,* Chardonnay, Kusenie; you met her at your meeting."

There was that woman who owned the market and the butch-chick who told him she didn't give a damn about his motel. "She that little dyke?"

"Honestly, Trent, just because a woman is independent."

"You telling me you sat with her for two drinks and you didn't catch onto that?"

"Not at all

"What did you talk about?"

"For starters, the meeting you didn't tell me about."

"I'm not going to bother you with all I do."

"Have anything to do with the fact they nearly had you tarred and feathered?"

"She told you that?"

"She painted the picture. I think it was something worth sharing with me. You, I mean, not her. It's that lighthouse they don't like."

"I suppose."

"So, take it down."

"No. It's up and it's ours. All that time and I'm all you talked about? Flattering."

"Did you know that Abe Carver has sheep?"

"Didn't you?"

"I've never been down there."

"You can see them when you walk the shoreline."

"There's a private property sign."

"Yeah, but it's like a hundred yards up from there."

"Trent don't go doing that kind of thing. It's not like a sign put up by the power company. People here strike me as the type who take private property seriously."

"And you know that because of your talk with the dyke?"

"Yes. She and her partner have a sheep farm on the other side of the island."

"And you still didn't get she was gay?"

"No. Working a farm doesn't make her gay."

"No, having a partner makes her gay."

She'd have thought wine would make sleep come easy. It didn't happen, neither did the lovemaking. This night disturbed her, the Barbers, Rachel Kusenie, the island meeting, Abe. While Trent breathed heavily beside her, she listened to the howling along the beach. The dogs, Abe Carver's dogs, traveled in a monotonously distinct pattern that started a great distance away then gradually neared until they seemed to be just outside the window. They didn't do it to announce their presence or the presence of a stranger, it was more of an omnipresence. Every night she fell asleep to their baying. It was all she knew of Abe Carver, those howls, and he became indistinguishable from them. She came to the realization she had a neighbor whom she not only didn't know, but who nobody seemed to know. Trent assured her the howls would soon be like crickets to lull her to sleep. So far it hadn't happened. Though her sleep suffered, she felt triumph in defying the things that threatened her world.

Eleven

As Tabitha expected, Memorial Day weekend was a bust. But by the Fourth of July they had all three cabins filled and three of the six rooms. That was a sixty-seven percent occupancy rate, Trent crowed. Not bad for the first two months in existence.

Trent had worked hard to do it, hard enough for Tabitha to feel a pride for him and in him, enough to make her pull a heavier load. It didn't make her want to stay. She hated every minute of it. She wasn't enamored with having to make beds and clean up for her own kids, doing it for strangers she found to be miserable and degrading. Her kids would grow out of it, but guests were forever.

The boys chipped in willingly once she made a game of it. Not athletic contests where Ricky was a heavy favorite. It was always about teamwork where beds were made one boy on each side; for furniture one sprayed while the other dusted; one vacuumed while the other moved furniture. Then how long in room one? Can they cut it by a minute in the next room? How much time can they spend cleaning room three if they wanted to finish ten percent faster than room one? Ricky would be in charge of one cabin with things done his way. Then it was payback with Jeremy barking the orders in cabin two. To keep if equal, Tabitha handled the role in cabin three.

Reservations were coming in through August. It wasn't luck or even word of mouth. Because of Trent's tireless efforts, there wasn't a business within twenty miles of Stryker John Island that wasn't advertising for *Aress Landing.*

Bring in a receipt of more than five dollars from *Collier's Donuts and Ice Cream* and get ten dollars off the room rate. Twenty dollars spent at the *1941 Cafe* or *McDuff's Barbecue* was good for ten percent off.

And that lighthouse, though not popular with the islanders, was a hit with the guests, everyone of them posing for the camera beneath it. So much so that Trent had new flyers made up that featured it rather than the cabins. And postcards they couldn't keep on the rack. Trent was ordering up miniatures that would be ready for the next season. The light with its soft green-yellow firefly glow was another attraction. Guests bringing chairs out to sit beneath it at night gave Trent another idea; a patio around it with open fire pits.

The lighthouse, followed in varying order by the views, the grounds, and the serenity topped the positive comments on the check out cards. But the howling dogs at night was a clear winner on the negative side. Trent couldn't use the "you'll get used to it" line on them. They didn't want to. "For the first five minutes it was a wistful sound, " one woman wrote. "After that it became unbearable."

"That sonavabitch is doing it on purpose," Trent told Tabitha.

He was talking about Abe Carver, of course. It was his land, his dogs, causing the disturbance. Tabitha didn't know why he would leave his dogs out at night to wander so close. From what she gathered from Rachel Kusenie and her own vision of him, she took it that he neither knew nor cared enough to corral them. "It could be he just isn't used to having neighbors," she said, more to calm down her husband then defend their neighbor.

"Not used to people period, crazy bastard. Think it's time we talked."

She didn't argue. It didn't take long for Trent to get customers; it wouldn't take long to lose them.

The next morning, after a quick cup of coffee, he headed out. "Don't get crazy," she warned him.

"Hey, just relax," he said, agitated by her admonishments that never failed to irk him. "I've done this type of thing before. I know how to handle people like him."

She crossed her arms as she stood in the doorway. "Ah-huh. You'll get no witness here."

This time Trent drove. He wanted to make a dramatic slamming door, spinning tires arrival and exit. Carver's place was still when Trent arrived. The dogs must have been asleep, exhausted from their night foray. But there was a restlessness about the place. Trent thought back on the ghost hauntings and descendants of Malaga Island. *Yeah, he thought, if I was one of them, this is the place I'd come.*

He stood outside the truck, off the property. He knew the kind of man Carver was by now, the kind who would scream "trespassing" at a flock of resting gulls. He also expected what came next; Carver stepping onto the front porch with his shotgun in hand.

He didn't burst through the door as he did at their first meeting. He came out casually which would normally mean to Trent that he came out for a chat. Bringing along the shotgun indicated he came out for a confrontation. "We need to talk, Carver," Trent said from where he stood.

"You just stay back now."

"I'm back far enough, no need for that gun."

"Always need for a gun. What is it you want now?"

The boys raced down to the cabins ahead of Tabitha. Mop struggled to keep up. Her yips reminded Tabitha of Jeremy calling ahead for Ricky to slow down whenever they were at the park. The motel had been nearly full this past week and would be nearly empty the next. There could be dozens of reasons for that, but Trent chose to believe it was Carver's dogs. Tabitha didn't believe word could travel so fast.

A horn beeped in the parking lot behind her. She was excited by the thought of a last-minute guest. That was the struggle inside her, to get off the island as soon as possible but also to see her husband's hard work pay off. Her hardship was his glory, and as a dutiful wife she felt it a legacy of sorts to see it through to the end with him. To be honest with herself, it wasn't all that horrible, and she wasn't lonely. And it was more than nice to have her hospitality be genuinely appreciated with money, tips, and compliments.

She recognized the black Durango. It was Rachel. She had called a few times, saying she was free to lend a hand. "Heard you were doin' well," she'd say.

"Better than we thought."

"Well, hope I'm having something to do with that. I dropped the *Aress Landing* name on the mainland in a few choice areas," Rachel said.

When she told Trent this, he just grunted, "Didn't notice any dykes registering."

Tabitha appreciated her efforts while graciously declining her offers. It wasn't her style to take near-daily visits from a woman she still considered a casual acquaintance. Rachel was persistent; now she was here. Too late for Tabitha to fake it. Rachel was out of the truck and heading down.

She was dressed in a black sundress. Her legs were absurdly white against it but very taunt with square calves and thighs that knotted as she walked down the gentle slope. Tabitha couldn't help noticing how disturbingly tight it pulled around her hips with each long step. She may have been a sheepherder, but she knew how to strut.

Her hair was down and full. It was darker than Tabitha remembered, and longer, though at the bar she wore it tied back. "Hello," was all she said as she neared, but already Tabitha could see a breeziness she didn't know Rachel possessed.

"Hi." It came out as a startled response, as if Rachel had snuck up on her.

"Don't recognize me?"

"No. I mean, yes, course. Ahhh, taking a day off from the farm."

"Sorta. Shopping on the mainland. Wanna come along?"

Tabitha, still confused and taken aback, could only manage a schoolgirl-like response. "Well, gee, I'd love to but there's work I need to get done here."

"I'll give you a hand."

She backed herself into that one and only rudeness would get her out of it now. They continued down to the cabins where she assumed the boys had started work. "Your hubby not here?"

"He's gone out. But he's not far."

"I figured that. How far could he go?"

They were about the same height, five-four, but Tabitha felt as if she was the entire time staring up at Rachel. Rachel had probably ten more pounds on her, solid muscle. Her neck and arms were chestnut brown from the sun. She seemed intent on staying within shoulder nudging distance as they walked, though she didn't feel a need to carry on a conversation. And what was that scent? *Tommy Girl?* Tabitha casually breathed it in. Yes, definitely *Tommy Girl.* It was awkward, and Tabitha felt as if she was coming up for air when they finally made it to the cabin.

The boys had stripped the sheets from the beds. Ricky was chasing a squealing Jeremy around the rooms, attempting to toss a sheet over him. Tabitha hadn't related to them all the possible fluids the sheets could contain; Pee was sufficient to have them donning disposable gloves and for yet another motive for Ricky to torment his brother. "Make him stop, mama!" Jeremy begged as he ran behind her.

She straight-armed the charging Ricky as she swept her other hand around the back of his neck. "Why weren't you here?" Jeremy said. "You were supposed to be with us; he does this all the time you don't come in right away."

"You," she said leaning into Ricky, "knock it off." She turned to Jeremy. "And you, I'm sorry. Okay to you both?"

"Yeah, yeah," Ricky said, twisting out of her grasp.

"No," Jeremy said as he stormed outside.

"I can see why you need no help," Rachel said.

"Usually not this bad."

"My sheep are easier to control." Tabitha didn't know how to take that Weren't sheep easy to handle? Follow like sheep, meek as a lamb? "Tell you what, we can get this place cleaned up in no time," Rachel continued. "Hey, big fella, go ahead and see to your little brother."

"We're the same age," Ricky said indignantly.

He looked to his mother as if Rachel was out of her mind.

"They're twins," Tabitha said.

"Oh. Cool. Go 'head, then," she said to Ricky. "Shoo." She made a move as if to chase him out. She was cat-like enough that Ricky scooted as if his life depended on it.

"You didn't need to do that," Tabitha said.

"It was nuthin'; we'll get it done better without them around."

No, Tabitha wanted to blurt out, *you shouldn't have done that.* She wanted these mornings with the boys, the boys-being-boys' antics being much a part of it. But she thought it better to go through the morning in hopes Rachel would get this out of her system. And the next ferry to the mainland was in less than forty-five minutes so she'd be on her way soon enough.

"Cute place," Rachel said as she stood at the window watching Ricky race to the house. "You folks *have* been working your asses off." She lifted her arms to the nape of her neck and flipped her hair into a bun. She held it there and her biceps flexed while her fingers kneaded her hasty hairdo. She caught Tabitha staring too intently. Tabitha dropped her eyes to the bed and found herself reaching for the sheets that had already been removed.

Somewhere between Rachel's greeting and now, Tabitha must have given off a vibe. She half wondered what it was, half scared she was still giving it. Rachel frightened her by doing a sudden back flop onto the mattress in front of her. She somehow managed to maneuver herself insidiously beneath Tabitha's busy hands. Her eyes sparkled and she let out a soft laugh. "Comfy," she said. "You make a good bed."

Tabitha was at a loss, not knowing where this was all coming from. It had never happened to her before, not even a hint, least not that she was aware. But Trent had read it right whereas she was unwilling to pass judgment. She was passing it now, but never should have done what she did next.

Twelve

Trent knew Carver wanted nothing more than for him to step across that line known only to him that separated his precious private property from the rest of the world. Carver even stared at the dirt easement at Trent's feet, waiting for the opportunity.

"It's those dogs, Carver."

"What about 'em?"

"Bring them in at night."

"Neva bring 'em in."

"Then tie them up nearer your place; they're howling right outside my guest houses."

"They need to be out in the field to guard the sheep."

"No wild animals gonna get your sheep, 'cept maybe your own dogs."

"And to keep trespassers away."

"Nobody's gonna —."

"You did, Aress." He brought the shotgun in tighter to his chest.

Trent couldn't deny it. A lie wouldn't work either. He thought back on that night. Unlikely Carver had CCTV out there. He heard the dogs but really didn't stick around to see them. Maybe Carver was right behind them, or had them on long leashes, like bloodhounds leading the charge through the English moors. "I'm sorry about that," he managed to say. Despite his resolve to stay on the offensive he found himself in a bit of a retreat.

"Don't accept apologies any better than I do trespassers."

"Carver, I've tried to be neighborly but—."

"Don't accept neighbors neither."

"Yeah, I heard. Especially neighbors who buy property you wanted. It was for sale for a while, you know. You had your chance."

"Didn't have a bad enough desire."

"Yeah, well I did. And I bought it. And it belongs to me now so get over it. And call off the dogs, literally."

"You bought *that* property," he said, bobbing his head up the road towards the motel, "didn't buy mine."

Trent was as close to furious as he had ever been at a man. But it was just one wrong move Carver was waiting for, and something told Trent trespass shooters were well represented up here. "Got yourself another dog, I hear, what's that give you three, four?"

"Enough for now."

"You're fuckin' with me and my place," Trent said through a tense jaw. "You got those mutts roaming up and down the property line."

"Not mutts and not roaming."

"Where then? Where you keeping them out there at night?"

"Keepin' 'em on my property, is where, and that's all you're gonna know."

It left Trent speechless. At night Trent was forced to lie awake by the damn hounds until exhaustion took him. From there he tried to determine where the dogs were. Hard to know. They seemed to be strategically moved nightly along the shoreline. If it were one spot, the same spot, maybe a sound-deadening wall could help. Not only was that expensive but talk about pissing off the islanders. On a more personal note, it would indicate he'd been beaten. And he wasn't about to be beaten by the likes of Abe Carver.

But Carver, ironically, was not much different than certain people he had met in Washington. It wasn't education or money, position, or status, that gave them the edge. It was the ability, innate or learned, to disregard standards of behavior. And it wasn't out of ignorance, far from it. It was a genius on another level. "I can call the police, you know, make a formal report."

"You could. Waste of time, yours and theirs."

"Not mine."

"Dogs on my property. Dogs bark on my property it's my business. Deciding to bed people down within earshot of barking dogs is plain stupid, you ask me. Now you wanna call the police, well, they won't come over for that, I know, but if they do, I'll make a report myself, 'bout you trespassin.'"

"That was then, Carver. I'm doing this in a righteous manner, face-to-face, no threats, no shouting. It's you standing there with the gun, not me."

"I know where you stand; you know where I stand," Carver said. "We're done here."

Tabitha wished she had handled the next few moments better, that she had gathered her senses and taken all emotions being played out into account. After all, if this was a man, she would have had no problem handling the situation directly and delicately, depending upon the dictates. Then again, she had experience in that area and the signals didn't sneak up on her as they had now. Having no familiarity here outside of novels she read, she could only rely on instinct.

Rachel stretched her arms over her head, accentuating not only her sinewy neck but her nipples against the thin fabric. Then she smiled, encouraging Tabitha's next move. But Tabitha had none. To use the boys being just several yards away would indicate there was another time in another place. To say she was married would suggest regrets of some kind. The truth was she was severely put off by this, "disgusted" being a more accurate word. When Rachel lifted herself and wrapped her arms around Tabitha's neck, Tabitha could think of no delicate way of saying it. "Goddamn you, stop it. What do you think I am?" She then muttered sentiments she couldn't recall as she wrestled out of Rachel's grasp, though it really wasn't much of a struggle as Rachel was the one doing the recoiling. Whatever it was Tabitha said, it shook up Rachel as much Tabitha was.

Rachel scampered off the bed, close enough to tears to stop Tabitha's outcry. She put her hands up defensively or in surrender. "I'm sorry," she said. "I thought ... maybe ... I'm just sorry," She hurried around the bed, ducking as she passed Tabitha, as if a swat on the head was in the offing.

The awkwardness of the moment had Tabitha reeling. Why had she been obtuse, so ignorant of the signals? Trent had seen her once in a crowded room and picked up on it. Yes, she was gruff and tomboyish, but that was most of the field hockey and volleyball players she knew in high school. And she certainly didn't come off that way today. As a matter of fact, had it been Trent doing the bed linen, he may have been tempted to put a move of his own on Rachel.

What bothered her most, though, was the truth. She did know Rachel, and she knew of her intentions. She knew of them when she was invited to *Trugards* for a drink. She knew from Rachel's touch across the table. She knew from the comments after and the multitude of phone calls that followed. She knew when Rachel drove up and stepped from her truck as a tomboy Princess. So, what followed shouldn't have spooked her. But rather than rehearse a subtle, but candid, rejection, Tabitha focused on the disgust that was building inside her.

Seeing Rachel race off in what could only be seen as humiliation had its effect. What Tabitha saw as repugnant now had a face. It was no longer a concept, an underground lifestyle glorified in magazines, movies, and daytime television talk shows. Did she lay into Rachel because of that disgust, or did she feel threatened? Not a threat of hidden desires, Tabitha surely had none in that direction. But all things being equal, she truly admired Rachel. She enjoyed her free spirit, her independence, her candor, her trust. She was childlike in her innocence in spite of her experiences. When Tabitha took inventory, these were the qualities she searched for. She learned she had none of them.

Too late she made the decision to chase her down. She now had the response she wanted to give. *I'm sorry, Rachel, I'm flattered, really, and while I accept you and your lifestyle, it's just not me*. Or something like that, toned down so as not to sound so much like an after-school TV special. She hurried to the door, met by Trent on his way in. "I wish I had a big freakin' gun!" he screamed.

"What?"

"Yeah. Not to use, just to hold."

"What are you talking about?"

"I'm talking about my visit with that crazy bastard."

"Didn't go well I take it." She turned back to the bed to give the illusion she'd been changing them the entire morning.

"The man's a menace. No class, no regard. He's pissed at us for buying the property."

That was a surprise; she had no idea of an issue there. "He said that?"

"Yeah, I told you."

"No, not until just now."

"What difference does it make? It's ours."

"Sounds like he's still sulking over it. He may grow out of it."

"You shittin' me? I'll grow out of my teeth before—."

"What did he say about the dogs?"

"Oh, well, he apologized profusely. Said he'd take care of it as soon as possible. He hoped it wasn't an inconvenience to us. Oh, and asked how you were making out and whether he could slaughter a lamb for you."

"Slaughter a lamb? You're kidding."

"Of course I am; haven't you been listening to me."

"I mean, does he really slaughter sheep there?"

"The dogs, Tabitha, it's about the dogs, don't you get it. What are we supposed to do, offer guests a mint and two Ambiens on their pillows?"

Tabitha was forced to finish the other two cabins by herself since Rachel chased the boys off. Trent followed behind, going on about his visit with Carver and occasionally tossing, then fluffing, a pillow. He was working himself into a frothy lather.

"Wasn't that that Rachel woman?" he asked as they headed back to the house.

"Yeah. Mind carrying something?" She was loaded down with three laundry bags of dirty towels and linens while he walked causally with a half-filled trash bag.

"Sorry. Preoccupied." He grabbed two of the bags from her.

"Think she look different today?"

"A little. What she want?"

"She was going into town, asked me if I wanted to go along."

"Don't. She's just trouble."

"Why would you say that? You don't know her."

"I know her type. She can clean up all she wants, can't fool me or change my mind; she's still trouble and still a dyke."

The summer that started slow, then picked up for nearly a month, had become a crawl again. Slow economy, late marketing, could have been reasons to satisfy Tabitha, but when a family that signed on for three days left early the next morning after a particularly punishing night of dog howling, she fell into agreement with Trent. He made calls to the police department in Nuthatch Cove. On that first call they told him they didn't have the manpower to patrol the island. By the fourth or fifth they told him they weren't going to waste their time, energy, or money dealing with a barking dog complaint. They had just seven reservations the rest of the summer. It put Trent in a very bad place.

The boys loved the respite. It was summer. Their school days were over. They were at the ocean. They couldn't understand daddy's foul moods. "We want to sail," Ricky said. he pleaded as he watched the ships and boats heading out to the Bay of Fundy. Trent's answers were curt, when he answered at all, and they didn't sound promising to the boys.

Trent spent his nights and many early mornings at the edge of the property listening to the dogs. It became an obsession. He wandered the stony ridgelines between his tract and Carver's, feeling how close, how far, they were from him. They knew he was there, his scent carried in with the salt on the stiff sea breeze. The howling grew more intense, more impatient, the more he paced. And so, he paced faster, running at times, driving them mad tracking this phantom.

One night, when the howlings were a safe distance inland towards the house, he toured the other side of the ridge in an area he calculated the dogs to be most nights, dipping low enough to keep his silhouette off the moon-washed sky. A rancid smell greeted him. Not dog piles. This was rotting flesh. The ground was an assortment of grasses, sand, and stone, easily distinguished underfoot. He was toe-tapping for anything peculiar.

He kicked up something soft. Wet grass. No, not here where all the other grasses were dry. He knelt to knead the pile gently. The smell was strong but if it was a dead thing, it had been so for a while. He picked up a tuft of dry gray fur or hair. Then another attached to a thick branch. He held it against the light sky. The branch was a bone. He dropped it and rubbed his hand in the dirt, but he was in the midst of a pile of dry hair, bone, and gristle. He stood to search out the area further. More piles. They seemed to stretch every twenty, thirty paces apart. Sheep carcasses.

The flock he had seen were hundreds of yards inland near the house. And even the slaughter shed was a ways back. Strays? So far out? He had his theories. He knew these dogs would never be satisfied with only barking. They wanted much more. Carver had made sure of that.

Thirteen

Two weeks before Labor Day had two groups of college kids stay for a Friday into Saturday morning. They didn't mention the dogs when they left. They spent the day touring on bikes they brought over, and the night at *Trugards.* They came back late, spent the night at the lighthouse, and made more noise than the dogs. Tabitha had to roust them for the eleven A.M. checkout. They left a lot of wine bottles and no tips. Trent thought it could be a good niche market, college-aged drinking groups. Tabitha wanted no part of it. They were the last guests of the year.

Tabitha felt horrible for how she had handled the season. She didn't sabotage the endeavor, but worse, she felt happy there was no need to. She talked the experience down so badly that her parents found more than one excuse not to come up. Her mother told her, "Next year, when you folks are more settled."

Though the home-schooling experiment went well with even Ricky fully absorbed, the island was no place to bring up kids. The proof being there were only two others on it, both infants. Keeping to a normal school schedule, Tabitha had the boys back at the kitchen table for short periods of reading and math the day after Labor Day. It was not going well. The boys were having a rebellious first month and Tabitha thought strongly of saying "screw it," they'll be out of here soon enough. It didn't help that the second week of October was an Indian summer with temperatures near the seventies.

She relaxed the schedule for a few days, at least for the duration of the warm weather. It would be best for all of them. The boys were restless; Trent was growing more depressed, making him more distant. With good timing he'd be ready to leave with them as soon as Christmas. But right now, time away to Bangor or Augusta would help them all unwind.

But Trent was staying up all night and into the morning hours. Most times he just sat outside or in the living room with the lights out. He slept late, at times past two in the afternoon. He no longer articulated dreams for the motel, but Tabitha caught him lost in unknown thoughts. Staying at the motel as it died around him was torture, but leaving it, even for a day, was to abandon it to Abe Carver, and that was unthinkable. "Go," he told Tabitha curtly when she suggested the trip.

"I'll bring some flyers," she said. "We can drop them around."

"Don't patronize me, Tabitha."

"I'm not."

"I'm okay. Just trying to find my way around this setback, you know me."

That next day Tabitha gave space to Trent, and to herself. She and the boys set off for Bangor. The trip would have been a good one for Mop. She loved the car, and though Tabitha wasn't sure what dogs did and didn't comprehend, perhaps Mop would sense they were leaving for good and be briefly elated. Or maybe enjoy the change of scenery as much as the rest of them. For as bad as it was for Tabitha, as lonely as it would be for the twins, and as desperate as it was becoming for Trent, Stryker John Island was no place for Mop, either.

For her it was too vast, too wild. The smells, sounds, and sights were all larger than life, at least the life she knew. At night she tucked herself tight against Tabitha's feet as she sat in the armchair. She was never allowed in the bedrooms to sleep, but her whimpers became so incessant and so animated when Carver's dogs were put in place that Tabitha carried her up every night.

Still, the nights were intimidating. The confines of the bedroom did nothing to deaden the howls outside. Mop's ears perked, her heart raced, and she shook steadily through the night. Her days were spent brooding in the sun. Worse than the terrifying night sounds was being alone. Sensing a kindred spirit in Jeremy, Mop tried to stay close to him most days, avoiding the boisterous and rambunctious Ricky. But Jeremy found the attention a burden. Trent was preoccupied by events quickly spinning out of his control, and so Tabitha took the extra efforts to attend to her.

The boys wanted Mop to come along. Tabitha told them she'd be good company for dad. "I don't think so," Jeremy said, "dad doesn't like company anymore." That hurt Tabitha but it was true. She made mention of it to Trent who was more angry than hurt. "Take the dog; take them all. I don't much give a damn right now." She left Mop behind, telling the boys their dad was thrilled to have the company.

She was blocked into the drive by Rachel's Durango. It came skidding to a stop, and just as fast and furiously, Rachel came flying out. Tabitha saw this would not be an opportune time to make amends but opened her window and tried to offer a smile. Rachel ignored it as she flipped an envelope though the window and turned without making eye contact. Tabitha opened it, a $1200 bill for vehicle damages.

Trent didn't watch them leave. He knew that within a short period of time it would be for good. Maybe by Thanksgiving; for sure by New Year's. By saying little, Tabitha had said enough. If *Aress Landing* had played out as he pictured it, as it was promising to be, he'd have a prayer in hell of convincing her to stay. Now, not only was it turning to financial ruin, but she had the opportunity to say, *I told you so*. That she hadn't, he was grateful.

He turned his attention once more to Abe Carver. Diplomacy, compromise, gamesmanship, those were the principles that guided Trent throughout his career. In Washington there were always contingency plans, always a back door, a side door, an end around. He was impotent here. This was a negotiator's nightmare, a man like Carver with no affiliations, no ties, no constituents. He had no connections to anyone or anything. No strengths but no weaknesses, no visible reason to live or die. Except for his half-wit nature, he'd be a great John le Carrè protagonist. If Trent was to lose, and he'd done so many times without brooding too long, he refused to do it to a man of such low character.

Businessmen knew success, like failure, depended on many variables. These variables had to be constantly evaluated. Trent saw only one. If it were not for Carver and his dogs, *Aress Landing* would be booming. He had overcome all other obstacles: the renovations, the logistics, the remoteness, the naysayers, the hostility of the islanders. Carver, he now knew, was not something to overcome. More drastic measures needed to be taken.

Most of what was left behind by the long-ago owners of the place was thrown out by Trent during renovation. He joked that he ferried as much material off the island as he did onto it. But he kept some for no apparent reason: a bundle of brittle roof shingles, three exterior oak doors, a twenty-foot length of aluminum gutter, and five unopened cans of rat poison. He kept it in a locked wooden shed, the type only rodents could get into. Contrary to the boys' story, he hadn't seen a rat since moving in. Just last week he made a mental note to carry the cans off the island on his next mainland trip.

He read the label for the ingredients: warfarin, tetrahydro, naphthalenyl, hydroxy. He had no clue what they were, or how lethal, but even the color, Aqua, was inoffensive. Recommended dosage was one packet. He didn't know if that was for one rat, or a herd of them. He didn't know the size of dog he was dealing with, but knowing Carver, it was sure to be a big one. He guesstimated ten packets would do, then recalculated that up to twelve.

No one much cares how a rat is poisoned, but a dog, that usually leads to an investigation. But that was in civilized places, with civilized dog owners. Hell, Carver didn't even bother to name his. Still, if he suspected Trent, he would call in the police, who may or may not give it their time. Trent grabbed an even twenty packets to ensure success the first time, then buried the rest of the cans and packets.

It was mid-morning. The dogs weren't put out until early evening. But they could be heard somewhere most times of the day. It was part of Carver's chess game. Trent wandered the ridgeline between the properties with four pounds of warfarin-packed raw hamburger, throwing stones and whistling. When he was confident the dogs were elsewhere, he found the area of carcasses. He tucked some of the meat inside the carcasses but the majority he placed in piles nearby, not knowing if it was a habit of dogs to revisit old stocks of food.

Tabitha and the boys didn't get back until nearly eleven. The boys dragged themselves to bed. Tabitha sat to talk and gauge her husband's day. He seemed back to his old self with a positive attitude about the place and the future. "It's like the Baltimore Ravens," he said, launching into a metaphor using his favorite football team. "They always had the team; they were always close. They just needed to stay with it and work hard."

He was content enough to let her put her feet on his lap and talk about the trip to Bangor. The boys were wild. Tabitha tried to visit the Farmer's Market, but the kids complained and tugged at her legs so much she had to leave midway through. They were constantly running off at Waterfront Park so shopping was not going to happen. They ended up at Blackbeard's Family Fun Park and the Discovery Museum. "So ... what'd you do?"

"Thinking mostly," he said.

"About what in particular?"

"Our options."

She didn't repress her excitement at the prospect of cashing in. Her feet nearly slapped his face she jerked so eagerly. She wished she had played it cool; she had no doubt he knew the option she wanted. "Oh?" she said as she recovered her composure, "What kind of options."

"We can move the cabins to the other side of the house. They're on slabs, it wouldn't be all that hard. The motel rooms would take a bit more work."

"Okay. But that's what, a hundred feet, you think that will be enough to keep the guests from hearing the dogs?"

"Not completely, but I've done my own sound checks and with the house in the middle, it deadens it enough."

This was only slightly more daft than his twelve-foot high steel wall idea. But his eyes were clear, no glassiness, no far-off stare. "What was that, a love note the dyke gave you?" He asked.

"Huh?"

"When you were leaving."

"Hardly."

"Didn't think so, the way she pounced then left."

"Yeah, well, I wished it was. We gotta come up with twelve hundred bucks to fix her damn truck, now."

She thought that would set him off. It didn't. "Small enough price to pay to get her off your back and any other body parts she's wanting to jump."

"Yeah, well, that's another thing, Trent, where are we coming up with all this money?"

"I got it."

"I know. Just I don't remember us ever—."

"I told you, I saved it. Don't sweat it."

She accepted that. Money was always a concern for him, the eternal battle between what he earned and what they paid him. The two were never close. "Was Mop good company for you? Where is she?"

Fourteen

The look on Trent's face told Tabitha all she needed to know. She was hoping Mop simply tucked herself into a corner to sleep for the day, but it wouldn't be like her, knowing how she adored traipsing after the four of them. It was sweet and often annoying. She wasn't a seventy-pound Retriever who would push you aside; she was a seven-pound Biewer who would trip you up. Often you heard the yip before even feeling her underfoot. But neither your cursing nor her pain discouraged her. That's what had Tabitha concerned.

She went about calling and searching the house, Trent at her heels, telling her if Mop wasn't inside, she must be curled up under a bush outside. "She'd never do that," Tabitha said as her searching became more frantic.

"How do you know what—"

"Jesus, Trent, how dense were you while we were away. Mop's always underfoot, always. If she was left outside, she'd be yipping at the door."

It was at that word, "yipping," that both stood dead still as the dogs just beyond the hills began to bay menacingly close.

Mop knew when tension was in the air. It was usually around Trent. Still, she would wait nearby for the air to clear, keeping her distance, staying quiet until it tapered. She did that this evening.

Trent was walking the shoreline. It was one area Mop avoided. It was filled with the wind and the spray that soaked her from the inside out and took hours to shake off. Trent marched the grounds in a fevered urgency that kept

Mop hunkered down in the safety of the tall grass. She moved to follow only when it was safe, when Trent made his last trip to the shed and disappeared over the ridge.

It took time and great effort to cross the field and climb the hill. The sun setting and the tall grass had Mop blind to things a foot away. She stopped to listen to the rustling. She followed it right, then left, moving further inland, or maybe in a circle. Now that's all it was, rustling as the wind picked up. If Trent was out there moving, he was now indistinguishable from all other sounds and his scent was lost in the swirl.

And she was alone. Never had she been outside unable to see at least one of them. Never had she perked her ears and not heard a familiar voice. She sniffed vigorously; the only sense left to her. New smells were coming to her, rotting meat and strange pheromones. Suddenly everything around her was new, all new in this new world. Then the strange voices. She stopped. No, not voices, dogs, the dogs she had listened to night after night in the safety of the bedroom. She whimpered as she crouched low, lower, pawing the wet dirt beneath her. She tucked her snout into the shallow grave, working the dirt with her chin, licking the iron-rich mud from her paws. Closer they came, deeper she pawed and crept, yet they were closing so much faster than she could dig. The heavy paws beat down like thunder rising up from the bowels, shaking the ground. She whimpered, then wept, then there was the blur of black swallowing her whole.

"The dogs sound different tonight," Tabitha said.

Trent thought so, too. "Louder than usual."

"No, not that. Wilder."

Yes, that was it. More beastly. There was no control to it, no unity of a pack honing in on a sight or a scent. There were no barks, or even growls, but an array of mad wails and yelps. It was an orchestra warming up, each instrument tuning itself to its own needs. The rat poison couldn't have taken effect so quickly. Trent now suspected what had the dogs at their fever pitch.

Tabitha's mind wasn't far behind. It had her tearing out the back door towards the hill where the dogs seemed to be gathered. Trent grabbed her. "You can't go up there," he said. She pulled hard to break free.

"Mop," she screamed.

"We don't know she's up there."

"Did you go up there?"

He wanted to ignore her, pretend he didn't hear or understand. But at least her contemptuous question, or was it an accusation, calmed her down. "For a minute," he said, "to look around."

"Then she went up there. You know she wouldn't let you out of her sight. I can't understand how you didn't see her, not one time all day."

"I swear I didn't." But it wasn't true, the swearing part. He hadn't seen Mop, he was sure of it, but no, he couldn't swear to it. *I was preoccupied,* he needed to tell her, though really, it shouldn't be necessary. She had to know he couldn't put up with Carver and his dogs forever, and while she was out relaxing with the kids, he was back here, formulating a plan. He had to; if not him, who?

Tabitha sat and cried into the early morning hours. Then she lay in bed and cried. Trent snuck out early after she cried herself to sleep. He found pieces stretched out along the ridge. Hard to tell but they had to be her. The sheep remains were days old, mostly bone now. These were fresh droppings of meat and blood, and multi-colored fur of whites and browns. Not a lot, which gave him more proof it had to be Mop.

She was awake and at the kitchen table, three-quarters of the pot of coffee already gone when he returned. She looked as he would expect her to. Without his asking she told him, "I don't want to hear about it; I don't want to know." He sat across from her. He wanted a cup of coffee but felt sharing what was left would steal the moment from her. They were both remembering the day he brought her home, the hard time they had of breaking her of nipping at anything that moved, the battle of supremacy between her and the boys, the irritating things she did and the loving way she did them. But while Trent's remembrances were tender and doting, Tabitha's were mired in a deep-rooted loathing, if just for the moment.

"Now what do we tell the boys?" It was a murmured question she asked herself. Trent was tempted to answer but like the coffee, this was a time he left for her. She gave no answer and her look dared Trent to find one.

"I don't know; she ran away?"

"We don't bullshit our kids."

Sure, we do, he could have said. *We do it all the time.* Not cool, not now. "Then it's the truth, I guess."

She stared hard into him. There was a moment of hatred in that look. Had the moment lasted she would have followed up with her brutal accusations of his disregard for her and his children. His disregard for their safety, their well-being, their needs, their desires. There were also her naggings doubts of his motives. *Why here? Why now? Why not admit it's not working?*

But he would never admit such a thing. It was what she loved, now despised about him. To never give in had its merits. It had its pitfalls. There was a measure of defeat in all victories, a measure of victory in defeat. That was why she didn't let the moment linger. Between her fiery accusations and his passionate defense, nothing would be gained.

"What?" He snapped. "What am I supposed to say to make it right?"

"Nothing."

"That's right, Tabitha. *Nothing* is what I can say, not a goddamn thing. So why are you looking at me like I'm supposed to come up with something?"

She rose from the table. "Because the boys will be up any minute now, and you'll need to."

He did tell them something, that Mop got caught in the tide and was swept out to sea. It was a measured lie. Mop was dead, that part was true, so the boys wouldn't think she was just lost. And it was a horrible mishap, another measured lie. So, the two lies made up a truth of sorts, that there are things out there not meant to harm you but can.

They cried simple tears that day. Their dog was gone. Life didn't go on forever. That it was so for all living things hadn't made its impact on them, and that was good. Their young lives had no business being complicated.

Fifteen

"Dad said she did, that's why."

"Well, I don't think so; Mop never went near the water, even when we tried to make her."

"You tried; I never did."

"Well, I'm going to look for her anyway."

Jeremy followed Ricky out just so he didn't have to answer questions when asked where his brother went. He hated lying to his mother; he wasn't good at it. Telling her he didn't know Ricky was out looking for Mop would make him queasy. She'd get mad at Ricky for going then Ricky would get mad at him for telling. That would make the queasy in his stomach worse.

So, he followed and tried to keep up. When Ricky started going inland up the rocky slopes, Jeremy re-thought the whole project. "You can't go up there."

"Why not? Dad does. 'Sides, what are we supposed to do, look for Mop in the whole ocean."

"Mom told us —."

Ricky stopped and turned to Jeremy. "Go on home then if you're scared. You see dad's face when I asked if he saw Mop in the ocean? He didn't say nuthin'. I think he's wrong; I think she mighta came up here and got caught in the rocks."

"Why would she come up here?"

Ricky waved him off and continued up the rocks. He was already far inland by the time Jeremy got to the top. By climbing onto the rock outcroppings, he saw just the roof of their house. Behind him was the roar of the crashing waves without sight of the ocean. In the distance was a house and a barn he had never seen before. And a shed Rick was fast approaching. All this just over the hill from them.

He caught up to Ricky who was standing just outside the shed door. "Smells," he said, breathing heavy.

"Yeah. Bad."

"We shouldn't be here I don't think."

Ricky ignored him and slowly opened the door.

It was dark, save for the widening sliver of light as the door moved. "What's that buzzing?" Jeremy whispered.

That buzzing and smell greeted them in the form of two gutted, hanging sheep which Jeremy never got to see. Ricky screamed and pushed past him out the door. "What's the mat —," but Jeremy cut the question off as Ricky bolted across the field. He wanted to look back in the shed but didn't dare. He wanted no part of whatever it was that could send his brother sprinting away in horror.

Ricky stopped at the edge of the field at the rocks, more to catch his breath than to wait for his brother. "What happened?" Jeremy asked. Ricky was doubled over on his knees.

"Something," Ricky stammered, "I don't know ... maybe ... two boys ... I'm not sure."

"What were they doin'?"

Ricky shook his head. "Nuthin'. Hangin'"

"Hanging? Why'd you run away screaming like that?"

Ricky stood up after recovering most of his breath. "'Cause, they were hangin'. Like by a rope or chain. I don 't know, somethin'."

"What? No way."

"I think so. Let's go back to see."

"Uh-ah." Jeremy bounded down the rocks.

"We gotta."

"No, we don't; we gotta tell dad."

"We can't; he'll kill us for coming over here."

"If you go back, I'm gonna tell."

"Baby. You're always such a baby." Ricky climbed down the rocks, deriding his brother as he did.

Just as he landed on the shore, a grizzled man shuffled out from a crack in the rocks like an old hermit crab. Ricky made an unsteady sidestep towards the water. Jeremy kept his distance. The old man looked as if he was trying to smile. It made him look more disturbing; head cocked, brown teeth, gray face, and craggy, like the back side of a hippo. "You boys kinda far from home," he said, his voice dry as sand.

"No," Jeremy said, pointing behind them, "we live just down there."

"You're not within arm's reach from home on this island, you're too far away."

Ricky gave him a tight-lipped smile and continued to walk up the shoreline.

"Explorin', were you?"

"No, just walking."

"See anything ... interesting?"

"Jeremy let's go home."

"Know why they call it Stryker John Island?" Abe Carver said. "'Cause he still makes 'em call it that."

Ricky stopped. "Who makes 'em?"

"We gotta go, Ricky, c'mon."

"The pirate, that's who."

Ricky cocked his head. "What pirate?"

Jeremy knew he lost his brother at that. He was intrigued himself, though not enough to walk back to the old man as Ricky was doing.

"Didn't know Stryker John was a pirate, did ya? Dad didn't tell you that, did he?"

"Uh-ah."

"Know what happen to 'im?"

"What?"

"Well, see, I was hopin' *you* did," Carver said. "Seems nobody does."

"He's gotta be dead."

"Think so?"

"All pirates are dead."

Abe Carver nodded slowly as he backed himself into the crevice, drawing Ricky with him. Jeremy came forward and stood at the opening. It blocked the wind and deadened the ocean. A great hide-out, Jeremy thought, and a fun spot to sit if not for the scary old man.

"Lot's of spaces like this all over the island," Carver said. "Some bigger. Some so tight can't barely fit a boy size of you in."

"Stryker John, did he live on this island?" Ricky asked.

"Pirates don't live on any land; they live on their ships. Land, like this, is where they do things."

"Like hide treasure," Ricky said.

"And other things."

"Like what" Jeremy asked, leaning in closer.

It wasn't that the old man had a seductive way of telling a story; he didn't. And he didn't send off friendly vibes. It was the story itself that had the boys absorbed. Pirate tales were what their mother had been reading to them. It was how she got them to relate to the ocean; how it sustained people, how it transported them as the ancient highway across the world. And the islands, thousands of them, big and small, populated by thousands and dozens, warm weather and cold, temporary shelters and permanent civilizations. Yes, she read to them of Columbus and Magellan and Polo. But none held their rapt attention like Blackbeard and Bonnet and Calico Jack.

"Well, I'm not an expert on pirates, but I can tell you about Stryker John."

He had their attention.

"He was real friendly with the Indians up here. Not because they liked him, they didn't, no one did. But he got them things. He got them guns and bullets and horses and cattle. Know how?"

"Uh-ah."

"He stole 'em. Stole 'em up and down the coast, from here to Cape Cod, and up into Canada. Stole 'em anyway he could."

"Did he kill anyone?" Ricky asked.

"Killed lots. But it wasn't just them things he gave to the Indians."

He waited for the thought to sink in, waited for Ricky to look back at Jeremy, waited for Jeremy's mouth to match his eyes, opened wide with fright. "He brought them kids from the villages. He kept them on this island until the Indians could take 'em."

"Why?"

"Because they hated settlers. Some of them children, the lucky ones, were raised as Indians."

"What about the others?" Jeremy asked, his lips trembling so he could barely form the words.

Carver shook his head. "They were given back to Stryker John who would make them pirates if they were strong enough. Them that weren't, he'd bring 'em back to this island, string 'em up on a tree and gut 'em down the middle." With that he lowered his voice to a hideous timbre as he made a slow slashing move from Ricky's neck to his belly. "And some say he and his pirate crew still do. Say they see 'em all over this place. Come in on the fog, howling when they do, like a pack of wolves. See, the Navy come in and shot 'em all dead, right there where your house sits."

Ricky shot a look back at Jeremy before telling Carver, "Up there, in that shed, I saw —."

"We gotta go now, Ricky." Jeremy was insistent. "We gotta go."

"Wait. I think I saw some in that shed."

"That one up the hill?" Carver said. "Been nuthin' in there for years. I used it for my lobster traps back when I was lobstering."

Ricky had heard and said enough. As he did at the shed, he pushed past Jeremy who gladly joined him in pursuit and actually overtook him. "Stay out of the rocks," Carver yelled after them. "That's where the pirates wait."

"That's the man with the dogs," Jeremy said when they were safely away, "the man dad hates."

"I know it."

"Believe that, 'bout the ghosts?"

"Course I don't."

"You ran like you believed it."

"I was just gettin' hungry, that's all. And don't tell Mom or Dad we was up there either."

Sixteen

Without warning, Tabitha's parents came up for Thanksgiving. They called just before driving onto to the ferry. Tabitha explained to Trent they had been trying to call since Portland but there was no service. The poor service was true enough, but Trent had his suspicions Tabitha not only knew they were coming, she instigated it.

Under normal circumstances he would have welcomed them as guests. They all got along. Phil and Jeanine weren't in-laws, they were friends. There was never any "take care of my little girl" stuff. Trent never felt as if he had to earn their trust or respect. And they were easy. They didn't fuss with fixing or rearranging; they didn't murmur innuendoes; they didn't criticize or judge.

Phil, his father-in-law, had great stories that told second and third times just got better, albeit always a bit restructured. This, Trent owed to his myriad of jobs from magician at a traveling carnival to food taster at a bakery to bicycle messenger at forty-three years old. But full-time he ran his own property investment firm until the market went south, filling in the lean years with these other pursuits. And the boys were getting old enough to appreciate his stories, as well. Yes, under normal circumstances, Trent would have truly appreciated their company.

Tabitha would have been wiser to drop it to him, say, the weekend before, make it look natural and un-orchestrated. Little quipped lies such as, "they miss us," and "they really want to see the boys," would have worked well. Or even, "they don't believe it's as bad as I've been telling them; they want to see for themselves." That would have been closer to the truth.

Phil and Jeanine did no better when they arrived. Their smiles were reserved, the hugs brief, the greetings cautious, even with the boys. Trent caught the sideward glances between Tabitha and her parents. *Paranoia,* Tabitha would call it if he made mention, so he didn't. He feigned pleasant surprise at their arrival and mustered all the cordiality he could stand.

"Show dad around the back," Tabitha said, smiling. "I'll take mom around the house." That did it. She said it with such animation, such pride. The fix was in; Trent was about to be lambasted on three fronts.

He played it out, but he wasn't going to make it easy. "Jeremy," he said, not wanting to deal with Ricky's manic style, "you come with us, show Grandpa all we've done to the place. Ricky, stay here and help mom show Grams around."

Jeremy grabbed his grandfather's arm, talking non-stop about the things he learned about the ocean. "And guess what, Grandpa, the island's haunted by the man it's named after, Stryker John."

Phil chuckled. Trent was taken aback. "Who told you that?" he asked, sure that he hadn't.

"Ah, I think we read it."

He wasn't the most observant parent around a house, but he was sure he hadn't seen such a book. And Tabitha would never introduce it, even if there was one written, which he doubted.

"I don't think you did, Jeremy. Now, who told you?"

"No, we did, I think we did read it."

"Jeremy?"

"Just let it go, Trent," Phil whispered. "Boy's just trying to impress his old granddad, don't embarrass him."

Trent ignored him. "Did you talk to our neighbor? Were you talking to Mister Carver?"

They were on the shoreline now. Jeremy stared over at the rocks where Abe Carver confronted them. Trent followed his gaze. "Tell me Jeremy."

"I don't know. I think so, maybe."

"When?"

"I don't know."

"Where?"

"I don't know."

"Jeremy, you do know. Now where did you talk to him?"

"On the beach, down there. Ricky and I were just walking, and he came out, I mean, he came down the rocks."

Phil picked up on Trent's alarm. "This guy a problem, Trent?"

Trent reached down and gripped Jeremy's shoulders. "First off, Jeremy, there's no ghost here on our property or anywhere, okay."

"Okay."

"And I don't want you talking to Abe, I mean, Mister Carver again. If he ever tries to talk to you, I want you to run home and tell me. Understand?"

"Dad, you're squeezing me hard."

Trent hadn't realized how disturbed the thought of Carver reaching out to his family was making him. He released Jeremy and stood. "Go up see your mother."

"But I haven't shown —"

"Go."

"Little rough," Phil said. "What shook you, the ghost or his talking to that Carver fellow?"

"Carver's crazy but not a demon, and place like this, well, legends are gonna happen because fools believe."

Trent pulled his coat around his neck as the chill came up with the stiff ocean breeze. How to tell a little boy that spooks and monsters weren't real, that the horrors he'll face in his life, the real horrors, are from real people, people like Abe Carver.

He felt Phil's eyes measuring him and now regretted not letting the ghost story slide, it giving his father-in-law the opening he was looking for. "I don't know the ghost story," Phil said, "but Tabitha's mentioned the problems with your neighbor. Wasn't it his dogs that got to Mop?"

Trent was too enraged at Tabitha for relating that beyond the two of them that he ignored the comment.

"This venture worth it to you, Trent?"

"You ran a business; you know better than I do."

"But I also knew when it was time to call it quits."

"Did you really, Phil? When did you ever do that? It took me and the best corporate lawyer in Virginia to convince you to file for Chapter 11 when the housing market collapsed."

"Shameful of me to ride it out long as I did," he muttered. "Shameful. But I did quit. In my heart I knew it had to be done. So, I'm telling you, don't make the mistakes I made."

"I won't," Trent said, "but I want the opportunity to make exactly those mistakes."

"But this? Here?"

"Why not this? Why not here? Going from one trough feeder to another isn't changing anything. That's the shit that makes you old. It's what happens when you stick around after realizing you're just a brick in the wall. Soon enough you're replaced. And it doesn't make a difference if you were a better brick 'cause the next brick needs to break down what you've done to prove it's needed. Only in the end it's not, 'cause another brick is waiting to do the same. Within two years no one even remembers or cares you were there.

"My job, my old job, being a mouthpiece for all that crap I didn't believe in, a spin doctor for those with so much money that the only thrill left to them was stealing it from others." He chuckled. "'Spin doctor, know why we're called that? We spin around so damn much we spend our days sick and dizzy."

The faster the words came out the more they sloshed as his mouth numbed to the cold.

"I don't disagree with anything you're saying," his father-in-law said. "but being your own boss has its drawbacks."

"I know that. Pioneering is what I'm doing. What I'm doing here is a good thing for so many people. If my kids decide to go the trough route, so be it. But it won't be because they didn't know any other way."

They had walked up to the house and were outside the back door. Through the kitchen window Trent heard his wife and mother-in-law chatting. The voices were muffled but the topic was solemn. He knew because Tabitha let go with that brooding laugh meant to break the tension but, really, just made it thicker. "About the boys," Phil said, "they getting the future they need out here?"

"They'll find their way."

Phil rubbed the back of his neck. "Trent, I don't see how —"

"We're always so concerned with the children. And the children of our children." Trent said, looking back at the ocean. "We put a brake on the environment, and the economy, and social issues, insisting that each generation is responsible to worry about the next. But if we don't take the opportunity to move forward ourselves, we don't make much to leave to them now do we?"

It was past sundown. The wind was whipping with the delicate sting of sand and salt, and the November gales brought the temperature into the teens, but Phil wasn't finished. "Tabitha seems to think people on this island don't like what you're doing."

"That's because they're on this island. Most have been here for years, and some have never stepped off it."

"Maybe they have a reason. Could be you're pushing the envelope here."

"Evolution, Phil, it's part and parcel. Computers, the world couldn't do without them, *can't* do without them."

"Could if they never happened."

"But they did happen, and reversal is impossible."

"So, your being here is what? Their destiny?"

Trent hadn't thought of it in such terms, but he supposed everything was part of someone's destiny, action causing reaction, every wind altering forever the pattern of sand. Perhaps his presence on Stryker John Island had its purpose beyond chance. He walked up the short flight of steps to the back door. Phil grabbed his arm.

"Okay, Trent, maybe I'm not getting through so I'm telling you straight up; I don't like it. I don't like it for my daughter or grandsons."

"Don't care if you do, Phil. She's my wife and their –."

"Yeah, got it, your kids. This has nothing to do with ownership. When I say I don't like it for them, I'm saying *they* don't like it. Only the boys are too young to say it; Tabitha's too devoted, and you're too obtuse."

"She tell you that?"

"She didn't have to."

"She's adjusted."

"Adjusted," Phil shouted. "You sound like a prison warden. What's it mean to be adjusted? You prop them up against the wall to keep them from tipping over? You smack them in the face and tell them it's better than being beaten upside the head with a baseball bat?"

"I've never laid a hand on them."

"I called you obtuse to spare you my real feelings here. If you don't get that metaphor than I guess it's worse than being obtuse. You're just damn thoughtless. What is it you want out here? On an island in the middle of nowhere?"

"You're never gonna get it."

"Yeah, I do get it. You can talk all you want about it being great for the kids and best for the island, but this is about you, no one else."

The door pushed open. It was Tabitha. "What's all the noise out here?"

"Just guy talk," Phil said as he wedged past her into the house. "Just guy talk."

Living alone all his life, Abe Carver had developed a sense of things around him, both natural and unnatural. Often, he heard voices that he never spoke to, no matter how much they chided him. Even that of his foster mother whom he feared above all others. She was long dead. And though her spirit continued to curse him from the grave she could no longer beat him. Nor could her stories torment him, the ones of his ancestors from Malaga Island that came to him nearly every night, especially after heavy drinking, and the angry voices they brought. They were old stories of people long dead. Nothing from that world could harm him, and life had hardened him against beliefs in unearthly specters such as ghosts and gods.

Still the voices were there, and if they weren't real, then he was going mad. Madness was the one thing he believed in for he had seen it. First his father, then his mother, both by the time he was eleven. Two years after his father's suicide, his mother was committed to the Bangor State Hospital. His foster mother, whom he lived with until he was sixteen, refused to let him see her, believing her madness to be contagious, or at least highly influential. Yet somehow a piece of it found him.

Loneliness can make a man go mad; he'd been told along the way. Isolation put a man in a bad lot. But secluding himself on Stryker John Island all those years ago was the ideal life for him. Otherwise, he may have killed or been killed.

So why the sudden slice of hatred?

Until now, his had been a simple, singular madness. Its effects were well confined. It tormented no one but himself until he not only came to terms with it, but had come to appreciate it. It was, he recognized, his only identity.

It was the neighbor, he decided early on. But no, he had had neighbors before. He never met them. It hadn't occurred to them or him to be neighborly. They were there; he was here. Be they good folk or as mad as he was of no consequence. There was not a thing connecting them. He was a single standing Domino whose tipping would affect no other.

This neighbor's visit was unexpected and unwelcomed; Abe did his best to convey it as such. Aress had the nerve to imply, no insist, that the animosity between them was about owning land. Abe wasn't even sure he owned the land he was on; nor did he much care. Malaga Island was the only knowledge he had of land ownership, and it didn't sit well with him.

Life to him had no basis in what others thought or tried to dictate. He didn't know what it was to be "neighborly," or "courteous," or "gracious." He knew the words, having heard them at *Trugard's* from the mealy-mouthed patrons who paraded themselves as rugged individuals come to live rough in the backwoods of Maine. But not a man was among them and he'd told them so many times, drunk and not. The only thing he had in common with any of them was his disdain for Aress.

The talk at *Trugards* was of little else. What real man would come to this island to run a motel? And put up a model windmill and neon sign for photo ops by brittle men in Dockers and boat shoes, picnic tables for overweight wine-drinking women, and bonfires for wild drinking parties? Not even the pretenders on Stryker John would act so pitiful.

What really amused Abe, if that was the word, was the scraggly rat-eared dog that traipsed around the grounds at Aress's heels. A wife, young kids? Who cares, drag them along. They can at least do windows and laundry or whatever small chores a motel took. But a dog no bigger than a woodchuck, and nowhere near as scrappy? What use was that?

He didn't see the attack on the thing, but he heard it and saw its aftermath. Aress had just come over the ridge. Abe was out there out too, in a depression just beyond, too deep for Aress to notice.

He called his dogs forward to scare Aress off as he had done dozens of times before. But Aress was gone by the time they came up. They caught the scent of his dog and were then out of Abe's control. He tried calling them back as they galloped over the crest. It didn't take long for the slaughter to begin and end.

Wasn't much to go around between three dogs. Still, the sport of it kept them riled as they tore through the field and fought hard over the tiniest bits and pieces. Abe couldn't say he was sorry about it. Having a pint-sized dog out here was no smarter than having pint-sized kids. At least the boys he could talk to, scare them a little, maybe make their dad think twice. Didn't seem to be working. Aress could live where he wanted but he had no business trying to be a neighbor. The dogs were the fence between them, and smart men knew never to cross fences.

Seventeen

Except for Ricky's steady needling of Jeremy, the meal was worse than quiet; it was edgy. With no cable on the island there was little to do after dinner but talk. When that failed, the two women read, Phil napped, the boys needled, and Trent reflected.

There was nothing wrong in his plan or his planning. It was still a great opportunity for the boys, to grow up on an island. Already they were reaping its benefits; their mother confessed as much. The trouble with the islanders was the cost of doing business; what occurred with Carver was unforeseeable. Trent was experienced enough to know that for every problem there was *not* always a solution, least one he could direct. So, at times punting was the only option. Despite this good advice, it wasn't an option he was going to take.

Shortly after he planted the rat poison and Mop was dismantled, there was a noticeable decline in dog activity. For four days after there was none at all. And not a word from Carver. No visit, no cops, no shotgun blast across his cabins. It had Trent feeling more than satisfied of victory. It wasn't a subject he broached even obliquely with Tabitha. The loss of Mop still stung and talk of dogs, even nasty ones, made her bleed all sorts of pain and angst. But then it started up again on that fifth night. He wasn't sure if Carver had a pack of two, three, or more. He had no clue as to how many had died, if any, or if they just turned ill. Or if these dogs were new or the others had been treated and returned. Or, a combination of the above.

Tabitha reacted as if she never heard them stop. When they began again that night during dinner, she and the boys turned their faces toward the sounds then resumed eating, almost in unison, without a word said, as if acknowledging their existence would cause further disaster. It was, Trent felt looking at it now, as if the dogs were no longer simple tools used by Carver but rather masters in their own right, capable of dictating absolute obedience by virtue of their mere presence.

Phil and Jeanine were both fast asleep now, Tabitha drifting. The dogs were baying a good ways down the beach, barely audible, but Phil's snoring was a close substitute. The boys were nowhere to be seen and it gave Trent a start, fearing they had headed outside. But Trent heard them on the staircase, behind the wall that separated them from living room. He crept close to catch their murmurings.

"Wooo," Jeremy was saying, "hear that?"

"That was just you," Ricky said.

"Wait, listen again." There was a period of silence where Trent listened, as well.

"There, right there, hear it?" Jeremy said.

"Yeah, the ghosts," Ricky said.

"Think so?"

"Could be."

"Know what I think," Jeremy said, "I think that's Abe making that noise. 'Member how old and scary and creepy he was?"

"So."

"Just like a ghost."

"Okay, if that's Abe-the-Ghost making all that noise, then what noise are the dogs making?"

"Well, maybe ... what if ... there are no dogs. It's only Abe and there aren't any dogs."

"That's crazy. Dad's seen them, and mom ... you hear them fighting all the time about it."

"Hey," Jeremy shouted loud enough to make Trent jump, "what if Abe is the ghost *and* the dogs, too?"

"No."

"Yeah? Well, what if old man Abe turns into one, like a werewolf?"

Later, when Ricky was sound asleep, Jeremy lay in bed thinking well into the night. He wished he could be like the rest of them, easy to sleep. He fell asleep late and didn't sleep long. He didn't like this place, not as much as he pretended. He did it to keep his father happy, and to not look like he was siding with his mother to gang up on him, and to not look chicken. It was a lot of things. There were no friends. There was no real school. His parents fought all the time now. His mother rarely smiled. But mostly, it was the ghosts.

Talk of ghosts was forbidden by his father and laughed at by his brother. And so he hadn't mentioned it, no matter what he heard and felt. He didn't speak of the howling that was not winds and not wild dogs. Mop wasn't dead. She was part of the island now and was telling him things.

This place is not right. It wants to be left alone. He didn't need to hear it from his mother, or the creepy Abe Carver. He didn't need to see it in the eyes of the people at the store. How could the others not feel it? They were not wanted here. His mother knew it, but it was more a matter of *her* not wanting to be here. Didn't she know she had no choice?

He wondered what really happened to Mop. Ricky now believed she simply wandered off and was swallowed up by the ocean as their father had said. After all, it was something Ricky could have done. But Mop was more like Jeremy, shy and skittish, neither prone to wandering off. As painful as it was to contemplate, Jeremy could see his father leaving Mop outside. Not by design, but the motel, and now the neighbor, seemed to dominate his attention. It would be easy to overlook something as small as Mop.

Jeremy's awareness intensified as his father's waned. He attuned himself to the schism between his parents. Not their words, they were easy to understand, but their movements. His mother's mimicked those of a mime stuck in a box while his father's were trance-like, his entire being an out-of-body experience. He was, to Jeremy's horror, like the island ghosts of his nightmares.

"Gonna be a cold, cold winter, Missus Aress," Hack Corlin said as the family boarded the ferry.

"Colder than it already is?"

"Oh, yeah, much colder, so says the Almanac if you can believe that stuff. Got hot chocolate down below and tell the boys there's some marshmallows in the cabinet beside the fridge." He leaned nearer to her ear. "Save 'em for myself, mostly."

She passed, but told the boys about the hot chocolate, figuring the boiling would probably burn off anything infectious. She wasn't comfortable with anything solid so didn't mention the marshmallows. "The pilot said it was going to be real cold this year, said he read it in the Farmer's Almanac," she told Trent sarcastically when Corlin went to cast off.

"Guess it is then."

"Yeah, well, not real comfortable riding in a boat driven by a man who believes medieval astronomy over the Weather Channel."

They were heading to the mainland to rent a car for Trent while she and the boys were in Virginia. Trent made it clear he wasn't going. They had grown more distant in the past few weeks. Very distant. Since the last tourists left the only enduring talks they had ran the gamut about the motel. She railed while he made his plans in great detail, and then made constant adjustments. They consisted of establishing gardens, planting a hedgerow around the cabins, a white picket fence along the roadway, the patio under the lighthouse. And there was the on-going advertising campaign for which he was reaching out to big firms as far south as New York now. For a time, she was waiting for him to announce the money for such things was gone. That never happened. Seems that stream was as endless as his commitment.

Then came the day the planning stopped. It was around the time the dogs began again to patrol the ridgeline. Maybe it was just his articulation of them that ceased. Maybe he was tired of her rolled eyes, her deep sighs, and her general dismissiveness. But then even his topical magazines and books went untouched. She conducted an experiment by stacking them into a closet, waiting for him to explode. Nothing. Whenever Trent left the house, she knew where to find him, especially near sunset. He'd walk the coastline from end to end of their property. He formed the loneliest image, so small against the boulders just beyond, so insignificant before the thunderous waves. At times he'd stop, listening for the dogs, even when there was no sound but for the unrelenting ocean.

He retreated further after her parents' visit, still refusing to believe it wasn't her idea. He didn't get into her face over it. It was his silent treatment technique. Not the one where he'd ignore her. Instead, he would nod and bite the inside of his lip, showing her he was paying attention but wasn't buying it. It was infuriating, and it didn't make what she had to tell them him easy.

"What do you say we turn the tables and surprise them at Christmas," she said.

He nodded and chewed his bottom lip.

"Things are slow; we ... er ... you, can use the break."

Trent never made mention of the barbed discussion he had with her father. It was her mother who told her. Her father was beyond furious and threatened to take them all off the island that day.

"I want to leave," she told her parents, "But I can't. It's not the right time."

Her parents demanded to know when the right time would be. She told them truthfully; she didn't know. During the holidays was unthinkable. But wait too long into the spring, when he was prepping in earnest for the season, would be heartless.

"You want, you go," Trent told her.

"I can't leave you back here."

"I'm a big boy."

"But at Christmas, and the boys." She looked woefully at him, as if this was the beginning of a last farewell.

It was now three days before Christmas. The drive to Virginia they could do in two. Corlin asked when they were returning. Trent looked to Tabitha, as he and Corlin awaited her answer. "I haven't decided." She stared at Trent, awaiting an order or a suggestion, but he said nothing and left to join the boys below. "I don't know," she told Corlin, "By the third at the latest. Why? Won't you be running?"

"Depends. The Almanac gives or takes a couple of weeks. Might get the freeze over as early as New Year's Day or by the fifteenth."

"You believe in all that?"

"Didn't use to. Gettin' stuck in a couple of Nor'easters will make ya, though."

"I guess I should take a number where I can reach you," she said.

"Be smart, considering never can trust cell phone service out there," he said, nodding to the now distant island. "And give me yours so I can let you know if you'll be needing to come north sooner. You are planning on coming back north?"

"I said I was, why wouldn't I?"

Corlin curled his lower lip. "No reason, I guess. I'll get you my business card."

"Mister Corlin?" she said as he turned.

"It's Hack."

She peered down the ladder into the below compartment, insuring Trent and the boys were still out of earshot. "Hack, do you ... hear things about us?"

He removed his New York Mets cap and scratched his balding scalp. "Well, I suppose I hear lots of things about lots of people."

"Please, don't be coy, you know what I mean."

"Not sure I do. Do they like you and but not the motel idea, that it?

"For starters."

"Seems like you're ready for some straight talk so here it is. Your old man is cocky and self-centered. You're aloof and self-centered. That lighthouse is an eyesore, and the motel is an intrusion."

Tabitha didn't ruffle. "I hear a theme here."

"Does it surprise you?"

"Not at all. I have been aloof, and it has been self-serving. Anything nice to report?"

"You got great legs." He shrugged. "Just something else I've been hearing when the women aren't around. Think, ah ... your husband would be surprised?"

"Better not be about my legs. But he may take issue with the character cracks. It wouldn't change his mind about staying, though."

"Well, I wouldn't worry much about the comments, Missus Aress. Some of the greatest ventures started out as misadventures. Like I told your old, I mean Mister Aress, new things here become old things pretty quick. It's the novelty they don't like. I wasn't a favorite myself back when."

In Bangor, after dinner at *The Fiddlehead,* Trent bought a slightly used Dodge Ram pick-up.

"What happened to the little economy car you were going to rent?" Tabitha asked.

"I never said I was renting economy."

"But this?"

"You heard the man, bad winter. "'Sides, I need it for hauling."

"Again, don't want to know what, and again, the dumb question ... can we afford it?"

"Yes."

"Of course, we can." She offered her tight-lipped grin. "Sure, you'll be okay? Our first Christmas apart."

"I'll be fine; you'll be fine."

"Not lonely?"

"Course I will be."

"What will you do?"

"I've been thinking about getting new carpet for the motel rooms and painting the cabin walls. This'll give me a good start. Matter of fact, I'll check out carpet on my way back."

Tabitha wasn't so sure. On the drive south she questioned her decision not to tell him what she heard from Hack Corlin. She said he wouldn't care, that it wouldn't change his plans. But perhaps it would if he knew for sure. Worse than that, she knew if anything was to happen to him, an accident or the weather, there was no one there to give a damn.

Shortly after they parted, she called his cell phone but there was no answer. Not surprising, he probably left it home since he hadn't received a call in months. She'd give it a few hours, give him time to get home. Maybe it wouldn't change his mind, maybe nothing would. But her arguments had failed to move him, maybe a stranger is what it would take.

A trip to a carpet store was not on Trent's agenda for tonight. He had been mulling over this next move for months, never thinking he'd have the opportunity. The family being gone was the one he needed.

He never let himself be driven by untested desires. He never gave into that near-psychotic approach to problems, that inner-voice that kicked and screamed and shot first. But this, this idea, was so bizarre it frightened him. That he was capable of envisioning it was certainly a step in the wrong direction, one he could well be incapable of returning from.

The ferry was making its last trip of the night. Corlin was on the deck, directing the three vehicles loading up. Trent parked beside the ferry, ignoring Corlin's arm gestures to board. Trent bid him to approach the truck. "You boarding or what?" Corlin asked when he got to within earshot of the window.

"Not tonight. I need you to tell me where Dutch's place is."

Eighteen

"Why?

"Just need to see him."

"No. That man has nothing you need."

"Now how would you know?"

"Mister Aress, Dutch is about one thing, and it's not selling family dogs to good homes."

"Corlin, just point me in the right direction."

"I'm trying to."

Trent had met the man and seen his dogs. Both disturbed him greatly. Corlin was telling him nothing he didn't at least suspect, that Dutch raised and sold his dogs for one task, fighting. As Corlin said, Dutch didn't advertise them as such. They were "guard dogs," but the line between the two was a fine one. No, Corlin had no direct knowledge. If he did, he would certainly use it against the man he referred to as evil. But he had ferried enough of his customers to the island and brought back enough of his dogs. If not for the extra money Dutch paid, Corlin would honor his conscience.

Trent was not dissuaded. He knew what he was getting into. Corlin didn't have an address but sent Trent to a man who would. He sent him back through Nuthatch Cove then north for four miles to Thorpe Road. Two lefts later he'd fine Taig's Auto and Truck Salvage. "Alvin Taig's his best buddy," Corlin told him. "Get there before dark when Taig puts his dogs out, see if you still wanna get involved after that."

He found the yard just as the sun was setting. It sat in a bowl behind the main road with acres of rust and junk as far back as Trent could see. Even on the back hillside, metal hulks hung precariously like Kudzu. Over the eight-foot chained-linked fence, he saw the snow and mud-covered corridors that meandered throughout the yard. The dogs howled though he could see no customers in the yard. He supposed it was him the dogs had alerted on.

He had never feared nature, but as of late, the cold and the snarling dogs were getting to him. The yard had at least five of them that were scattering now, searching out his scent, as he rolled down the window, peering through the dark for an entrance to the building. A man he suspected to be Alvin Taig came out to find the cause of his animals' consternation. He eyeballed Trent hard as the truck rolled forward. As he neared the man, he had no doubt it was Taig; he had the kind of face that could only belong to Dutch's best friend. Trent reflexively looked for a rifle but saw none. It didn't comfort him much; Taig could be a handgun guy. Got a minute?" Trent called over to him.

Taig didn't speak, just cocked his head, and squinted into the car.

"Need to get hold of Dutch."

Taig closed in. He shuffled like an old gold prospector, hunched over from years in the mine. "Who?"

"Dutch."

"No, who are you?"

"I live on the island. Met Dutch there, said I should call him."

Skittishly, Taig ducked his head through the window. One gray eye flashed around the cab while the other stayed on Trent. It was glass with no life behind it. Though creepy considering the scene around him, Trent found it mesmerizing, as if he was dealing with two men, one dead, one crazy. Taig shook his head. "Don't know you."

"I know. I was told you know where I can find Dutch. Do you?"

He ran his tongue across his two bottom teeth. "What fer?"

"That's not your business. Can you, or can't you?"

He nodded. "Gotta name?"

"Trent. Trent with the motel."

"Wait here."

Alvin Taig seemed crazy enough to be paranoid for no reason, but if what Corlin said was true, it could be his suspicion kicking in. *I'm not a cop,* he wanted to tell him, but paranoia, real or imagined, can be a good thing, long as it's not your own.

The dogs found him. There were six, their snouts oozing juices through the chain links. He left the truck so as to peer around the rear fender at them. He surveyed the fence line to ensure its integrity. Still, though satisfied the barrier was safe, he dared to venture no further. He didn't know dogs, not dogs like these. He knew dogs sold in pet stores to old women who lived in apartments; dogs that crawled up to your lap to lick your face, dogs that wrestled with squeaky toys. These dogs were like bikers, with names like Spike and Psycho and Hammer, or maybe no name at all. They were thick and hairy with tails that dragged, and fur matted with crusted fluids. They pushed their way into the fence looking for a way to break through to devour him. They were Shepherds, Pit bulls, Boxers, and mad mixes stirred together in a cauldron by some sinister creature, a creature Trent was about to make a deal with.

Guard dogs, my ass, Trent muttered. It hit him that nasty Mister Taig may get a bad notion and release his dogs on him. He hustled back into the truck just as Taig came out the door and called to him. "Be here in a few," he said. "Wants you waitin' inside."

There was nowhere to sit. The upholstered chairs that weren't overflowing with car parts were covered with oil, grease, and such. Trent stood, unwilling to make himself at home. "Coffee?" Taig offered.

"No. Thanks. What did Dutch say?"

Taig poured himself a mug. It was hours old; Trent could smell it. "Said to come in. Wait."

"I mean about me."

"Nuthin'. Just kinda laughed."

"Laughed?"

"Sit, ya want. Move some of that shit."

Trent continued to stand. He heard the dogs now sniffing and clawing at the back door which he supposed led to the yard. He didn't get the sense they were wanting to protect their master. It was more probable they wanted to rip them both to rags. "Those Dutch's dogs?" he asked.

"My dogs."

"I mean, did you get them from Dutch?"

"Me? Nah."

He found himself on an island, the pun unintended. Now it was sinking. With Tabitha and the boys gone he was willing to sink with it, to depths he had never gone to before. He was in the very darkest part of this world he barely knew. It didn't really matter if Corlin was right about Dutch and his dogs because in his heart, Trent was hoping he was. That laugh Taig mentioned, Trent knew its meaning. It was to welcome him in.

The dogs were making him nervous. Taig was making him nervous. Standing was making him nervous. He pulled an air filter, distributor cap, and manifold cover off a chair and sat. Ten minutes later a truck's headlights creased the window behind Taig's head. Taig didn't move, telling Trent it had to be Dutch. To say he was relieved just went to show how nerve-racking it was to be alone with Taig.

Dutch came in with a sordid grin, the type Trent envisioned him wearing when he took the call from Taig. He hadn't time to close the door when Trent was on him. "We'll talk in my truck," he said, pushing past him.

The dogs were still at it as Trent got into the cab. He was about to burst from the maniacal yelping as his stomach knotted and the blood ricocheted through his skull. "Got any that don't go on like that all the fuckin' time?" he said to Dutch when he got in.

"What? The dogs?" He laughed. "You want dogs that don't make noise you're comin' to the wrong guy."

"Musta heard," Trent said, "My dog was killed."

Dutch was non-committal per his custom on such matters.

Trent squirmed in the seat. "I was thinking, nothing as vicious as these things, but maybe you got something for me?"

"Why?"

"Thought you made it a point never to ask?"

"I don't ask what you're gonna do with 'em, just why you want 'em."

"I don't see a difference."

"You want 'em so you can sit by the fire and rub their bellies, ain't gonna happen. You want 'em to cuddle with you, the missus, and the kids in bed at night, ain't gonna get that neither."

"Like you said, guard dogs for my place."

Dutch nodded then smiled almost pleasantly.

"What's the cloak and dagger routine with creepy Alvin in there?" Trent asked.

"We all need our guard dogs, Mister Aress."

Nineteen

Trent followed Dutch along the darkest road he had ever seen outside a nightmare. Whatever might go on out here was sure to stay a mystery, murder included. It took forty minutes to arrive at a dark pole barn. He followed Dutch past it to a double-wide with a yellow porch light.

Without a word being said the two walked back to the pole barn amidst the now familiar sounds of snarling dogs. Dutch pulled a large ring of keys from his coat pocket. As he unlocked the three padlocks he asked, "Your wife, she okay with this?"

"Yeah. Yeah, she's okay with it."

Dutch, bent over as he worked on the bottom lock, peered up and squinted at Trent. The vapor from his breath, the dull light, and his grizzled face put Trent on the English moors in an old horror flick. "Sure?" Dutch said.

"You really care?"

He snapped the lock open and pulled it free from the hasp. "Nope."

Their entry into the pole barn brought the decibel level to nauseating depths. Dutch turned on the three rows of florescent lights that illuminated the packs of dogs in stages. He waited for the scene to be set while Trent stood nervously behind him.

Dutch began to walk the floor. There were rows of cages, some woefully small for the size dog it held. Trent made a quick estimate based upon the configuration and came up with fifty to sixty cages. "You've never handle anything like this," Dutch yelled above the snarling beasts. "Kinda like an Indy car versus a Ford Escort, takes some getting used to."

There was no way Trent would be able to control one of these animals. His plan was to get three, tie them up outside to a post, and put a salvage Army tent over them. It would just be for the winter, enough to let Carver know he was ready to match him dog-for-dog. But three was going to be too many, a post not going to hold them, and a single tent not going to work.

The echo of snarls and growls bounced off the corrugated walls. Not one dog sat back to allow the sights and sounds to go on around it. They strained mightily as they pressed against their cages. But these animals weren't striving for his affection. That instinct had long ago been torn from them, or perhaps for these animals, never was. They fumed as the men approached. They snorted and rattled their cages with head butts. Some tore at the bars with broken teeth. Their eyes blasted ice shards and reflected no recognition of them as anything other than a danger. Their duty in life was to defy, to challenge, to distrust. Passing, Trent felt the heat from their breath at his legs. He didn't know if anger was an emotion of animals. Maybe rage. And though it was part of their wild nature, it took men like Dutch to nurture it into something more malevolent.

He pulled Dutch's arm to get his attention. "These dogs ever get out?"

"Huh?"

"Out." He pointed at the back wall of the barn. "Exercise, play?"

Dutch laughed. "Yeah, play. They play real nice." He added something but Trent couldn't make it out. He shook his head and motioned to the outside.

Dutch brought him to the double wide where it was quieter but only slightly warmer. "Beer?" he asked.

"No."

Dutch was a momentary necessity, like an emergency visit to the dentist. He wanted no small talk. The sooner he was out, and on his way, the better. This wasn't a world he wanted to get used to. Standing outside the pole barn while Dutch opened it, Trent recalled frigid days playing pond hockey as a kid, where the sting on his cheeks and in his nostrils was invigorating. Here, he found it suffocating, like being shoved into a freezer chest.

Dutch opened a bottle of Alagash Black. He flipped the cap onto the countertop and fell back into a worn-out armchair. Trent waited for him to take half the bottle in one gulp. "How much?" he asked. "For two?"

"Depends. Like cars. Depends on what model."

"It's nuthin' like cars. You can't tell one of yours apart from one of Taigs."

"Or one of Carver's?"

"It's not like I'm buying a sled dog here. Their just wild animals and most look worse for the wear so stop bullshittin' me like you got something special to offer."

"If it ain't nuthin' special then why you comin' to me? Lots of little pups you can get at the Mall."

Trent glared impatiently, but old Dutch just wiggled himself into the comfort spot of the chair. "Aress, you're missing the big picture here. My dogs, they *are* special, very special, and you'd better know that comin' in."

Dutch leaned forward. "Go back down to the barn and poke around. Go put your face against them cages. Maybe reach in to give 'em a pat. Go 'head, you just do that." He settled back down as Trent contemplated his next move. Dutch finished the beer and stuck the empty between his thighs. It was sleeting now, the hard rain slapping against the aluminum box.

"I don't need 'em for long, how much to lease?"

Dutch laughed. "For someone who claims they ain't like cars you seem to think I deal 'em like they are."

"Fine, how much?"

"Mister Aress, I don't think you're—"

"Your most expensive dogs, damn it, how much?"

"Well, I think I know what you want. I think I got what you want. But you tell me and then we'll get to work."

Trent took that beer. And two more as he listened to Dutch describe the feeding and care of the dogs. "They're all different," he said, "and I'd be bullshittin' if I told ya I know how each of 'em are with strangers and each other. Some of 'em are wild and others are too wild, is the best way to describe it. You start thinking of 'em as pets, you're doomed. You control 'em the same way you do a forest fire. There's no part way, keep at it and keep it contained. Never turn your back 'cause it comes at you from all sides, know what I mean?"

Hell no, Trent had no clue. He would have left in a panic had Dutch not touched on certain hot-button issues. "They been trained for one thing," Dutch stated matter-of-factly, "and they'll do it. How well?" He shrugged. "Some have been there and survived. Some, barely. Others are waiting. How much will it cost? Depends on the type, like I told ya."

Dutch offered to help train him on handling strategies. He was reluctant to have Dutch on his property. He supposed it was no different than having a plumber or drywaller, but somehow, it was very different.

Dutch wanted to know where they'd be housed and fed, and how much contact they'd have with Tabitha and the boys. None at all, would be about right, Dutch advised. Then he wanted to see the cabin Trent had in mind. It was the smallest one with the stove, refrigerator, and bathroom fixtures he hadn't yet updated. It was also the one the college kids used so the carpet needed replacing and a crack in the wallboard needed attention.

Trent took two dogs for $2,500 each. They were both pit bulls, just under two years old. Neither had injuries. Trent took his word for that but could see from a distance there were no obvious scars. "They're both prospects," Dutch said. "Got game. This one here," he said pointing to the larger one, "had her in The Keep awhile back."

"The Keep, what's that?"

"Training."

Dutch took the two out of the cages and both sat staring back at their cages then up at the two men. Trent looked to Dutch. "They're confused," Dutch said.

"They gonna get along?"

"If you do what I tell ya, they should. Like I said, don't assume nuthin'; they got some breedin' in 'em."

Dutch delivered them the next morning, and for the next two days he worked with Trent and the dogs. They were every bit the handful Dutch said they'd be. Trent was given lessons on how to keep them calm and controlled. It wasn't done with pats and soothing tones. Dutch threw in a couple of thirty-five-pound chains which were bolted into the cross beams at either end of the room. Their lengths were such that the dogs could get to within just two feet of each other. And a truck tire was hung on a red spruce, high enough for the dogs to grab onto and drag their hind legs. Dutch brought in a half dozen rabbits and tied a hind leg on a long rope one at a time between the two chained dogs.

Trent was sickened by the barbaric scenes that were structured for one, disturbing purpose. But in his mind, it would be over and done before Tabitha and the boys came home. He would set the two dogs loose at dusk when Carver's dogs were roaming the ridge lines. Carver would give up his antics, and next summer would be the promise he made to himself. His family would never know. He'd remove the chains and tire, clean the blood, send the dogs back. The means were of no consequence for the ends were never in doubt. He was in the right, and it never occurred to him that Abe Carver could believe he was, as well.

Twenty

Hack Corlin was right, or at least close enough. The end of December was brutally cold and the wind off the coast was relentless. Trent couldn't hear Carver's dogs and worried Carver was keeping them chained nearer the house since there was no need to disrupt the flow of guests to the motel. That would make having his own dogs useless, just a drain on his time and finances. There wasn't time to wait.

He spoke with Tabitha and the boys on Christmas. The plan was for them to return on the third of January. Trent tried to fend her off by telling her she may want to wait, with the weather being so iffy, but it nearly backfired when she offered to come back earlier.

He decided a proactive approach was needed. It was a strategy his old boss used when the other side was uncooperative. And in doing so he was fond of issuing the command, "release the hound." It was no longer a metaphor.

It was a ray of hope for Tabitha in an otherwise dismal Christmas season. Thoughts of returning to the island caused her nightmares and day sweats. Her parents empathized, having spent time there. Part of her savored their sympathy while it caused consternation on another level. It wouldn't take much to push her over the edge, make her and the boys stay, forcing Trent to make a decision, them or the dream. While her mother subtly nudged, her father violently shoved.

"He's lost touch," became her father's catch phrase, and her mother agreed to an extent.

"It's not like he's crazy," she'd say, "just ... confused."

"He's not confused. He knows what he wants," he pushed back, "and to hell with anyone else. I'm telling you it's like a wife beater, once down that road, they don't turn back. If I knew this about him from the start, I'd have stopped the wedding."

"Oh, cut that out, Phil, you'd have done no such thing."

"Oh, wouldn't I now?"

For her part Tabitha agreed with neither of them. She was too concerned with keeping Jeremy and Ricky out of earshot. But she had her own mind on the issue. An ultimatum was in order. Of course, Trent would have answers, a plan, more options, so if she was to issue an ultimatum if would have to be just that. It would take a reckless disregard for the sanctity of marriage and family for her to not return to him, but she was willing to do it. A sinister weather report would have made it so much more convenient.

She'd think on it. Amidst the holiday visits with friends and relatives, the boys' sugar buzzes and late nights, and the horrendous traffic, she'd find time to give it her attention. She'd filter out all the criticisms from her parents, the concerned looks of relatives, the sideward glances from here friends. She could tell them it was fine, really, the island was wondrous and peaceful, the boys were thriving, and she, well, she was adjusting. But she didn't think she had it in her any longer.

Trent spent the first few days working with the dogs. He mimicked what Dutch had done with the chains and tire, foregoing the rabbit exercises. He was right, they were civil to each other, nearly apathetic. The only mixing between the two was when he brought the food. As an exercise to control them, he tied each to a hundred-foot rope and let them run the yard. He lured them back with a whistle and ham bones, two dozen of which he picked up on the mainland from a source Dutch turned him onto.

Still, Carver's dogs were nowhere to be seen or heard. He walked the ridgeline at various times of the day, hoping to come across them. If he couldn't deploy his dogs soon, he'd have to get rid of them, sell them back to Dutch for half of what he paid.

Returning from a morning surveillance he spotted a red F-150 on the road at the house. He quickened his pace for fear whoever it was would come down to the cabins. It was Hack Corlin, coming around the side as Trent arrived. "Knocked but didn't get an answer," Corlin said, stating the obvious.

"Well, it's just me home right now." Trent continued his walk to the front of the house.

"Yeah. Seems like a few folks I was expected to be ferrying haven't made an appearance."

"Cold, wanna step in?"

Corlin obliged.

"Coffee?"

"Why not. Startin' to freeze up the crossing, just like they said it would."

Hard for Corlin to tell what Trent meant by offering shelter and coffee. He didn't seem to want company, and neither the weather report nor his ferry manifest seemed to hold much interest for him. Corlin took a seat at the kitchen table at the back window overlooking the cottages and ocean rocks. The wind was rustling up some ferocious spray. The sea water that didn't make it back to the ocean hung in icy strips like paper machè on the boulders.

"If you get to talk to her, might wanna tell her that," he told Trent.

"What? About the weather? If it delays her a while that's fine."

That took Corlin by surprise. The Aress's didn't seem the type, the type like him and his ex who could easily dismiss one another for days and weeks on end. "Could be more than just a while, could be weeks." He pointed out back. "That wind stops whippin' like it's supposed to, and the temps stay in the negatives like they are, ice comes in to stay. It gets too thick I can't move. Already getting a substantial plate of it."

"Well, what is it you want me to do?"

"Just sayin'."

"Black all right? The milk's gone sour."

Trent didn't sit. He stood looking out the window. "That's life on an island, right," he said. "It's rough. It takes a special type of person."

"Different maybe, not necessarily special."

"People go too far out of their way to avoid things like this," Trent said. "Back in Virginia, in my old neighborhood, I'd stand at my window like this at quarter to six in the morning to watch seven garage doors go up, and seven luxury cars and SUV's all start up remotely. Those candy-asses couldn't bear to even sit in a garage in a cold car for two minutes."

"Know the type. I don't suspect those people thought about much else in terms of lifestyle, least of all changing them substantially like you have," Corlin offered.

Already Corlin noticed the winds starting to fade, and that wasn't good. "So, like I was saying, I was expecting some return fares that didn't show."

"Yeah, we talked about that, remember?"

"I'm talking about Dutch."

Trent turned. "What about him?"

"He came over with you a few days ago and hasn't gone back. Doesn't usually do that."

"Maybe he took a boat back with someone?"

"Nobody takin' their boat out in this. And that would mean leaving his good truck over here, wouldn't do that in winter. Haven't seen him, have you?"

"Not since that first day; he came over the house for a few hours."

"Hmm, he's not the visiting type. Then he drove out in his own truck, by himself?"

"In his own truck, all by himself. What's up, Corlin, you been deputized to find a missing person?"

Hack shook his head and smiled. "No, no, still just a ferry boat pilot here. But when you got the only source to get on and off the island, you don't miss much."

Trent emptied his coffee mug and put it on the table. He dug his hands into his pants pockets and hunched his shoulders against the perennial cold that blasted past the window at this spot. "Corlin, just what is it you think you're not missing?"

"Like I told ya, Dutch hasn't been —"

"Yeah, been brought back to the mainland on your ferry, but what is it you're implying?"

Corlin cocked his head as he recognized where Trent was going. "Implying? You think I'm sayin' you ... I mean, you think I suspect something happened to old Dutch? Like something bad? Something you might have done? First off, and no offense to your manhood, but unless you got the drop, you're no match for him. Second, Dutch is a strange bird all right, but he's predictably strange. He comes and goes on the same day. Always. You saw that first time you met 'im. What I mean here is, yeah, I know he stayed on the island. Just curious as to why."

"Can't help you there. Seems to me Dutch is his own man who comes and goes as he pleases."

"True enough."

Corlin finished his coffee with a heavy sigh. He held onto the cup, massaging it gently with his thick, grease-stained fingers as he looked casually out the window. Trent looked for signs that he was noticing things out of the ordinary, such as the muddied snow surrounding the area of the hanging truck tire.

Hack had no trouble sitting in silence. He appeared able to pick up on the sounds. The distant waves, the circling winds, creaks, and groans of old wood. Trent supposed it had much to do with being a ferry boat pilot, bolstered by his prior avocation as a sailor.

Corlin snapped the silence. "Why not go to Cape Cod? Long Island? Kennebunk? Somewhere it'll matter, and frankly, someplace right for a wife and kids?"

"We back on that, why am I here? First off, that's where everyone goes to try to make a name for themselves."

"And the second part is?"

"I like it here."

"Not because you're afraid of competition?"

"Not it at all. It's just about what I like and where there's a need. Simple. And I like my name up on that lighthouse sign board. Like you, I want people to know me, to know I was here."

"I don't have my name on the ferry."

"You should."

"Nuthatch Ferry Service is fine for me." Corlin pursed his lips. "I can see the point though, but the question bigger than what and where is *why?* Why the need? Now a ferry, that's a need here. Didn't have to be me, could been one of a dozen folks, I guess. But a motel where there're no overnight visitors, that's a stretch, don't ya think?"

"No."

"To folks like you, the end of summer means death for an island. Tourists leave, ice cream shops close, hotels lower their rates, restaurants reduce their hours. But on a place like this, everything has a purpose of its own. It's not like an ecological chain, like if one farm fails, they all do, or if *Trugards* goes under another store can't take its place. But it's all ... economical. Just need you to know, Stryker John's a place to forget and be forgotten. No one starts here, they just go on. Know what I'm saying?"

"Yeah. That you were either sent here by my wife or the islanders to get me to close up shop."

Corlin let go a genuine laugh, more authentic that the tight-lipped smiles he'd been giving up to this point. "Me? Offering advice on family matters? Or an ambassador for the Strykers? Now that *would* be different. But ... it did kinda strike me as strange you didn't go south for the holidays with your family."

"Neither did you."

"Going *to* them is different than going *with* them."

"You don't mind, I have work to do here; good time when there are no distractions."

"Those dogs you and Dutch brought over ... weren't his now, were they?

Twenty-One

"Too much activity out back for two little boys," Corlin said. "And it's snowed since they left."

So, he had noticed. And his mind was working on it. It was the motive for his coming. Not the weather, not the concerns for his family, not the question-and-answer session on the motel. He'd make a good lobbyist. He was patient, a good listener, and manipulated the conversation with ease. Then again, he was a businessman at heart.

Trent could deny it, like a child confessing innocence for breaking a window. He could ignore the comment or straight out tell Corlin to go to hell. But hostility worked best when there was an escape route. Here, he had none. "There a problem with that?" was the best he could manage and it frustrated him that he had allowed himself to be caught off guard.

"Yeah, Corlin said. "I told you there was. Like I said, I hear a lot and I can tell you Dutch is being watched."

"By who?"

"By the county and probably State Police. Which means you may be in their sights now. I don't know what your plans are with them, but I do know what those dogs do. I like you, Mister Aress. I like your family. You mean them well and I think you have a good heart. But somehow ... this island's getting the better of you."

Trent took a deep breath, held it, and worked his lower lip along his teeth. He stared down, nodded, and worked his hands into loose fists. He found himself giving off the signals of vulnerability he schemed others into. "This got anything to do with the beef you got with Abe Carver?" Trent asked.

"I have no beef with him," Corlin said.

"Not what I hear. You know, Corlin, that old ferry of yours ain't nuthin' more than a Farmer's Almanac of legends and myths when it comes to reality."

"Been right enough in my experience."

"Like I said, I got work to do." Trent walked away.

"You can't handle those dogs." Corlin called to him. "Nobody can. I've seen it firsthand. Hell, Dutch can't. Says he can but he can't. That's the way he's made them, and the worst of it, he doesn't give a shit. You get hurt, dog gets hurt, no business of his. No insurance policies on it; no one's gonna call in the cops. It's dirty business. He's dirty. He's got one thing on his mind, and you and I have been there. We know how twisted it can make a man."

When Corlin left, he did so without another word, as if to let his warning sink in in its own time. Trent went back to the window. How obvious the scene before him was, even to someone not looking for it. He shouldn't have let him in. He should have carried on the conversation outside where two minutes, four tops, would have done them both in.

He waited twenty minutes to ensure Corlin wasn't circling back. Why he would and why Trent was concerned made no logical sense. The dogs howled as he approached. They were getting hungry. He went to the shed where the dog food was stored, then gave thought to tonight being as good a time as any to let them loose on Carver. It would be dark within an hour; the dogs would be that much hungrier, more aggressive and loud. He'd stake them to anchor points on the ridgeline further down the beach, closer to Carver's house. Maybe his sheep would be wandering about, putting the dogs into a frenzy wild enough to alert Carver.

When he released them they went straight to the shed. Already they learned where their food came from. He'd have to do this more often, starve them, then perhaps bring the rabbits in, and let them hunt. Nothing makes him bad-tempered like an empty stomach. Same for dogs, he reasoned.

He grabbed the six-foot steel rod he found while cleaning out the cabins, one of the many items he didn't throw out for no obvious reason. He hadn't a reason to use it on the dogs yet. The sound of it flush against the cabin walls and even against the tire was enough to subdue them for a short time. When they settled down enough to be approached, he attached the chains to their choke collars and led them off like Blood Hounds put on a scent.

He knew securing anything substantial into the frozen ground would be near impossible. In anticipation of this he brought along a couple of crowbars to wedge into suitable rock piles. The dogs caught a scent. Could have been anything from Carver's dogs, his sheep, or the scattered remains of Mop, and it was all he could do to not have himself dragged over the rocks like a downed kite as they made their mad rush up the ridge. He threw a ham bone down to keep them busy while he wedged in the crowbar and fastened the chains to them. When that was done, for good measure he tossed a bone just outside their reach.

He heard their wild calls as he made his way back to the house. He certainly couldn't distinguish their yapping from any other dogs, but he knew Carver would. His cell phone rang which surprised him as the service had been getting seriously weak of late. It was Tabitha. The connection came in and out, making her voice stammer. He had her hold on until he got out of the wind.

"Where are you?" she asked.

"Painting. Just coming back from the rooms. Windy and cold, I could barely hear you."

"What else is new?

"How are the boys?"

"Fine. Me too if you're asking."

"Course."

"Trent, I'm thinking about things, about not returning. Not right away."

"But for the season?"

The lack of a response on her end could have been her not having one or the poor connection. "You hear me, Tabitha? You'll be back for the season?"

Her answer was a garble with the only recognizable word being "why."

"Why what? Why come back?"

What he got next was another string of disruptive discourse with words and phrases centered around the boys schooling, their social development, and her father. That set him off. "Stay then," he yelled. "Stay back there with mom and dad where it's warm and safe. But let me remind you how much you idolize those big-shot captains of industry and politicians I had to work with; those same people I came to loathe. I did admire them for one thing and let me tell you what it is since you can't seem to grasp it. Risk, Tabitha, they all took risks."

Tabitha was trying to break in on the other end. He didn't know if she was even getting any of this; he didn't much care. If she wanted out, if she thought she had no other choice, then she could just up and do it. He could make it work without her. She had a right to be cautious but an obligation to be supportive. That her father wielded greater influence had him questioning any sort of future together.

"I've had it with what we had. This is my dream, my hard work. I'm going to create something on this Podunk Island. I won't sit back and wait for someone else to do it."

Somewhere along his diatribe the connection was lost. For the first time since she and the boys left, he broke into the bottle of scotch he picked up for himself in Bangor. Not even on Christmas Eve or Day had he the inclination, so obsessed was he in training the dogs. He drank himself to sleep this night. His mind wrestled with strategies, tactics, thoughts of territories won and lost, and hardened battle lines. There were contingencies to be dealt with, and further logistics for his dogs. Slowly his body succumbed to the scotch; his mind fell quickly in step. For just a while, it was the most restfull of sleeps.

Twenty-two

The familiar scent of ham bones had their full attention, making them oblivious to this new land. They had worked up a lather over the past thirty minutes despite the frigid cold. But now, straining against the chains had tired them out enough to make them lay in the crusted snow to rest before resuming their efforts. Here, the sights, sounds, and odors confused and frightened them. They had no knowledge of having been bred and trained to be fearless beasts. The unknown disoriented all living things. It sharpened only the senses needed to survive. With nothing to fight, all they could do was wait for something, anything, familiar enough to grasp hold of.

At first there were the ferocious winds alone. Slowly the dogs picked up the scent of raw meat. Not the ham bones they had become used to, something wondrously new that had them back on their feet. Then, almost immediately, they backed away as far as the chains allowed, back towards the stone outcropping and beach. A new sound was on the wind that did not illicit the same captivating response as the new odors. It had them yipping, looking at each other for comfort, and pulling frantically yet futilely. The sounds grew. Now came the smells that choked the air with danger. Terror throbbed in the winds, and rapidly overtook every sense, even that powerful sixth sense, all focused laser-like on this on-coming menace.

The snow picked up, swirling in the winds. Ghostlike apparitions appeared, charging low and hard through it. The dogs hastened their frenetic attempts to loosen themselves from the chains. They backed quickly to the rocks. One turned to make a fateful attempt to flee behind them but was snagged at her hind leg. An attacking dog launched itself into the mix, pressing its prey against the boulders. It was a flurry of browns and grays, and flashings fangs, set to the mad music of demonic howls.

The commotion alerted her companion to the uselessness of a retreat. He turned valiantly to do battle, baring his teeth as he lowered his rear haunches, muscles spring loading his planned attack. He snapped at mid air as if a shadow boxer throwing loosening jabs. Within minutes his companion, out sized and out maneuvered, lay on her side, breathing heavily to her last, and gushing blood into the fresh snow.

The attacking dogs were feeding now, tearing at the barely breathing carcass while the dying dog lay whimpering as her vital organs were shredded. The fresh blood incited their frenzy as it did the companion dog who was torn between the hunger to join in and preparing to defend himself from a similar fate.

Realizing there was no escape, he set himself to do what he had been trained for. He watched and waited for the dogs to turn to him. He pulled and snapped whenever he felt he could seize a tail or leg as the attackers pounded recklessly within reach. He could grab hold only for mere moments, so feverishly were the dogs pouncing on their prey. Then, from the blind side, a wave of black fur hurled him against the rocks, and for all his training, all his posturing, he couldn't regain a footing to do battle. They were joined by the others. So thick and riotous was the heavy canopy of fur that no sky, no snow, no stars could be seen, there was only the suffocating smells and sounds of an imminent death which mercifully took him.

"It's a sick business."

"Yeah, well, don't come on all full of disgust. You came to me. You came to me twice."

"I'm not operating the business."

"Yeah, you're just a customer."

"Seems to me you have a few customers on the island."

Dutch smiled. "Why they call it a business, Aress."

They were in a rusty trailer behind Dutch's pole barn. When he arrived, Dutch was slumped in a worn, fat armchair, smoking a Marlboro, bottle of Gritty McDuff Black Fly in his lap. He glanced up casually when Trent burst in, like he was expecting the company.

He had come to Dutch fuming after finding his two dogs torn and shredded like old carpet. Fortunately, the carcasses were partially snow covered and the blood was frozen into the new snow. It made the scene easier for him to take. Out of curiosity he overturned several body parts that had been disbursed as far as a hundred feet from where he posted the dogs. He found them unrecognizable except for an ear and a stripped hock and hind foot.

Tracks were still visible leading to and from the bloody melee. As expected, they led across the field to Carver's house. Anger and loathing had him wanting to follow them to accost Carver, fear and common sense kept him from doing so.

For weeks, not a sound from Carver's animals, then he sets them loose. Sets them loose on the night he hears Trent's dogs on the ridge. It was more than a shot across his bow; it was a volley into his midsection, designed to cripple him before he could make a move. Carver was true to his malevolent nature, Trent had to give him that. It was more than Trent could say for himself. His actions were a warning; Carver's were a statement.

He searched further out for signs that his dogs may have inflicted their own degree of destruction but found none. It was a massacre. It was impossible to know how many dogs attacked. Had he not tied his dogs down they may have had a chance.

"How many dogs does Carver have?" Trent demanded.

"You know me, Aress, I ain't talkin'."

"That why you're hanging around the island, isn't it, to sell more to him?"

"I sell to everyone, and I'm not sure I like your tone."

"You knew. You knew what he'd be up to."

Dutch grinned, and not cordially. "Up to, Aress? Not following you. I sell dogs to people who want dogs. I sell them when I'm asked. Didn't ask Carver, didn't ask you, don't ask nobody."

"You said my dogs were trained."

"You were there when we worked with them."

"Five grand and they didn't last a week. And you said no money back. I don't like the way you do business."

Dutch nodded. "I gathered that. Let me tell you, Aress, I don't advertise; I don't have a sales pitch; I don't take testimonials; I don't make promises, and I don't apologize. I don't go around defending what I do, mainly 'cause I don't usually have too."

"Because what you do is illegal."

"Makes you an accessory. We done here or is there some transacting you want to do?"

Twenty-three

He got nowhere questioning Dutch on the status of Carver's pack. Not numbers, locations, types, colors, or ages. He was torn between continuing the argument, telling him to fuck-off, threatening to go to the cops, or restocking his own arsenal.

There was less than five days before Tabitha's scheduled return, if she did at all. If he waited even another day or two, he might as well give into Carver. Then it would be over; the dream, the reality, all gone to some psychopathic, antisocial, descendant of madmen. "Corlin says you been on the island longer than usual. Says you usually do your business then move back to the mainland."

"That's right."

"So, you're still doing business here?"

"Guess that's for you to be telling me."

Eight of his finest specimens were in the pole barn on this very day, Dutch told Trent. Trent checked them out. This time he by-passed the meeker ones, the smaller ones, the ones without noticeable wounds. If they growled or rattled the cage, he noted them for a second look. "How much?" he asked.

"Like before. Depends."

"Don't give me that shit. I want a good price for the next ones, regardless of what I pick. If I'm getting no refunds for the last two, then I should get a deal here."

He wanted four. That would be his guess for what he would need, believing Carver had three at least. Dutch calculated numbers in his head while the two stood before the cage of the biggest German Shepherd in the mix whose left ear was only half there, and right lip and cheek had healed over in a most gruesome design. "You want this one?" he asked.

"He's still here so I'm figuring he won a few."

"And three others?"

"Yeah."

"Got 'em picked out?"

"Think so."

Trent took him around to the cages. He waited for Dutch to cast an opinion, but he offered none. Perhaps so as to have deniability in the event they were busts. "Tell you what," Dutch said. "All four for six grand. Now that's a bargain anywhere."

Trent took it. There wasn't an hour to waste bargaining. He paid and decided the logistics wouldn't allow for him to transport all four together. He opted for two trips but when the smallest one, a Jindo mix, fought the company of the Shepherd, he made a third trip to accommodate it.

Either it was coincidence or conspiracy but when he got the Jindo home, Carver's dogs were out. They weren't near his property. After all these months he could pinpoint their precise location by sound. And there were more than just two, as he suspected. He was satisfied in getting his four.

He had two dogs in one cabin, one in the other. On the ride home he was contemplating where to board the temperamental Jindo. Might just be a good time to give them exercise, he thought. It was nearing sundown. The wind was picking up. Snow squalls were coming in. He let the Jindo loose. It picked up on a scent as it ran in loose figure eights, pausing on occasion to get its bearings. He released the other dogs who stood confused at the doors.

He expected a mad dash, like the un-fencing of a wild bull at a rodeo. But he recalled catching raccoons and other critters as a kid. When it came time to let them go, he and his friends scattered when they dumped out of the box or opened the makeshift cage door. Instead of a furious scramble, however, the animals would sit and look them over with a casual disregard. They'd hop or crawl or slither slowly as they surveyed their surroundings, assessing the strengths and weaknesses of their predicament. Only then did they skitter off.

Trent always believed it was part of their ignorant nature. They weren't human; they couldn't make the cause-and-effect relationship. Every change of scenery, every new sensation, every fresh event, could only be evaluated in the present context. Once released from the cage, the episode was forgotten. Where they came from, where to go next, had no connection to a past or future. He was their god and by altering a moment in their lives he had recreated them.

He understood now it wasn't that way, that animals' lives were as complicated as humans with decisions to be made and choices to be had. It fascinated him. Not that wild creatures could evaluate in such dimensions, but that they could do so better than humans. Had it been him suddenly uncaged, he would have sprinted as fast as he could, as far as he could, before formulating any type of plan. He could run headlong into another disaster, and another. Survival instincts in the wild were so much more acute when death loomed imminent, impersonal, and indiscriminate.

The dogs ignored each other as they sniffed and inspected the door jambs and stoops, which though covered with new snow, must still have held the scent of the previous dogs. He allowed those moments before luring them to the top of the ridge with two ham bones, just enough to put the fight into them. Then he walked away.

He stood at the back door and listened. First to the howling wind, then to the crashing waves. Then, like carelessly leaving embers burning in a leaf pile, he went inside the house. He didn't know what he was expecting, what he was wanting, what he was avoiding. There was no sound inside, nothing to bother him, nothing to alarm him. The world outside was theirs for the night, and he didn't want to belong to it. He poured what was left of the Highland Park Scotch and collapsed in the chair. Tabitha was right, the windows were drafty. He held the Scotch in his mouth and let it trickle down his throat for warmth. The wind was ferocious now, and angry, as if calling him out. He slipped deeper into the chair, deeper into the glass, deeper into sleep, deeper into himself.

Twenty-four

Tabitha finally managed to corral the boys in the backseat of the Land Cruiser, with no help from her parents who had spent the last two days convincing her not to return to the island. "It can't be just about you anymore," her mother said, "you and him. If this is an experiment for him — "

"It's not an experiment, mom."

"Well, your father's right this time. It's not healthy and it's not safe. You need to stay here, with us if you need to."

"And what message does that send the boys? Commitments be damned; bug out at the first sign of trouble?"

And the questions and answers went round and round. No one right, no one wrong. Was she doing right by her children, by her husband, by herself? She didn't know the right answer; she didn't know if there was one. All she knew for certain was calling Trent on the phone and telling him they weren't coming back wasn't fair. To which her parents would respond it was Trent being unfair. And so, it would begin again. She kissed them both and said good-bye while hurrying to the car.

The boys weren't happy about leaving either. Partly, she believed, they sided with her parents. But of more immediate interest was the re-bonding with friends and places. As was usual, Jeremy kept his feelings to himself, not wanting to impart influence on his own behalf, trusting in her to make the right decision. Still, she knew his moods better than she knew her own. Ricky, on the other side, was willing and able to be heard at anyone's expense. "They have loud dogs and ghosts up there," he said. "And no beach to swim at and dad hasn't even bought a boat yet."

The long ride north was filled with regrets and worries. Nothing the boys expressed was out of line. To a child, these were important issues. Childhood needed to be swathed in trust. "Swathed" was the word she used, and Trent hated. To him it sounded Biblical which is why she used it. To her it signified comfort, tradition, and faith. Childhood brought with it a sacred union which, though accosted by certain realities, was held together by certain others. Her thoughts at those times were her boys' thoughts. She took pride in growing as a family, in being a good mother where her devotion let them grow while still protecting the child in them. A child had no business knowing or caring of politics or religion or financial crisis, and she cringed at the stories of nine-year-old cello aficionados, twelve-year-old Wall Street wiz kids, and fourteen-year-old Harvard graduates.

But Trent's thoughts on the issue were as honestly acquired as her own, in a youth that barely was and passed too quickly. To him childhood had an imposed expiration date. The *Age of Innocence* was so-called because it denoted a demarcation. Self reliance was to be obtained as soon as possible, and anything along the way that promoted and accelerated it was to be embraced. "It's about being adaptable," he would say. "Look at me." How many times she wanted to argue back, *Yeah, look at you.*

The nightmare he came out of was so deep, so intense, it followed him into consciousness with a jolt that nearly knocked him from the chair. He had followed a pack of wolves along the ridgeline. The moon was low and full, nearly blinding, as was the snow he plodded through while the wolves hurtled themselves onward, becoming dots on the horizon as the roar of their beastly howls split his skull. He wore a T-shirt, shorts, and a tool belt, and carried a hammer which he swung wildly against the dark and swirling snow. He cursed, fell, stood, cursed more, then lay near dead in a snow drift while a heavy rainstorm drenched him.

But no, not rain, heavier, like syrup, and sticky. He forced himself to roll onto his back and immediately was awash in streams of blood. Though his mouth was shut tight he couldn't keep from drinking it in. The more he tried to spit, the more he drank.

The snow was now a field of burnt orange under the moon's glow. And on it lay an endless row of lifeless dogs whose bodies lay parched and stretched like rugs. Eyes, dozens of pairs, death-black pupils in icy white sclera, staring at him from heads torqued at impossible angles. Soon the howling wolf pack had him surrounded as the ridges rose to interminable heights. A hot breath parted the hairs on the back of his neck. A heavy, disturbing whisper implored as to what he was feeling.

Fear, he tried to say, though nothing would come. Still, the beast heard.

"Fear for whom?"

Myself, again with no voice.

He turned his head slowly into the snout of Abe Carver as a sneering wolf. His hot breath felt to be melting his face. "When you awake the fear will stay in you; the kind you can't explain to others because they can't feel it as you do. How can they? The nightmare is yours."

His cell phone went off, playing *Hero,* the Spiderman theme Ricky pleaded for him to set as his ring tone, just as the sweat was starting to turn him frigid with the onset of the winter blast waging outside. It was Tabitha and it unnerved him that she was calling so late at night. "Hi," he said in greeting, cheerful, in hopes it dusted off the cobwebs of the nightmare.

"Just wanted to tell you we're on our way back."

"Back where?"

"To Maine."

"Oh, okay, why you starting so late?"

"We fixed the boys breakfast, so I didn't have to stop," she said, leaving out the hour-long argument her parents put up.

"In the middle of the night?"

"Trent it's almost nine-thirty in the morning."

"Oh, geez, I guess I've overslept."

"You feeling okay?"

He was debating whether to tell her about the dogs. It was hardly an insignificant event he could feign he'd forgotten when she returned. Yet it couldn't be explained over the phone. Like Carver warned him in his dream, the terror was his experience, impossible to know for anyone who hadn't been there.

Tabitha broke in. "Trent. You still with me?"

"I'm sorry. Yeah, I'm fine, just ... don't know where the time went."

"Your breathing's heavy," she noted. "You having any chest pains, numbness?"

"God, Tabitha, I'm not ready for a heart attack. I'm fine; it's all fine. Just take it easy driving up here, there's been quite a bit of snow."

Trent's head was thick from last night's thoughts, drinks, and deeds. He was anxious to attend to the dogs he had left out, but not overly. He sat up slowly, leaning forward to stretch his back and massage his face with his fingers. The snow had plastered the window behind him. It made it impossible to see beyond, impossible not to imagine the cold desolation that awaited him. He wanted to hear the dogs whimpering at the back door. But they weren't Mop; they didn't know to rely on him. Once released, they belonged to instincts that didn't include him. It made the nightmare more real, for if they were waiting for him at all, it wasn't as their champion.

Twenty-five

Blinding squalls whipped him. They dashed about to their own dictates. To his north where the ridge line lay was a blur of white on white. He maintained a bearing by using the jagged rocks of the shoreline whose distinct silhouette defied the storm. Snow and cold had his head down and pounding. If he happened upon a dog, it was sure to be dead at his feet.

He brought the leashes and now realized now useless they would be He tried whistling but couldn't catch enough air. His calls were lost in the frozen wind. He didn't dare venture far, and so stuck to staggering in pitcher-mound sized circles where his tracks were blown clean after each lap. Already he was feeling the numbness settling into his fingers, signaling the horrific pain to follow. His bare face was frosting over, saliva crystallizing at the corners of mouth, running mucus solidifying beneath his nose. The harshness of the environs only confirmed the harshness of the reality: no dogs could survive this. The wolves of those documentaries and his nightmare, perhaps. Or the storied dogs of Jack London tales. But as raw as his animals were, they were domesticated and cared for to a degree that left them too frail for days and nights such as these. In a vulgar gesture he allowed himself to envision them taking out Carver's pack before they succumbed. He retreated to the house, assuring himself that the evening would reveal answers. It had too, he had run out of time.

Hack Corlin hadn't seen snow like this since 1978 or felt cold like this since ... well never had felt cold like this. Ice. Death to boats everywhere up here. Mid-winter and the harbor was nearly seventy percent frozen according to reports with minus zero temps forecasted for the next five days. The Coast Guard had warned ferrying operations to cease. If not for the islanders making stock-up trips back to the mainland he would have heeded their warning. And yesterday for sure had he not received a phone call from Tabitha Aress saying she'd be at the dock by three the next afternoon.

If he were a betting man, he would have wagered he had seen the last of her and her kids. Either she was very devoted or an emotionally abused wife. The latter didn't seem to fit him or her, but you could never really know without living under the roof.

It was nearing four and not a word from her yet. He was in the boat house with three space heaters on high. He convinced himself to give them another fifteen minutes. It was an hour and forty-five-minute round trip with docking thrown in. That would have him coming back to home port in the dark. He hadn't yet charted the ice flow and even if he had it was changing daily, and always increasing.

Surprised he hadn't heard from Trent yet. Shouldn't he be up here to greet them after all this time? Isn't he a bit concerned they were an hour late? He was certain she hadn't called her husband with an update; if she had why wouldn't she have called the ferry? Maybe Trent was supposed to relay the message. Typical for service folks everywhere, always an after-thought.

He spent the next fifteen minutes fixated on the young couple. He was old and past the years when getting into a flap over a woman was prudent on any level, though he allowed himself leeway for the fantasy. Then he let himself wonder. If those two were here for a weekend or daytrip, yeah, they'd be wrapped up in each other's arms at the port railing and rocking B&B's at night. But a lifetime? She shouldn't be changing linen on the very beds she should be wearing out, turning wind burnt and leathery, buying beef jerky by the gross and beer by the case. Not that woman.

His daydreams brought him to 4:25 when he made the decision to shut it down, perhaps for a few weeks. As he stepped from the boathouse, he heard an urgent car horn. Tabitha gave him a nervous wave as she leaned out the window. "I'm late, I know."

Hard to stay angry at a face like that. "Better hurry," he said and waved her on board.

They had the deck to themselves with lots of room for the boys to roam but Hack urged them not to. "It's gonna be a rough ride over for you," he told them. Then, mostly to himself, though she heard and gave a sheepish grin, "rougher and darker ride for me on the way back."

"I tried calling since Massachusetts but couldn't get through," she said.

"It's really not a problem."

"Mind if I stand up in the cabin with you?" Tabitha asked.

"Get's pretty cold up there, and rough. I wouldn't advise —."

"I'll be fine."

"Me too," Ricky insisted. Jeremy was about to chime in until their mother uncharacteristically raised her open hand at them and screamed. "Damn you two, I've had enough of your demands. Get in that car and don't dare get out. I mean, don't open a damn door or window."

She sat on a back bench until they were underway. The ferry lunged from its dock. It felt as fragile as an aluminum canoe in a rocky shoal. The ice flows shifted the craft left, then right, effortlessly. They beat against the hull sending ghostly echoes and vibrations throughout the ship. Tabitha felt a pang of guilt for leaving the boys alone; surely the effects were multiplied below deck.

Without asking permission she stood alongside Hack who was handling the ferry as if it were a scalpel slicing alongside a major artery. While the horizon was a brilliant field of orange, already the sky at forty-five degrees was a darkening blue. No doubt he would be returning to the mainland in rough darkness. "I'm sorry," she mumbled.

"'Bout what?"

"This. Making you come out this late. Trust me, if I knew it would be this bad – "

"Not a problem, it's what I get paid to do. 'Sides, I've seen it worse."

"Really?"

For the first time he took his eyes off the seas to look at her, "No. Not really."

She allowed him to clear the largest flows before addressing him again. "Not a good time to be asking, Hack, but it's the only time I've got. Trent. He been acting strange since I left?"

Hack gripped the helm firmly as the ship scraped alongside a chunk of ice. His face tightened as he did. "No," he said. "Tell the truth, barely seen him."

"But you have seen him."

"Yeah, guess I did, a while back."

"How'd he seem to you?"

He shrugged as if he didn't understand the question, but of course, he did. "Little lonely, I guess. Okay other than that." Why get himself involved? He liked these people well enough but barely knew them. And if she wasn't sure about her own husband, why would he have any better insight? Best to keep things like that to himself.

"Where'd you see him?"

"Where?"

"Yeah, where? Here, on the ferry? At *Trugard's?"*

He stared across the bay, hoping for a large ice flow to take them off topic. Saying on the ferry would have her asking where he was going; *Trugards,* she'd be asking if he was drunk. What the fuck he care? "Don't really remember, just around I guess."

Bored or tired of his disregard, she went below. He felt guilty. She was asking questions that didn't call for specific answers. She was starting conversation of a personal nature that needed only an ear, not a voice. He could have shown concern without divulging any truths. Occasional nods, knowing glances, "ah-huh" and "I see," would have done it. Let her talk it out of her system.

As he expected, there was no one to greet her at the other end. He waved half-heartedly as she drove off. She had the most tormented look on her face. Perhaps he had said more than he thought.

Twenty-six

The Almanac was right, Hack Corlin was right, she was right. This place was where winter came to exercise, to explode, to experience its full potential. Its fury scared the boys, even Ricky, who was in the front seat, his chest pressed to the dashboard, feverishly scraping frost from the inside of the windshield. "Mom, I can't see."

"Sit back, Ricky, if we swerve or hit—."

"We might hit something?" Jeremy screamed from the backseat.

"Swerve, Jeremy. I meant swerve. Ricky, I said sit." She reached across and heaved him backward.

It was the longest one and a half miles she'd ever driven. White knuckle, sweaty palms, tight shoulders, scared-to-the-marrow, driving. She was incensed Trent wasn't there to meet them. He could have guided them back, knowing the roads so much better than she did. For all she knew they were inches from sliding into the ocean. She knew there'd be few if any cars on the road, but if there were, it'd be her luck they'd be coming from *Trugards*. She had been calling him since getting on the ferry. Hack Corlin told her cell phone calls weren't going to happen.

There was no keeping the frost off the inside windows, so she pulled Ricky back up to work the scraper while she rolled down her window, trying unsuccessfully to free ice from the wipers. They were driving blind. The car was filling with snow. Drifts were forming in Jeremy's lap. "Put up the window, mom," he hollered.

"I can't see. I have to clear the windshield."

"But it's cold."

"Shut-up, Jeremy, come up here to help," Ricky said.

"We only got one scraper."

"Use your fingers."

Jeremy ignored him. "We can walk."

"That's stupid," Ricky said. "Too cold in here, how cold you think it is outside? That's stupid."

Tabitha was in a panic, and at first thought Jeremy's idea wasn't the worse thing they could do. The road was gone, filling rapidly with snow drifts. The house was straight down this road, or nearly. Driving was getting impossible. She closed the window and looked over at Ricky and back at Jeremy. They were all dressed for a Virginia winter with the heavier gear in the cargo space.

Either way, staying in the Land Cruiser or walking, they were needing those clothes. They sat silent for a few minutes as the car rocked and whistled. "Stay put," she said as she opened the door.

"Where you —."

"Just going to the back to get more clothes."

"We gonna walk?" Jeremy wanted to know.

"I don't know," she said.

The door budged but a sliver when she pushed on it. The boys were watching intently. She didn't want to alarm them, but the drifts had increased dramatically in height since she had her head out the window. "Ricky, Jeremy," she said calmly. "See if we can get out your doors."

Ricky's barely moved. Jeremy had some success. "I can squeeze through," he said.

"No, don't."

"Let me," Ricky said, climbing over the seat. He pulled Jeremy away from the door, but Tabitha managed to manhandle him.

"Don't," she said, straining to keep control of his arm. She knew that when he got himself into such a state, he was near impossible to restrain. "Let's ... just think about this for bit."

"It's just going to get deeper," Ricky said.

"And colder, mom," Jeremy added.

They were both right. They could stay warm in the car as long as the gas lasted. But she didn't care how deep the snow was; it was the drifts that worried her. And while the rational side of her hoped for a four-wheel vehicle to come by, her paranoid side wanted no one to come near them.

"We'll wait here," she said.

"How long?" Ricky wanted to know.

"Not long. I just need to decide the best thing to do."

He woke to the howling winds. It was cold. Damn this house had drafts.

His head was still fuzzy. He didn't drink as much as the other night, but he obviously had enough. He checked the time, past six. Tabitha and the boys should be at the ferry by now. He looked out back, but it was like looking into a deep cave. He opened the door which the wind yanked from his hand. It cleared his head and vision. The light afternoon snow had turned violent, terrifyingly violent. No way Corlin was taking the ferry out in this. He closed the door and checked his cell phone which had no new messages. He tried calling Tabitha but as he suspected there was no signal.

To drive to the ferry would be foolish if not suicidal. It was a sure bet that Tabitha and the boys were safe on the mainland, waiting out the storm. There was nothing to do but sit and think, and there wasn't a thought on his mind that didn't make him want to drink again.

Trent was finding his comfort in the fierce and frigid winds. Warmed within by the Scotch, he now welcomed the cold winds like the passing of an oscillating fan on a humid summer night. He even drew his comfort from the dogs whose howls now came to him romantically. He felt passion in their freedom, living amongst men yet without them. Yes, there was romance in that. How could one not feel it?

The Scotch soothed him. The things of an island winter had an appealing affect on him. Its brutality; its relentlessness; its indiscretion. He welcomed its raw insensitivity. He had made enemies here and few friends. He had alienated family and done contemptible things for questionable reasons. Yet he was content in what he had done and failed to do. He put his head back on the chair and howled along with the dogs. They were back, calling for him to join them. Finally, something that believed in him, something waiting for him to lead.

Twenty-seven

Abe had just come in after securing the sheep in the barn to wait out the storm, and now the damn dogs were scratching and howling to come in. They rarely did, even on the bitterest nights. Abe beat that out of them at a young age. Must be the wind scaring them. Dogs were crazy that way. No fear of any beasts but give them something they can only sense, they go all sorts of mad. Still, he agreed this storm had that kind of anger. Came up hard and fast and was making a ghastly roar as it heaved massive waves against the rocks on its way across the island.

Abe took his eight-foot oak walking cane with him to the back door, intent on laying it stiff on their backs. Better they should fear him more than they did the storm. He hiked the greasy old Carhartt around his neck, anticipating the blast sure to come when he opened the door. But the blast that came was not from the nature he expected, and its attack was more furious.

He saw the snarling shepherd mix for just an instant. It had heard him working the door and prepared itself. It was crouched low on its hind legs, its front paws stretched far forward. There was no time for Abe to level the cane. Instinctively he grabbed at his neck and took a step backwards. It was just enough so that the attacking dog managed to barely lay its paws on his chest. But Abe was old and unsteady, and the surprise of the attack and its ferocity toppled him onto his back.

The dog went instinctively for his throat but would have to push through Abe's hands to get there. It grabbed hold of Abe's wrist and twisted like Abe saw them do to a dead pig's hip joint. Abe pulled back enough to anchor his hands to the thick jacket collar. He flailed his elbows into the dog's head, ordering his dog to heel. The dog didn't relent. It began tearing at his hands while madly digging its paws into Abe's chest as if trying to unearth a soup bone.

"Damn dog," he cursed. "Fuckin' mutt." He tried to roll onto his stomach but damn it was heavy. To let go of his jacket collar would be a tactical disaster, and so he flung his knees up wildly and twisted his torso, looking for any weapon, any leverage. By now he was too exhausted to feel pain or take notice of the blood flowing from his hands.

He felt a sharp tug at his left foot. He kicked it away. Before he could recoil his knee, the dog's teeth sank deep and held tight. This was the first intense pain he had felt from the attack. He screamed and lunged up to unhook the dog. He found himself in a forest of thick, wet fur. Heavy coats of blacks and browns and grays moved madly on top of him. It was two dogs now, maybe more, and the weight and ferocity of them threw him back to the ground. And worse, they weren't his dogs.

The first dog had taken advantage of the opening and attacked his throat. It missed, catching a fang in Abe's mouth, digging into his gums, and ripping the corner of his mouth open. It was searching out fleshy parts to get to the meat but with the heavy jacket, the neck up was all it had. The second dog was working his way up his leg. It had found his thigh and would have savaged it good had Abe not been kicking and hollering. *Not the groin,* he was either thinking or yelling out hysterically, *shit, not the groin.*

The room was filled with their ghastly snarls. His face was covered with his blood and globs of dog saliva. He could now imagine how it felt to be on the ground in a dogfight. And the horror Aress's little mutt must have experienced in the last few moments it had left to live. As exhausted and cramped as he was, he couldn't let up. He had to get to his stomach, out of this submissive posture, wrap his bloodied hands over the back of his neck, and hang on for his life. But the dogs were too big and enraged. They had tasted blood and felt flesh. As prey, Abe was fighting back, which threatened their meal. And with two of them, there was competition for the spoils. Abe was no match and so needed to create a diversion.

The cane was nearby somewhere. Despite the clawing and biting, he threw his hands out left and right, grasping for it, or anything loose. He was in no position to use it as a weapon. Best he could do was slide it across the room. Or toss a boot or a plate. Something to distract them. Then hope to hell they tired themselves out.

It was there, just over his head. But his wild swinging knocked it out of reach. The dog hadn't stopped digging into his midsection since the attack began, understanding instinctively its position of dominance. The result was the Carhartt had been shredded, and the wool sweater beneath was no defense against claws that could dig a three-foot hole through packed clay in a matter of minutes. It was as if his belly had been flayed by a blow torch.

He closed his eyes and grit his teeth, ready to submit himself to an agonizing demise, just begging a dog would find a vital organ quickly, when there was a sudden shift in the weight above him. For an instant the clawing and digging stopped. He took the moment to roll over. There was a mad struggle above him, and he realized a third dog had joined the fray. It was a turn that was sure to make his predicament more perilous in the next few moments.

His right knee tendons must have been destroyed; he could barely bend it. On all fours he managed to crawl to the table and haul himself to his feet as the battle behind him raged. It wasn't a struggle for territory or dominance, it was for him; he was the prize. He looked over his shoulder, not wanting to turn fully in a confrontational attitude. There were three. Two he had never seen before. There didn't appear to be sides, just three mad dogs snarling and snapping, lips turned, teeth bared. Abe's shotgun was at the front door just ten steps away, ten long steps.

The dogs were intent on each other's movement. Just maybe his would go unnoticed, After all, he wasn't the threat here. Moving was excruciating. He dared to look at his right thigh and knee. The jeans were shredded. Wet blood had the torn fabric clinging to his skin. What he thought was blue jean or blood were knots of chewed muscle and gristle. It made him sick, knowing it was his, and the blood kept coming.

He hobbled on, nearly there. One more hurdle around a coat stand. He reached awkwardly for it and made a grab, but his badly torn hands couldn't hold on and it crashed to the floor. The dogs scattered but for only a moment. They turned on him in unison. As if the trio signaled an understanding of cooperation, they spread themselves out across the small kitchen to corner him at all angles.

It was no longer a matter of stealth but of quickness. He turned and grabbed the shotgun. Realizing getting one shot off, never mind three, was an impossibility, he raised it as a club and swatted at the on-coming commotion behind him. Had the dogs the time or sense to fully coordinate, all three would have attacked. As it was it was just the one, the one he recognized as his own. The stock of the shotgun grazed its shoulder but had the desired effect. It let go a yelp as it crashed to the floor, springing up quickly but with less ambition.

His grandmother, he was told, conversed with the animals of Malaga Island. Dogs, birds, cats, sheep, cows, rodents, even fish. She was storied to siren fish into the nets if the desperate need arose. She didn't like to do it for it upset the trust she had developed. She was thought a witch, and one of the excuses for the folks of the Island to be dispatched. For a fleeting moment, he wondered about the curse they said his grandmother had put upon the Maine islands, vengeance from nature.

He felt it now with the storm and the dogs' sudden turn. He knew well what they wanted. He had seen it in their eyes as they awaited the slaughter of a diseased or deformed lamb. What was it they were sensing from him now? His fear, his vulnerability? He determined to give them none of it, and so he cursed and wailed and swung the butt end of the shotgun. They moved but showed no signs of retreating as they matched his screams with ghastly howls of their own.

Abe was in no physical condition to carry this on much longer. He had the front door to his rear, but the storm had piled snow so thick and high that he had no chance of getting off the front stoop before the pack turned the pure white to a deep crimson. This, the dogs were sensing and it emboldened them. They were now content to let him exhaust himself.

A fourth dog entered, another one of his. He caught its eye, hoping for recognition. Its stare was blank. There was no solidarity, nor were there signs of animosity. It was as if to say, *this is all about business and I know what I have to do.* It circled behind the others and waited.

Abe was barely able to hold onto the gun. Slowly, he pulled the stock to his belly and weakly racked a shell into the chamber. At the sound the dogs only inched back, even his own two who knew well the sound and power of it, having heard and seen it dozens of times when Abe used it to show his own dominance. A fifth dog entered. No, it was the same one. He was seeing double and getting dizzy. He was nauseated and his hands fumbled in confusion with the gun, the type of gun he had used since he was nine years old. That was what scared him most. Did he just rack a shell? Buck or slug? How many were left in the chamber. Was the safety on? Where was the safety?

The room was now filled with dozens of snarling, frothing dogs, or so it seemed. Dogs like his, like the ones he had trained to attack and kill without regard. He raised the gun like a clumsy kid. He was unsteady in his aim. The dogs approached cautiously while he jabbed the gun at them. They snapped and one caught the barrel. He would have squeezed off a shell had the dog put the business end down its throat.

He was done. As done as a slaughtered lamb hung in the shed to bleed out and dry. One round. If he could get off one, clean round into a beast the pack might descend upon the more convenient meat. He pulled. It wasn't the precision squeeze he had perfected, and the clumsy grip did nothing to lessen the recoil. He was thrown against the door. The shotgun was thrown an impossible distance away. He lay on his back while the echo dissipated. For a moment it was still. He was losing consciousness, accompanied by his own pathetic moaning. He was begging for mercy, then found himself trying to recall a prayer. His own moans were joined by a guttural chorus moving slowly towards him. With great effort, he lifted his head. It was to be his last great effort.

Twenty-eight

Ricky was not happy about being told to wait it out. He was hungry and getting cold. He stopped complaining only because his mother stopped listening to his reasons; she just yelled and told him to shut up. So now he muttered while Jeremy sobbed.

He watched his mother intently. She was worried. She fidgeted, breathed deeply, sighed, stared out the frosted windows as if she could see. If his father ever worried, he didn't show it, least not in front of Ricky. He now appreciated that. If he picked up on it, he knew Jeremy did, which was why he was sobbing. His mother chastised him for it without understanding she was the cause more than the storm.

Jeremy infuriated his brother at times like this. There were differences between them he didn't understand. Like when he hid in the corner with a flashlight on the nights the dogs howled. And how he shook uncontrollably for hours after hearing the ghost stories from Abe Carver. He cried every day when Mop was lost until dad yelled at him, telling him to grow up and get over it. And he cried at school more times than his parents knew. How many fights Ricky had defending his brother from the taunts of *mama's-boy, cry baby, wimp.* "Don't run away from them," he would advise Jeremy. "You need to fight back." "I know," Jeremy would say, his head bowed, his shoulders stooped, already in defeat of the next confrontation.

He'd never fight, though. He cowered, like he was doing now. But this time Ricky had no one to beat up for him. He could yell at him but that would make it worse, and his mother was already saying everything he wanted to.

Having driven just a few times to the ferry and never paying the drive much attention, he wasn't sure how far they were from home. He scratched at the frosted window. The world was swirling white. He saw hills now where he could swear there were none before. The island was boring away from the water. It didn't have hills and rivers like his old house. It didn't have many trees. The rocks were cool, but they couldn't play on them so what good were they?

They couldn't be very far from home. He could be there in minutes They all could; his mother just hated walking. She'd drive around a parking lot three times waiting for a spot up front. His father had a pick-up truck like most of the people on the island. Must be because they were so good at driving in snow. If he could just get to his father, he could come out to get them and drive them home where it was warm and they could make hot chocolate.

No sense asking. He tugged at the door handle. It gave way of the latch. Already he felt the wind swirling through the slight opening. It wouldn't be long before Jeremy and his mother felt it too. He pushed into it. It opened barely enough for him to squeeze through, and into a brutal wind gust that tossed him against the side of the car. He tried but couldn't get the door closed behind him. His mother was yelling frantically for him to come back. Jeremy pressed his faced against the side window and watched him struggle onward through the storm.

It didn't take long before he realized how under-dressed he was, no matter how short a distance he had to go. If not for his mother, he wouldn't have on boots. But his jacket was the wool one his grandmother bought him for Christmas, not the goose down one that let him slide in wet snow without getting the least bit chilled. And he was wearing worn jeans, not even the thick corduroys he hated.

He kept his head down; he had too, or the gales would have pushed him back to car. As it was, he was barely making any progress. He heard high-pitched yells, could be his mother, could be the wind. He didn't dare turn around for fear of losing momentum.

Where was the road? Where was the ocean? He thought back on his drives. The road was straight from the house to the ferry. No, there were two turns. Did they already make them? This didn't seem like very good idea, after all. He had fallen half a dozen times. His jeans were soaked through. His fingers and toes were getting numb. He could no longer move his mouth and his ears stung. And it had been less than two minutes since he started.

He turned to look at the truck, hoping for his mother to grab him by the collar and drag him back. She wasn't there and truck was gone, least he couldn't see it. He could make it. He could get to the house in this and be a hero. His mother would be angry at first; his father would be so proud. Then his mother would wrap him in a warm blanket and sit him on her lap while she scolded him and stroked his hair like she always did.

Straight ahead he pushed. "Blinding snow," his mother had read to him and Jeremy from *Call of the Wild.* He knew it now on an intimate level. But were his eyes not seeing, or rather was there nothing to see? He had cast himself into a white box pushed down a steep hill, and no matter how the box tumbled and turned, all views were the same. He was no longer cold. He found some comfort in this, having no idea how serious his situation was becoming.

Twenty-nine

The headlight glow came back to her mockingly and the horn faded in the blasting wind. She tried to follow him, but it was as hopeless as she had suspected and feared. After spinning the tires uselessly for several minutes, Tabitha was able to plow forward about twenty yards before careening into a snowdrift. In a morbid gesture, she scanned the area left and right along the drive for Ricky's body. She ran after him but made it barely a truck's length. It wasn't the cold; she could ignore that. The snowdrifts were at her knees, and so at Ricky's waist. And the wind pushed her as if commanding her back into the truck.

Jeremy went into a panic when she left him alone. She didn't blame him, being in her own panic while trying to calm him. And very suddenly her fear for Ricky gave way to hate for her husband for not only bringing them here but leaving them. It was he who sent Ricky out into the blizzard. He who had her stuck in a snowbank. He who had Mop killed and Jeremy out of his mind. She shook this off quickly. Not for Trent's sake but for her son's. "Jeremy," she said as calmly as she could, "we're fine as long as we stay here, understand?"

He was working hard to contain his fears. "But Ricky's not."

"I know. So, I need you to keep it together. I need to think about how to get Ricky back here."

"How?"

"I need to go back out."

Jeremy lost it. He climbed over the seat back and clung to her. "You can't," he screamed.

"Jeremy, I need to find him."

"You can't," he repeated. "You can't." She understood this to have a double meaning, that she couldn't leave him, and she couldn't find Ricky.

She now regretted winning the small battle with Trent of conserving money and energy. She had him shut down the neon sign on the lighthouse, once an irritant that was now in critical need. Without it, Ricky would have no beacon to guide him. Her small victory for control, now back to haunt her.

They were low on fuel and no doubt low on the battery, two things she needed to keep from her son. Filling up the gas tank was one of the many things Trent harped on that she ignored. They were on an island, for crissakes, where half a tank lasted them two weeks. She had less than a quarter now.

She clicked on the dome light as she leaned across and fumbled through the glove compartment in a contrived attempt to locate a flashlight. "I thought I put one in here," she mumbled loud enough for Jeremy to hear.

"What?"

"A flashlight."

"Maybe it's in the back." He crawled over the seat.

Tabitha took the moment to examine the dome light that flickered dimly. She quickly killed it. She had no choice but to keep the car running. The battery wouldn't last long in this cold; restarting the car wasn't something she wanted to chance. A quarter of a tank would last them a few hours. The agonizing question was, how long would they need?

She turned on the radio looking for a weather report. AM was out of the question. Only one FM station came through, an oldies playing *God Only Knows.*

"Dad said you shouldn't keep the car running when the snow's deep," Jeremy said from the back floor where he was searching under the seats for the phantom flashlight. Tabitha ignored him.

"The snow can block the exhaust pipe and the smoke gets inside the car. That's how people kill themselves." He was just making conversation, his way of showing her how brave he was, not really paying attention to what he was saying.

Here they were in this mess, his mess, and still Trent was influencing them. It was the craziest thought that came to her just then, the type they said that comes just before a tragic death; she couldn't remember the last lingering kiss he gave her. That's when it came together. She wasn't his future, or even his present. He was finding himself here long before they ever met, and that future wasn't changing for her, the boys, or anyone.

Nothing, perhaps not even this incident would change the course of his heart and mind. And now she blamed herself. She had seen it all along. She knew she wasn't changing him. She knew the birth of his sons was not an influence. If anything, the boys cemented in his mind that this foolhardy ambition was not only right, but his destiny. His resolve, his discipline, his unrestrained spending had nothing to do with her. She was as far removed from him as that last lingering kiss.

"I can't find one," Jeremy said sliding back into the front seat. Tabitha looked him over. He looked so frail, so frightened. He was shivering, more from nerves than the cold.

Finally, the Oldies were interrupted for a weather report. Bangor expected six to ten inches, ending near midnight. Heavier amounts near Augusta but it would taper off closer to ten o'clock. The coast from Biddeford to Brunswick would be heaviest hit with the worst nearly over. She scraped the frost off the window for the third time since Ricky left; it hadn't let up here, and already there was close to a foot. Not even the national weather service thought enough to point its Doppler at Stryker John Island.

Maybe Ricky was right. Maybe making a dash for it was the best plan. It wasn't much more than a half mile away. And he had always landed on his feet no matter his antics. She'd seen him mesmerized by a five-inch gash in his shin before telling anyone he had it. He broke his wrist on a Sunday but didn't complain about discomfort until Wednesday. But that wasn't Jeremy. She'd have to shame him out of the car, then shame him onward. "Jeremy, this isn't going to be easy."

"I know."

"I don't know how long this storm will keep up."

"I guess we need to get out and walk," he said.

She tried not to let his remark surprise her, but he saw it. "We can; Ricky did."

"I know but he shouldn't have."

"But he did. And he didn't come back so he must have gotten there."

She felt him watching her intently for any sign that he was wrong. Anything that gave into his gut feeling that all was lost, that Ricky was swallowed up by the storm as they would soon be. She leaned over, but rather than grasp his hand, a sure sign of a mother's comfort, she rubbed his head as his father always did. She hated mimicking the gesture but at this moment, it worked for Jeremy.

"Let's wait," she said. "It has to stop soon. Then we'll do it; we'll walk home."

There wasn't much for Tabitha to do but worry and twist left and right in the seat to alleviate the cramps in her butt. It was impossible to know if the snow had stopped or the drifts were being whipped by the winds. Was she watching snow accumulate or drifts rise? She turned her anger from Trent to nature. That irony amused her, that she had no influence over either force.

She slept in fits and starts, a combination of anxiety, cold, and soreness. Jeremy stretched out in the back. He slept surprisingly well. Of course, he was small enough to stretch full out, and he wasn't a mother.

She threw good sense to the gales and kept the car running most of the night. Her original plan was to warm up the inside, then kill the engine until the heat was needed again. But the freeze was impossible to keep out as the gusts rocked the car. Even the headliner and console were cold to the touch. It all served to intensify her anxiety over Ricky. Only his dogged stupidity would keep in safe in a night like this.

Thirty

The sun came up with a blinding whiteness. She awoke in phases that brought her through varying degrees of the same nightmare. All of them had Ricky laying lifeless beneath the motel's lighthouse while Trent chastised him for frightening the guests.

The gas tank was empty and the battery dead. She leaned into the door to force it open. The door swept the snow like spreading frosting.

It was painful to look in any direction. She fumbled in the glove box for sunglasses. They weren't much good but at least she could focus. There was no wind. Never had she seen a world so white and untouched. The snowy landscape around her hadn't been shared by a soul. Above the birds were carrying on. The scene beyond would have been magnificent had it not been the place her little boy was lost in.

She reached back to shake Jeremy awake. He was curled in a ball that unraveled like a stuck caterpillar upon her touch. He told her he was awake all night. He wasn't but with deep sleep so elusive it probably felt that way. Neither of them was ready to trudge out but they had no choice.

"Ricky back?"

"No. But the car's out of gas. Good thing is it's stopped snowing so we're gonna be walking home."

He surprised her by getting himself into a full-length stretch and yawning while telling her, "Good, ' cause I'm cold and hungry. Dad and Ricky'll have breakfast ready for us."

It was surprisingly mild outside, the effects of the sun's rays off the snow. But she knew it wouldn't take long before the wet snows penetrated their clothing. No sense taking a change of clothing, there being no place to make the change. It would be a teeth-gritting trek she told Jeremy who seemed to get it.

The cold was in them now as they trudged and sweated. It was hard to keep their heads up, though Tabitha did it in search of the lighthouse and her son. They traded off the sunglasses to fend off the splitting headache they got from the blinding sun every few minutes. The visage no longer held an appeal. Every snowbank could be covering her son. Short of digging through them all, she could only hope not to see an appendage sticking out from one. "There it is," Jeremy shouted.

"What? Where, Jeremy?"

He pointed off to their left at ten o'clock. Shading her eyes against the glare while wiping away tears, she caught sight of the lighthouse. Christ, she thought she had them heading way east. They would have hit the ocean, then wandered up or down the treacherous coast, perhaps miles in the wrong direction. At night and in blinding snow, it wouldn't be hard to imagine Ricky doing the same.

Jeremy began pushing through the snow towards the lighthouse. As small as he was, he was able to run, fall, roll, and right himself in stride. Tabitha couldn't keep up as each step burned her quads and cramped her hips. She looked for Ricky, happy for not seeing him laying broken in the snow, back in that panic for not seeing him at all.

She quickly lost sight of Jeremy as he disappeared over the hill, beyond the lighthouse, hopefully to the house. It had taken them nearly forty-five minutes. It would have been just dumb luck for Ricky to have made it in that time. The storm had passed, the sun was that of a June day. Still, her face, fingers and toes were frozen. She knew to expect the agony of the thaw. What would be her son's condition after what, an hour, two, more? And during the height of that storm?

Jeremy's boot prints seemed to be the only ones leading to the house. She followed them in. Jeremy was on his father's lap. Trent's hands were wrapped loosely around his shoulders. He was slumped in the armchair. His hair was disheveled, an empty bottle of scotch on the side table There was no reason to believe he had any clue as to what had transpired over the night. Still, she had to ask. "Where's Ricky?"

He was having a hard time focusing. Sleep and booze, she knew. She had no time for either. "Where?" she screamed. "Where is he?"

Trent slid Jeremy off his lap and made an attempt to stand. "I .... I don't ... I mean, what —."

Against all logic she ran upstairs calling for him. She went room to room and back again, forgetting where it was she left off, praying this was one of his insensitive games or that he had fallen asleep under a bed or in a closet. She scurried and searched incessantly, anything to avoid settling down to the unimaginable truth.

She caught Trent halfway on the stairs. She stared down at him. She pushed past, nearly knocking him backwards.

He was easy enough to topple, still woozy from last night's drunk. Or was it this morning? She was staring out the back door when he came up behind her. "He's out there," she said with a desperation.

"He's fine," she heard from behind. His voice was hollow. Not just the words and the tone, but the character. There was no integrity to it, no compassion. It instilled no comfort or sense of trust. His words were not of the same desperation as her own. There'd be no miracle coming from him. Not today. Not anymore.

"He's not," she said stiffly. She was trying to hold on to any humanity she had left for this man. But more, she was creating distance from him. Like staring at a photograph, knowing that memories, good and bad, were far behind.

"We'll find him." She felt his fingertips, like spindly, bare tree branches, on her shoulders. She stepped away from his touch and turned. "Don't you ever get it? We're supposed to protect them. It's what they expect; it's what I expect, and it's what ..." She couldn't finish the thought. It was so basic she was ashamed to be reminding him.

He stood awkwardly in front of her. He was afraid to tell her the truth. She knew he had been drinking, knew he was still partially drunk, but to tell her he wasn't even conscious of the severity of the storm and therefore had no idea of the danger they were in last night would be too shameful. He turned it around on her. "Jesus, Tabitha, you mean to tell me you tried to make it through this storm?"

"I did make it."

"But why would Ricky try — ."

"Because he's Ricky, that's why. He thought he could make it; he thought he'd be the hero, just to impress you."

"Maybe he did. Make it, I mean." He pushed past her and scraped the frost off the back window. He peered through.

"What?" Tabitha asked.

"The cabins, or the rooms, I think I left them unlocked."

"Go look."

He left to get his winter gear.

"I'll do it," Jeremy offered.

"You'll stay here," Trent said.

"But I'm already dressed."

"We need you here, in case Ricky comes back," Tabitha said.

Trent was in the laundry room. She took the opportunity of being out of Jeremy's earshot to make her demands known. "I'm going."

"Don't need us both."

"We got more than one building to look in. And when we get Ricky, we're leaving."

"In this snow?"

"We got here; we can get out of here."

"Might wanna rethink that."

"Don't .... don't you dare tell me what to think anymore." She was cognizant of her anger and how it rose brutally up her throat. It wasn't what Jeremy needed to be hearing at this point. Trent bent over and busied himself tying his boots. He stood and worked his gloves under the cuffs of his coat and pulled his knit hat low over his face, all without acknowledging her presence in the room. His cursory interest in what she had to say was typical, but a thing she would no longer tolerate.

"How are we here?" she demanded. "I want to know where you stole the money?"

"We're wasting time," he said.

"Jesus, you arrogant bastard. You can't be the hero now. Not anymore. Answer the damn question. Answer me you coward."

"I didn't steal anything. I found men who did."

"Who?"

"Too many to count. I gotta take a leak."

She waited at the back door to scan the snow-blown landscape down to the cabins and motel rooms. There was no sign of activity, recent or past, as if the slate had been wiped clean.

"Take the motel keys in case," Trent told her. "I'll check the cabins."

The sky was still clear with the sun a brilliant yellow. But the wind had picked up considerably. It caught them immediately out the door. The walk to the outbuildings would be a rigorous one, with the snow up to her thighs and Trent's knees.

He pushed on, leaving her further behind. It intensified the abandonment she felt during the past year. *At least turn around, you bastard. See that I haven't been swallowed up.*" You'll drop this mess you've dragged all of us into," she said to his back. He kept struggling through the snow without acknowledging her.

"You hear me? You're dropping it. Right now."

He cocked his head enough to call back under his armpit. "Are you saying something to me?"

"You heard me."

He stopped, letting her catch up. "What?"

Both were pitching in the wind. Snow drifts settled against their bodies. If they stayed in place for twenty minutes they'd be buried.

"This mess you got us into ends today when we find Ricky." She was screaming now, knowing that indeed the wind was carrying off her words as fast as they came out.

"My mess? I'm looking for my son 'cause you let him run out in a snowstorm."

"You sonavabitch."

"Yeah, so you've said. And for the last time we're not dropping anything; too much invested here, time and money."

"Tell me you got paid a reward for being a whistleblower."

A sardonic smile crumpled his face. The snow crystallized the moisture at his eyes and nose. "And spend months recording phone calls and meetings while the Feds fiddle-fuck around with legal red tape?"

"Damn, Trent, how many hells can you throw us into?"

"All you ever saw was the money. And all the stuff it bought. You didn't see what I had to give up of myself to get it. You never gave a shit about that. I brought us out of a hell, Tabitha."

"Then get another job."

"I can't go back there."

"Why?"

"A lot of people want to see me dead. Don't ask who and don't ask how. You know the work I did and the people I did it with. I saw what was going on and I made my plan a long time ago. That plan involved rich and powerful people."

"You talking bribes or are you blackmailing?"

"I gave you all you need to know."

The cold was now in her bones. The storm didn't put it there. She had the truth, as she wanted, but it did nothing to comfort her.

Thirty-one

They weren't happy again. Back home when they argued it was over with quickly. Someone would get mad and the other would make a joke, which made the other one madder. But just for a while. Sometimes it was about him and Ricky; he understood those arguments. Ricky said they were crazy for getting mad over the things they did. Jeremy didn't think so. Mad was mad.

This place, though, had made them all change. Mom and dad were fighting all the time. It used to make mom cry; she didn't cry anymore. Now she yelled and got angry. Jeremy understood it was because crying didn't work anymore.

Today it started in the laundry room. Mom wanted to leave this place. That was no surprise to Jeremy. Jeremy wanted to leave too but didn't dare tell his father, afraid he'd call him a sissy. Watching them outside just now in the snow was very different. He started out watching them, trying to hear them through the window or read their lips. Slowly they blurred as his focus drifted across the field and past the cabins to the ocean. The world there moved in slow motion. His senses became acute. Impossibly, he heard the crashing waves. He could make out the individual snowflakes as they thrashed about in the wind before being pounded into drifts. And there were the long, deep echoes.

So many times, he wanted to tell them all he knew about this place. It was what happened to you when you listened too hard and too often. Hearing things no one else did, things you wished you hadn't. Believing in the very things others wanted to doubt. He was the quiet one for the contrary reason Ricky was the loud one. He wanted to hear what Ricky wanted to ignore.

He knew of the ghosts who wanted them gone. He had heard and felt them. His family could laugh, scold, and tease all they wanted. They did it out of fear. Jeremy had learned not to be afraid. They were just that, ghosts. Things that once were but are no more. Memories, as he once heard on a television show, that lingered on. Spirits of people who didn't know any better, who didn't know they were dead. He knew they couldn't hurt you unless you let them. He knew this much too; Ricky was never coming home.

Tabitha pushed on towards the motel rooms. The walk was slow and labored. Her quads burned; her lungs ached with each step. Trent was at the first cabin, staring into the window. She shaded her eyes to watch him, waiting for Ricky to run out. Trent showed no sign of success He bent over as if examining something in the snow. He turned back to her with no sign of encouragement.

She made it to the nearest room door. She was close enough that calling his name could have been heard from inside. She did this while fumbling with the doorknob. *Please be asleep,* she pleaded when there was no response.

The door was unlocked as Trent suspected. She pushed through calling his name as if doing so would make him instantly materialize. The room was small; she could see the entire place from where she stood. Still, she wasn't satisfied, and wouldn't be until searching every foot.

The blood on the sill confused and scared him. If it was Ricky's, where did he wander off to? Trent called inside for him several times, hoping the broken window was his doing, but he was convinced the boy wasn't there. Tabitha hadn't noticed or she would have headed over rather than going on to the motel. That was a good thing; one less scene to contend with.

It wasn't fresh blood. But it was still deep scarlet, obviously frozen. He put his head as far through the window opening as he dared, given the precarious positioning of the remaining glass shards. He caught the putrid stench of rotting flesh. For that moment he thought the worst before remembering this as the cabin he used to train and feed his dogs. He kept the soup bones in the cabin while the dogs often dragged the dead rabbits back inside.

Tabitha was at the motel about fifty yards away. He nonchalantly entered the cabin. Immediately heard a low humming from around the corner where the beds and bathroom were. He moved towards it cautiously. It grew in intensity, accompanied by scratching along the floorboards. A thick German Shepherd lay on the bathroom floor in a dried patch of blood. His winter coat gave him the enormity of a brown bear. Needing shelter and smelling the rotting food, it must have thrown itself through the window. It looked to be close to death, yet its eyes locked onto Trent in its last great act of self-defense.

Trent backed away slowly. He didn't recognize it as one of his, but then, he hadn't spent much time with them before sending them out to the field. The big Shepherd was baring its fangs with all the ferocity it could muster. It drooled uncontrollably. Trent watched it ready its hind legs which were terrifyingly sturdy for a dog near death. That's when Trent noticed the masses of gray fur around the bathroom and bedroom floor, fur that certainly wasn't part of this beast. And the odor, too powerful to be old bones. It was overpowering to him now, but he had to stay focused on the dog.

It seemed content to let him retreat. No doubt it had staked a claim here. But what was it? Old bones or something more recent? It wasn't Ricky, a thought that both comforted and sent shivers through him. The god-awful smell had him wanting to race from the cabin. But he had seen these dogs move, and with the two sharp corners he had to negotiate around, he'd be no competition.

He made efforts to search the area as he moved away. The dog sensed now that Trent was a threat to whatever it was protecting. It came to its feet. Trent saw no gaping wounds. This animal was healthy enough, and capable of doing serious injury. But there was blood from somewhere. Then he spotted it, the trail of blood that led to the closet.

She called frantically as she went room-to-room. There was no space too small she didn't search. He may have been unconscious or in shock. She could only hope as each call met with silence, every space, empty.

Surely Trent had finished searching the cabins. She looked down at them several times praying to see them crossing the yard back to the house. She sat on the bed and let herself sob. Quietly at first, but it didn't take long to let it go. So many times, the three of them had cleaned these rooms while going through lessons. Ricky was gone for the reasons that drove her into hysteria. He was impulsive; he was rebellious; he was candid; he was assertive; and he was everything she wished she could have been.

She was brought back to the present by the wailing of a pack of dogs that seemed to be just outside the door. She saw nothing outside the windows so dared to poke her head out. There were three of them, at least, down at the cabins. They were circling the one Trent entered, pausing expectantly at the window he had been peering into.

Trent had seen destruction of this kind before. And though it didn't shock him as it once had, this scared the hell out of him. Then, he was the dominant force. He was the one in control. The territory was his and he bent their will. Now the tables were turned.

He couldn't keep his eyes off the bloody carcass, half in, half out, of the closet. Behind him the dog was moving up slowly with a low, guttural snarl. Trent could see its shadow in his peripheral vision. It was sizing him up. Not as a meal, Trent didn't believe, but as a competitor for the meal it had stashed away.

Trent didn't move. He stood mesmerized as if witnessing a dazzling feat of magic. As macabre as it was, the scene fascinated him on many levels. How did the two dogs crash through the window? Did one follow the other through or did they work in unison? Why? For shelter, the scent of rotting meat? What made the one turn on the other? Were they fighting over the meager scraps, or did they see the other as a more substantial meal? And more intriguing; was it the epic battle Trent secretly desired to witness?

He had spent piles of money and dedicated substantial effort and time on his dogs, only to have them killed before he could see what they could do. It was as big an enterprise as the *Aress Landing*, and an integral part of its success, so interconnected that Trent no longer distinguished one from the other.

The carcass had been mutilated, torn into several pieces, the hind portion chewed to the bones. The head was detached, dragged several feet from the body, or more likely the body having been dragged away, as if to separate its identity. It was an old kill, least not within hours, but what did he know of such things?

How would a beast even go about eating live prey? These dogs, though wild and vicious, had been hand fed. It must have been close to starvation to turn to cannibalism. He wondered if there was another word for it in the animal kingdom. It didn't seem necessary, one word being enough to describe such an act, no matter who or what was involved.

Trent stepped over the dead dog and straddled it. It was the only floor he had left as the Shepherd crept closer. It now had Trent's complete attention. Its tail was low, ears backs, salivating as it ran its tongue over gray gums. It didn't look wounded but definitely unstable on its feet, and woozy. That didn't give him an easy feeling; a dog not in its right mind can be more dangerous than one you can communicate with. Trent tried. "Easy, fella, you want to be let out? Let me just step around – "

At that move the dog snapped, propelling its head into Trent's thigh. He was rethinking his initial observations, that the dog was only protecting its food cache. There didn't seem to be much meat left inside the dog carcass, and it was hard to know how long it had been trapped in the cabin. Trent knew that look. Mop was never shy about letting them know when he was hungry, albeit it to a lesser degree and never for a piece of him.

He searched for any weapon of offensive or defensive potential within arm's reach. The only thing he saw was the bedspread. Tabitha insisted on a heavy material even though this was a summer resort. She chose something called chenille. The chance of being able to pull it from the bed and cover the dog before it resumed its attack seemed remote, but it was the best chance he had. Slowly he slid his hand towards the bed. The dog followed it, seemingly mesmerized as it stopped its low growling, creating a silence that allowed them to contemplate each other's next move.

Thirty-two

That silence was broken by a pack of dogs that had inexplicably gathered outside the broken window. It merely startled Trent while fully capturing the attention of his captor. As it backed off and turned its head to the window, Trent swept up the bedspread and tossed it at the dog in one motion. It caught its head as the dog went into frantic convulsions, backing out enough for Trent to make a move.

It would take but a moment for the dog to free itself. Not enough time for Trent to escape. And the dogs outside left Trent with nowhere to go. The new arrivals snarled and propped themselves on the windowsill while he kicked at the shrouded dog sending it yelping towards the closet. In Trent's experience, a few well-place kicks were all it took. This experience, however, was very different.

The dog shook off the bedspread and turned on Trent, staring defiantly from inside the closet. This time, the snarling, hurtling beasts outside did not distract it. It focused in on Trent. It seemed to know it had him cornered. It not only had the advantage of strength, speed, agility, and primordial canines, it had been here before. While nature gave it its gifts; it was nurture that prepared it for this moment. Trent had watched his dogs in training attack without remorse, without conscience, and he watched with equal indifference. But he did have a conscience and in the midst of this life and death struggle, he was forced to confront it.

He was the architect of so many events, one leading explicitly to the next. He realized the consequences of each at inception. None of them surprised him. Worse, none of them scared him, and that was his sin. Now, a life would be taken. Instinct in both animals knew what had to be done, forcing Trent to disregard his conscience one more time.

He made a dash for the bathroom, expecting to outrace the dog who had to negotiate around the bed. But the dog leapt onto the bed instead, and in one succeeding bounce managed to crash into Trent. This time there was no mistaking its meaning when it grabbed onto his thigh.

It set its teeth in deep, the effect of which had Trent screaming while burying his fingertips into the door jam. To jump, even the slightest, would give up a ham-size chunk of himself. To stay still would allow the beast to chew him through to his spine. He found he was to witness the epic battle after all. Not as an observer but on a level such as he had never known.

He attempted to dislodge the dog with futile punches to the head. He read grabbing its ears was effective. He pounded on its nose which made the dog release only to re-position its mouth further down his leg. The dog was no longer content to hold on; it was actually starting to feed. Mauling was the word that came to his mind. Blood soaked through his pants. And bloodied tissue matter. If shock had set in, it hadn't deadened the pain.

Somewhere in the cabin was the rope he used to tie his dogs. He hadn't seen it. The closet; it had to be in the closet. There was only one way he knew for a rope to be used as a weapon. He needed to create enough time and space to work it. He reached down with outstretched fingers on the dog's head, working his thumbs into its eyes. Trent felt the eyelids close tight. The dog flinched but did what it was trained to do, hold firm to its kill. Trent had no choice but to dig as deep as he could.

The eyelids were amazingly difficult to penetrate, a point he should have recalled from experimenting as a child. It had to be done as violently as if breaking ice on a frozen pond. Cruel as it was, it now had to be. If it worked out as planned, the dog wouldn't be alive long enough to suffer. If it didn't, it would be his own demise. As he groped and peeled, the dog began to give way. But that wouldn't be enough; he needed to incapacitate it.

As the dog let go and backed off, Trent pushed in and lifted up, raising the dog's head as it emitted a piercing howl. It pawed madly at its snout while blood streamed down. Trent had no time to watch the results of his own grizzly attack. He took a moment to examine his thigh before dragging himself to the closet. It was difficult to tell the fibers of his jeans from the tissue of his leg, both soaked with blood and shredded. He saw no geyser-type eruptions of blood, a sign an artery hadn't been punctured.

The dogs outside were pacing and snarling. He feared one would take the initiative to leap through the window. His nearest threat was still howling in agony. Trent, as intent on ending its misery as he was on neutralizing it as a threat, search the closet for the rope. Frantically he twisted the dead dog out of the way. It didn't take much to move for as he grabbed its hind leg it separated from the torso. He found the rope underneath.

A mad dog is a dangerous dog, and as Trent stood cautiously over its writhing body, he found himself talking soothingly as if it were Mop after getting accidentally stepped on. "You don't deserve this fella," he said. He stretched the rope to tie a slip knot. "Don't know how you ended up here or why we got together like this. Thing is, this was my choice and you had none." He finished the knot and expanded the loop. "If there was a god for dogs, you'd be setting this rope for me."

It was easy to cradle its head. Spared the curse of ego and with the battle lost, it humbly yielded to the victor. A calm overcame Trent in his desire to end the animal's pain. He slipped the rope over its neck. He saw one eye had been removed, either torn out or pushed back into its head. He gently tightened the noose with the knot under its throat. He stood to snap the rope taunt. At that, the dog made a valiant effort to stand, forcing Trent to pull back like the reins on a horse. The dog did not submit; it didn't know yet that it had to. "Just die, you bastard, die." Trent pulled back as the dog struggled forward, unaware it was facilitating its own execution.

Tabitha walked out of the motel but stayed close to the open door. The dogs, she counted four, were swarming under the cabin window. She didn't dare call for Trent, fearing she would get the dogs' attention.

She'd never seen dogs behave this way. If they belonged to Abe Carver, Trent had his reasons to be scared and angry. Watching them attempt to climb through the window had her nauseated with worry; was Trent still in there? Was Ricky with him? Did he, or they, even know the dogs were out there. Of course, they had to know, unless they weren't there, or worse.

It was the "or worse" clause that made her forget consequences and call out. All except one ignored her, but when the one raced at her, the others followed. The snow was deep enough to make their going slow, slow enough for her to wait and see if they meant her harm. Her comparison was Mop, whose tail would wave like a metronome set to presto, her mouth, she swore it was smiling, and her ears stayed perked, awaiting another sound of her voice.

She couldn't see their tails, so deep was the snow. But their ears were pinched back, and foam and spittle coated their mouths. She was on her way back into the room when she saw Trent at the door. "Get inside," he was screaming and waving wildly with one arm. "Back inside." She froze. As she had never seen dogs behave in such a manner, neither had she seen Trent in such a panic. Something had spooked him horribly, and so, she foolishly watched the dogs close in an effort to understand what it was.

The dogs had picked up steam, sensing her as easy prey. Only Tabitha was still unaware of their intentions. She was barely aware of her husband's now-hysterical warnings. The closer they got the more beastly they became. They seemed to be flying several feet above the snow. She could see the tails now, spear-like, and that's what snapped her out of it. She turned her back and ran to the door. She was in the room mere moments ahead of them. Breathing heavy for such a short sprint, she leaned her back on the safe side of the door, then felt the horrific thuds as they slammed hard against it in quick succession.

She dared to peer through the window. Two dogs peered back. They looked docile now as they cocked their heads, as if wondering why they couldn't come in. The other two were scurrying around, sniffing the snow, scratching at the door, looking for a way in, looking for her. She felt safe enough but knew just how relentless hungry dogs could be. And sick dogs, for the first attacker, now scratching incessantly, appeared to be rabid.

She sat on the end of the bed to think. With all his screaming Trent could have told her if Ricky was safe. Maybe he did; she couldn't remember. She struggled to get refocused. She was trapped; Trent was trapped. And Ricky was still lost for all she knew. "Jeremy." She mouthed his name. She jumped up, racing back to the window. She could see the house but not the back door If Jeremy was to come looking for them, it would be too late. By the time she saw him, he'd be halfway to the cabin. In this snow, and being Jeremy, he'd be no match to outrun the pack. She closed her eyes and mumbled a telepathic prayer, "Please, Jeremy, be watching now. Be watching and just ... just stay in the house. Please."

Thirty-three

Jeremy had witnessed the entire episode since his parents left the house. From the heated argument they took outside with them to the dog attack on his mother.

It was dark now. Jeremy could no longer see the dogs but was sure they were out there. He was starving, and sure his parents would be as well, and Ricky when he got home. He cooked the only meal he could; bacon and fried eggs. All the while he watched and waited for Abe Carver to come take his dogs home. Unless ... unless he and the dogs were one in the same.

That was his thought when a large dark animal slowly approached the cabin. It was dusk and the wind tousled its fur, making it appear twice the size of the other dogs. At first, he thought it was a bear, or a wolf, like a werewolf. While the other dogs down at the motel howled and jumped madly, this one was content to patiently study the ground. It sniffed at the packed snow, along the windowsill, then lifted its head to test the air. At one point it sat under the window to take in the scenes around it.

In time the four others spotted it. They raced back to the cabin, thrashing and howling. When they arrived they encircled the big animal. Jeremy expected a brutal melee to ensue. But the dog stood its ground. One-by-one the dogs approached to sniff and nuzzle against it, but none dared stay too long. Then, they were gone.

Jeremy was sure it was the old man, come back for his dogs. But he didn't take them far. Jeremy opened the door, hoping for silence, but always there was the sound of the dogs somewhere close by.

There was a light on in the room his mother was in, but the cabin where his father was, was black. On a few occasions Jeremy braved the unprotected outside and called to him. The last time he called two dogs returned. It was a gibbous moon, a term his mother taught them, so he saw their shadows approach. It put a new fear into him, for he saw them only because they came in fast and clumsy. Had they come in with stealth as the man-dog did, he wouldn't have seen them until it was too late.

He stumbled back inside, shutting the door hard. When he looked outside the dogs were gone. He shut off the kitchen light to reduce reflection off the windows in hopes of regaining sight of them. Nothing. He was raising the window when a dog leapt up and crashed its snout into the screen. Jeremy fell onto his back as the dog continued jumping into the screen, tearing it loose of its frame.

He went for the only weapon close and long enough, the broom. It was in the corner beside the carving block. He slid out the largest knife, feeling its weight. It was the first time he dared to hold it, but now that he was alone and in fear for his life he didn't want to use it. The thought of cutting a dog, any dog, was unnatural to him. He could poke it with the stick end of the broom, that would work. He waved the knife through the air several times before putting it on the kitchen table. But this dog was attacking his parents; it would attack him. He had to cut it. It was the only way.

Trent dragged the dresser and mirror over to block the window. It covered the bottom two-thirds. It would take a very cunning, very nimble, very desperate dog to get through. He killed the lights and sat with a wet face cloth over his nose and mouth to diminish the intake of stench. He found it impossible to control his heavy breathing and stifle his yowls of pain, though he knew it was the smell of rotting meat, not noise, that brought the dogs around.

The dogs were circling the cabins. He heard them panting and pounding on the snow. The pounding had him worried. They were dashing between the cabin, the motel rooms, and up the ridgeline. Back and forth, two at a time. First one, then the other, beating down the heavy snow. They were making a hard packed trail for themselves; an express line to their food source. What was once heavy going was now made as smooth as their grassy pasture. It wouldn't be long before they began crashing at the doors and windows again.

He had no watch but figured it to have been nearly five hours since the dog attack. Seemed like twice that. Mercifully he had managed to pass out on several occasions, nature's remedy for pain. He took a moment to inspect the wound closely. He gingerly tore the pant leg as much as he could. Like a flash weld, the jeans were now interwoven with his leg. The bleeding seemed to have stopped. He wasn't sure that was a good thing. There were three distinct wounds where the dog had bit, slid, released, and bit again. Where it slid down was the worst, like being ripped open with a dull bread knife. Hunks of insides mushroomed into the outside. He touched a glob of himself. It sent an intense burning up his leg, so yes, nerve endings were intact.

Dragging himself to his feet and over to the window, he peered through the portal he left uncovered above the mirror. The moon was high enough to allow him to see into some corners while leaving others a mystery. He searched the yard left and right as far as his peripheral vision allowed. Had it not been for a flash of a shadow to his front, he would have assumed it safe to work his way back to the house.

A dog was darting beneath the kitchen window. Trent could swear he smelled bacon in the wind. A second dog appeared and stood expectantly at the window on its hind legs. They must have been the smelling bacon, too.

These dogs were starving. He hadn't fed his own much before releasing them. But Carver's dogs should be well fed, dead lamb or whatever it was he gave them. But any food laid out over night was sure to be buried and frozen. Maybe frozen food lost its smell, even for dogs. In any event, the dogs needed food and now knew where to find it.

He wouldn't make it ten feet in this snow before being brought down like the wounded prey that he was. He collapsed against the dresser. In spite of the outdoor freeze, he sweated and shivered profusely. He'd kill Carver if he walked into the room; kill him as he had killed the dog, only without apology. Fighting to kill the pain and fear, he worked his mind back to how it was he lost control of his world.

There was no law or leadership to get involved here. And all attempts at civility failed. He wasn't about to back off. But he chose to fight with Carver's weapons, and that's where his plan faltered. What was it Hack told him, 'Dutch has nothing you need.' Trent wondered about the psychology behind fleshing out a man like Dutch. Never would he have given this man a sideward glance back in Virginia, other than as an oddity.

But up here, Dutch was the power broker. In a wild world with little order, command and control was forged with the most primitive means. It made sense to Trent, for people to manipulate their world with the tools they had at their disposal. Then, as now, it was a juvenile notion to think beating Carver would define him. But that was what he needed from Dutch, a means to create his identity in a world that demanded creation.

Trent had to lure them away from the house. Anything stronger than the smell of cooked bacon. A stench was what he needed, and a stench was what he had. He went to the closet to pick up the rotting dog. It oozed something putrid that wasn't blood as he bent over to move it. He could suffer living with it all afternoon while it rotted and reeked but handling it would take some strategy. He put on his heavy gloves and soaked a facecloth. Then, pulling the top sheet from the bed, he dragged the carcass pieces onto it. He folded the sheet over it with one hand while holding the facecloth over his mouth and nose with the other. He dragged it outside quickly, leaving it ten feet in front of the cabin, enough space for a buffer zone. He stripped the sheet away and made wild banshee screams up to the house.

The dogs ignored him. The wind was swirling. He had no way of knowing if the scent was making its way up to them or sweeping out to the ocean where it would fade uselessly away. It was dangerous to leave himself so exposed. He looked down to the rooms for Tabitha. Calling to her could remind the dogs someone was down there. "Christ," he muttered, "I'm making the damn things seem human." Yeah, it was sarcastic, but they had shown strategy. Perhaps this was another, a diversion by sending a couple up to the house while the others lay in wait. Were they just around the corner, down at the motel rooms, perhaps both? He listened but heard no howling. That he didn't like, starving dogs howled. Or did they?

He could make it to Tabitha on the trail forged by the pack. From cabin door to motel door was less than thirty yards. Ninety feet. Those were Ricky's feet. He counted it out when Trent claimed the cabins to be a stone's throw away from the motel rooms. "Wow, you can throw a rock that far?" he said, impressed yet skeptical.

He heard them coming out of the shadows, their desperate panting coming moments before he saw them. A fortuitous turn for Trent who would have found himself in a position of no return had he set out for Tabitha. He made a wild dash back inside as they descended.

It was like standing at a shark tank during feeding. He didn't think they even noticed him with the raw meat in their path. There were three, with two thinner than the others. Again, he couldn't say for certain which, if any, were his. For all his research on the motel, how to run it, how to rebuild it, he paid scant attention to the how-to of the living things he brought to it. For all his disdain of Dutch, he sure knew his dogs.

Tabitha hadn't heard a thing since the pack's feeding frenzy at the cabin. Her phone was dead. Another of her few successful coups, she convinced Trent not to put phones in the room to save money. And the clocks, they were of the wind-up vintage. Cute pieces and cheap, but now as worthless as her cell phone. No communication, no time, no heat, no clue as to where Ricky was or how Jeremy was doing. And now, it was hitting her hard, no food.

No problem getting water from the snow, but the howling, in the distance or not-so distant, kept her from being out too long or venturing too far. She couldn't sleep, though she was sure she had dozed for minutes, maybe more, at a time. She calculated the last meal she had. It was a snack, a Hostess Cherry Pie, from the service station along the way to the ferry. That was, what? A hundred miles from Nuthatch Cove, so two o'clock yesterday afternoon. It was now ... dark. Maybe four o'clock, maybe eight. Hell, it could be three in the morning.

The only clear view she had out the window was down and across to the house. The lights were still off, and now the moon was down. She may as well be blindfolded in a box. It was more terrifying than in the car where she had a modicum of control. She stretched out on the bed for what seemed like minutes. She didn't come to in the usual slow, groggy state. It was fast and ruthless, accompanied by a blood curdling scream.

Thirty-four

He couldn't hold out forever. The dogs weren't leaving, especially now they'd found food, food he provided. And Carver hadn't shown himself. If he knew what was happening, he didn't much care. When did dogs sleep? Did they sleep deeply? Did they sleep near their food? Again, questions he couldn't answer.

He stepped outside without a plan. He stood motionless to adapt to his surroundings. The sun was coming up behind him. It was as peaceful a morning as he could recall, no winds, and quiet but for the winter waves which sounded bigger and angrier than in summer. The one sound he waited for, though, was that of the pack. Each time he thought they were present, he convinced himself it was just the roar of the ocean.

He had to make it to the house. It had weapons, and his cell phone which he could charge in hopes there was now coverage. And food, and Jeremy, the passive, sensitive son, cowering, he supposed, in a closet.

He moved out cautiously. Any path he made on his way down to the cabin the day before was a memory. The otherwise flat landscape now undulated with drifts. As the sun erased the shadows, he saw he was in the deepest drifts, with snow up to mid thigh. To his left about ten yards was the lowest point. Believing the dogs were still close by, every extra step, every extra second, could be costly. But in the shallows, he had a fighting chance of outrunning them.

Moving was tough. Though the snow numbed the leg wound, he had no strength, and his motions could be considered more falling forward then walking. Still time to turn around and head back but he saw no strategy in that.

The ground was slightly uphill. Strange he never noticed the varying grade before having to trudge it in this snow. He stopped upon hearing a change in conditions. He hoped it was the wind that had picked up, echoing around him. He removed his knit hat and did a three-sixty turn. There was no wind but there was a new sound, erratic and high-pitched, and coming from the ridge to his right. The dogs.

Trent moved out faster than he should have, he stumbled face down into the snow. Pushing to right himself was like pushing on water. He sank deeper until his entire head and torso was buried. He went to his knees to lift himself out, but his burning quads were not up to the task.

He managed to make it to his feet, losing valuable time. He brushed snow from his face as he lunged forward, careful not to fall again. He dared not look to the ridge and tried not to listen. Every second counted. Every one away from that back door forty yards away was one less to live.

He never heard them coming. Just a hard tug at his hamstring. Another jolt knocked him forward. He refused to fall. Like an orchestrated infantry attack, two more came at him on either flank. Fortunately, they hit near simultaneously, keeping him upright. The attack was furious and relentless. His thick jacket and gloves were giving him temporary protection. Had it not been for the deep snow, exposing less of his jean-clad legs, he'd have been dragged down in a bloodied mess.

He pounded them with closed fists, aiming for their heads. But he had no leverage, and his swings were frantic and wild, rarely connecting. Their guttural snarls were terrifying. When they grabbed hold of his arms, they took a moment to stare him down before he batted at them and shook them off.

He hoped the deep snow would exhaust the dogs, but they appeared to have developed a strategy of taking turns attacking two at a time. He was in no shape to fight off four crazed dogs. He snarled back at them. Screamed insanely. Flailed his arms. *Stay up,* he urged himself. *Just don't go down. They'll tire. They'll quit soon.* Christ, they had too.

Outside the pack a fifth dog appeared, the Jindo. It stood uncommitted, seemingly confounded by the riot before it. It cocked its head. Trent hoped for a measure of recognition.

The back yard was still half bathed in dark. Malevolent shadows were all Tabitha could make out. They jumped and shook manically. She stepped outside. It was Trent, stooped over in the middle of a charging pack of dogs.

It was his screams she'd heard. They were unrecognizable, high-pitched and frenzied, animal-like. She moved towards them instinctively. She'd be no help joining the fight; her intentions were to create her own commotion to frighten the dogs off, like shoeing raccoons from the trash cans. Instead, she found herself screaming at him, "You sonavabitch, you couldn't let it go. You had to make a point, you crazy sonavabitch, you had to prove something."

She went on without a pause. As long as she screamed, the rest of reality couldn't take hold.

Up until last night Jeremy was content to believe the dogs were ghosts, and Abe Craver was their phantom leader. As ghosts they were harmless. They had no power over real people. That was far less terrifying than the reality.

He wrapped the duct tape, the tape his father said could secure a car to the bottom of an airplane, around the butcher knife and broom handle. He filled a glass with gasoline his father kept in the back closet. He hoped that between jabbing with the knife and flame, the dogs would scare off for good.

They were all trapped as long as the dogs were free to run wild. If they got as insistent and violent as they did last night, if the jabs and flaming broom weren't enough to discourage them, he'd have to kill them. He hated the thought, hated that it would have to be him to do it, but it was the dogs or them.

They were too sick to know better. His mother read them *To Kill a Mockingbird*. The scene where Atticus shot the dog still upset him. It didn't seem the dog needed to be killed. But Atticus was a good man who said the dog was sick and in pain, and that it would attack someone. If Jeremy had a gun, he'd do it that way, like Atticus, make it quicker for him and the dogs.

He liked his bacon juicy, but this batch wasn't for him, so he let them get crispy enough to fill the kitchen with a good amount of smoke. He turned on the fan then opened the window to get the aroma flowing so the dogs would get close enough for him to use the knife and broom. But it was too late. The dogs were back and not content to wait for burnt bacon.

He heard the commotion outside, his dad surrounded, his mother stumbling to help him. Why couldn't they have waited five more minutes? Five more minutes and he would have lured to dogs back to the house where he was ready for them.

The Jindo edged forward. She was too small to make her presence known. She drifted as close to the pack as she dared, not wanting to commit. She wasn't particularly hungry anymore, yet there was an impulse to join in.

This was a strange world she found herself in. That day she was brought here, she wandered aimlessly, searching out the strange odors and new sights. Most of the time she found herself running from those angry sounds of other dogs. When at last she was forced to face them, she suffered a nip to her muzzle and hind heel before being allowed to follow behind at an acceptable distance.

Nothing gave her comfort. At night, when it was time to rest, there was no shelter from the wind. No bowl of food appeared from the cruel man who made sure to rake the screen of each cage with a metal pipe before moving along.

Now, behind the pack, a figure was approaching. It trudged through the snow as if it was severely wounded. She moved away from the pack to get a better view. The fragile figure approach. It was howling, in obvious pain, as it stumbled closer. The Jindo crouched low into the snow to hide her haunches that were flexed and ready to spring. If the creature noticed her, it didn't let on as its wails continued. She sprang to the attack The creature was slow to react; when it did it froze. With its heavy brown coat, the Jindo didn't blend into the white background. She heard another dog coming up behind her. She glanced back to see a large shepherd that had broken from the pack. It also found this strange, slow creature an interest. Unless she attacked first, she would find herself on the edges again.

It became a race. She was lithe and bounded effortlessly through the drifts like a snowshoe hare while the cumbersome shepherd labored under its bulk. Ignoring her initial trepidations, she threw herself at the creature who toppled easily. She straddled the prone body and braced for the shepherd's arrival, but the shepherd pulled up short, letting her keep the dominant position. Comfortable the creature was controlled, and the shepherd was conceding, she tore into the hide that was surprisingly easy to penetrate.

Jeremy watched in horror. His father was stumbling, occasionally going to his knees allowing the dogs to climb on top of him. He grabbed his weapons, leaning the knife-edged broom against the back door and pouring the gasoline onto the straw bristles. The matches? Where were the matches? Somewhere near the window. He searched the sill, the counters. Now where? His mind went blank. This was no time for that; there was no time left for any of that. The sunlight was just beginning to clear the roofs of the cottages and cabins. The ground between them and the house was lined with daggers of darkness. He saw his mother, or what he supposed was her, lying in the snow, a thin, coyote-like dog pawing madly at her while a larger stood in wait.

The matches, where were the damn matches? "Think," he muttered, "you put them right here when you were cooking the bacon."

That was it, the bacon. His mother hated it when they left trash on the counter. This in-progress training was becoming his obsession, another matter to make his mom happy and proud. He dug into the trash and grope around. The package of matches had fallen to near the bottom. They were damp. He sniffed. It smelled like bacon grease, felt like it too.

How he hated lighting matches. Ricky would do it to flick the lit matches at him, chasing him around the yard, the house, too, when he could get away with it. And now covered in grease. His mother had warned him about grease fires, how quickly they went up and spread when the grease spat out.

Her screams were still coming; so were his dad's. There was no time to fear lighting matches or remember being tormented or worrying about grease fires. He grabbed the broom and opened the back door. One, two, three, four strikes. The match head disintegrated. With the door open their screams were more terrifying. Jeremy was horrified by his father's begging and cries of agony. He breathed deeply as he tucked the match head under the book cover and snapped the match out as he had seen Ricky do. It sputtered to life. Quickly he touched it to the straw. It responded immediately with a satisfying crackle.

He raced out the backdoor minus his gloves and boots, and won't his mother be pissed at him for being outside in his stocking feet. The dogs on his father responded to his screams and the torch right away. They backed off, leaving his father collapsed in the deep snow, surrounded by patches of blood. Jeremy continued onward. The snow was above his thighs. His initial charge had turned to a waddle, like pushing through the waves at Virginia Beach.

The broom, back heavy with the butcher knife, was taxing his right arm. Every two steps he'd stop while keeping the flaming torch pitched forward like a jousting lance. The dogs, once skittish, now turned intrigued. They stopped their retreat and stood entranced.

A low, communal howling commenced. Jeremy closed as the dogs crept forward. There were three. The largest came up to Jeremy's chest. The two others, the ones who had his mother grounded, were oblivious to Jeremy. He sidestepped to his left, or tried to, moving towards his mother while keeping sight of the dogs.

"Dad," he screamed, "Dad, you okay? It's me, Jeremy. I'm out here with fire and a knife. The dogs are afraid so you can get up and run. Dad, you can get up." The sight of the blood and motionless body of the intrepid man who seemed immortal had him feeling very alone and vulnerable. "Dad, get up. Get up now. I'm going to get mom."

Dad didn't get up and the dogs weren't afraid anymore. They shadowed Jeremy's move toward his mother. Soon, Jeremy realized, it would be five on one. The flame was dying. The dogs seemed to sense that danger would soon pass. There was just enough flame to get him down to his mother, he hoped. The thought of using the knife end still made him uneasy but he was ready.

Jeremy hurried his awkward side-to-side movements. He called to his mother to meet him halfway. As he feared, she didn't answer, didn't stir. But the two dogs on her, now only about ten yards off, did, and the other dogs were no longer impressed by the flame.

It was the sight of his mother's blood that emboldened him to turn *Lord of the Flies.* He twirled the broom clumsily like a long baton to bring forth the butcher knife. It was then he realized how badly numb his fingers had become. The broom tumbled over his shoulder. The flames caught the fuel-saturated sleeve of his coat. His entire arm went up in that instant. It took precious seconds before he resumed enough of a thought process to fall into the snow.

The sleeves and front of the nylon jacket were gone, melted into his flesh. His arm was already blistering to a wet, fleshy goo. He pushed himself deep into the snow. The flames were gone but not the burning. He withdrew his hand to see strips of red skin dripping from it. He couldn't move further. He couldn't recall why he was out there. Out where? The whiteness of the snow was all around him; left, right, up, down. It was a strange consciousness he had fallen into, or perhaps a stranger sleep.

Rumblings, he heard, quiet, consoling rumblings. He curled himself under the freshly laundered sheets his mother put on his bed. How he loved the coolness of fresh sheets on a warm, summer night such as this. "Ricky, you awake? It's so warm. Open the windows, Ricky, I'm too tired to move."

Thirty-five

They were all gathered at *Trugards,* every resident of Stryker John Island, plus two, that being Hack Corlin and Dutch. And it was uneasily quiet.

The owner, Mel Cready, was setting up eight-ounce glasses of beer which were being drained as soon as they hit the bar. It was his way of keeping busy while the State Police occupied his office. They asked him not to serve those not yet interviewed. He nodded his understanding but didn't much care if his patrons abided by it or not.

He did a comical double-take when Rachel Kusenie's partner came out of the back office and downed a glass, then a second. She came in with Rachel for lunch on that rare occasion where she nursed an unsweetened iced tea while Rachel downed a bottle of Chardonnay. Rachel grabbed her arm, but her partner pulled away to sit alone in a corner.

There was no room for doubt, the Almanac was spot on: the coldest, snowiest winter in fifty-seven years. It took until now, mid-April, for major chunks of earth to appear. And that, in part, was what brought them here.

The Troopers were calling them interviews, but really, it was just talk as far as Mel Cready could see. For some reason he was the first one they spoke to. How well did he know them? Were they friendly? Were they aloof? Enemies? Problems? Concerns?

The cops weren't saying much. He supposed they just wanted to paint a picture which was a waste of resources because the media was all over the island painting their own.

Anything the islanders knew came from innuendo, gossip, implications, inferences, and a sprinkling of facts. Same way they got all their information. Dutch was the last and longest interview of the three-day event. He sat at the bar a few hours each day, nursing a beer, smiling in that chilling way as he listened to the occasional comment about what really happened down at the Aress place.

Dutch cocked his head and spoke to Hack Corlin at a table nearby. "You know, give Aress credit. Man of his word, wanted to make the island somethin' special. Well, he did that in a big way, least till the buzz dies down. Know what else? He loved legends. Gonna be a one hisself now."

Hack listened to the comments around him. There were six or seven of them leading the conversation.

"They found one of the boys about a mile away; think he was runnin' away from home."

"Shoulda been that wife runnin' off."

The guys saw that as a thing to laugh about.

"Who the hell was he, anyway, come in here to make problems and changes?"

"Didn't even know enough to protect himself against the winters. Didn't ask no one here for help with that, did he? Hell no, he had all the answers."

"Learn more by listenin' than talkin', ain't that truth, and boy did that man like to talk."

"Just came in here, grabbed prime real estate, and wanted more. He did, too, just wanted more for himself."

"Yeah, and all that crap about the island getting the benefits. Heard that shit before."

"There were little boys out there, too, you know," Marla Barber said.

"We all know that Barb," her husband drawled. "Ain't no one sayin' anything bad 'bout the ankle bitahs."

“I heard he was friends with Abe Carver, how crazy you gotta be for that?”

Hack knew it was nervous chatter, meant to keep the shame away, keep this a one-man problem. He knew because since the day he heard the news, he occupied his thoughts with the same notions. "There was room on the island for him," he said to the crowd. "Just like there was room for me."

"Yeah, but you didn't try buy the place up."

"I bought my own corner of it, just like you all have. It's why we all came."

"I came to get away from people like him," one said.

Rachel Kusenie spoke up. "You saying it was our fault somehow?"

"Don't go thinking we're not upset about his wife and kids; we're not heartless." That was Todd Barber. "But the fact is, he was irresponsible."

"Not saying it's your fault or that anyone's heartless. It just seems simple to me, like if you all think he was out of his element, why not go over there to help him out."

"How 'bout you?" Cready said. "Didn't you drop the wife and kids off in the middle of that big storm?"

It was a distasteful detail of the story for which he offered no mitigation. This was an island, and an island to him could represent isolation or community. He saw Stryker John as community, but this event will forever change that viewpoint, for him and the islanders.

When it was apparent Hack had nothing more to add, the spontaneous talk started up around him again. "He shot her and then the kids, I heard. Then ate his gun. Blew the back of his head out."

"Sounds like 'im, something he'd do."

"Still, just a shame is all."

Then a gentle voice from the back. "Didn't happen that way at all." All heads turned to look into the shadows at the small, seated figure to the left and rear of Rachel Kusenie. It was Rachel's partner, Carmine. She dared look out at the crowd for but a moment before dropping her stare back into her lap.

"What do you know about it?" Rachel said.

Carmine didn't look up. "I was there."

"Where?"

"At the motel."

Rachel looked back at the crowd, feeling as if she had to deny her partner's involvement for fear of being judged a negligent parent. "When?"

"The day they came, the police."

"Now why the hell'd you go – "

"I found him. I'm found the boy." She started by looking directly at Rachel, then, remembering it was an island issue, spoke out to the full room. "Like Mister Corlin was saying, everyone here seemed to have an opinion of the man. And the woman." She gave a penetrating gaze to Rachel. "Most opinions weren't too good. It was a bad winter. We needed help down at the farm. I know we helped others get through. When I came up to get supplies, I heard about all sorts of problems people were having. Anyway, I didn't see or hear of anyone going down to that part of the island."

"Now wait just a minute, Carmine," Todd Barber said. "We woulda given 'em help had they asked."

"I guess I'm wondering why didn't they ask any of us?"

"Ego, you ask me," Mel Cready said. "Know what he said to me once? Said, 'Don't you want to leave something behind to be remembered by, something with your stamp on it?' Said, 'Hell, even this bar has someone's else's name, not even your own.' So, I says to him, 'nothing wrong with leavin' things just the way you found 'em.' Ego, that's what it was with him."

Carmine had never met the family, though she felt as if she had. For months she had been listening and watching the islanders' response to them. They were disliked, distrusted, and dismissed, except for the missus who had Rachel's full attention those first few months.

"Where was he?" Marla Barber asked. "The boy, where'd you find him?"

"He was in a snowbank, down on the beach. I saw his leg sticking out of a drift."

Having been emotionally exhausted and drained from reliving the scenes during her interview, her delivery was deadpan. She had no desire to relate the experience in a manner intended to enthrall. Nor did she feel the need to share the family's fate with people unconcerned with their existence. "I thought maybe he was just playing in the snow. But he wasn't moving. I thought maybe he got stuck, you know, just a while before. But it wasn't just a while. It was months."

"Now how would you know that?" Rachel's tone was meant to deride the storyteller, but Carmine was having none of it.

"I was there; I dug him out."

At the start of Carmine's talk, there were murmurs of quiet conversations, the sound of beer bottles tapping on wooden tables, and glasses bumping glasses behind the bar. Now it was dead still so she gave them what they wanted.

"I drove to the dock, told Mister Corlin. He called the mainland. I stuck around to show them where the boy was. Ricky. His name was Ricky."

"I found the rest of them too." They waited for more details.

Such a small island. So close they all were, yet so dull and empty on many levels. From her first day there she knew it wasn't going to work. But why leave? Where to go? She already knew she didn't belong with many people, and now "here" was just another place not to be.

"I knocked at the door. To be honest, when they didn't answer I was relieved I didn't have to tell them about finding Ricky. I went to the back door. I could smell it."

There was no sound. No one walked out. No one told her to stop. No one said they had heard enough. Were they getting any of this? While they were settled into their homes and lives, helping each other through, being the good neighbors, this odd family was literally thrown to the dogs and torn apart by them. Finally, one asked. "What about the dogs?"

"What?"

"The dogs, what happened to them?"

"They killed them."

"Who did?" Rachel asked.

"The police."

"Couldn't they have just caught them?"

She had witnessed the most gruesome, horrendous sight of her life; one she'd have nightmares about for the rest of it, and some here were concerned with the dogs. "They ate people and at least two were rabid."

Carmine looked at Hack Corlin who seemed to get it. He was shaking his head, looking over his shoulder at Dutch. Dutch was leaning back in his chair, beer in his lap, eyes half closed, but she knew he was listening. Yes, he would certainly be listening.

"Probably Carver's dogs that did it," one said. "I been scared off his property by them just by the barkin'. Vicious things."

"They got him too," Carmine announced. She refused to give any more details, so she ignored a request to do so. And they waited. It had been a long, hard winter. With the thaw, this type of story was just what they needed. But no more details would come from her.

She spoke coldly, the words stripped of emotion. Yet this moment had her living the disturbing details as if for the first time, starting with Ricky, staring up at her. She knew he was dead, but his eyes were locked on her, as if he was about to ask for something. He was like a China Doll, bleached white, his eyes opened and frozen like shooter marbles. He had his hands balled into little fists and held them tight to his chest, as if that would keep them warm. His hat was lying about three feet away. She wanted to put it on him. Crazy. He was gone, but she thought maybe it could keep him warm.

Freezing to death, she had heard, was a painless way to die. That hardly seemed a consolation, and though Ricky was may have been spared such agony it was not so for her. Mercifully, he had escaped the fate of his family.

They had been torn, chewed, and dispersed throughout the yard. The island had no wolves or coyotes or other predator capable of such slaughter. It had to be dogs that got loose. Closest dogs she knew, closest ones with such ferocity, came from Abe Carver.

She preferred to think they had gone like their son, frozen to death in the snowstorm, before the dogs descended. The clothing made it difficult for the dogs to penetrate into the flesh but not impossible. They went for the face and neck mainly. The sight of that had her avert her eyes to the hands which were also mauled. A boot was across the lawn, meaning a foot had been had. There were large paths of blood on the remaining snow. To her that meant the dogs had spent the winter, however long, returning to the bodies.

In fear for her own life, she sprinted back to her truck and raced to the ferry, hoping it would be at the dock. Hack Corlin remained calm and thankfully didn't ask for details while they traveled back to the mainland to pick up authorities. Two deputies were ready to go over. They had only their sedan so when it was time to load the bodies, they asked if they could load them into her pick-up. She wasn't happy about that but the thought of leaving them on the ground to suffer more savagery was abhorrent to her.

It was a painful thing to watch. The two deputies were younger than her. It was obvious they'd never seen anything like this. They neglected to bring body bags. She went inside the house and pulled sheets off the beds, then, in a bizarre gesture, switched them out for the heavy comforters. They wrapped the bodies and parts without looking at them.

They asked her about relatives. She didn't even know their names, but for the woman, Tabitha. Or where they were from. She offered her theory on what had happened and who owned the dogs. With the blanketed bodies in her pick-up bed, she led them up the road to Abe Carver.

They found the back door open. Snow had filled the entryway. It was warm enough inside to allow the dead flesh to rot fully. It was too much for any of them to take but the body would have to be recovered. The deputies went in bravely, having become war-tested veterans within the span of an hour. She followed as a show of solidarity.

The gag reflexes took effect upon entering. The dogs had the comfort of dining in and so seemed satisfied in making themselves at home there. They left little of him. That was, little that resembled a human. The one deputy turned to her, his mouth and nose tucked into the sleeve of his nylon jacket. "This him?"

"Ah-huh," she said, only to get the process moving. Later she would tell them she wasn't for sure, there being so little to go by, but Abe Carver lived alone and hated visitors, so the odds were the pieces they wrapped and tossed into her pick-up were him.

But the putrid odor didn't stop at the house. All three of them turned to the barn. A deputy opened it to the sight and stench of twenty-four rotting sheep. It was one more unbearable scene none of them wanted to handle. "We're leaving that mess for the EPA." he said.

"Guess we can figure the old man was killed months ago," he said. "Enough time for the sheep to starve to death."

"Shame," his partner added. "That barn been unlocked it would've been the sheep the dogs got hold of 'stead of the family."

Hack Corlin broke the silence. "Ferry's leaving in twenty minutes."

It was only Carmine who responded. She walked to the front door, donning her coat with the determination of one vowing never to return.

"Where you goin'?" Rachel demanded.

She stopped without turning. She knew the tone of voice, knew the stare down that would accompany it. She could have ignored it, for once, kept moving passed them all, through the door for the last time, leave her belongings behind. There wasn't much she wanted to keep, even less she needed.

The truth was, she hadn't gone to the motel to see about the family. She wanted to see for herself the woman that had Rachel in such a dizzy state. Months ago, when she asked about the damage on the Durango and Rachel mentioned it was backed it into by the ditzy new woman on the island, she began counting the number of times Tabitha's name was dropped. She stopped counting at thirty-three in about six weeks. And that didn't count the references to the motel or the phone calls to it. When Carmine mentioned trying to make a go of the motel years ago, she was shot down, told it was an insane idea. But this Tabitha, Rachel bragged, could make a go of it. She was charming and would make the perfect hostess.

Rachel came home after a day of crying, though she tried hiding it. That was when her obsession with Tabitha stopped. Not only didn't Rachel mention her or the motel again, she forbid Carmine from doing so. If Carmine had deluded herself into thinking this was one-way and unconsummated, this latest turn showed it to be otherwise; no one fell so hard from a flirtation.

Carmine had to see for herself and would have done so earlier had it not been for the impassable snows. As perverted as it was, she took an extra minute to examine Tabitha's obliterated face, attempting to put it back together, wanting to see what had so consumed Rachel.

"I said, where you goin'?" Rachel demanded.

Turning around would be the end to her escape. Stryker John wasn't home, and the people here weren't family, but no other place seemed to work much better. To stay, she'd become just the person who found dead bodies once upon a time. And though she didn't give details, she would in time. She'd be at *Trugards*, retelling the story to residents and visitors for history's sake. That history, like all history, would change with time. Fact and truth will give way to myth and gossip. Over time she, herself, will forget one from the other as heroes became villains, villains the heroes. When she turned old, she'd be that curiosity that folks would just have to see.

All eyes were on her, but that wasn't what made her shoulders droop and the coat slide from them. It was Dutch's eyes she caught. He was upright now in his chair, paying attention. He gave her a wink that disgusted her and made her heart sink. She collapsed into the closest chair, the one almost at the exit door.

"Ten minutes," Hack said.

"Gotcha Cap'n," Dutch said. "Finish my beer first. I'll be there."

Hack wanted to leave him behind. He thought hard about it. Empty gesture, he decided. "'When the whirlwind passes, the wicked will be no more,' he said to Dutch. "Hell is where you'll be."

Dutch smiled. "Ahhh, Proverbs." He held his finger to his lips and whispered, "'Debate your case with your neighbor himself and do not disclose the secret to another; lest he who hears it expose your shame and your reputation be ruined.'" He raised his glass. "To hell with both of us, Cap'n. To hell."

John Ouellet is a retired Special Agent of the Detroit FBI office. He is the author of The Captive Dove and numerous short stories. He still resides in Michigan with his wife. They have no cats or dogs.